Skinny Berry

Skinny Berry

Terry Olson

Draumr Publishing, LLC
Maryland

Skinny Berry

ISBN: 978-1-933157-23-8
PUBLISHED BY DRAUMR PUBLISHING, LLC
www.draumrpublishing.com
Columbia, Maryland

Printed in the United States of America

Dedication Page

For Barb and Tom
the architects of my life

And for Bud
whose stories cultivated the fields of my imagination

Acknowledgements

Thanks to my editing posse—Nicole Appleberry, Emily Bach, Gary Byrne, Jo Byrne, Alicia Davis, and Jeff Foldie. Thanks to my lovably pedantic wife. And to my children for hugs that magically refresh the mind and spirit.

Special thanks to Jeffrey M. Smith, the author of *Seeds of Deception*—an eye-opening book that lays bare the corporate driven world of genetically modified foods. Special thanks to Dr. Arpad Pusztai, whose research on the negative health impacts of genetically modified foods earned him the wrath of corporations and governments who would alter our food supply without adequate scientific testing. Dr. Pusztai was kind enough to provide background information to a lowly writer working on a book about genetically modified organisms. Special thanks to Don Vig, an organic farmer in North Dakota, who embodies all the wisdom of Ike Stiles, but has none of Ike's vices, to my knowledge. Mr. Vig's insights helped bring the Stiles' Family Berry Farm to life. Special thanks to Brian Depew. When I had the good fortune to meet Mr. Depew, he was a graduate student at Michigan State University, working on rural and farm issues. His observations on the interplay between academia and the farm culture helped flesh out the imaginary Michigan A&T University. And finally, special thanks to Rida Allen and Draumr Publishing, for helping turn a sheaf of unruly electronic bits into this novel, which I hope you enjoy.

Chapter One

Tom Hughes usually took the long way when he went to Perkins, Michigan. He liked to drive the back roads into his hometown. It was like a self-guided tour of his lost youth. But when Ike Stiles had called to invite Tom to a late dinner, there had been an unmistakable urgency in the old man's voice. Thinking of Ike's tone, Tom turned onto the expressway.

Finding the Stiles' farm was easy enough. Several barns that dotted the landscape along US-27 had been turned into pastoral advertisements. White paint on the sides of the red barns heralded a tantalizing countdown and a promise of the glorious products that might be purchased. First there was:

Only 6 miles to
The Stiles' Family Berry Farm
U-Pick Berries All Season
Blackberries * Blueberries
Raspberries

And a mile on:

Only 5 miles to
The Stiles' Family Berry Farm
Fresh Produce All Season
Exit Right on US-10
Don't Miss the U-Pick Pumpkin Patch

And so on. It was hokey, but Tom knew how effective it was from his own days working on the farm. Hundreds of tourists detoured off busy vacation schedules to pick sweet, swollen fruit on perfect summer days. It made Ike Stiles one of the most prosperous farmers in Wabeno County.

Tom's mind wandered as he exited west on US-10, the car driving itself. His higher brain function was preoccupied by memories that felt like leaves pressed in wax paper. He remembered driving this same highway with Claire the first time he brought her home. It was Thanksgiving and they drove up from Lansing. They were in love. And having no family of his own, he needed to introduce her to Ike and Kaye Stiles.

He took the Perkins exit and drove slowly south through the one-stoplight town he called home. He remembered Claire, a worldly denizen of suburban Detroit, telling him how cute Perkins was on that first shared homecoming. And he remembered deliberately not telling her how boring a place it actually was, not wanting to spoil her illusion of idyllic small-town life.

The memory of Claire was a painful ghost now. She had died in March, effectively ending all that was good in the world. Every trip now, be it a simple walk to the grocery store, or a homecoming, was a living reminder of two worlds. The first, a world of relative perfection where Claire still lived in his memory. And the second, a cold and hollow world where Claire had ceased to exist.

Three miles south on Perkins Road, Tom came to his childhood home. It was a small A-frame house, wooden shingles painted brown, as they had been for all the decades of Tom's life. He had left for college when he was eighteen, with his mother selling the house and moving to sunny Phoenix that same year. But the rural neighborhood was still home to Tom, thanks to Ike and Kaye

Stiles.

Next to the A-frame where he grew up was Ike's farmhouse. It was a two-story white home with a wrap-around porch. On it he could see Ike rising from his chair to greet him. Behind the farmhouse was a red barn, its wall serving as the final billboard:

You have arrived at
The Stiles' Family Berry Farm
Welcome!

"How the hell are you, young man?" Ike said, coming down the porch to meet Tom in the driveway. Ike was seventy-six, but his step was still lively, and his voice did not betray his age.

"Not bad, old-timer," Tom lied. He could not bring his eyes level with Ike's. He had never felt worse in his life. Claire's absence was a crushing pain that would never let him breathe again. "Not bad."

"Come here." He pulled Tom close and thumped a heavy farmer's hand on Tom's back. "I am so sorry. But you're gonna get through this. There's always light at the end of the tunnel."

"I know," Tom lied again. "How are you and Kaye?"

"We're still going," Ike said. "And at this age, that's all you can ask, I think. Come on and have some dinner."

Ike led him up gray stairs and offered him a cedar deck chair on the porch.

"I got you a cold one all lined up," Ike said, handing Tom a bottle of Stroh's.

Tom was grateful. A case of Ike's favorite beer might take him to a place where he could forget. "So what's up?" Tom said. "You sounded kinda worried on the phone."

"Well, it's probably nothing much. We'll take a look after supper. Closer to sundown. You'll get a look with your own eyes."

Tom took another drink. There was no rushing Ike. He talked in his own rhythm. It was soothing and slow. He was a man raised before twenty-four-hour cable television and high speed Internet access. His mode of conversation was an art form. It was like hearing the old farmer in *American Gothic* speak.

"Tom! Come here, you," Kaye Stiles said, hipping her way out the screen door, a TV tray under each arm. She handed the trays to Ike and gave Tom a long hug. "It's good to see you."

"You, too," Tom said.

"I hope you brought your appetite," Kaye said. "You're looking a little on the scrawny side."

"Just trying to watch what I eat." He patted his stomach. This was another white lie. He had lost twenty pounds since Claire died. On a good day, his diet consisted mostly of beer. On a bad day, mostly bourbon. And while his pot belly had not melted completely away, Tom could see himself growing gaunt when he looked in the bathroom mirror.

"I'll get a couple of pounds back on you right tonight." Kaye laughed, then turned back for the house as Ike set up the TV trays.

Kaye did all she could to fulfill her promise. She brought them plates of fried chicken, mashed potatoes, homemade pickles, and slices of cantaloupe.

"Come on and sit down, Kaye," Tom said.

"No," Kaye said, patting her trim waistline and smiling. "I'm still watching my girlish figure." She went back into the house, returning periodically to ensure Tom was eating at a healthy pace.

Ike and Tom finished a six-pack between them before a dessert of fresh strawberry shortcake with whipped cream. What room the men had in their mouths for conversation was filled with talk of the cool spring, the lack of rain, and the entirely average record of the Detroit Tigers. There was a deafening failure to mention Claire, though Tom thought of her with every change in topic. As they polished off dessert, the shadows of the summer evening fully engulfed the porch, and the sun fell low in the western sky.

"Come on, let's have a walk," Ike said. He drained his beer and rose from his chair. Tom followed as Ike walked him back to the barn. An office and tool room was tucked just inside the barn door. Ike walked to an ancient refrigerator in the back corner and opened it. "Another one?"

Tom nodded and Ike cracked two beers. Then the men headed out of the barn and into the fast growing paradise of fresh produce, berry fields, and orchards.

"See that cornfield there?" Ike said, pointing south through his own cherry orchard, across County-Line Road.

"Yeah," Tom said. "That's Behmlander's old place, right?"

"Yep. He died back—when was it—'95, maybe?"

"So who's running it now? Did he have kids?"

"None that stayed. Michigan A&T bought the whole damn thing up. The North Central Research Center, they call it now."

"No kidding," Tom said.

"You know anything about genetic engineering?" Ike asked.

Tom paused for a moment, his mind trying to keep pace with Ike's rapidly evolving topic. "No, not much. You mean like the sheep cloning thing in England?"

"Hold up a second," Ike said, stopping by a cherry tree and nestling his beer bottle on a low branch. He fished an aqua package of Bugler Tobacco and a rolling paper from the enormous front pocket of his overalls. He tapped a small amount of the tobacco into the paper, expertly rolled a cigarette, then licked the paper to form a seal.

Tom had seen the ritual a million times. It still amazed him that Ike was breathing with no difficulty into his seventies.

"That sheep," Ike said, as he drew a breath and lit the cigarette with a match. "I guess that's genetic engineering, too. But I'm talking about plants. Man-made plants that are resistant to herbicides and pests."

"Yeah," Tom said. "I've heard of them. I guess they can do those things in a lab nowadays."

"Do 'em in a lab, for cris'sakes. They've been growing 'em in fields for the last ten years. You eat 'em at damn near every meal."

Tom shook his head, unsure of Ike's point. They walked on down a worn tractor trail that ran between Ike's orchard and the acres of berries that made up the rear of the farm. The sun had reddened and touched the tops of the fir trees that lined the west end of the berry patch, casting long shadows across the land.

"They call 'em Frankenfoods over in Europe," Ike continued, as they approached a drainage ditch that ran along County-Line Road on the southern end of his farm. "American farmers are having a helluva time selling their crops there."

"No kidding," Tom said. "I had no idea."

"Yes, sir." Ike took the cigarette from his mouth, coughed deeply, then spat on the ground. "Something like eighty percent of the soybeans you eat and thirty-five percent of the corn. It's all unnatural. Genes spliced in from bacteria and all kind of crap."

"No way," Tom said. He doubted Ike's education on the latest technology. "That would have to be on the label, wouldn't it?"

"No, sir," Ike said, and spat again. "Hell, some of those starvin' countries in Africa won't even accept our aid shipments."

"That's crazy," Tom said. "They'd rather starve?"

"Look there." Ike's massive hand again pointed across the road to the neighboring farm. It lay before them in the dying sunlight. Rows of brambles lined the western edge of the field, which sloped down toward an uncleared lot.

Tom followed Ike's direction and saw four deer walking cautiously out of the woods. They made their way through the brambles and into the cornfield that sat on the eastern half of the farm. "You wanted me to come out to see the deer?" He smiled. "You know—"

"Hush up and watch, boy," Ike said without venom.

The deer stopped and nibbled at the corn plants on the edge of the field. Then they moved comfortably into the corn rows as if they had paid for the all-you-can-eat buffet. The corn was still low enough so that Tom had no difficulty watching their progress. Several rows in, a buck paused as if he sensed the men watching. He changed direction and started marching up one straight row of corn, pausing to nibble along the way. His harem followed suit, and the deer formed a single-file chow line.

"That's the edge of the buffer there," Ike said. "They plant real corn as a buffer on some of these crops. The genetically modified stuff is in the middle. Them deer won't touch it."

"You think the deer know about the crops?" Tom laughed so deep and rich that the deer looked up startled.

"I know they do," Ike said. "I watch 'em almost every night. The same thing."

Tom looked again at the deer. There did seem to be an imaginary barrier beyond which they would not graze.

"We've been organic here since '99," Ike continued. "Helps with the yuppies on their way up north. Some of 'em won't eat non-organic, y'know."

"So if it's organic, it's not genetically modified?"

"That's right," Ike said. "We have to be certified. No synthetic pesticides, herbicides, or genetically modified crops."

"Man," Tom laughed again, "farming sure has gotten complicated since I moved on." He followed Ike into the berry patch, the old farmer cutting a path between two rows of blackberry brambles. Several yards into the patch, Ike walked over to the row bordering the southern edge of his farm.

"Look at this," Ike said, grabbing a stem from the bramble, his leathery hands impervious to the soft thorns. "Look there. See them berries. Looks good, huh?"

"Yeah." Though the berries were still burgundy, their form was perfect. A berry ripened on each stem.

Ike walked a few rows nearer to the center of the blackberry field. "Now look here," he said, pulling another stem toward Tom.

"Not bad," Tom said. Some of the berries had been eaten away, but the plant looked healthy to him.

"But it's not perfect," Ike said. "Right?"

"Well, some birds got at a few, I see."

"That's right. Perfectly natural. Birds always get at a few. That's how the plants spread their seed. Get eaten up and crapped out all over God's creation."

"So what's the problem?"

"Problem is that the birds aren't getting at those rows on the southern edge. I've been watching. Birds won't touch 'em."

Tom looked at Ike. The farmer's voice had grown agitated.

"It's not just the blackberries," he said defensively. "It's the corn, too. Those same deer make their way over here after nightfall. And there are parts of my field they won't eat from. It's not a straight line. But mostly on the southern edge."

Tom looked back at the deer, still grazing single-file along the same imaginary line in the old Behmlander cornfield. The hair raised on the back of his neck, closely followed by an involuntary shiver. "So what are you saying?" he asked, trying to sound confidently dismissive. "You're saying these animals won't eat genetically altered crops?"

"They're smarter than people like that, Tom," Ike said. "They know the wheat from the chaff."

"And you're saying that those crops over there somehow migrated across the road into your fields?"

"I've heard of it before," Ike said.

"So what are you going to do about it?" Tom said. "Isn't this something for the Department of Agriculture or someone?"

"I doubt they'd much care," Ike said. "They approve these genetically modified crops as fast as they're made."

"You're not thinking about some legal action?"

"It's crossed my mind," Ike said.

"So you're looking for a lawyer?" Tom said.

"I'm not looking for any old lawyer." Ike laughed now, loud and resonant. "I'm looking for the best damn lawyer to ever come out of Perkins, boy."

Tom tried to smile. "That's a very nice compliment. But it's not saying much."

"It says it all for me," Ike said. He spat again, an exclamation point.

"Well, even if you could prove all that you say, I'm not sure you'd have much of a case," Tom said. "What are you going to say about damages, 'Ladies and gentlemen of the jury, these people made my client's berries resistant to all forms of pests. Increased his yields and his profits.' A jury's not gonna give you a million dollars for that, Ike."

"If my crops are genetically modified, I could lose my organic certification," Ike said. "And if the animals won't eat this crap, it can't be healthy. I'm going to have to keep the bad stuff away from the good. I don't want somebody's kid eating that stuff."

The pair hiked back toward the farmhouse, serenaded by cricket song, as darkness settled on the farm.

"I'm really not taking new cases right now," Tom said, his head down to avoid Ike's eyes. "And a case like this is way out of my league."

"Can't you just look into it, Tom?" Ike said. "You're the only lawyer I know. And this ain't something I can do myself."

"Well," Tom sighed, "maybe I can make a few phone calls. Find you someone who could help."

"Fair enough," Ike said, plucking a leaf from a low branch.

Kaye turned the porch light on for them and waited with a basket of homemade jams, honey, and canned pickles. She gave it to Tom with a hug. Ike bid him farewell with a handshake and another thunderous clap on the back.

"Things will get better," Ike said. "Just keep getting up in the morning. Keep breathing."

"I know," Tom lied. "I know."

Taking the long way home, Tom remembered how much Claire had liked the Stiles' Berry Farm. He glanced at the basket seated in Claire's place and remembered how she loved Kaye's blackberry preserves on fresh baked bread. Since he was a boy working in the brambles, the Stiles' Berry Farm had been synonymous with delicious, wholesome food. But that image had been tainted by the thought that some of the crops on Ike's farm were possibly high-tech creations. Driving through the darkness, Tom was reminded of Ike's warning. "They're smarter than people like that," the old man had said. And Tom's appetite for blackberry jam was lost.

Tom's dry eyes did not crack open until well into the morning. When daylight finally coursed through his pupils to his throbbing brain, his first thought was of Claire. She was gone, and he would have to nurse his own hangover. Just get up out of bed, he told himself.

He willed his feet to the floor. His errant arm flailed and knocked a nearly empty bottle of Jim Beam off the nightstand. As he rose and trudged to the bathroom, his vision swayed. A hot shower, a glass of ice water, two Advil caplets, and a cup of coffee set him as right as he could be. He arrived at his office before lunch and considered it a small victory.

Tom rented the one-story brick office building in his second year of practice. It was a prime location for a small-town office— on the corner of two of the busiest streets in Milton— only a block and a half from the courthouse. He and Claire had settled into the office like a home. This would have been their nineteenth year, he thought, opening the locked front door. He had avoided the office as much as possible because he could not enter it without remembering everything about her. Looking at her empty chair behind the reception desk made his eyes burn.

Tom's first job after law school was as an associate at an insurance defense firm in Lansing. Claire was the belle of the secretarial pool. She had long black hair that framed her porcelain face. She wore her classic beauty with the elegance of royalty, and balanced it off with intelligence and competence. Tom never understood how such a woman could have chosen to spend her life with someone as average as himself.

Intensely shy, Tom found that he could hardly speak to her when she was assigned as his secretary. But she put him at ease over time, in her understated way. When Claire began to show interest in him, their office flirtations began in earnest. Tom frequently wondered that if they had met in today's atmosphere, with its keen attention to sexual harassment lawsuits in the work place, whether he would have carried on as he did. They were engaged within six months and married within the year. And as soon as they had saved a enough of a stake, they set off to build a small law office all their own.

While the office flourished, more because of Claire's business sense than his own lawyering skill, there were no children in those first years. And when Doctor Brown confirmed that there would never be children, the young couple was bound closer together by an aching pain of loss.

They threw themselves into work. The little business became their child. And it grew healthy and strong, nurtured by their love. Fortune was good to them, in a way only a personal injury attorney can understand fortune. In their sixth year in Milton, there was the C-2 vertebrae fracture to the seventeen-year-old boy from Whitfield. A cement truck operated by an amphetamine freak veered across the center line causing a head-on collision. The boy had been unfortunate to survive the carnage. And Tom and Claire were fortunate to take a third of the seven-figure settlement. Fortune struck again in their tenth year of practice, when they made a cool million for simply referring a horrific roll-over SUV accident to Putnam, Putnam & Vale, a personal injury firm in Detroit.

The rest was nickel and dime. Simple auto negligence cases.

Slip and falls. Dog bites. Minor misfortunes that paid college tuition for all the children they never had. Along the way they bought their office building. Paid off their mortgage, student loans, and car payments. And had a large enough business account to run the office until their retirement. Daily they remembered they had each other and didn't need anything more. Life had been very good to them.

And then everything changed. It was a cold spring morning. A Sunday like any other. A comforter kept them warm in bed. Coffee and toast and *The New York Times* were shared between them. Tom heard her breath, suddenly raspy, and thought she had swallowed wrong.

Her asthma had been a mild annoyance in their life together. A barely noticeable companion. She kept an inhaler under the bathroom sink. He could count on two hands the number of times he had seen her use it in their nineteen years together. But that morning in March, the inhaler did not give her relief.

Claire's face, still beautiful at forty, contorted in agony. She turned blue as she fought to breathe, an image Tom would carry to his own grave. He spent the last minutes of her life strangely torn between two worlds. In one world he begged the 911 operator for help, as if by will he could make the ambulance arrive in time. In the other, he sat by her side, helpless as a child, while she slipped away. When her eyes rolled up into her head, Tom knew she would die. They had often joked together about the poor quality of health care in Wabeno County, but as she lay dying Tom kicked himself for not moving his beloved somewhere more civilized. A place where the ambulance would arrive in the nick of time. But in rural Michigan, Claire had simply died in his arms.

Closing the office door behind him, Tom locked the dead bolt. He did not turn on the lights. He could do Ike's bidding in the dark. He walked through the reception area, down the hall to his own office, resisting the urge to hurry. In the cabinet of his oak credenza he found a half-empty bottle of bourbon and a dusty glass. He poured a full glass and sat in his leather chair.

The bourbon burned going down, and the fumes cleared his sinuses. He did not feel better. He would never feel better. But the sting of the drink might let him get through a day of acting like

an attorney. He brushed files and dust out of his way, making a
clearing on his desk. He grabbed a legal pad and jotted notes to
himself:

Ike Stiles v. ???
Facts: Plaintiff believes genetically altered crops from
neighboring farm have spread to his fields. Plaintiff is an
organic farmer. Damages?
Issues of fact: Are his crops altered? How much $$ lost?
Issues of law: What cause? Products Liability?

It was definitely not the run-of-the-mill slip and fall case. He
really had no idea how to approach it. His first call would have
to be to a plaintiff's attorney who was well-versed in all manner
of litigation. Tom thumbed through his Rolodex, then punched a
Detroit number into his cell phone.

"Putnam, Putnam & Vale," the cheerful female voice of a
professional screener answered. "How may I direct your call?"

Tom identified himself, and Franklin Putnam was on the line
in two minutes.

"How are you, Frank?" Tom said, pleased that his own
schmoozing lawyer voice came back to him so quickly.

"Great. Great," Franklin said. "You hanging in there?"

"I'm doing okay," Tom lied.

"Great," Franklin said. "A few of those cases you sent over
have already settled. You should be seeing some referral fees real
soon."

Putnam, Putnam & Vale had taken over almost all of Tom's
caseload after Claire's death. Franklin Putnam was the chairman
of the Bar Association's Trial Lawyer section, and was among the
most respected plaintiff's lawyers in the state. Tom knew he was
placing his clients in good hands.

"I know you'll do those folks right," Tom said. "You have a
couple of minutes, Frank? I have a new case, and I'm not really
sure what to do with it."

"Sure," Franklin said. "Shoot."

"This is a good friend. An old farmer. He runs an organic
berry farm up here. A place I used to work at when I was a kid.

Anyway, there is a university research station across the road that is supposedly growing genetically altered plants. And the old guy is convinced that it is affecting his crops. He wants to sue. You ever handle anything like that?"

"We wouldn't handle it," Franklin said, and Tom knew that his lack of hesitation was a bad sign for Ike's case. "Can't make money on a case like that. Not on contingency. I know the Canadian Supreme Court just had a ruling on a similar case earlier this year. In favor of the corporations. The biotech companies fight these things tooth and nail. Definitely a money trap."

"Well, the old guy has some money. Could he find someone to help him on retainer?" Tom asked.

"No one any good," Franklin said. "Best he could do is find a young lawyer who would take it and end up costing him a lot of money for nothing. I'm sorry. I'd love to help. But a case like that is a dog."

"No," Tom said, "don't apologize. I was only looking into it for him."

A few more calls confirmed everything Franklin had said. No credible lawyer was going to help Ike in this situation. The best the old man could do was throw good money at a bad lawyer for no result. For most clients, this would have ended Tom's inquiry. But Ike wasn't most clients, and Tom knew he would have to roll up his sleeves and find some answers. He poured himself another shot of bourbon and took his notes with him to the Milton Diner for a quick lunch.

The bowl of potato soup did not sit well on top of the bourbon. Another drink when he returned to the office settled his stomach, but caused an insatiable need to nap. Tom barely made it to the couch in the reception area before he collapsed. His own snoring woke him sometime later. He could tell it was late afternoon by the brown hue of daylight that permeated the office. He checked his watch. Four-thirty, and there was still work to be done.

He shuffled back to his desk and glanced at the bottle of bourbon. There would be time for another drink later. It could even be social. Tom returned to his legal pad and refreshed his memory.

Franklin Putnam had an encyclopedic knowledge of most areas of tort litigation within the state, and he was never at a loss to deliver a quick lecture to anyone who was willing to listen. Franklin's failure to rattle off a condensed legal treatise on the law governing Ike's case led Tom to believe that the legal issues would be mostly novel ones. That meant research. And probably a lot of it.

The office's conference room was lined with all the law any local lawyer would likely need. It had the cases, statutes, practice manuals, and treatises that governed most issues of general practice. For anything not covered in the books, Tom had full access to the WestLaw database from his desktop computer. But Tom could barely operate the computer and he hated research. His forte was being able to talk a good game in the courtroom, without much regard for the written law. He was persuasive, if not precise. And when it came to research, he usually paid a younger lawyer to handle it.

He pawed through his Rolodex again and punched a number into his cell phone.

"Law Office of Nell Yeates," a familiar voice answered.

"What are you doing answering your own phones?" Tom laughed.

"Not everyone's as lucky as you, Tom," Nell said. "Some of us have to pay for office help."

Nell had done an internship in his office five years earlier, before moving on to practice in Alpena. She was a competent young lawyer, and Tom had used her for research ever since. Nell obviously hadn't heard about Claire, and Tom was in no mood for gracious condolences.

"Hey, I have a job for you that might pay a few bills," Tom changed the subject.

"It's about time," she said. "I was beginning to think you'd closed up shop."

"Well, I'm cutting back a lot," Tom said. "But I've got an issue here you can sink some good billable hours into."

"Sounds great," she said.

Tom outlined his problem in broad strokes, and Nell promised a research memorandum for him as soon as she could turn it around. Tom would cover the cost out of pocket. No sense in making Ike foot the bill just yet.

With Nell working on the legal issues, he needed an expert to help him understand the facts of the case, and there was still time in the day to find one. Tom turned to a separate Rolodex on the credenza that contained hundreds of doctors and academics arranged by area of expertise. After flipping idly through the catalogue of human knowledge, Tom realized he didn't even know what kind of an expert Ike's case would require. Tom's practice had always focused on making a dollar. He cared about his clients, but he was not a cause man. He had never litigated an environmental issue in his life. He leaned back in his chair and searched his mind. Did he know anyone who was even into environmental causes?

There was Charlie Sage, the local prosecutor. While he was no environmentalist, he was dating that activist professor who had caused all the trouble for the Blue-Mart development. It was a start. He dialed the prosecutor's office and caught Charlie before he left for the day.

"Tommy," Charlie said. "Glad you called. I've been meaning to get a hold of you."

"Good," Tom said. "Let's have a beer and catch up."

Charlie was silent too long. "I'm not sure that's such a good idea, Tommy," he said finally.

"What are you, my mother?" Tom said, irritated.

"C'mon, Tommy. How about I buy you dinner instead?"

"I'm drinking my dinner tonight, Captain," Tom said. "Just like the old days. Five-thirty at O'Hara's. Don't be late or I might start without you."

Tom was confident Charlie would show. He leaned back in his chair and listened to the numbing silence of his office. He'd gotten off to a reasonable start on the case. It was only a couple hours working the phones, but it felt good to be doing something. But now the silence, and Claire's absence, were overwhelming. He locked the office hurriedly and walked down the block to O'Hara's. It was five-fifteen, and though Charlie was not late, Tom did start drinking without him.

Tom was working on a second beer when Charlie Sage plopped down on the bar stool next to him. There were only a handful of lawyers in Milton, and Tom was not particularly close to any of them. But Charlie was by far Tom's closest colleague. Charlie had been the town's public defender for years but had been elected prosecutor the previous fall when the outgoing prosecutor seriously overreached on a case and charged Charlie's young associate with aiding a "terrorist group." When the "terrorist group" turned out to be a bunch of peaceful activists, the old prosecutor found himself in a political nightmare. The case against Charlie's associate was without legal merit and was quickly dismissed, but it had riled up the local electorate enough to oust the prosecutor and install a bunch of Green Party candidates on the county board. Charlie got swept into the prosecutor's office as a reform candidate.

"Old Milwaukee for my friend," Tom said to the bartender.

"You started without me," Charlie said, feigning disappointment.

"You'll catch up."

They drank and chatted about nothing for a time, avoiding talk of Claire or Tom's drinking.

"You still seeing that professor from Central?" Tom asked at the first lull in their conversation. "The leader of that activist group."

"Wilma Quinn. Yeah," Charlie said, finishing off a beer. "It's pretty informal. She's cool."

"I saw her down at the courthouse a few times last year. At those rallies she was leading. She was pretty gung ho?"

"Oh yeah," Charlie said. "Passionate, I would call it."

"Big into the environmental causes, huh?"

"Ph.D. in social ecology," Charlie said. "That covers a lot of ground. She wants to save the world from everything. And pretty well knows how to do it, too."

"I got a new case where I might need some expertise like that," Tom said, hailing the bartender for two more beers and tossing a twenty on the counter.

"You're taking new cases?" Charlie said, honest surprise in his voice.

"Well, I haven't taken it yet. I'm just investigating it. You know the Stiles' Berry Farm?"

"Sure," Charlie said. "Wilma likes to stop at that place."

"Stiles has got an environmental issue with one of his neighbors, and I'm having a hard time finding an expert."

"You grew up around there, didn't you?"

"Right next door," Tom said, taking a long drink from a fresh beer.

"So what's the issue?"

"I guess the neighbors have some genetically modified crops or something, and they're spreading onto Stiles' land somehow," Tom said.

"Oh yeah. Wilma's always talking about that stuff. She hates bio-engineering," Charlie said. "She shops at that farm because it's organic. Isn't it?"

"Yeah," Tom said. "He's been organic for almost six years now."

"Oh, I'm sure she'll know something about it," Charlie said. "Or at least get you in touch with someone who does."

"Cool," Tom said, raising his bottle in a toast to his friend. "Here's to a million-dollar settlement, and a big old expert witness fee."

Tom tried to order shots, but Charlie vetoed the plan. He was obviously uncomfortable with Tom's drinking. Tom could feel the judgment. He knew he had a lecture coming from a fellow member of the bar. Charlie hemmed and hawed. He complained about the prosecutor's office he had inherited, and they talked about old courtroom battles, before Charlie finally came to his point.

"You know, Tommy..." Charlie said, and hesitated, obviously trying to choose kind words. "There's rumors flying around the courthouse. People are talking."

"I don't give a goddamn," Tom said matter-of-factly.

"I was in Parr's chambers the other day, and he was asking about you," Charlie went on. "People are worried."

"Nothing to worry about," Tom said, taking a self-conscious drink from his beer and accidentally splashing some on his chin and neck.

Charlie didn't let it go. "We all know how much you're hurting. It's natural. But, I don't know, maybe you should find someone to talk to about coping with this?"

The words stung Tom's pride. He knew Charlie well enough to know that the words carried good intentions. But he didn't want to admit that nothing in the world would ever be right again. He didn't want to talk about her, or his loss.

"C'mon," Tom said, trying his best laugh. "You and me have been getting drunk at this bar for what? Almost twenty years now. I'm not gonna stop that because she's gone. It's one of the only things I've got left."

"I didn't say to stop—"

"Yeah, I'm still sad," Tom cut him off. "Yeah, I don't want to get out of bed some days. But that's natural, ain't it?"

"Yes," Charlie said. "Grieving is natural. All I'm saying is there is talk. And if you're thinking of practicing law again, whenever you're ready, you should probably think about seeing someone. Because living like this, I mean, people have seen you out and about, drunk in the morning. And this is a small town, Tommy."

"What are they saying about your decision to de-emphasize drug prosecutions? How do the locals feel about that one, Charlie? I mean, who gives a shit?"

"It's not the same thing," Charlie said.

Their exchange paused, and Tom burned a little as both men stared ahead at the mirror behind the bar. The truth hurt. He had always considered himself to be a strong, independent man. But Claire's passing was really the first great test of his life, and he was failing miserably.

"I'm working on it," Tom said finally. "But I don't need no shrink."

"All right," Charlie said. "I didn't want to upset you. I just thought you should know what's going around."

"I know," Tom said. "Like *Peyton Place*, this little town."

With that, Charlie's lecture was over. They talked about nothing and drank beer. And by the time last call came, Tom had drunk the world into partial oblivion. He had little memory of his journey home from the bar. And his hours of fitful rest were black. Another small chunk of life taken away. Another day without Claire in the world.

Tom's sleep was rocked by the telephone. He opened one eye to let in the least amount of light that would orient him to time and place. His own bed. Bright daylight. The ringing continued, exploding in his head. It had to be stopped.

"Hello," Tom said in a muffled voice.

"Tommy." It was Charlie's voice, too exuberant. "Good news."

"Why are you awake?" Tom struggled for words.

"Some of us gotta work," Charlie said. "Hey, you got a pen and paper handy? Wilma's got a guy you need to talk to."

"I'll call you back in—" Tom said, dropping his head back on the pillow.

"No, no, no."

"What?" Tom said.

"This guy's up in our area today," Charlie insisted. "Get a pen and paper. You're going to want to talk to him."

Tom took down the information, then started to nurse another hangover.

Chapter Two

R yan Romanelli followed his doctoral student as she led him through the experimental tomato field. He sensed excitement in her hurried gait.

"Pretty unbelievable, isn't it?" Wendy Isaacson said, stooping to examine a single plant. "Only the third generation and look at it. What do you think, Professor?"

Ryan bent down next to her and examined the transgenic plant. The quarter-inch hole on the growing tomato was an obvious indicator. He leaned close to the fruit and looked in the hole, where a tomato fruitworm rested, fat and happy.

"This little guy definitely looks resistant." Ryan smiled at his student. "What do your samples indicate? How much of the crop is infested?"

"Right around ten percent," she said.

He had warned Wendy about her research topic when she asked him to supervise her thesis. Setting out to prove that a genetically modified tomato plant would cause harm to the environment by making super pests as a side effect was no way to earn accolades at Michigan A&T. But Wendy was an idealist, like himself, committed to basic research no matter where the truth led. And he was happy her research was succeeding.

Ryan walked with Wendy through the field at the Beaverton Experiment Station, examining plants and discussing her methods. It was her fourth year in the program, and she was already a good scientist; she needed his guidance only for formality's sake. As they made their way through the field, he saw a conspicuous black Cadillac turn onto the dirt access road. It drove to the research station leaving a trail of brown dust in the air behind it.

"I'm expecting someone," he told Wendy, who looked surprised by the presence of a visitor at the isolated research center. He excused himself and made his way to meet the lawyer.

"So Professor Quinn told me you had some questions about GMOs," Ryan said after an exchange of pleasantries.

"GMOs?" Tom laughed. "I tell you, I know so little about all this, I don't know what questions to ask. What's a GMO?"

"Genetically modified organisms," Ryan said. The lawyer's eyes were bloodshot and there was the faint smell of alcohol Ryan normally associated with undergraduates in the front row of Friday morning lectures. "Like my tomato plants here." He introduced his field with a gracious sweep of the hand and a slight bow. Wendy waved at Tom from the middle of the field, where she was stooped-down collecting soil samples.

"These plants are genetically modified?" Tom asked. He looked like a typical American to Ryan. Blissfully ignorant. "How can you tell?"

"These are Bt-tomatoes," Ryan said.

"They look normal."

"Look normal. Taste normal," Ryan said. "But they are really part tomato, part bacteria."

"Part bacteria?" Tom looked at the field and swallowed noticeably.

"Uh-huh," said Ryan, smiling. *Bacillus thuringiensis*. Or Bt for short. Found in the soil you are standing on. It produces a natural insecticide. So we take a gene from Bt that makes the insecticide and put it into a tomato plant, and *voilà*, we've got a tomato plant that makes its own insecticide. A Bt-tomato."

"Is that good?" Tom asked.

"Well it's not good if you're a tomato fruitworm," Ryan said. Wendy looked up and gave a half-hearted chuckle. "But Bt isn't toxic to humans. Organic farmers have been using it for years to get rid of pests."

"So it's good," Tom said, his posture relaxing.

"Well, we don't really know," Ryan said. "The Bt the organic farmers use gets broken down by sunlight in a few days. But when we put the Bt gene in a plant, the plant just keeps on pumping out more and more of the stuff. It doesn't have an on-off switch. So the Bt levels in some of these plants are insanely high. At least according to some studies."

"So they aren't made for eating, then?" Tom asked.

"You might think that." Ryan smiled wider. "But Bt-tomatoes have been approved for human consumption for years. They never really took off. Kind of creeped people out. But you've probably eaten a bunch of Bt-corn and soybeans, if you shop at a supermarket."

Ryan loved to watch the looks on people's faces as he explained the miracle products found in modern grocery stores. Tom was silent for a time, as Ryan led him into the field and introduced him to Wendy.

"Wendy is studying the effects of the Bt-tomato on the tomato fruitworm," Ryan said. "Her hypothesis is that the use of Bt crops will create resistant pest populations. She thinks we are creating super bugs that will be resistant to regular applications of Bt. Not such a good deal for organic farmers, if she's right. Which is what your case is about, right? An organic farm problem?"

Tom gave Ryan the highlights of Ike's story.

"Genetic pollution," Ryan said, when Tom had finished. "Once these plants are released into the environment, there's nothing stopping them. Life, Mr. Hughes, it just keeps on spreading."

"So you don't think that sounds crazy?" Tom said.

"On the contrary," Ryan said. "It would be crazy if the GMOs didn't spread. They are alive. They procreate. Cross-pollinate. Given a year or two, a GM field is bound to mingle its genetic material with neighboring fields of the same species."

"So is that something you could test for?" Tom said. "Can you take a sample from my client's field and determine if it is GMO or whatever?"

"You said his farm is next to the North Central Research Center," Ryan said.

"Yeah."

"That place operates on a private grant from GenAgra. They've been field testing there for about three years," Ryan said. "So I've got no doubt they are growing GM foods there. But, I'm not sure what specific research they're doing. I'd have to check into it."

"GenAgra," Wendy smirked. "Making *life* better."

"But if it came down to it, you could do some tests and find out if there was genetic pollution, right?" Tom asked.

"Probably. But, why don't we go and have a look," Ryan said. "I'm headed back to the university. We can stop there, and I'll give you a quick tour of the place."

Al Bullard reluctantly disembarked the corporate jet. The concierge flight attendant had rebuffed his every advance on the two hour flight from D.C. to Chicago, but he was still sorry to leave her behind. Two attendants were offloading his bags into the trunk of a limousine, and a chauffeur held the rear door open for him at the bottom of the stairs. GenAgra certainly acted like a first class operation. His father had been right about the revolving door from D.C. to the corporate world. The perks were definitely better in the private sector.

"Good afternoon, sir," the chauffeur said pleasantly, as Bullard squeezed himself into the back seat. Bullard made no effort to respond. Effort on his part was reserved for audiences that mattered. The chauffeur closed the door on the light blue sunshine of a Chicago summer, leaving Bullard alone in the cool gray of commercial opulence. He sank into the soft leather seat surrounded by a full entertainment center and complimentary wet bar.

Bullard was relaxed to the point of boredom as the limousine conveyed him to his first meeting with Wes Zimmerman. Zimmerman was the CEO of GenAgra, the fourth largest biotech company in the world, and Bullard knew that the old man had more power than the leaders of most countries. But Zimmerman was small potatoes to Bullard, who had spent the better part of the last six years with instant access to the vice president of the United States. He had even met with the president personally on several occasions. And after such heady days, a meeting with a CEO was nothing to get excited about.

He dozed as the limousine fought interstate traffic, dreamed of a flight attendant with a slightly more accommodating mind set, and was awakened by the chauffeur when they arrived at the Sears Tower. Zimmerman's assistant was waiting in the lobby.

"Mr. Bullard?" the assistant queried. "I'm Cal Ickes, Mr. Zimmerman's personal assistant."

Bullard shook the assistant's hand silently.

"We'll see that your bags are taken to the Four Seasons," the assistant said. "If you will follow me, Mr. Zimmerman should be ready to see you shortly."

The assistant led him to a private elevator, swiped a magnetic card before a control panel, and ushered Bullard to the 70th floor. They moved briskly through a bright lobby, the assistant's smile the only apparent security clearance. Past a maze of bureaucracy, the assistant showed Bullard an understated conference room.

"I'll let him know you've arrived," the assistant said. "May I get you anything to drink while you wait?"

"I'm fine," Bullard said.

"May I say, sir," the assistant ventured, "that I am a great admirer. Your book on framing of issues was priceless reading for those of us trying to work our way up the corporate ladder."

"Thank you," Bullard said, pleased. "I've always thought public relations should have a more prominent role in business education today."

"And I never missed your show on CNTV, when it was on," the assistant gushed.

Bullard was flattered and annoyed at once. The assistant must have been a real news hound to have watched the show, which had survived only three weeks. The ratings were abysmal and the network brass as much as told him that he would never be telegenic enough to make it in "infotainment."

"Thank you," Bullard said. "You know, I was always happier working behind the scenes, though. You should bring me a copy of the book sometime, if you'd like. I'd be happy to sign it."

The assistant left. And Bullard basked in the assistant's obvious awe. He loved the attention brought by fame, even small fame, but knew at a professional level how fickle public attitudes could be. The compliment for his book owed more to the million dollar marketing campaign than to the merit of his writing. The world was far more about marketing than about ideas. He looked out the room-length window, over the cityscape and down onto a misty white fog that was drifting across Lake Michigan. It was a scene that might make men think of fishing or sailing or swimming among the whitecaps. But to Bullard, the view brought to mind the price of advertising on signs among the skyscrapers.

The door opened and the assistant entered, followed by a stout, elderly gentleman in an impeccable blue suit.

"Mr. Bullard," the assistant said, "this is Mr. Zimmerman. Mr. Zimmerman, Al Bullard." The assistant deftly bowed out of the room.

"Al, nice to meet you," Zimmerman said. His handshake was like a vice, dispelling any illusion that age had made him frail. "I've met your father on a number of occasions. He's still with Interior?"

"Yes, sir," Bullard said. "Undersecretary. He has spoken of you, too, sir."

"Great guy," Zimmerman said. It was obvious from the old man's charm that Zimmerman had worked his way to the top as a salesman, not a technocrat. "Can I get you a drink?"

"No thanks," Bullard said. "They took very good care of me on the flight."

"Good," Zimmerman said. "Well, why don't we have a seat."

They sat separated by a corner of the cherry conference table, and Zimmerman proceeded to talk about yachting on Lake Michigan to break the ice. He then pumped Bullard for information from inside the Beltway. Bullard was relieved when Zimmerman ended the mandatory banter about non-business items, but did his best not to show it.

"So, I'm very sorry I have not had a chance to meet you in person since we brought you on board," Zimmerman said. "I've been meaning to set something like this up for months, but things have been crazy here."

"Well, a new marketing campaign for such an old company can do that," Bullard said. GenAgra had been around for nearly a hundred years. It started its corporate life as Midwest Chemical, making petrochemical products for the emerging American market. In the early '80s, its image and balance sheet were decimated by its hand in producing Agent Orange, asbestos, and several toxic suburban wastelands. Midwest Chemical sought protection in the corporate cocoon of Chapter 11 Bankruptcy. It was reborn in the mid-'90s as GenAgra. Gone were the ugly old chemical lines that had stirred up intense litigation. GenAgra concentrated on its profitable business in agrochemicals, and on the emerging field of biotechnology. Bullard was impressed with the company's transformation. It was worthy of comparison to modern PR techniques.

"The guys over in marketing are in love with your new campaign," Zimmerman said, smiling. "Making *life* better. They just love it. They tell me our recognition and favorable numbers are through the roof, in historical terms."

"Yes," Bullard said. "Our focus group testing says the new slogan and logo are really making good headway. It's funny, though. We're getting some contamination from the pharmaceutical advertising. From Viagra."

"Really?"

"Yes," Bullard said. "They're spending a ton to make Viagra a household name. And it sounds so much like GenAgra. We're getting some customer confusion with our ads. It shouldn't hurt, though. Viagra is a great product in terms of its positive opinion ratings. No one wants to tell you that up front, but when we start to sift through the numbers, we know the public loves it."

"You ever use it?" Zimmerman laughed. "Well, you're probably too young still. But that stuff—well, I digress."

Bullard let a polite laugh cover his boredom.

"This new campaign is great," Zimmerman went on. "But it's only the start. We're about to launch a product that will revolutionize the biotech industry. That's why I hired The Bullard Group in January. I want you to do for this new product what you did for the conservatives in Washington for the past six years. I want it to steamroll the world like Coca-Cola."

Bullard's work for the conservatives in D.C. had made him the guru of the public relations world. He had helped solidify their control of Congress, because he knew how to work a focus group to perfection. He had helped elect a disturbingly unpopular man as president of the United States twice because he knew how to manipulate words to recreate reality. Selling rabbit turds as a new cereal would be child's play.

"What's the product?" Bullard asked.

"Well, we haven't actually named it yet," Zimmerman said. "We were hoping you might do your magic there. But the guys in the field have taken to calling it the Skinny Berry."

Zimmerman filled him in on the details of the Skinny Berry. Bullard was amused at first, then became distracted. A blackberry that would help people lose weight sounded too good to be true. They could have hired the chauffeur to sell the Skinny Berry and found success. But, so long as the price was right, Bullard was happy to sell the product to all the world.

Tom willfully declined Ike's offer of an afternoon beer, as the old man showed Ryan around the farm. The afternoon wore on toward dinnertime, and it was easily the longest Tom had gone without a drink since Claire's funeral. His legs were shaky as he followed Ike's guided tour.

"The closer we get to the southern edge of my field, the less bird damage you'll find," Ike explained to the nodding professor. Ike told the story so much better, Tom thought, as he watched the two converse.

Ike waved to a family picking strawberries in his field. "You finding the big ones?" he hollered with a smile, and the children with the family tumbled over one another to tell him how well they were doing on their search for berries.

"I'm not aware of any genetically modified blackberry," Ryan said. "But, with GenAgra running the field next door, it wouldn't surprise me."

"I thought it was Michigan A&T that ran that farm," Ike said, surprised.

"Well, technically, GenAgra owns the land," Ryan explained, "but it's a joint venture with Michigan A&T. And for the money

GenAgra pumps into the university, you'd better believe that they're calling all the shots."

Ike snorted and spit, showing his obvious distaste for mega-corporations. Ryan cut small shoots from several of Ike's blackberry plants and placed them in airtight plastic bags. He used a felt tip pen to write a nearly illegible identification on each sample, and then repeated the process in Ike's fast-growing corn field.

"I'm going to take Mr. Hughes with me, and we'll see what we can find out over at the research center," Ryan said, motioning to the fields across the road.

"You ought to take a torch to that place." Ike scowled. "Goddamned GenAgra."

Ryan laughed. "Probably be much more efficient."

Tom observed the way the professor communicated with Ike. Ike was the epitome of the common juror in Wabeno County. Tom, who had deposed hundreds of experts in his day, thought Ryan showed a great rapport with the old farmer. And if he could charm Ike, then the professor would probably have a jury eating out of his hand, Tom surmised.

The men made their way back to the farmhouse. Tom hopped in the passenger seat of the professor's Volkswagen Jetta for the short trip down to the research center. The professor drove down, across County-Line Road, and passed a flourescent green and white sign that welcomed them to Isabella County. Ryan turned right onto a private drive, passing signs warning them they were entering the private property of the North Central Research Center.

Ryan parked the Jetta near a one-story house that had been converted into an office complex. The sign above the door said "North Central Research Center—Main Office." Ryan showed his university credentials and signed Tom in as a guest.

"What brings you out here today, Professor Romanelli?" the student clerk behind the desk asked.

"Just taking a look around," Ryan said rather slowly. "On my way back to school and was passing by. Considering some new lines of research for the fall, and looking for the right environment."

"You should check out the back-half, then," the student said cheerfully. "Once that blackberry crop passes its final testing phase, it should be outta here. I guess GenAgra's all hot and bothered to get it on the market."

"Really?" Ryan said. "What is it? I hadn't heard about any blackberry crop."

"Around here we call it the Skinny Berry." The student grinned. "It's a transgenic blackberry, crossed with a gene from *Hoodia gordonii*. A handful of 'em will suppress your appetite all day."

Tom was lost in the technical talk but saw the surprise register on Ryan's face.

"Is the *Hoodia* gene actually expressing itself?" Ryan said.

"Oh yeah. Try a few, Doc. Everybody working the field does." The student winked. "They work like a charm. Somebody's getting rich with this one."

Ryan led Tom out the back door of the office complex, then along a narrow blacktop path. The path swung to the west between two lush, green fields of corn.

"What's a hoot-eye?" Tom said, when they had passed a safe distance from the office complex.

"*Hoodia gordonii*," Ryan corrected him like a tutor. "It's a cactus that grows in the Kalahari Desert in South Africa. Pharmaceutical companies have been trying to commercialize it for about a decade now, but it's very hard to cultivate. It takes your appetite away when you eat it."

"Like a diet drug?" Tom asked.

"Like the king of diet drugs," Ryan said. "The Bushmen have been using it for centuries. One serving supposedly takes your appetite away for an entire day."

"You don't see a lot of fat Bushmen, do you?" Tom joked.

"If they've really isolated the appetite suppression gene from the *Hoodia*," Ryan said, "and they are getting it to express itself in a plant indigenous to North America, it's no joking matter. This is big business. It's like a winning lottery ticket."

Ryan glanced around, then stepped off the asphalt path. He made his way a few rows deep into the cornfield. Tom followed, admiring the young doctor's agility as he found a sample ear of corn, bagged it, and jotted a note on the bag in a series of quick motions. But Tom's attention to the doctor's work was soon averted, as an electric golf cart made its way around the corner of the opposite corn field, and headed down the path toward them. Its driver and passenger were both older men dressed in white lab coats. Tom strained to make out the badges on their lapels. As they drew near, he recognized the green and white logo as one he had seen frequently on television. GenAgra. Making *life* better.

Ryan hurriedly bagged a second corn sample and stuffed it into his front pants pocket. The passenger in the golf cart turned to study them, but the cart rolled past silently, without incident. Ryan hurried Tom along into the blackberry field. They headed down a path between rows of thick blackberry brambles. Tom looked closely at the blackberries that weighed down their stems. They were farther along than Ike's patch. Most were not yet fully ripe, but numerous berries were deep purple already. Tom snatched a few dark berries as he passed and mindlessly popped them into his mouth.

The flavor exploded. It was the pungent sweet taste he remembered from his earliest years as a boy playing in Ike's late-summer fields. But it was followed by a slightly nutty aftertaste. The strange aftertaste was only a hint and passed quickly. It was not unpleasant.

"Man," Tom said, sucking at seeds lodged in his teeth, "these are good."

Ryan shot him a look of a disdain. The professor was Tom's junior by at least ten years, but he carried a wise demeanor that made him seem older.

"This stuff hasn't passed FDA approval yet," Ryan said.

"But that kid back there..." Tom started, then stopped. He wondered if the slight burning sensation he felt on his lips and tongue was just his imagination.

"Not that the FDA is going to do anything to stop this. They'll rubber stamp any GMO as safe for humans as long as it is deemed 'substantially equivalent.'" Ryan said with disgust. "Have you ever heard of StarLink corn?"

Tom shook his head, convinced that the tingle in his mouth was psychosomatic.

"It was a corn product grown back in 2000," Ryan said. "It was a Bt-corn, but the toxin it manufactured could survive longer through the human digestive process. So it was more toxic to humans and bad enough that even the EPA wouldn't approve it for human consumption."

"You think that corn back there is like that?" He was unsettled by his new-found knowledge about the food supply.

"No." Ryan smiled. "I mean, I don't know. But I doubt it. StarLink was never approved for human consumption. But they did approve it for animals. Problem is, there was no way to keep animal grain and human grain separate in the supply chain. So the StarLink corn ended up contaminating all kinds of corn products before it was recalled."

"Yeah, so," Tom said, swallowing and feeling a slight burn where the berry juice had touched the corners of his mouth.

"Well, a bunch of people ate tacos and tortillas in the fall of that year. People without any history of allergies. And a good number ended up going to the hospital with anaphylactic shock." Ryan laughed.

"How come I never heard of that?" He tried to spit the remaining juice out of his mouth.

"Because when they complained, our government said it was all in their heads," Ryan said. "They could never prove what corn products were contaminated and whether these people actually ate the StarLink corn." He stopped at a bramble and expertly clipped a sample for comparison to Ike's crop. "Nice berries though, huh?"

"Yeah, they're great," Tom said sarcastically. "I feel so much better."

"I'll get these checked out at my lab and let you know in a few days," Ryan said.

"Thanks a lot, Doc," Tom said.

They walked back to the office complex, entered the back door and were about to depart when the student at the counter stopped them.

"Doc, could you hang on a second," the student said, his voice raised with a hint of authority.

Ryan and Tom froze. Slowly, the professor turned and headed back to the counter to meet the student.

"One of the guys from GenAgra said he saw you out there sampling some of the corn," the student said, his natural smile fading slightly. "You know this is a cooperative site, Doc? No samples allowed to leave without express approval."

"Oh, I'm sorry," Ryan said, a sincere apologist. "One of my students is working on a corn comparison survey, and I couldn't resist snagging one of these ears. I wasn't even thinking." He pulled one of the bagged ears of corn out of his pants pocket and handed it to the student.

"Thanks, Doc," the student said. "Those guys from GenAgra can be real assholes." The young man rolled his eyes, and Ryan nodded agreement as he turned to leave with Tom.

Ernie Vasquez felt a cold shiver run up his spine, a mixture of fear and ambition. It was only his second week as regional epidemiologist, and a young doctor was on the other end of the phone line explaining a shocking illness. It was the fourth such account Ernie had heard in just under two weeks. And while the illness sounded ferocious, Ernie was excited to be on the front lines with a chance to help save the world. He was already having delusions of grandeur. He could imagine the headlines: Fast Action by State's Newest Epidemiologist Averts Public Health Nightmare.

While the illness was small in terms of the number of suspected cases, its symptomatology was alarming. The first two cases were treated by the same small town physician, Dr. Donald Brown of Milton, or the illness might have gone unnoticed for weeks. Doctor Brown saw the first case in his office on June 1st. The patient was an otherwise healthy 22-year-old construction worker who left the job to visit Doctor Brown's office. He presented with severe muscle cramps, swollen extremities, a rash, and respiratory distress. Doctor Brown initially thought the worker was experiencing anaphylactic shock, but the man reported no allergies. The worker showed poor response to an epinephrine injection and was taken by ambulance to the nearest hospital in Perkins. It may have been a steroid injection that Doctor Brown administered before the ambulance arrived that kept Patient Number One alive. The worker made it to the regional hospital and was later medevaced to Ann Arbor where he remained, paralyzed, in extreme pain, and breathing with the assistance of a ventilator.

Patient Number Two arrived at Doctor Brown's office on

the morning of June 3rd. She had been driven in from the town of Watson by a neighbor. She was a senior citizen of moderate health, battling obesity and type 2 diabetes, but she presented with symptoms similar to that of Patient Number One. She was writhing in pain from head to toe and had edema in her lower legs so severe that the skin had fissured and oozed water. While at the office, she suffered an ascending paralysis, and her breathing was so distressed that her face turned blue. Doctor Brown skipped the adrenaline and injected the patient with a cortico-steroid. She was stabilized and transported to the regional facility in Perkins, where she remained bedridden but off a ventilator. There had been some minor improvement in the elderly woman's condition, but she was still not ambulatory.

Doctor Brown made a call directly to Ernie, the regional epidemiologist, because of the severity of the symptoms. The doctor's firsthand account of the illness had frightened Ernie a bit. He immediately called his supervisor, Herb Underwood, manager of the Bureau of Epidemiology. Ernie wanted to put out an alert for this new syndrome so hospitals would be required to report suspicious cases.

Underwood spent a half-hour laughing at Ernie for being too green in his first week on the job. The supervisor condescendingly explained that two cases of anaphylactic shock did not make an epidemic. He lectured Ernie about the proper balance between risk and cost to society, and told him to keep an eye on it, but to settle down.

Ernie spent the weekend feeling like a fool. He had made the unidentified syndrome sound like the Ebola virus. But the ferocity of the debilitating new illness stayed with him, and by the time he came into the office on Monday, he was ready to roll up his sleeves and go to work. Ernie ordered his own investigator to start calling hospitals across his region, actively looking for instances of the new illness that might have gone unreported. It was labor intensive, but by Tuesday their search had results.

Patient Number Three was a 48-year-old auto-worker. He had just died at the hospital in Bay City, with the initial cause of death being listed as an acute asthma attack. But when Ernie finally got through to the emergency room physician, the death sounded very much like a case of the new syndrome. Severe swelling, ascending paralysis, acute respiratory distress, and intense muscular pain—or "myalgia" in doctor-speak. Ernie ordered blood and tissue samples from the deceased be forwarded to his office.

And now, only two days later, Ernie was speaking with the doctor for Patient Number Four. Number Four was a college student from Michigan A&T. The student went to the campus clinic complaining of severe cramping, a rash, and difficulty breathing. He was a picture of health prior to the onset of the syndrome, but now his young body was hooked to a ventilator at the local hospital as he fought for survival.

"Thank you for taking the time to talk about this case, Doctor," Ernie said. "Do you think you could get me tissue and blood samples?"

"You got it," the young doctor said. "You have any idea what we're dealing with here?"

"Not yet," Ernie said. "But a couple of the early patients responded well to prednisone injections. It stabilized them to some extent."

As soon as he was done with the doctor, Ernie dialed Underwood's office. He fenced with the secretary to get access to his supervisor and was eventually put on hold. He tried to organize his thoughts as he waited, but was distracted by the Muzak.

"This is Herb Underwood," his boss said. His voice was clipped and curt, a fitting tribute to his personality.

"Herb. Ernie Vasquez here, up in Isabella County," he said with as much cheer as he could muster.

"What do you need, Vasquez? I'm getting ready for a meeting with the director tomorrow, so I'm kind of pressed for time."

"I've got two more cases of that unidentified syndrome I was telling you about last week," Ernie said.

"Where'd they come from?"

"One in Bay City. The other in St. Johns," Ernie said.

"And the other two were in?"

"Milton, sir," Ernie said.

"So it's not localized," Underwood sneered. "Not likely a single event."

"No, sir," Ernie said. "And, the cases have been spread out

over two weeks now."

"No pathogen? No idea what the incubation time is?"

"No, sir," Ernie said. "Just a group of very acute, very deadly symptoms. But I really think we should go to condition yellow and issue a statement to hospitals in the state, sir."

"These symptoms don't amount to much more than a very severe allergic reaction, Vasquez. Until you can identify some connection between these isolated cases, we are not going to put out a statewide alert. Has anyone made you aware of the budget crisis in this state, son?"

"The man in Bay City is dead, sir," Ernie said. With Underwood as his supervisor, Ernie didn't think he was going to last very long as a regional epidemiologist. "Two others are on a ventilator. Something serious is out there, sir. And you said last week, it's about risk versus cost. I think the risk is pretty high here."

"People die every day, Vasquez," Underwood said, playing the gentle mentor now. "Thousands of them. And lots of times there are questions about the exact cause. It's something you are going to have to get used to in this job. Right now, all you've got is a few unrelated allergic reactions. Until you get me a cause or a source, there's not much we can do."

Ernie managed to maintain a polite voice. He had a career to think about now. But, the sound of concern he had heard from the treating physicians convinced Ernie that Underwood was making a big mistake.

Chapter Three

Tom drove the back roads from Perkins to Milton. For the first time in weeks, his attention had been diverted away from Claire. His sober thoughts danced about the potential case of Ike Stiles v. GenAgra. If all that Ike had said proved to be true in a trial, a jury would want to run a scientist or two out of town. And Tom was impressed with the expert he had retained to investigate the case.

He mulled over Ryan's potential as an expert witness, as he drove back to his office. The doctor looked a bit younger than Tom would have liked in an expert, but his authoritative command of the subject matter more than made up for this deficiency. There was an easy credibility that oozed out of the doctor's running commentary about genetically modified foods, too. And he talked a good, common English that was able to make difficult topics sound as simple as addition. Better still, Ryan was pleasing to both the eye and the mind, in his manner and appearance. Any hint of grunge could be ironed out with a good casual jacket. On the whole, Tom would feel confident having a case rest on the expert opinions of Professor Ryan Romanelli.

Having gotten a good start on his factual research, Tom was eager to check Nell's progress. Tom hated people who talked on cell phones as they drove, but he was stuck in Milton's equivalent of rush hour traffic. Ten cars lined up to turn into the new Blue-Mart superstore. And since the end of the business day was fast approaching, Tom decided to break his own informal ban on in-car cell phone calls.

"How's it going, Nell?" Tom said. "Can we sue the bastards?"

"You know your office phone is out?" she asked. "I've been trying to call you all afternoon. And your fax isn't working either."

"Oh, yeah," Tom said, pausing. "Well, I'll have to get it checked, but what's the news?" He felt guilty for not telling her about Claire and resolved to get the story out as soon as he got his legal briefing.

"Well, there's good news and bad news," she said.

"Gimme the good first," Tom said. "I can use it."

"All right," Nell said, and Tom could almost see the wry smile on her face. "Of course you *can* sue the bastards. The law runs all the way back to jolly old England. The basics. Trespass is the most obvious cause of action, so long as there is some physical element to this genetic pollution you described."

"Uh-huh," Tom said. "That makes sense."

"And of course you'd have alternative counts. Nuisance for interference with the use and enjoyment of the land, in case the court's found no physical trespass. And a count in negligence, for the research facility allowing the pollution to escape. There might be a cause for product liability too, but I'd need to know more about the specific crops involved."

"So that's the good news," Tom said. Traffic was moving again. "We've got a cause of action."

"Yes, that's the good news," Nell said. "There is a cause of action in *theory*."

"And the bad?"

"As far as I can see, no one has successfully sued under these theories. All the litigation is really going in a different direction," Nell said.

"What direction is that?"

"There's a ton of federal case law out there where these companies—Monsanto, GenAgra—are suing farmers. Patent infringement cases. And they're very aggressive."

"The biotech companies are suing farmers?" Tom said.

"Uh-huh," Nell said excitedly. "And kicking the shit out of them. These biotech guys just don't seem to lose, Tom."

"Patent infringement," Tom repeated. "I'm not sure I follow."

"There's patent infringement. And breach of contract," Nell said. "Basically, the companies are making the genetically modified plants and then patenting them. Then they sell the seed to farmers for a premium. They're basically saying to the farmers, 'Here is your new and improved plant seed. The plants make their own pesticides, so you won't have to spend as much on pesticides. And the plants are immune to our herbicide, so you can spray as much as you like right on your own crop and kill all the weeds. No fuss. No muss.'"

"Uh-huh," Tom said, intrigued.

"But the plants themselves are all patented life forms. So the farmers sign agreements that they won't keep any seed and replant it, and they won't resell the seed. So the farmer has to keep coming back every spring to buy new seed from the biotech company. You know. Making *life* better."

"I am getting sick of hearing that," Tom said with a disgusted laugh. "But it's downright frightening when you say it in this context."

"Yeah, I know," she said. "I would've never imagined these outcomes. So anyway, when the farmer tries to skim some seed for himself, and the biotech company finds out about it, bam, the farmer is dragged into court. And ends up paying tens or hundreds of thousands of dollars in damages. Pretty amazing."

"How do the biotechs find out?" Tom asked.

"Oh, glad you reminded me," Nell said. "This is classic. They've got riders to their contracts that let them come and knock on the farmer's door at any time. 'Just here to test your crops, Mr. Farmer. See if you've got any of *our* genetically modified plants in your field.'"

Tom let it sink in. It seemed kind of un-American. "Wow. Somebody call the ACLU, huh?" he said. "But this wouldn't apply to our case. Ike hasn't signed any agreement to buy this stuff. He hates the thought of it."

Tom pulled up into an empty parking space in front of his office. He hopped out, cricked his neck awkwardly to hold the cell phone to his ear, and unlocked the front door. He saw Claire's empty chair and felt guilty again for not telling Nell the full story.

"That's what you'd think, but it gets even worse," Nell said.

"What?"

"There's a case—*Monsanto v. Jones*—that's been winding its way through the Canadian court system for years," Nell explained. "Monsanto sues a farmer for patent infringement because they find their genetically modified corn in his field. Farmer claims he knows nothing about the crop being genetically modified. It could have blown over from a neighboring field, or it could've ended up on his land as a part of highway spillage. He doesn't know. But the Canadian Supreme Court just ruled earlier this year. He got the benefit of a genetically modified crop. It was in violation of Monsanto's patent. The farmer had to pay damages."

"Yeah, I heard about a case up there," Tom said, plopping into his office chair. "But Christ, you'd think Canadian courts would be more liberal."

"It was a close decision at least," Nell said. "Five to four. But these guys always win, Tom. Or at least they always have."

"They used to say that about tobacco companies," Tom said.

"Oh shit," Nell said. "I don't like the sound of that. It wasn't a mom and pop law firm that took down big tobacco, Tom. These companies will chew you up."

"So what's the bottom line?" he said.

"Bottom line," Nell said, pausing a moment. "No way you sue anyone involved in this unless you have money to burn. You're at least as likely to end up paying damages as you are to get them."

"But there is a valid cause of action?" Tom said.

"In *theory*, yes," Nell said. "But in practical terms, it hasn't been done yet. And I wouldn't be the first to try it."

Tom laughed. "So you'll draft a complaint for me if I give

you the facts?" He checked his watch. It was 4:55 p.m., and if he was going to start practicing law again, he needed to make another phone call.

"As long as you're paying, boss," Nell said. "But I won't put my name on it. Tell 'em you drafted your own complaint this time, okay?"

"They'd never believe that," Tom said. "Hey, are you going to be around for a few minutes? Can I call you right back?"

"Sure," Nell said. "I've got to get some of my own work done since I spent all day doing yours."

"Okay," Tom said. "Let me call you in a minute, okay?"

Tom hung up the phone and went to Claire's desk. He pulled out the phone book and methodically found a number for the classified department at *The Milton Beacon*. The local paper only published on Sundays, and he needed to post his help wanted ad before the office closed for the weekend.

He punched the number into his cell and was disappointed to hear an automated message asking him to call back during regular business hours. At least someone got an early start on the weekend.

He called Nell back. He did not know how to broach Claire's death, but he had to tell her at some point. Nell's sorrow cut through his embarrassment, and he politely listened to her attempts at comfort.

As she turned, Wendy Isaacson caught a glimpse of her own face in the mirror behind the laboratory sink. She felt betrayed by the slight downturn at the corners of her mouth. Sulking like a schoolgirl, she chided herself. Her hands moved mechanically, preparing samples for the immuno-assay tests.

Ryan wanted preliminary answers for the attorney today. And Wendy learned long ago that what Professor Romanelli wanted, he got. She spent hours in the lab at times, wondering what she saw in the strange, little man. He was seven years her senior, and his dark, unkempt hair was already graying. He wore those awful black plastic-rim glasses. And he had ignored her in any personal way for over three-and-a-half years, despite her best efforts to make him take notice. Really, what was there to like?

But the intense jealousy she felt as he closed the door to his office to meet with the new graduate assistant surprised her. For the most part, Wendy had a monopoly on the professor's attention. She was his only graduate assistant. And even if his attentions had always been professional, she always thought he would come around in time. But the way the young redhead had twisted her hair and fawned over him made Wendy want to vomit. Perhaps it was time to finally write him off as an experiment that never germinated.

She turned to look at herself in the mirror again. At twenty-six, Wendy was not getting any younger. Her face still looked good, but she could already see faint crow's feet at the corners of her eyes. She looked down to her hands. Weathered and well-worked from all that damned time in the tomato field. It was definitely time to move on. Brilliant as he was, she could not wait on him forever.

Wendy removed the final field sample Ryan had collected from its baggie. She placed the corn leaf over the top of a small plastic test tube and depressed the cap. A tiny circular piece of the corn leaf fell into the narrow bottom of the tube. She quickly ground the circular piece with a sterile plastic pestle, added ten drops of water and repeated the grinding. Once the sample was prepared properly, she copied the identification information from the baggie onto the test tube and placed the tube with the other test samples in a small rack.

Before he had to run off to meet with little miss redhead, Ryan had given Wendy some basic background on the testing she was now conducting for him. An organic farmer was concerned there had been transgenic pollution onto his land. It was becoming a more frequent request in the testing world. Big agriculture wouldn't be happy until one hundred percent of American acreage was populated by GMOs.

The likely source of the pollution was a genetically modified variety of GenAgra corn, and Wendy decided to start her testing with the immuno-assay test for GenAgra's most prolific GM product: Weed-Away Corn. Weed-Away was GenAgra's top line herbicide. They had made a fortune during the agricultural revolution selling Weed-Away to farmers. Weed-Away was a deadly effective herbicide, however, and a farmer had to be careful using it. In trying to get rid of weeds, a sloppy farmer might end up killing his own cash crop.

But GenAgra had solved that problem by the late '90s and figured out a way to make billions in the process. They found a plant in South America which was resistant to Weed-Away, patented the plant, isolated the resistant gene, and genetically engineered that gene into a corn plant. Weed-Away Corn was born. Now farmers bought Weed-Away Corn seed from GenAgra and grew corn plants resistant to Weed-Away herbicide. They could now spray as much Weed-Away as they wanted on their crops, killing all the weeds without hurting the corn plant.

She placed a test strip into each of the samples she had prepared. The strips would tell her which plants, if any, were Weed-Away Corn. Wendy set a timer for five minutes and walked to the other side of the laboratory so she could get a better view into Ryan's office window. Out of the corner of her eye, she could see the redhead laughing coyly at jokes Wendy had heard years before. She pretended to work as she watched, and the minutes passed in a slow burn.

When the timer went off, she went back to interpret the test results. Bingo, she thought, giving the rack a quick look. She was a genius. Six out of the fourteen samples had two distinct blue lines across the center of the white test strip. Positive for Weed-Away Corn. The other eight samples had one blue line, which meant that the test had worked, but that the tested corn was not genetically modified Weed-Away Corn.

She took a closer look at the labels on the test tubes, searching for the one sample that came from the GenAgra field. She smiled, seeing that it was one of the positives. It was safe to say that GenAgra was growing a Weed-Away Corn field up there, and that the organic field had started to grow some Weed-Away Corn of its own.

"I'd like to see little miss redhead have the intuition to do that on the first try," Wendy said under her breath.

She hurriedly recorded the test results on a laboratory form and considered breaking in on the professor's meeting. She smiled. He would probably like to know how quickly she had solved his problem.

Tom made it to the office by ten. Insomnia the night before had kept him awake until he finally gave in to the desire for a drink. One glass of rationalized bourbon quickly became two, and the next thing Tom knew, he was venomously smacking the snooze button on his clock radio.

A very slight hangover slowed him down, but a fresh determination was growing inside of him. There was a new battle to be fought. An injustice was happening not only to Ike, but to everyone. Tom had learned a great deal about GMOs in the past forty-eight hours. He doubted that most Americans knew they were eating genetically modified foods on a daily basis. When they became aware, they would probably be pissed. And that meant making someone pay.

Making the bad guys pay was a rare, essential good of being a personal injury lawyer. People liked to focus on the money "ambulance chasers" made off others' misery. But to Tom, the real fun was punishing the wrongdoer. And his brain was already working overtime casting GenAgra as the villain.

He spent the first part of his morning dancing around the office like a bee in a hive, straightening out desks and clearing away junk. He then sat down at Claire's desk, the central nervous system of what had once been a thriving enterprise, and tried to think as she would have. Tom was a far poorer manager than his deceased wife, but if he could only imitate her, he might divine some of her administrative genius. He jotted a "to do" list on a yellow Post-It Note, as he had seen her do so often in the past.

The simple trick gave Tom direction. He checked items off the list as he went and had soon nudged the office back on course. He called the phone company and ordered a restoration of their service. He sorted through a volume of old mail and paid the essential bills. He called *The Milton Beacon* and placed a help wanted ad in the weekly paper. Finally, Tom made himself a manila file folder for his only active case. Stiles v. GenAgra, he typed on the label, and attached it to the folder.

With the office rounded into some order, he left Claire's station for the comforts of his own executive chair. He placed his newly prepared file on the desktop, opened it, and read over his notes. He scratched and scribbled new thoughts, and re-read the pad:

Ike Stiles v. GenAgra
Facts: Plaintiff believes genetically altered crops from neighboring farm have spread to his fields. Plaintiff is an organic farmer. Damages?
Issues of fact: Are his crops altered? How much $$ lost?
Issues of law: What cause? Products Liability?
Count I - Trespass
Count II - Nuisance
Count III - Negligence
Count IV - Products Liability?
Counterclaim likely - Patent Infringement

His own practice had been so focused on auto negligence that Tom had to strain to remember the elements of a trespass case. A physical intrusion was required, Nell had said, and that was enough for Tom to dredge up a chunk of law from his memory. A chunk that he had forgotten twenty years earlier. A trespass was a physical intrusion onto the land of another, in its most basic terms. If Tom's memory was correct, it didn't even require actual damages. A landowner could sue for nominal damages, or damages in name only, to protect his land against a trespasser.

Having clarified the law in his own mind, Tom let the facts of Ike's case drape themselves like a grapevine over the legal framework. If Tom sued GenAgra, he would need to prove there was some physical invasion. Ike's own testimony as a witness would not suffice. The invasion that had occurred, if any, was invisible to the layperson. Judge Parr, who would likely end up hearing the case, would never allow Ike to tell tall tales about animals not eating berries as evidence of some physical change in his crops. That evidence would not hold up to scientific scrutiny. Tom would need an expert to say that GenAgra's crop had physically intruded onto Ike's farm. With that much, Tom could make out a *prima facie* case for trespass, and that was enough to file a lawsuit.

He found Professor Romanelli's phone number on his cell and

dialed it. "Doc, Tom Hughes here."

"Hello, Mr. Hughes." The professor's voice sounded older over the phone. "I was just talking about your case with my graduate assistant."

"Great," Tom said. "That's why I called. You find anything yet?"

"Here, let me put you on the speakerphone," Ryan said. There was a click, and it sounded like the phone had been placed inside an electronic tunnel. "I've got Wendy Isaacson with me. You met her yesterday. She's been running tests this morning."

"Hello, Mr. Hughes," the young woman said, her voice cheerful and assertive.

"Hello, Wendy," Tom said. "Or is it Doctor Isaacson?"

"No," she said. "Not until Professor Romanelli gets me through my thesis, anyway."

"We have some positive results," Ryan said, breaking in. "I was just getting Wendy to fill me in."

"Okay," Tom said.

"I did an initial test on your samples this morning," Wendy said. "I used a standard ELISA test, which is an immuno-assay test—"

"It is basically a kit," Ryan interrupted. "Kind of like a home pregnancy test."

"Uh-huh," Tom said.

"Well, according to the immuno-assay test, GenAgra is growing a genetically modified corn crop at the facility next to your client's organic farm. It's called Weed-Away Corn. It's a corn plant engineered to be resistant to GenAgra's Weed-Away herbicide," she said.

"Uh-huh," he said. "I've heard of Weed-Away." Anyone who had ever tried to maintain their own lawn had seen it in stores. A jingle from the Weed-Away commercial popped into his mind, and he suppressed the urge to sing out, "Kills weeds fast."

"Five of the thirteen corn samples that were taken from your client's field also tested positive—that is, these samples came from genetically engineered Weed-Away Corn plants," Wendy said.

"These immuno-assay tests are qualitative, not quantitative," Ryan added. "We can't say how much contamination there has been in the field based on this testing, only that the six sampled plants tested positive for being Weed-Away Corn plants.

"So would you say there's been a physical invasion?" Tom asked the legally operative question.

"Well," Ryan said thoughtfully, "those plants got there somehow. Either your friend planted Weed-Away Corn seed, or the plants cross-pollinated with the GenAgra field, or there is some other source."

"Something physical had to pass onto the land to effect this change in his plants, right?" Tom instinctively sought to clarify the response. "Either that or Ike planted the genetically altered seed himself."

"Pollen is the most likely source," Ryan said, "based on what you and Ike have explained. So that would be something physical, if that's what you're getting at."

"What about the blackberries?" Tom said.

"That's a more difficult question," Ryan said. "The immuno-assay tests are available for the more common types of GMOs. But this blackberry is something relatively new. That's going to require a complete DNA test. I have access to testing facilities here on campus, but they're over in the Biotechnology and Breeding office. And I'm not so sure I want to use that lab."

"Why's that?" Tom asked.

"That office gets a good chunk of its operating budget from GenAgra sponsored projects," Ryan said. "If I use that lab to test the blackberry, they're going to get wind of it. But I've got a friend who runs a private lab down in East Lansing. I was going to ask if you'd like me send the blackberry samples to him."

"Sure," Tom said.

"I can't get it tested for free, though. That's going to run you right around four hundred dollars," Ryan said.

"Well within my budget," Tom said.

"Must be nice to be a lawyer," Wendy said.

Tom could hear the smile in her voice and strained to remember her face from their meeting yesterday. "I'd rather be a professor, to tell you the truth," he shot back. "You wouldn't believe the headaches I've got trying to run this place by myself."

"Okay," Ryan said. "I'll get the sample out to my friend's lab today."

"How long's it going to take to get an answer back on that, Doc?" Tom asked.

"Usually, one to two weeks," Ryan said. "But, I'll see if I can get him to rush it."

"I can't thank you enough for helping me with this stuff," Tom said. "Charlie told me you were the guy I needed to talk to, but I had no idea how much I didn't know."

"It's my pleasure," Ryan said. "We have common interests in this one."

"I'll be needing an expert witness to make this case, Doc," Tom said. "Assuming I actually file something. Would you consider coming on board?"

"I've never been a witness before," Ryan said. "Never really wanted to be a hired gun."

"Well, you could do it for free," Tom laughed, "but I'd feel mighty funny not paying you for your expertise."

There was a pause.

"What do you pay?" Ryan asked finally.

"It varies by expert," Tom said. "Let's say one hundred and fifty per hour. Two hundred for court time."

"I'll do it," Wendy chimed in.

"Thanks," Tom said kindly. "But, there is something about a full-fledged doctor that juries really like. You'll have to wait until you get your Ph.D., my dear."

"I'd certainly consider it," Ryan said.

"Great," Tom said. "You'll let me know when you get the tests back on the blackberries?"

"We'll keep you posted," Ryan said.

Ryan's testimony about the corn coupled with Ike's testimony that he planted only non-GMO crops would be enough to make out a basic case for trespass. Theoretically, they had enough to proceed. But not every legal claim that was supported by evidence ended up as a lawsuit. The real question was not one of theory but one of practicality. Was it wise to file the lawsuit? Nell had pretty much answered that question. Only a fool would think this suit was going to make money.

Tom remembered Franklin Putnam's warning. At best, Ike

could find a young lawyer to take the case and charge him a lot of money, Franklin had said. It was crazy to even consider a case like this against a giant like GenAgra. A pragmatic lawyer—something Tom had been for decades—would have a serious talk with Ike and nip this case in the bud.

It was an easy call to make. One he had made a thousand times. But now, Tom wavered. If the law was all about money, then this case was a loser. The risks far outweighed the potential gain. But if the law was about ethereal concepts like justice and fairness, then someone ought to help Ike fight off this multi-national giant. It was a real *Mr. Smith Goes to Washington* moment. Tom chuckled at the hint of idealism he felt—a sliver of real feeling that had miraculously survived decades of practicing law for profit. He needed to speak with Ike.

Al Bullard had the old CEO eating out of his hand by the time he left Chicago on Friday. Wes Zimmerman was old school. Bullard knew this from what he had heard about the business magnate before his trip. But in their face-to-face meeting, Zimmerman proved exactly how old-fashioned he was. It was obvious that the old man didn't care much for lawyers or boardrooms or hundred-page licensing agreements.

Zimmerman's evaluation process was clear to Bullard from the first handshake. The old man wanted to evaluate prospective business partners by looking them in the eye. For those who made a favorable first impression, the old man would want a more careful social evaluation. He would insist on having a drink or playing a round of golf, and he would spend the hours weighing his target. And in the end, if the man running GenAgra liked what he felt in his gut about a prospective partner, then they would be welcomed with a trust normally reserved for family. All this, Bullard surmised in his initial contact with Zimmerman.

Zimmerman was a dinosaur, Bullard decided, as he cruised along in the GenAgra corporate jet, again in the care of his favorite personal stewardess. In the globally competitive market that Bullard witnessed during his years in D.C., Luddites like Zimmerman, who did business based on intuition, were a dying breed. Any wolf—like Bullard—could play along. Invade the inner-circles of their empires and wreak havoc from within.

He shared none of Zimmerman's old-boy-network mentality. Bullard had simply smiled and nodded and maintained a perfect face of sincerity in every platitude he heaped on the old man. After a steak dinner at the Chicago Chop House and an evening of drinks on Zimmerman's yacht, the old man was ready to let Bullard guide the company's image into the twenty-first century. Bullard ended the evening by gaining full managerial control over the Skinny Berry product line. It was the way he worked best. And Zimmerman, completely fooled by Bullard's performance, had given it willingly.

"Nice perks, huh?" Phil Stevens said, flashing a ceramic smile and reclining his seat. Stevens was GenAgra's director of marketing and had been sent along as a guide.

"Yes," Bullard nodded unenthusiastically. He hoped Stevens would shut up, but the silent treatment had not worked so far.

"You know, everyone in the department was just ga-ga over your image campaign," Stevens continued. "Such a catchy jingle. Da-da dum, dee-da," Stevens sang the last few notes out of key. "I walked in on my kid playing video games last week, and I swear to God, his little friend was singing it. Da-da dum, dee-da. The kid is friggin' eight. I mean you got total market saturation there."

Bullard smiled and nodded again, then turned to look out at the clouds beneath him. He let Stevens drone on, feeding him only an occasional polite affirmation. He wondered how soon Zimmerman might consider shaking up the marketing department. Phil Stevens was not going to cut it as a travel partner for any length of time.

The jet touched down in Lansing in just under an hour. A white SUV, with the GenAgra logo that Bullard's firm had designed, picked them up for the ride to GenAgra's North Central Research Center in Perkins. The drive was longer than the flight, but Stevens still managed to talk through most of it. Judging from the look on the driver's face, Bullard thought that Stevens had alienated him as well.

Bullard noted the lack of development as the SUV neared its destination. He noticed a distinct absence of service centers and fast food restaurants on the rural highway exits. And the country road that led to the research center cut through a virtual wilderness. A few farmhouses and barns dotted a land filled by forests and green fields. The only sign of commerce was a small farmers' market. He estimated the considerable development potential of the land and wondered how much money could be made if this property were situated anywhere near D.C. or Chicago.

"Here we are," the driver said as the SUV turned onto a gravel drive and brought them to a renovated farmhouse.

"That's Doctor Malec," Stevens said of the older gentleman waiting for them near the front entrance. "He's the director of development for the Enhanced Foods Division."

Bullard liked the name of the division. Someone had framed that well. "Enhanced foods" sounded far superior to "genetically altered foods." He smiled, but it quickly faded to a grimace as he stepped out of the SUV. He didn't like the feel of gravel beneath his four-hundred-dollar loafers. He paused to see if the sides were scuffed by the stone drive and frowned at a white chalk mark on the leather.

"You must be Al Bullard," Doctor Malec said warmly, extending a hand. "I'm Dr. Otis Malec. Welcome to our facility."

"Thank you," Bullard said.

"Hello, Phil," Malec said, and Stevens nodded in reply. "Chicago called and said you were coming. Wanted to talk about marketing the Skinny Berry."

"Yes," Bullard said. "Just to take in the operation."

"Let me show you around the place," Doctor Malec said. He instructed the driver to bring a golf cart to the back entrance. The doctor narrated a field trip of the facility, including the interior of the revamped farmhouse and layout of the fields. Bullard was shocked at how low-tech the place looked. When he thought of biotechnology, he thought of beakers and surgical masks and ultra-clean white rooms. But this place looked almost exactly like a small farm. It was squalid. It was not an image that would sell Skinny Berries.

"We are about to have our weekly staff meeting, Mr. Bullard," Doctor Malec said, as the tour ended. "Won't you join us, and then I'll have some time to spare for you afterwards."

Bullard gladly agreed. Malec was well-spoken, professional and a huge upgrade in companionship from Stevens. Bullard politely nodded when introduced at the staff meeting and settled back to listen. His mind wandered as the group of scientists, technicians, and student workers hashed over the business of the day. It was a language Bullard didn't understand and one he knew America didn't speak. Americans, to be blunt, were uneducated sheep who needed to be herded to market. And to proper consumer decisions.

When the meeting finally ended, Bullard stayed behind with Stevens and Doctor Malec. Bullard rose from his chair, closed the doors so he could talk candidly with the two men, and paced inside the room for a moment, before launching a question at Doctor Malec.

"Does the Skinny Berry work?" Bullard asked.

"You bet it does," Doctor Malec said. "In our tests on laboratory mice, there was a reduction in the amount of caloric intake of nearly seventy percent daily. The mice lost weight. Some of them might have withered away if we kept on feeding them the berries."

"Any side effects?" Bullard asked. He wanted to get right to the point, to educate himself on the salient aspects of the product he was going to have to sell.

"Well, aside from the weight loss," Doctor Malec said, smiling, "there is a very mild aftertaste. Other than that, they are substantially equivalent to a blackberry. We should get fast-track approval from the USDA very soon."

"Can it be made into pill form?" Bullard asked. He had never tasted a blackberry and wasn't sure if Americans would be thrilled about eating fruit every day. Especially if it had an aftertaste.

"Yes, it can," Doctor Malec said. Bullard liked the way Malec was straightforward with his answers. It wouldn't work in front of the national press corps, but it was wonderful for actually understanding a product. "The berries contain a gene from a cactus in—"

"Yes, yes," Bullard said, urging the doctor on, "I understand that it comes from the cactus and suppresses appetite. But it can be made into a pill, right?"

"As I was about to say," Malec continued, an annoyed edge in his voice, "the active ingredient in the plant is a molecule called

P-57—"

"We've licensed the right to produce P-57 in our genetically modified plants from Pfizer and Phytopharm," Stevens interrupted. "They hold the rights to manufacture, market, and distribute *Hoodia* products worldwide."

"As I was saying—" Malec continued, shooting an angry glance at Stevens. "P-57 can be extracted and manufactured in pill form, but the pills do not seem to provide the same level of appetite suppression as does eating raw *Hoodia*. Our blackberry plants will provide a higher level of appetite suppression than any pill on the market, perhaps as great as eating raw *Hoodia*."

Bullard liked what he heard. His body was growing weary pacing, and if he were being candid with himself, he, too, was carrying a few extra pounds. He might be in need of these blackberries.

"Do the berries have to be eaten fresh to lose weight?" Bullard said, taking a seat at the conference table. "Can they be processed? Like pies or jelly?"

"Our mouse studies indicate that the blackberries have the same effect on weight loss processed or fresh," Malec said.

"That was looked at in our first phase of testing," Stevens interjected. "In order for this product to be marketable—"

Malec shot Stevens an impatient look and the director of marketing trailed off in mid-sentence. Bullard was pleased someone finally shut Stevens up, but he was concerned about Malec's authoritative demeanor. These things had to be controlled.

"Good," Bullard said. He leaned forward, elbows on the table, and rested his jowls on his clasped hands. "What's our timetable? When will the product be released?"

"We're in the final phase of testing at this facility," Malec said. "The plant should be granted approval before the end of the summer. We have farms throughout the northeastern United States ready to begin full-scale production. The first berries should be produced next July. That puts the Skinny Berry in the hands of the American dieter by next summer. About a year off."

Bullard did not like the way "Skinny Berry" rolled off Malec's tongue. It sounded artificial, and the focus group that was internalized in his commercial brain told him it would turn off consumers. What would this gem be called, he wondered?

"That gives me just enough time to get them ready to buy it, Doctor Malec," Bullard said, a plastic smile widening on his face.

There was a knock at the door, and a short man with a moustache and brown hat poked his head into the room. "I'm sorry to bother you, sir," the man said to Malec. "But we just identified the individuals who had unauthorized access to the corn yesterday, and you said you wanted to know right—"

"Thank you, Karl," Malec cut the man off. The constant interruptions were obviously taking their toll on the scientist. "Why don't you have a seat in my office and we'll discuss it when—"

"No, no," Bullard interrupted Malec intentionally, taking advantage of the situation to mete out a lesson. "I'm almost finished here anyway. Why don't you come in, Mr.—"

"Watton," the short man said hesitantly, looking with uncertainty toward Malec.

"It's okay," Bullard said. "Come on in. I want to hear this, too."

"Excuse—" Malec started.

"I don't know if you got the memo yet, Doctor Malec," Bullard said, letting a friendly tone drip over pointed words. "But Wes has placed me in complete control of this product line. From production to testing to sales. Hell, Wes wants me to eat the damn berries myself, if I want to. And, I'm a hands-on kind of manager. I want to know everything. So there's no reason to send Mr. Watton away."

Bullard watched Malec's stunned surprise. It was clear he hadn't gotten the memo, and that would make things slightly more difficult. Bullard was certain Malec had not taken a direct order in a long time, and he wanted to establish dominance over the doctor immediately.

"So, Mr. Watton," Bullard said. "Please come in. I'm guessing you work in security here, from your uniform."

"Yes, sir," he said, still uncertain of his role in the new order. "I'm the director of security here."

"Go ahead, please," Bullard said. Stevens was smiling,

probably because the tables had been turned on Malec. "Tell Doctor Malec what it is—"

"These are internal GenAgra matters, Mr. Bullard," Malec said, regrouping. "What in the hell's going on, Phil? Has there been some change?"

"Mr. Zimmerman has put Mr. Bullard in charge of the entire Skinny Berry project, Otis," Stevens nodded. "You should've received an e-mail to that effect."

Malec's jaw hung slack.

"So what is it you needed to tell Doctor Malec?" Bullard returned to the diminutive security chief.

"Ah," the security chief said, still confused. "We had two guests on site yesterday, who tried to take an unauthorized sample from one of our corn fields. We've identified them."

"Excellent work, Mr. Watton." Bullard said.

"One of them is a professor at the university," the security chief said, emboldened. "He had the pass to get by the front desk. And the other was a local attorney."

"Well," Bullard laughed, "can't have attorneys running around unauthorized in our fields of gold, can we. What course of action would you propose, Doctor Malec?"

"I...I'd..." the doctor stammered.

"Doctor, you are still GenAgra's man on the point at this facility," Bullard said gently. "You will continue to run things on a daily basis here for as long as I'm managing this project. I didn't mean to startle you with the news of this reorganization. I assumed Wes would have passed it along."

Malec paused, as if to absorb Bullard's message and tone. "Mr. Watton," Malec said finally, "now that we've identified the intruders, get me their background information. Tell me everything there is to know. Who are they? Why are they here."

Malec recovered well, Bullard thought. "Wonderful to be a part of the team," he said, rising. "Well, I have a lot of work to do. Stevens, we should be catching the flight back to Chicago. Doctor Malec, it was a pleasure meeting you, and I look forward to working with you."

"Yes," Malec said stoically.

As he was leaving, Bullard turned and asked one last question, though the answer seemed obvious to him. "Doctor, who was it that invented this golden plant?"

"I did," Malec said.

Making Malec give up control of the Skinny Berry project was like taking the doctor's child. A seamless smile lit Bullard's face.

Chapter Four

Tom Hughes sat on the Stiles' front porch and breathed in the serenity. It had been a beautiful June day. The cloud cover burned off in the afternoon sun, and a slight breeze cooled the warm air to perfection. The setting washed away thirty years like erasing a chalkboard, and reminded Tom of summer evenings spent on the porch when he was a boy. He would drift over from his own yard, beckoned by Ernie Harwell's voice as it broadcast the bittersweet tale of Tiger baseball. Tom would fetch beers for Ike, and they would play two-handed Euchre as the sun ebbed. When Ike was sufficiently lubricated, his stories of the Korean War would be interspersed with Harwell's narration on the history of baseball, and together the men of Tom's youth wove a vivid tapestry of Americana. It was magic.

He brushed away the nostalgia and returned his focus to the Ike of today, a venerable man with a serious legal problem. Ike broke off a piece of Kaye's fresh baked bread, bathed it in honey fresh from the hive, and offered it to Tom. Tom took it from the old man, the bread warming his hand, and tasted it. The crust crunched between his teeth, but the core of the bread melted with the honey into a syrupy, sweet dough.

"Mmmm," Tom mumbled. "God, that's good."

Ike laughed with real joy and ate a piece of his own.

"I talked with Professor Romanelli today," Tom said, taking more of the sweet honey.

"Hmm," Ike said through a mouthful of bread. "He wasn't so bad for one of them pointy-headed college boys."

"Yeah," Tom said. "I like him, too."

"What did he have to say?"

"Well," Tom said, "he's got some of the test results back. You were right, at least about the corn. It's genetically modified, just like the stuff across the road."

Ike's leathery face broadened into a closed-mouthed smile. The farmer took a drink of his beer and gloated in silence.

"I wouldn't be so self-satisfied if I were you," Tom said. "The tests mean you've got a problem, don't they?"

"You didn't think an old man knew what he was talking about, did ya?" Ike said. "I told you. I knew it. Damn that place."

"Well," Tom said, trying to keep Ike level-headed, "we've still got a couple of weeks before the final tests are in, and we haven't gotten anything back on the blackberries yet. So this isn't conclusive."

"I know the blackberries are bad, too," Ike said. "I told you before, them animals aren't as stupid as we are, Tom. They know what's real and what's not."

"I know," Tom said. "And it's looking like you may be right, but a court isn't going to just take your word for it, Ike. We need an expert. And his tests aren't all in yet."

"That's okay," Ike said. "I know what they're going to show."

A white SUV drove north past the house. Tom recognized the green GenAgra logo on the side at about the same time Ike yelled out, "Goddamn GenAgra." He and spat over the railing of the porch.

Kaye brought out a plate of chops and a bowl of corn on the cob. "Now, Ike A. Stiles," she scolded. "You will not take the Lord's name in vain on my porch. And not in front of company. I'm sorry, Tom."

Tom nodded his forgiveness for Kaye's benefit and grinned at Ike when she left.

"Goddamn 'em," Ike whispered his curse.

Tom declined Ike's offer of more food, staring at the corn warily.

"What? You afraid of it now, too? Just like them silly old deer?" Ike teased.

"Maybe." Tom shrugged.

"I tell you," Ike said, taking another ear of corn. "I'm doing my best to separate the good from the bad. But other than burning the whole damn crop. I dunno..."

"I've made some phone calls to lawyers I know," Tom continued, "and done some research into your case."

"If they've contaminated my crop," Ike said through a mouthful of corn, "what's to research?"

"Every case has to be based on a legal theory," Tom explained. "This is a fairly unique kind of case. So if we're going to consider filing a lawsuit, you need to find the appropriate legal theory."

"They're ruining my crops," Ike said. "That's a theory."

"Well, it looks to me like this would end up being a trespass case, Ike. There are other theories, but I think trespass is the most on point. Any entry onto your land without permission is a trespass."

"So their pollen trespassed?" Ike said.

"That's probably the legal theory that would get us to court."

"Sounds good," Ike said, gnawing on a chop. "So when do we start?"

There was little hope of dissuading the old man.

"Well, we need to wait for the test results," Tom said. "So that's a couple of weeks. Then I'd need to draft the paperwork and get it filed. Maybe three weeks at the earliest. But, there's another step. A bigger hurdle."

"What's that?" Ike asked.

"Just because there's a legal theory that lets you sue, it doesn't mean you should sue. We have to decide if we *want* to bring this lawsuit."

"They're ruining my fields, Tom." Ike's voice was cross. "I'm going to sue."

"Hear me out, Ike. Every lawyer I've talked to about this case has advised me against taking it. This company you're thinking of suing—GenAgra—they've been very aggressive in litigation. So aggressive that they aren't the ones even getting sued. They're doing the suing for the most part. And they're ruining the small farmers that they've gone after. Hundreds of thousands of dollars in damages sometimes."

"But they've ruined my crops," Ike said angrily. "How in the hell are they gonna sue me for ruining my own crops?"

"It's called patent infringement," Tom said. "I know it sounds crazy, but they've patented the plants they've been inventing with the United States Patent Office, and if you grow one of their plants without being licensed to use the patent, they have the right to sue."

"That's ridiculous," Ike scoffed. "This is America. There's no way they can sue me when they've ruined my crop. If I lose my organic certification, there ain't gonna be no more yuppies coming to the fruit stand, goddamn it."

"Ike A. Stiles," Kaye called from inside the house. "If I have to tell you again, I'm going to send you to the barn with the pigs."

Tom smiled, but Ike was steaming. The old man's face reddened.

"This ain't right at all, boy," he said, "and I'm not going to take it lying down, either."

"Clients aren't the only ones who've been getting hurt in these cases with GenAgra, Ike," Tom said soberly. "Lawyers who take on this corporation can end up getting stuck with attorney's fees. Do you know what they pay their corporate lawyers an hour? Even I can't afford that."

"Well, I'd feel better with you being my lawyer, kiddo," Ike said. "But, if you can't do it, I'll just have to find someone who can. I'm not gonna let them bully me. I fought for this country once, and I'm not giving in now without a fight."

His client seemed to be fairly certain about what should be done, but Tom was still leery of taking on the case. Perhaps he should let Ike find a younger lawyer for battle.

"I don't know," Tom said finally. "It's a big risk you'd be taking if you go up against these guys, and I'm not sure I'm ready to sign on for that."

"Well, why don't you think on it while we wait for these test results to come back," Ike said. "I'll respect your decision either way."

Ike was a wise farmer. Tom sat back with the old man and listened to the Tiger game sans Ernie Harwell. When he rose to leave two beers later, the Tigers were trailing early in the ball game. It was going to be another long season.

Ryan Romanelli sat in the quiet of his office and poured over Wendy's data on the tomato fruitworm project. Her methods for the research were flawless, as with everything she touched. He was convinced this phase of the project would give her more than enough data to finish her thesis, and though it would be sad to lose her as a graduate assistant, she could probably be ready to defend her thesis by the beginning of the fall term. The work was better than other theses he had advised on, and probably good enough for publication in a major journal. *Plant Biology* possibly.

A single sharp beep sounded from his computer, spoiling the serenity of the office. He enjoyed the gray silence of late afternoons in the office and would have been annoyed by the tone had he not been expecting an e-mail.

He rolled his chair to the computer and used the mouse to access the incoming message. It was from his friend in East Lansing:

To: romanellig@mat.edu
From: ajmcoy@michgen.com
Subject: PCR test
Ryan,
Good to hear from you. Things are great here. Lab is overrun with business. Any time you're ready to leave the ivory towers, I could use you. If I get the samples by Monday I should be able to get you something back next week. No promises, but I'll handle it myself. You should drop down here some weekend. Call me.
A.J.

Ryan loved communicating by e-mail. He found it far easier to write his thoughts down and click them away than to pick up the telephone. He supposed it was an interpersonal deficiency on his part, but he was glad he lived in an age that catered to his idiosyncracies.

A.J. was an old friend from UMass. They had gone through the graduate program together and both had taken jobs teaching in Michigan. A.J. had gotten off to a better start, taking a position as an associate professor at Michigan State University, but he had not been as fortunate as Ryan in the long run. When it was clear he would not be tenured at Michigan State, he was forced into the private sector, starting his own testing firm. But from all indications, A.J. was going to get the last laugh. His financial future looked far brighter than that of any tenured professor.

As he typed A.J. a quick reply, he was interrupted again, this time by a knock on his office door. He pivoted in his chair to see Wendy. He waved her in, quickly sent his e-mail, then gave her his full attention. Ryan admired her beauty as she casually sauntered into the office and lowered her slender frame onto one of the chairs facing his desk. They had worked together three years now, and he was still awed by her face and the grace of her movement. He doubted that many seeing her on campus would mistake her for a gifted scientist. Fortune rarely bestowed such combinations of stunning looks and intellect.

"You wanted to see me before I take off?" she said.

"Yeah," Ryan said. He often found himself at a loss for words around her, but today was especially difficult.

"I just finished up grading the essays for the Intro to Botany class," she said.

"Thanks," Ryan said. The thought of her leaving pained him. He was never going to be able to replace her with anyone half as competent.

"So what did you want?" Wendy said. "You finally going to buy me that drink?"

Ryan smiled, trying to hide his anxiety. He had struggled mightily against himself to keep their relationship on strictly professional terms. Wendy had always been friendly, and sometimes flirtatious. He was used to it from female students.

But unlike so many of his brethren at the university, Ryan had always prided himself on his ability to keep himself free of such entanglements. He saw them have a negative impact on so many talented minds, and it seemed so unscrupulous to him to abuse the position of trust he had been given. But Wendy never knew how much she had challenged his integrity.

"Not tonight," he deflected her offer. "But before you leave. I promise."

"Sure," she said, her usual grin somewhat diminished.

"I wanted to talk to you about your research," he said, redirecting the conversation. "I've been going over your latest data."

"It's looking pretty good, huh?" Wendy said. "But I think I need to go one more generation with the plants before I can absolutely say the population of fruitworms has acquired a lasting immunity. Don't you think?"

"No," Ryan said. "You've got it right here in this data. You're ready to take this to your thesis committee as soon as you can get it written up. This is publishable stuff, Wendy. You've done it."

She smiled at his praise. She must have known how good the project was, so why would she want to waste another year?

"You really think so?"

"Without a doubt," he said. "That's why I wanted to talk with you."

She gazed at him attentively, brushing a long lock of sunny blonde hair away from her soft brown eyes. He was struck by a sudden instinct to avoid what he had planned to say, but resolved himself to go through with it. Every seedling had to be let out of the greenhouse at some point.

"I have a very light schedule this summer." He sighed. "No classes. No papers to publish. I think I may be in the field a good bit. Perhaps helping out our new lawyer friend. But, all in all, it's going to be very slow around here."

"Uh-huh," she said, showing no comprehension.

"It's really the ideal time to train someone new as a grad assistant. That is why I had—" he looked for a résumé on his crowded desk and found it, "—Ms. Freeman in the office this morning."

Her eyes, normally radiant, looked instantly cloudy, a mix of hurt and anger. At once, Ryan regretted his decision. But it was too late to turn back.

"You should really take the summer off and write," he said. "Get ready to defend your thesis and have it over with in the fall."

"But I, ah…" Her normally confident voice sounded shallow. "How am I going to afford that? I need this position, Doctor Romanelli."

"I know," he said. "I've checked with the financial aid office. There's a special bridge loan available for graduates working on their thesis. It's enough to get by for the summer. It should easily replace your paycheck here." He thought she might cry. He had expected she might be relieved or even happy. But he had not anticipated this reaction. He felt a physical ache in his chest.

"I don't want any additional loans," she said, gaining a resolve that he had come to recognize. "I can finish up while I am working here."

"I really think you need the time to work on the thesis," he said. "And I need the position to train someone new. I'm never going to be able to replace you, Wendy. But, after you're gone and teaching at some other university, I'm going to need to try to keep this place afloat."

He had tried for high praise and failed. There was the beginning of hatred in her eyes, and it unnerved him. He wished so many times they had met in some other setting, or even that her interest in him might outlive her position as his graduate assistant. But looking at her now, those hopes seemed a dim prospect.

"So you're letting me go, then?" she said, her words clipped.

"I'm not letting you go, Wendy," he said. "I'm merely encouraging you to get the thesis finished. You're ready to move on. I don't know if you recognize your own talent sometimes." He could see her actively struggling to hold back tears and wanted to reach out to her.

"So is that new girl that was in here…" She sniffed. "Is she going to work out, then?"

"She seems like she can probably do the job. At least while the workload is light," he said. "I'll get her trained this summer.

Remember, I'm a pretty good instructor. Look what I've done with you." He was relieved to see the hint of a smile on her lips.

"I guess maybe you're right," Wendy said, as she regained her composure. "But I'm going to miss this place."

Ryan thought he would be relieved once the conversation was over. Instead he felt an uneasy emptiness in the pit of his stomach when she left the office. He was going to miss her, too.

Wendy Isaacson felt a healthy guilt for the pollution her old Camry pumped into the atmosphere on her weekly trips to the Beaverton Experiment Station, but she secretly enjoyed the car culture of America as much as anyone. She had always enjoyed the solitude of her long commute with nothing but the intellectual banter of National Public Radio to keep her company. The trips were a weekly opportunity to find inner clarity.

Usually, she was able to think about life's bigger questions on her weekly jaunts. How to save the world? Was there any meaning to it all? But her thoughts on this final trip were far more self-absorbed. She was driving to clean out her office at the station, and to say good-bye to her chimeric plants. But the final trip to the experiment station was less a farewell to her plants and more a symbolic good-bye to the professor.

Ryan's push for her to leave the lab so she could concentrate on writing her thesis had been an unexpected blow. Logically, she could see that by telling her she was ready to move on, Ryan was complimenting her scholarship. But she had been unable to process his words solely in an intellectual framework. They rushed around her and sparked emotion. It had taken great effort to avoid tears, and even more to avoid anger.

She saved the emotional outburst for her younger sister. The weekend had been a series of phone calls home. Off and on, for forty-eight hours, they were connected by a long distance line. They laughed and cried and analyzed; it was more affordable than professional therapy. And finally her sister had encouraged her to leave the oafish professor in the dustbin of love's labor. It had all been clear on the telephone. But now, driving to the experiment station in mid-week, it seemed less so.

Halfway to Beaverton, with *The Diane Rehm Show* giving way

to *Fresh Air* with Terri Gross, Wendy needed lunch. She exited the highway in Milton and was not impressed with the typical offerings. There was a Big Burger, an Applebee's, and a British Petroleum gas station, which would have cold sandwiches in the cooler. She hated the fact that strip mall America was inching its way into northern Michigan, planting lifelessly familiar chains every ten or twenty miles. She was about to settle on the cold sandwich from oil-giant BP, when she saw a sign indicating the town of Milton was only a two-mile drive off the highway. She decided to lose sight of the freeway to see if the little town offered any rebellious cuisine. Her quest was rewarded near the center of the town, just off Main Street, where she found the Milton Diner. From its exterior, she was certain it would not serve meals microwaved from a bag.

Though the town itself looked sleepy, the diner was packed. There were no tables available, so Wendy took a seat at the counter. The walls told the story of the establishment, both in words and in pictures. Wendy saw a smiling old woman in black and white photographs, who had nurtured the little diner and turned it over to her grandchildren. She fantasized for a moment, of a life running a greasy spoon in a small town. A place where no one needed to be specialized enough to understand or even care about transgenic plants or recombinant DNA technology.

She ordered a pasty at the waitress's urging. When the dish arrived, smothered in homemade gravy and steaming a hearty aroma, Wendy noticed a familiar face enter the diner. She struggled for a moment to place the distinguished-looking gentleman, and just as her synapses made the connection, he walked toward her.

"Tom Hughes," he said warmly, his smile disarming. "You're Doctor Romanelli's assistant, right?"

"Wendy Isaacson." She smiled back. The cordiality of the scene made her think she had slipped back a hundred years in her trek from the highway.

"Do you mind if I join you?" Tom said, motioning at the crowded restaurant.

He looked harmless enough. He was old enough to be her father. Or at least her older brother. And from her surroundings, she figured politeness was the order of the day.

"Not at all," she said.

"What brings you to the diner?" Tom said. "This place is our local secret. They usually don't let outsiders in the door."

"I like to get off the beaten path sometimes," she said.

"Tuna on white, Marnie," Tom said to the passing waitress. "So how's the testing coming? I haven't heard from Professor Romanelli."

"I'm sorry, I haven't been in the office this week."

"Oh," Tom said. "You spend most of your time over in Beaverton, then?"

"Not really," she said. "Actually, Professor Romanelli wanted me to take the summer off to work on my thesis, so I haven't been in."

"Is that right?" Tom said. "That sounds great."

"Well," Wendy pondered her response. She could have hid the truth for the sake of polite conversation but saw no need. "Really, I wanted to keep working at the lab. But the professor kind of needed the spot for a new graduate assistant. So, I feel kind of idle now, with no job."

"Working on a thesis sounds like a full-time job to me," Tom said. The waitress dropped off his sandwich, and he thanked her.

"This is the first time I haven't had a job since I started college," Wendy said, taking a bite of the pasty. The dough and gravy were homemade. She paused to savor it. It was a taste that couldn't be packaged.

"Those things are good," Tom said, watching her eat. "But save some room for the Dutch apple pie. Incredible."

"You eat here a lot?" Wendy said.

"Only when I'm hungry," he said. "My office is right next door."

"Oh man." She smiled. "I'm glad I don't work that close."

"Are you implying something?" Tom said with a wry smile, moving his hand to his stomach.

"No, no." She laughed.

The conversation ebbed. Wendy could only eat half the pasty, and there was no chance of pie.

"That is some interesting work you guys do," Tom said after a time. "I really had no idea about all these genetically modified foods before last week. It's really eye opening."

"It really is an amazing field," Wendy said. "And I think there's a lot of good that will come from it. But it needs to be regulated more heavily. Or at least regulated. Right now they're just putting things on the market with almost no testing. No foresight about what the products will to do people. Or the environment. It's kind of like the Wild West."

"Well, maybe they'll get more serious about testing when I get through with them," he said, with mock bravado.

"So you think you'll be suing them?" Wendy asked.

"That depends on your professor's test results to some degree," Tom said. "And, of course, whether I can find a secretary capable of typing up the papers."

As the lawyer explained his difficulties finding office help, Wendy's mind began to spin deviously. The attorney needed office help. He might well be working closely with Ryan as an expert on the case. Her sister would scold her for even thinking about trying to use the situation to give Ryan another chance.

"So you're only looking for someone to answer phones and do light clerical work?" Wendy asked.

"Yeah," he said. "I mean it would be nice if they could type and file and help with research, but I don't want to ask too much. I mean, you should have seen these people I interviewed this morning."

"Would the person have time to read on the job?" Wendy said. "You know, like a student or something?"

"I don't suppose they'll be all that busy," Tom said. "If they're even halfway competent, they'd probably have time to spare. Why? Do you know a student who'd be interested?"

"Actually," Wendy said, "I might be interested. As long as I'd still have time to work on my thesis."

"You're overqualified," Tom said. "This is menial clerical stuff I'm talking about here."

"No, really," Wendy said. "I could use the money. And I type. And I should be able to assist you in understanding this genetic pollution case, too."

The lawyer leaned back on his counter stool, seeming to give the idea serious consideration. "Hmmm," he said. "You could work through the summer?"

"Sure," she said.

"That'd give me time to find someone else, anyway. Let me think about it."

Wendy smiled. She had never interviewed and not been hired. She was pretty certain the lawyer was going to give her a place to study this summer. And that place would give her the opportunity to keep tabs on Ryan. Her detour to Milton had been productive.

Al Bullard had taken an innate ability to manipulate people and turned it into a very lucrative business. In addition to the money, running a public relations firm gave him great personal satisfaction. In the last national election, he had told millions of Americans how to think. He was comfortable in every aspect of his business, from one-on-one surveys with individual consumers to high-powered meetings with the power elite. But nowhere did Al Bullard feel as comfortable as he did running a focus group.

The concept of the focus group was almost as old as marketing itself. But still, conducting the groups was as much an art as a science, and Bullard was a widely acclaimed maestro. He felt at home when he entered the testing room to talk with twelve carefully selected individuals about the Skinny Berry. He was a lion tamer entering a cage full of big cats. But he was armed with less conspicuous weapons than the chair and whip. He entered the testing room with his personal notes tucked in a black portfolio and a salesman's smile.

"Good morning, ladies and gentlemen," he said, his personal energy eliciting an audible greeting in response.

He introduced himself and eased his way into an explanation of the focus group. The twelve subjects listened attentively as he explained they were assembled to talk about a revolutionary new product. The researchers needed their honest assistance to make the product better. They should speak freely. Be candid. And then he started the group on its directed discussion.

"All right," Bullard said. "Our discussion today will focus on a new weight-loss product that is slated to come on the market sometime next year. By a show of hands, does anyone here think they're overweight?"

Bullard scanned the twelve-member panel. After a moment of peer pressure in action, all twelve members raised their hands. The focus group was seated in a semi-circle so they could see and interact with each other, as well as with Bullard, who casually paced about at the front of the testing room as he spoke. The panel was weighted to represent the target market of the Skinny Berry in age, occupation, race, sex, and most importantly, obesity.

"That's good. You're being honest. Look around. We can talk here," he said, placing his own hands on his abdominal girth and chuckling. "One of the criteria we used to select you for this panel was your likelihood to try a weight-loss product in the next year. So all of us here, and about two-thirds of the American public, would like to shed a couple of unwanted pounds." The group joined him in laughter and agreement, once the topic had been broached openly.

"How many of you would go so far as to say you were obese?" Bullard asked softly, raising his own hand.

"So we have two or three," he said, counting the scattered hands. He did not need to take notes. An entire team of in-house experts stood invisible behind a large one-way mirror on the interior wall of the room, recording and analyzing everything about the group. Responses. Body language. Social dynamics. "Good."

"All right," he said, moving on. "How many in this group have either been on a diet or used some weight-loss product in this past year?"

Two women raised their hands immediately. Bullard noticed another man and woman knitting their brows in active concentration.

"When I say weight-loss product," he said, "that would include anything as ordinary as eating a Healthy Choice frozen dinner to having gastric bypass surgery. And anything in between."

The man and woman who had pondered the question now firmly raised their hands, as did another woman. In all, five of twelve admitted to using weight-loss products, with four out of the five being women. From the statistics he had studied before the meeting, that was about right.

"Okay," Bullard said, feeling like the crowd was warming up, "let's give you guys a chance to talk. I'm going to ask a question, and I want each of you to respond. What is the single biggest factor, for you personally, that will make a diet work?"

Bullard looked to a paunchy black man at the end of the semi-circle with expectant eyes, and after a beat, the man said, "If my doctor tells me I need to."

"So, health reasons?" Bullard said.

"Yeah," the man said.

Bullard moved to a middle-aged white woman who was moderately overweight.

"Willpower," she said.

"Good," Bullard said, encouraging the shortest replies.

"Convenience," a Latino woman said. "I don't have time to weigh out food or cook special meals."

"Okay." Bullard felt the answers start to flow and moved a finger around the semi-circle, giving each consumer a chance.

"Yes, convenience."

"Convenience."

"Me too, convenience."

"Convenience."

"Too expensive."

"Convenience."

"Convenience."

"Taste."

"Taste. I can't stand diet foods."

The last answer made the group laugh together with cohesion, a herd of sheep, Bullard imagined, waiting to be fleeced.

"All right," Bullard said. "You guys are getting the hang of this. Let me throw you a curveball now. By a show of hands, how many of you would say you know a lot about genetically enhanced foods?"

Two hands cautiously rose.

"Okay," Bullard said. "You two keep your hands up. And I want to ask how many of the rest of you have ever heard anything about genetically enhanced foods? Specially engineered crops that allow our farmers to use less pesticides? Or treatments that allow our cows to produce more milk at lower prices?"

Another five hands went into the air. Over half the group.

"Okay. Now, by show of hands, how many of you think these enhanced products are safe to eat?"

Three hands remained in the air.

"And how many think that these enhanced products are in some way unsafe?"

Three different hands.

"And how many do not have any opinion?"

Six hands.

"You people just can't make up your mind, can you?" Bullard playfully scolded the undecideds. "Well, I'm going to bring out one of our analysts here at The Bullard Group, and he is going to tell you about the product we are unveiling next year. With your help. And then I'll be back to talk to you about it a bit later. All right?"

The group gave the affirmative, as he had requested.

Bullard left the room and met a senior focus group analyst in the outer hallway.

"Nice job, boss," said the analyst, who had been watching in the observation room.

"Save the ass-kissing, Stan," Bullard said. "You've got thirty minutes to prep them on the product, and I'll be back."

"You got it, boss."

"I have your teleconference all set up, Mr. Bullard," his personal assistant greeted him as he left the room.

"Good," Bullard said, stalking toward his corner office. "If I'm not off the video link by two-twenty, you let me know."

"Yes, sir," she said, walking after him.

Bullard's office was spacious, decorated in sleek modern tones. The windows looked down nine stories onto M Street. A gigantic flat screen television dominated the interior wall. The image on the screen was broken into four equal-sized boxes, three of which were occupied by the faces of GenAgra officials he had met earlier in the week. Bullard sat on a black couch in front of the screen and spoke in conversational tones with his new associates.

"Glad to see the new equipment I sent you is working, Doctor Malec," Bullard said. Malec, obviously unaccustomed to talking on the computer, gave a stiff smile.

"Yes," Malec said, from his office at the North Central

Research Center. "Thank you."

"This stuff is amazing," Kurt Watton said. The head of research center security wore the same brown hat and shirt that made him look like a cross between a UPS delivery boy and a Nazi youth. "Thanks."

"Well," Bullard said, "it will make working together a lot easier. Though I'll miss the corporate jet. So, how are we doing this week, gentlemen?"

"Wonderful," Phil Stevens said from his Chicago office. "How are things going on the marketing campaign, Al?"

"I'm getting some initial data today," Bullard said. "I think your berry is going to sell quite well though, Doctor Malec."

"It should," Malec said, his voice too loud for the microphone. "Obesity-related illness accounts for a growing portion of our health care spending in this country."

Bullard felt that the comment had been intended as a personal accusation about his own weight. Malec was obviously still angry at losing his pet project. "Everything is going smoothly there, Doctor Malec?"

"Yes," Malec said. "We're on schedule. We should have our last report into APHIS early. I am sure the berry will be approved for consumers."

"APHIS? What's that, now?" Bullard said.

"The Animal and Plant Health Information Service. They're the regulatory body under the USDA now," Malec said.

"And what's the process after that?" Bullard asked.

"Straight to market," Malec said. "Technically, the regulatory system is on a strictly voluntary basis. But approval is easy to get, so we have no problem working through the USDA. It's all about what we put in the reports. Nobody at APHIS does any independent analysis of our work."

"Good," Bullard said. "Sounds like clear sailing. How about your little security breach the other day, Mr. Watton? Any follow-up on that?"

"Yes, sir," Watton said. "Subject number one is Ryan Romanelli, Ph.D., professor of plant biology at Michigan A&T. His studies emphasize ecological factors associated with transgenic plants. He was a one-time consultant on GenAgra research but resigned, citing philosophical differences.

"Subject two is Thomas Hughes. A lawyer. Grew up in Perkins, only a couple of houses up the road from the research center. Now resides and practices in Milton. He runs a personal injury firm. Fairly successful ambulance chaser. One of the guards said he saw Hughes last week, walking near the northern property line with an old farmer named Ike Stiles, who owns a berry farm across the street."

"What do you think, Doctor Malec?" Bullard asked.

"Once Kurt gave me the report, I recognized Romanelli's name. He's definitely not an ally to the industry. Could be a potential problem," Malec said.

"What about the lawyer?" Bullard asked. "What do you make of him?"

"I don't know," Malec said. "I hate to speculate."

"Go ahead, speculate," Bullard said. "That's what smart guys like you get paid to do."

"If he's representing the farmer, I would think that there may be a problem with contamination," Malec said, his image and voice breaking down momentarily on the television screen.

"Contamination?" Bullard said. "Is that something to do with the Skinny Berry?"

"There have been reports in the literature of cross-pollination from GMO crops to non-GMO crops," Malec said. "Genetic pollution, so to speak. Such spread is rare and always minimal, and it doesn't cause any damage. But it is a possibility."

"Cross-pollination?" Bullard said.

"Yes," Malec said, his lips twisting. "It's how many plants procreate. Pollen from one plant fertilizing another."

"So the farmer's going to sue us because his berry plants got knocked up by your berry plants. What? A paternity suit?" Bullard cackled, joined by Watton and Stevens.

Malec stared soberly ahead. "I can't really think of any other possibilities, unless Romanelli has some interest in our crop. Perhaps a regulatory challenge or some type of intellectual property claim."

"What would you suggest as a course of action?" Bullard asked.

"Our legal department is excellent with these issues," Stevens said reassuringly.

"Yes," Malec said. "I'd refer the matter to legal. Let them deal with it."

"Sounds good," Bullard said. "I'd like to be in on the referral, though. Why don't you set up a conference call, Doctor Malec."

"There's no need for a conference call," Malec said, a look of disgust on his face. "I'll call legal and explain the situation. They usually take matters from there."

"I want to be in on that call," Bullard said. "Do you know how much money Americans spent on weight reduction products last year? $4.5 billion. This project is way too big to let things slide. You have my assistant's number, correct, Doctor Malec?"

"Yes," he said. "You gave it to me."

"Well, get your secretary to set up a conference call with the legal department," Bullard said calmly. "And make sure she checks with my assistant so that it fits my schedule. And if legal gives you any grief, let me know, and we'll see what Zimmerman has to say about it. Got it?"

"Yes," Malec said.

"All right, boys," Bullard said. "Thanks for the updates. I'll be in touch."

Bullard called for his assistant to end the teleconference link and headed back to the testing room. He slipped into the observation room and paused to watch Stan finish up the product introduction. As Stan's portion of the program wound down, Bullard eased his way back into the room.

"Thank you, Stan," Bullard said, projecting his stage voice again in front of the focus group. He surveyed the group as Stan left. They were over the hour mark and still seemed interested. The product introduction must have went over well.

"So what do you think of our berry?" Bullard grinned.

There was a wave of audible approval, with one voice clearing the general din, "We can't wait a year." Laughter followed.

"Now that you know about our product," Bullard said, "let me ask you again, how many of you think a genetically enhanced food is safe to eat?"

Six hands shot into the air, a gain of three votes after the product introduction. All risk analysis was a tradeoff, Bullard thought smugly. If these people thought it would help them lose weight without sacrifice, most of them would sign up to go over Niagra Falls in a barrel.

"How many think the genetically enhanced berry is unsafe to eat?"

One woman raised her hand hesitantly.

"That leaves five of you still undecided," Bullard said, laughing. "I guess you guys are just going to have to taste the blackberry pie before you make up your minds.

"Okay. Now, I would like to get your impressions of some product names and slogans we're considering." He walked to the dry-erase board and took the cap off a blue marker. On the board, in clear block letters, Bullard wrote:

Health-Ease Blackberries
"Losing weight is as easy as pie."

Bullard turned to look at his captive audience. He had several names and slogans in his portfolio, but watching the group read his first choice, his instincts told him that GenAgra had found its new product name.

Chapter Five

Tom said his good-byes to Wendy at the diner, but he couldn't shake her from his thoughts. She was polite and professional. She had basic office skills and an intellectual background that would probably come in handy on Ike's case. Plus she was very easy on the eyes. This last quality might become a distraction, but they had gotten on quite easily over lunch. It would be hard to turn down her help for the summer.

The phone rang for the first time since service had been restored. Answering the phone, it took a moment for Tom to remember what to say.

"Law Office of Tom Hughes," the words finally came from some automatic part of his brain.

"Mr. Hughes, this is Ryan. At the university."

"Hello, Doctor Romanelli," Tom said. "I was just thinking of, uh, you."

"I got your results back from Michigan Genetics," Ryan said. "Your farmer friend is the proud owner of two genetically modified crops. Weed-Away Corn—which our own tests confirmed—and the Hg-Blackberry according to these latest results. The same plants that are being grown across the street at the GenAgra facility."

"These latest test results—they are pretty conclusive, then?" Tom asked.

"It's a PCR test," Ryan said. "Polymerase chain reaction. Same DNA testing that is used in murder cases."

"Like the O.J. case?" Tom said, after a pause.

"God, I hated that case," Ryan said. "It did more to damage the public's understanding of DNA testing than anything I can remember. No. This is an absolute match. The chances of error are millions to one. It's as scientifically accurate as we can get. They're the same plants. All of them genetically modified."

"That would be your scientific opinion, under oath?" Tom asked.

"Unequivocally," Ryan said.

"And aside from Ike stealing the plant," Tom said, "what would your scientific opinion be on how the plant came to be in Ike's field?"

"Cross-pollination would be most likely," Ryan said. "It's either that, or GM seeds—or root-sprouts in the case of the blackberry—were used to grow your farmer's crops. And that would mean either someone physically moved them into the field or they miraculously got there through spillage or something."

Tom was running out of ways to avoid committing to Ike's case. The facts were in, and it appeared scientifically clear that GenAgra had, at the very least, trespassed on Ike's land.

"Have you given any thought to becoming an expert witness, Doc?" Tom asked.

"I have," Ryan said without hesitation. "I think I'd enjoy sticking it to them in court."

"Well, we may just give you that chance," Tom said. "If we decide to file suit, I'll put you on retainer as our case expert."

"Sounds good," Ryan said. "You have a fax number? I can fax you copies of these test results."

Tom gave him the number. "One more question, Doc. What kind of job recommendation would you give Wendy Isaacson?"

"She's going to be a great plant biologist," Ryan said thoughtfully.

"Well, I might have the pair of you working on this case, then," Tom said.

"What?" Ryan said, surprise coming through his voice.

"She was up in our neighborhood," Tom said. "I bumped into her at lunch, and she mentioned she needed work while she's getting her thesis ready. So I might take her on. Part-time at least."

"She was supposed to take the summer off to study," Ryan said. From his tone, Tom thought he had offended the doctor by considering Wendy for an inferior position.

"Well, apparently she really needs the work. You can't let good help like that go, Doc." Tom laughed, hoping to smooth over any awkwardness. "But don't worry. I'll make sure she gets plenty of chance to study. It's pretty quiet around here for the most part."

After hanging up with Ryan, Tom returned to his notes on the case. He jotted and scribbled:

Ike Stiles v. GenAgra
Facts: Plaintiff believes genetically altered crops from neighboring farm have spread to his fields. Plaintiff is an organic farmer. Damages? -- DNA tests confirmed
Issues of fact: Are his crops altered? How much $$ lost?
Issues of law: What cause? Products Liability?
Count I - Trespass
Count II - Nuisance
Count III - Negligence
Count IV - Products Liability?
Counterclaim likely - Patent Infringement
Witnesses: Ike Stiles -- 1) Planted organic corn/blackberries, 2) Didn't steal GM crops; 3) Lost certification - lost profits.
Dr. Ryan Romanelli -- 1) DNA tests - Stiles corn/blackberry = GMO-GenAgra corn/blackberry, 2) Trespass by cross-pollination
TTD:1) Contract with expert -- Romanelli.
2) Nell -- Draft Complaint.
3) Hire Wendy.

He looked at his notes and considered the case. As a rational matter, it was crazy to take on GenAgra over this, given their resources and litigious history. Ike could end up losing his farm. A conservative appellate court could make them pay GenAgra's attorneys' fees, costing Tom his own financial security. All that risk. For what? The damages were speculative at best. Ike was right in his forceful opinion that there had been a wrong committed against him. But when it came down to weighing the possible reward versus the risk, a prudent lawyer would walk away.

He jotted a final note on his pad:

4) Talk to Ike -- Last Warning

He knew the chances of convincing Ike not to go forward were about as poor as their chances of beating GenAgra in court. But he had to try, because Tom knew in his heart he would never let the old farmer take on the giant conglomerate alone.

Ernie Vasquez pulled the county sedan onto northbound US-27 and set the cruise control at seventy-five. With construction ahead it was at least a forty-five minute trip from St. Johns to his office in Mt. Pleasant. He glanced over at Jill Oswald, his investigator on the case. She was still organizing her notes from the interview they had just completed with the roommate of Patient Number Six.

A week had passed since Underwood ordered him to find a cause or a source of the syndrome, or to let the case go as a series of unrelated anaphylactic shock reports. Two more cases had trickled in since then, and though Ernie was no closer to a definitive answer, he felt the mystery illness was on the verge of giving up its secrets.

Jill had discovered Patient Number Five earlier in the week during her daily canvassing of hospitals in the region. A forty-two-year-old housewife from Milton had gone to the hospital in Perkins. She had a relatively mild case of whatever they were after, but the symptoms were present. Myalgia, a severe rash and acute respiratory distress. The woman had responded well to the steroid treatments but was still hospitalized. At least she wasn't on a ventilator.

The same ER doctor who had treated Patient Number Four had called Ernie yesterday. He had seen his second case of the mystery illness. Patient Number Six, the ER doctor had reported, was another student from Michigan A&T. She was a twenty-two-year-old healthy female who had been hit hard by the symptoms. Again, the patient had reported a rapid onset of cramps, severe edema, ascending paralysis, acute respiratory distress, and the necessity of a ventilator. Patient Number Six was clinging to life at the hospital in St. Johns, unable to speak.

Ernie had insisted on accompanying Jill to the field interview with Patient Six's roommate. The background data had not yet revealed a source or a cause of the syndrome, but as they had set out in the morning, Ernie felt confident that Patient Six's information would hold the key. Returning from the interview, he was deflated. His morning enthusiasm had been overly optimistic. The information provided by Patient Six's roommate was merely more data. A clear picture was not emerging. At least not one clear enough to spur Underwood into taking action.

"Same symptomatology," Jill said, straightening her notes. "But that's no help."

"No," Ernie said. "But there has to be something there. Let's go over it again."

"Okay," Jill said. "We've got six patients total now. All reported over a two-week period. Well, fifteen days."

"And the location?" Ernie said. "It has some geographical component, don't you think?"

"Fairly wide distribution," she said. "Two from Milton, one from Watson, one from Bay City, and now this makes two from St. Johns."

"They all have some connection to Wabeno County though, right?" Ernie said, struggling to pin the blame on any place, however broad the geographic description. "Milton and Watson. Both in Wabeno County. And both these kids worked in Perkins, right? At the same place, I thought."

"Yeah," Jill said, flipping through her notes. "They both worked at the North Central Research Station. But the guy from Bay City had absolutely no connection. And there's no specific location in Wabeno County that ties them all together. I mean if you are trying to pin this down to a locale, what are you thinking? Some environmental illness? If it was something county wide, you'd have more than six incidents trickling out over two weeks. Right?"

"I don't know," Ernie said, shaking his head. "I'm just trying to see some pattern."

Jill rustled through her notes again. "Okay, patterns," she said, after a quick study of the information she had collected. "Four out of the six ate regularly at Big Burger."

Ernie said nothing.

"Three out-of-six were drinking the same brand of ginseng tea," Jill said.

"That's no better than a chance connection," Ernie said. "Fifty percent sharing a common food means nothing, I'm afraid. Nothing that's going to help me get Underwood to take this seriously."

"I think you should take him to the ER to see some of these people," Jill said. "Man, this is a messed-up thing. I'm glad there haven't been any transmissions from person to person. I think we can safely rule out a communicable disease, huh?"

"Yeah," Ernie said. "I'd bet it is something environmental or food-borne. But it has a fairly long incubation period, whatever it is. That's why we can't pin down a source. Maybe something like West Nile, with the mosquito as a vector. I don't know."

Jill went back to her notes. "Two out of six ate at the Milton Diner regularly," she said, after browsing. "Two out of six ate at the Michigan A&T cafeteria, three out of six were under twenty-two, two out of six had gift baskets from the Stiles' Family Berry Farm.

"Oh, and listen to this. Four out of six loved broccoli. I mean, how many twenty-two year olds eat broccoli? There's your culprit." Jill waited for Ernie to laugh, but he was lost in thought.

Emerging from his thoughts, Ernie said, "Patient Six's roommate said something about her friend being happy she had lost a few pounds?"

Jill shuffled her notes. "Yup. Right here. She told her roommate she lost five pounds in three weeks. Roommate thought she was being a bitch for bragging about it, too." Jill smiled.

"There's been a few reports of that, right?" Ernie said.

"Let me see," Jill said, and paged through the case histories. "Three, four. And five. Five out of six reported recent weight loss. Five to fifteen pounds."

"Any weight loss pills? Or the same Lean Cuisine meals?" Ernie asked.

"Uh," Jill said, fingers and eyes sorting information. "Nothing. No foods or weight loss products in common with any of them. Man, I gotta get this information into the computer. I'm so behind on data entry."

Jill wasn't the only one shirking her clerical duties. He had been letting routine reports slide for a week as he focused on cracking the mystery illness. Maybe Underwood was right. Maybe he should be a good bureaucrat and let the illness come to him. If his syndrome did turn into something big, it would certainly make itself known in time, whether Ernie spent another minute investigating it or not.

As Ernie let the case slide from his mind for a moment, Jill started in about popular culture. Had he seen the latest network drama about desperate suburban women? What did he think of the celebrity criminal trial *de jour*, all the details of which aired nightly on CNN? When would the Tigers get their shit together? Ernie nodded and shook his head without comment, until they finally reached the office.

"If you shake something out of the data, let me know," he said.

"You got it, Ernie," she said. "Don't worry, we'll break this. And you'll have Underwood's job some day. Just don't forget to take me with you when you move into that big office in Lansing."

Ernie smiled as he headed to his office. He wasn't altogether comfortable in a supervisory role, but Jill made it easy.

"Those serology reports you wanted from Lansing came in, Mr. Vasquez," the pool secretary told him as he passed. "I put them in your box."

"Thanks," Ernie said. Almost two weeks into the investigation and the lab in Lansing was just getting him results on the early patients. Pathetic. If Underwood had given him authorization, he could have received the same reports in real time with the treating physicians. But, as it was, he felt like he was on the slow train.

Ernie slid open his desk drawer and took out his brown bag lunch. He ate while he worked. Since the patient histories were giving him nothing, Ernie looked over the serology reports for the first four patients, hoping for a break. His eyes scanned over the numbers. In a moment, Ernie had found the hallmark of the illness.

The eosinophil counts, a type of white blood cell, were too high to be believed. A normal eosinophil count was ten per cubic centimeter of blood. For people with severe allergic reactions or acute asthma attacks, eosinophil counts in the low hundreds would not be unusual. But his mystery patients all had eosinophil counts between 11,000 and 13,000 per cubic centimeter of blood. His syndrome had a definite signature, he thought, rolling his office chair to his computer and pulling up the medical research database.

He typed "high eosinophil count," "myalgia," and "acute respiratory distress" into the natural language search engine. Articles for two diseases came up on his screen. Eosinophilia-Myalgia Syndrome and Toxic Oil Syndrome. He quickly scanned the articles. A disease associated with a health supplement and an environmental illness, he concluded.

With quick phone calls Ernie was able to confirm that Patient Five and Patient Six also had strikingly high eosinophil counts. This was something concrete. Action was needed. He picked up his phone and dialed Underwood's office. While holding for Underwood, he considered what he would say to move his boss off his sit-and-wait attitude. They had a clear clinical description of this syndrome, and any blood test would show the signature eosinophil count. Further, there were two known illnesses in the medical literature with similar characteristics; one caused by a health supplement and the other by environmental exposure to toxins. Given this information, it would be prudent to put out a statewide notice for the mystery illness, and upgrade reporting of the new syndrome to condition yellow.

"I'm sorry," the secretary came back on the line. "Mr. Underwood hasn't returned from lunch yet. Would you like his voice mail?"

"Yes," Ernie said, glancing at the wall clock. Two o'clock in the afternoon and still out to lunch, Ernie scoffed to himself. He wondered how anything in state government ever got done.

Tom made it to the office early on Friday morning. He had scheduled an appointment with Ike and Kaye Stiles for 9:00 a.m. and knew that the old couple were always on time. He started a pot of strong coffee. As it brewed, he straightened the office. When the coffee was ready, he poured himself a steaming cup. He took it into the reception area and looked out of the large front window. It was another glorious June morning. The temperatures were still cooler than he remembered them as a boy, but the blue sky was draped cloudlessly around the Ohio Street business district Tom called home. The sun was breaking over the low brick skyline on the other side of the street, and he knew, looking through the glass, the sound outside would be almost as silent as it was in his office. As Tom surveyed his world, Ike pulled up in his vintage Fairlane 500. The farmer stepped out smartly, circled the car and opened Kaye's door like a chauffeur.

Tom greeted them at the entrance.

"This place is looking good," Kaye said, removing a sun hat and placing it on Tom's coat rack.

"It's not nearly what it was," Tom said, "but it'll do okay, I guess."

"Why the appointment?" Ike said, wearing an ill-fitting wool jacket pulled over his coveralls. "You've got those tests back already, don't you?"

"Well, we've got a lot to talk about," Tom said. "Can I get you some coffee?"

"Thank you," Kaye said, her stringent politeness a harmonic balance to Ike's, "Sure."

Tom made them each a cup to their liking and served the couple in his office. He had decided the day before that he needed the formality of the office to have a fair chance of dissuading Ike from the lawsuit. He needed to get the farmer away from his element and into the world of legal reality. With his audience arrayed before him in the stark office, Tom felt more like a lawyer than he had sitting on Ike's porch.

Tom opened the thin case file and began. "The tests have come back," he said. "And it's exactly as you said. Some of your plants are genetically modified. Both the corn plants and the blackberries. They're an exact match to the genetically modified crops being grown by GenAgra across the road."

"I told you, Kaye," Ike said smugly.

"Now you hush up," Kaye said, "and let Tom finish."

"It's okay, Kaye," Tom said. "He was right. Those animals he was watching proved to be very wise.

"The tests we've done so far do not show the extent of the contamination. There would need to be more testing in order to show what percentage of your crop was contaminated. But we can say, very definitively, that there has been contamination. Our expert would also say the contamination was most likely caused by cross-pollination. The only other explanations are that you somehow planted your own modified crops with GenAgra seed. Whether by accident or on purpose."

"My seed corn was certified organic," Ike said hotly. "And my brambles have been certified organic for years." Kaye pulled at his arm, and he quieted.

"I would never question your integrity, Ike," Tom said. "But GenAgra will, if we file this lawsuit. So we would have to prove that your crops were organic to start with, and then they were contaminated."

Ike nodded, his jaw set.

"Now, I've told you before," Tom said, "but I think I may not have been clear enough, so I wanted to be sure to bring you in again. Both of you. To discuss your options.

"In my legal opinion, you can lay out a basic case against GenAgra for trespass. You may be able to lay out a case for what we call nuisance. And probably negligence, too. There's a number of theories that would allow us to sue. I think that the law would allow you to bring a suit against GenAgra, and in a perfect world, I believe you would win that lawsuit."

Ike smiled, but Kaye was reserved. Tom knew she was hearing the subtle cues in his speech.

"That being said," Tom continued, "it is my legal opinion that it would be unwise, in this case, to file suit."

Ike's smile turned stony, but Kaye had his arm like a leash. It was a nuptial hold that Tom had seen before, and it was the very reason he wanted to have this conversation in Kaye's presence.

"We do not live in a perfect world," Tom said. "Just because you're right, doesn't mean you're going to win a lawsuit. I've consulted with two legal experts. I trust them both. And they both advised me that bringing this case would not be prudent.

"They found no cases where anyone had successfully sued a company like GenAgra, based on a theory like this. It has been talked about by lawyers and law review articles, because this genetic pollution is becoming a real problem for organic farmers. But no cases. No trials that GenAgra has lost. No appeals that they've lost. None.

"To be fair, that doesn't mean they've never been sued like this before. But if it has been done, we don't know about it. Maybe they've been sued and settled all the cases they couldn't win, so these cases never go to trial and never get reported. I just don't know the answer to that question."

Ike squirmed free from Kaye's grip. "Well this will be the first time then," he said before Kaye re-established her hold and shot him an icy stare.

"I understand how you feel, Ike," Tom countered. "I really do. You want to fight them. And they deserve to be fought. What they've done to your farm is definitely wrong. Even, legally wrong, I'd say. But you have to understand that just because something is wrong, it doesn't mean the legal system is going to make it right. And in your case, there's absolutely no certainty the system will work. In fact, the people I've talked to think filing suit has a good chance of making things worse.

"There are a ton of cases GenAgra is involved with that are reported. Contract disputes over genetically modified seed. Patent infringement cases, where they actually own a patent for the plants that are now growing in your field. And in every case we've found, GenAgra comes out on top.

"What's that tell me? It tells me they spend a lot of money pursuing their legal rights at all costs. They might settle their bad cases. We don't know. But if they have a leg to stand on, it seems they push forward with all their resources. These cases drag out for years, winding through courts as they go. All the way to the Canadian Supreme Court in one of the cases. And GenAgra comes out on top. It stops being a matter of who's right and who's wrong, and it becomes a kind of legal war of attrition. And they've got legal teams and high-priced firms and a legal budget that won't quit. Heck, they're richer than most countries on the planet. And they will spend that money to crush us in a court fight. There will be endless discovery and all kinds of hazy allegations. And in the end, chances are things will go their way.

"And that could mean you pay hundreds of thousands of dollars. You could lose your farm. I could pay tens of thousands in attorneys' fees. I could lose my practice. And we would risk all that on the hope we might get them to settle and pay you some damages without going to trial."

Ike was listening now. Tom could see he was still angered by the injustice of his situation. But now Kaye's grip on Ike's arm wasn't the only thing keeping the old farmer from speaking.

"And in the end," Tom said, "what are we going to ask for? Some money, Ike. That's all you can make them pay. Money. How much? I don't know. But it won't be enough to take the risk. It seems far more prudent to spend your money on remediation of the pollution to your crops than to take on this fight."

It was as quiet as a June morning in a small town when Tom finished speaking. He had laid out a convincing case for being cautious, and though the words left a bitter taste in his mouth, he had convinced Ike to think very hard about going forward. In the end, Ike and Kaye decided to take the weekend to think about their options.

"Why don't you drop by for lunch on Monday," Kaye said with a wink, as the couple left the office. "We should be able to decide by then."

Tom smiled but felt conflicted. Being a prudent counselor of the law too frequently cut against the grain of justice.

As he looked over the focus group reports, Al Bullard liked what he saw. The Health-Ease Blackberries really could be the new Coca-Cola, he surmised.

"Your car is here, sir," Bullard's assistant said, entering

the office. Bullard had almost forgotten about meeting with his father and Senator Tisdale, Chairman of the Senate Agriculture Committee.

"I'll be right down," Bullard said. He was tired of meetings with politicians. His new focus was on manipulating the masses for the benefit of the corporate world, and he was consumed by the task. As he nuzzled closer to the engines of the American economy, he started to see that politicians were mere shadows cast by the captains of industry, and he felt restrained when he was pulled back into the world of shadows. Bullard pulled on his black suit jacket, re-buttoned his collar, and straightened his tie as he walked out of the office.

"If someone from GenAgra's legal department calls, I want them put through to my cell phone," Bullard barked at his secretary as he left. He rode the high speed elevator down to the M Street entrance and hopped in the courtesy car that had been sent by the chairman.

"The Capitol Building, sir?" the driver asked.

"Yes, the senate entrance please," Bullard said.

Bullard watched the office buildings of the elite pass by his window, the streets crowded with lunching bureaucrats and spin-doctors, a massive parasitic horde. He thought of Malec's call in the morning. For a doctor heading up research on the premier product of a Fortune 500 company, Bullard found Malec to be substandard. He had phoned in to explain his failure to set up a conference call with the legal department. "They don't do conference calls with contractors," Malec had sniveled. Bullard shuddered at the thought of someone as mousy as Malec trying to sell a product so revolutionary. Even with the obvious advantages held by Health-Ease Blackberries, Bullard was sure that Malec could hinder the product's assured success if the entire project hadn't been turned over to a professional marketing firm.

As the car was halfway to the senate, Bullard's cell phone rang.

"Bullard here," he said.

"Mr. Bullard," his secretary said. "I have a Mr. Nunley from GenAgra's legal department on hold. May I transfer him to your cell phone, sir?"

"Yes," Bullard said, anxious to get some answers. The call clicked over. "Bullard here."

"Good morning, Mr. Bullard," the man said. "I'm Nick Nunley, director of the legal department at GenAgra."

"Thank you for returning my call," Bullard said. It had taken one quick phone call to Wes Zimmerman to light a fire under Mr. Nunley's dumb ass.

"Pleased to be of assistance," Nunley said. If he was angry at being cowed into returning Bullard's phone call, the lawyer's voice didn't give it away. "How can I help you this morning?"

"It's afternoon here in D.C.," Bullard jibed. Guess they didn't teach Illinois lawyers about time zones, he sneered to himself. "I instructed the project manager to schedule a teleconference with your department and was informed this morning that you didn't *need* a teleconference."

"That's right," Nunley said. "We have our own internal procedures for handling cases like this, and there's no need for discussion on the topic."

"Well, I hope Mr. Zimmerman's office has straightened you out on who is running this project," Bullard said.

"Yes," Nunley said, his voice now slightly rankled.

"So was the research team able to sufficiently explain the problem to you?" Bullard asked.

"Yes, the problem has been clearly defined," the lawyer said. "In fact, I already have some information to pass along on the case. We received a report earlier in the week that a lab in East Lansing tested plants belonging to one Ike A. Stiles. The testing found that Stiles is growing our plants without a license. We have already turned the case over to local counsel, a firm called Barnes & Honeycutt, out of Detroit. They handle all our litigation in Michigan."

"I trust that I will be kept well informed on legal issues in the future?" Bullard asked pointedly.

"I will personally make contact with lead counsel on the case and ensure they keep you advised," Nunley said.

"Thank you," Bullard said. Another lap dog. He was pleased with the eagerness of GenAgra employees to subjugate themselves. "And this firm, they are up to this challenge?"

"They're very aggressive," Nunley said. "They've never let us down before."

"Thanks for the update," Bullard said. "Sorry to have to go over your head."

"No problem," Nunley said. "Enjoy your weekend."

Nunley seemed competent at least, which was a step ahead of Malec. Competent lawyers were the foot soldiers of a company about to roll out a product like the Health-Ease Blackberry. The car pulled up through the Capitol security and parked near a heavily guarded doorway. The driver exited and opened the door for Bullard.

"The senate, sir." the driver said.

Chapter Six

Tom spent the weekend fishing on Watson Lake, catching little more than an early summer sunburn. He was alone on the water, sober, and felt better than he had in months. Even if Ike decided not to go forward against GenAgra, Tom was thankful for the push the case had given him toward resuming his life. Things were far from perfect, but he was getting out of bed everyday. Breathing in the world. And that was better than the alternative.

Late Monday morning he set out from his office to visit the berry farm, to get Ike's answer. As he approached the farm, he saw the fruit stand was bustling with activity. Strawberry season was in full bloom. Great weekend weather had stayed for the work week, and with the sunshine and the strawberries, came a steady stream of customers to the farm. Retired couples, housewives with newly freed school children in tow, and locals who had somehow escaped from a Monday routine to pick precious strawberries drooping ripe and low.

The porch was empty, but Tom saw Kaye at the stand, picking through produce. He parked the car and walked idly over the weedy lawn to the stand.

"You look like you could use a hand," Tom said to Kaye.

"Oh, Tom," she said, looking up. A smile blossomed on her sweet face and she reached out to squeeze his hand. "You're early, dear. I was just picking out some things to go with lunch."

"Can I help with anything?" Tom asked.

"No, no," she said. "I've got what I need. Let's go back to the house."

"So how's Ike?" Tom spoke in low tones as they made their way out of the crowded stand.

"Oh, he's doing fine," Kaye said. "A little rankled by all this, but fine."

"Have you made a decision?" Tom asked.

"I'm going to leave the final decision to Ike." Kaye smiled. "We've talked it over a good bit. But I promised him that he could make the final decision."

"Uh-oh," Tom said. "I was relying on your common sense."

"Now, Tom," Kaye said. "I am sure Ike knows how to be sensible when the chips are down."

Kaye's elegance permeated her words. Her manner was graceful and her demands light. She looked and sounded the same as she had since he was a boy. Always soft-spoken. But with a powerful essence.

"Let me get the door for you," Tom said.

"Thank you," Kaye said. "Ike's out back in the strawberry fields. You should go talk to him before lunch."

"Okay," Tom said.

"I'll call you when it is ready," Kaye said. She opened the refrigerator, removed a carton and poured a glass of juice. "And take him this, and make sure he drinks it."

Tom took the juice and set out for the fields behind the house. White clouds were fluffing up against the late morning sky over the fields of southern Wabeno County, fanned by summer's first true heat. Under the sky were the green fields of vegetables, fruit, and brambles. Customers were scattered throughout the strawberry fields, leisurely filling their quarts with ripe berries. Tom saw Ike's figure from across the field, squatting with a handful of student-workers, as they expertly plucked berries for the stand. Tom sauntered down the tractor path toward Ike. The berry patch was a maze of life. He breathed in the setting. Warm air heavy with pollen.

"What's an old man like you doing squatted down picking strawberries?" Tom crowed as he closed in.

"Well, if the world had to wait for lawyers to pick their food," Ike looked up, "we'd sure be in a helluva mess." He straightened up and met Tom with a slap on the back.

"Kaye said I have to make you drink this," Tom said, handing Ike the glass.

"Good," Ike said. He gulped the deep burgundy liquid down and belched proudly when he was done. "My damn foot."

"What?" Tom asked.

"Black cherry juice," Ike said. "For my gout. My foot is killing me. Don't get old, Tom. There ain't nothing good about it."

"Better than dying young," Tom said.

"Don't be too sure." Ike wheezed a laugh and rolled a cigarette. "Come on, let's head up to the barn."

Ike handed off his half-full quart to one of the students, and the two men set off. Tom walked alongside Ike, the old man slowed by a noticeable limp.

"That looks pretty bad," Tom said.

"Hurts like hell," Ike said through a grimace, "but it ain't nothing a week of juice drinking won't fix."

"You should go to the doctor," Tom said.

"Just be throwing money away," Ike said. "Ain't no remedy a doctor can give you that ain't been thought of a hundred years ago."

Tom did not want to dispute Ike's belief in folk remedies. It was a losing battle. So they finished the slow walk to the barn in silence.

Ike limped into his office, pulled a milking stool over toward his desk, and slumped into his chair. He propped his right foot on the stool and slowly loosened his boot. "Look at this puppy," Ike said.

"Holy hell," Tom said, looking at the gnarled old foot. It was red and swollen, starting at Ike's big toe and continuing toward his ankle.

"Too much of the good life," Ike said, slapping his gut. "Beef and beer. Give a man the king's disease."

"I think they've got medicine for that now," Tom said.

"Give me a week, and Kaye'll have me nursed back to health," Ike said.

"Looks like business is booming," Tom said, after a moment.

"Oh yeah," Ike said. "Been a good season so far. We could use a little more rain for the fields, but this weather has sure got the tourists out. On a Monday. Can you believe it?"

"Nope. It's busier than I ever remember it."

"Well," Ike said, "it's going to have to be, if I can't make GenAgra pay to clean up this damn mess they've made of my crops."

"So you've decided," Tom said, at once relieved and angry he had bent Ike's will.

"I've decided." The old farmer spat. "But, I'll tell you, if it wasn't for that woman." Ike motioned to the house.

"I know," Tom said. "I'm sorry, Ike. I really am. But you know this is the best decision, given what you were up against."

"Believe me, I don't like it," Ike said. "But you're probably right. Cost a lot less to clean up the mess and get on with it than to deal with those goddamned people."

Tom nodded.

"You're going to have to give me that professor's name." Ike said. "Professor Romanov, er—"

"Romanelli," Tom said.

"Romanelli, yeah," Ike said. "You think he might help me figure out how to get rid of these things? I don't really have any idea how to clean up this kind of stuff, or what it'll cost. And I sure as hell don't know how I'm going to keep it from happening again."

"Yeah," Tom said. "I'm sure he'll be able to help. Or get us in touch with someone who can."

"Good enough," Ike said. "It's a shame they've gotta go."

"What's that?"

"Them blackberries. You ought to see 'em. Here it's not even the end of June and some of them berries are already ripe," Ike said. "I could probably pick out the bad brambles just by looking. Earliest I've ever sold blackberries is the end of July. But I could open those fields next week, if it wasn't for not wanting people to eat what the birds won't."

"Really," Tom said. "You think they've done something to make them ripen earlier?"

"Something," Ike said. "I don't know. This old world is getting too new for me. I don't want to live to see the things you're going to, boy."

Kaye called them for lunch. Together the three of them munched on egg salad sandwiches and fresh fruit while watching the white clouds billow skyward. As they watched the world, there was no talk of modified plants or lawsuits. Tom was glad they had made a sound decision, but a part of him felt cowardly for not challenging the injustice. As the clouds rose, they turned dark, blotting out the sun. The air grew cooler and threatening, and the denizens of the strawberry fields filed out like ants from a picnic.

They paid for their fruit and piled in cars. A line of them carrying quarts of strawberries toward the interstate. Headed to dining room tables across the county and beyond. As he watched the traffic depart, Tom considered the pleasure of staying on the porch to watch the coming storm—protected by the roof, yet still able to feel the mist of rain as it drifted in. He looked skyward waiting for the downpour.

"What's this?" Ike said, his voice tense. He pointed toward the fruit stand. A white SUV had driven up the road from the North Central Research Center and was turning into the parking lot. It had the distinctive green logo of GenAgra, and it was followed closely by a gray Oldsmobile. "Shit." He was up out of his wooden porch chair and hobbling down the stairs before Tom could move.

"Now, Ike," Kaye said sternly. But Ike continued on.

Tom trotted down and ran to keep pace with Ike. "Settle down, old timer," he said, rounding the corner of the fruit stand just behind Ike. A man in a dark suit stepped from the Olds and walked to meet them as a gaggle of men climbed from the SUV and milled in the parking lot.

"Good afternoon, gentlemen," the man in the suit said. "I'm looking for Ike A. Stiles."

"You found him," Ike snapped.

"Hello, Mr. Stiles," the suit said, raising an outstretched hand.

"I'm John Percival, United States Marshals Service."

"You looking to pick strawberries?" Ike said, ignoring the attempted handshake. "I think you might want a raincoat."

"No, sir." The marshal laughed and pulled folded papers from his coat pocket. "I've been ordered by U.S. District Court Judge Michael Fuller to serve you with this temporary restraining order."

Ike snapped the paper from the marshal's extended hand. "I don't have my reading glasses," he said, handing the paper to Tom. "But I think I'll let my lawyer read it over."

"That's fine," the marshal said, all smiles. "You are named personally, as is the Stiles' Family Berry Farm. It orders you to close down your business pending a hearing on a preliminary injunction, and it allows these men here to come on your property and remove plant samples."

"The hell they will," Ike scoffed.

"Hold on a second, Ike," Tom said. He had scanned the restraining order. It appeared to be a valid court order, and Tom knew enough about criminal law to know that resistance could land Ike in jail. "He's right. This is a lawful court order. It gives these men the right to collect samples."

"You can speak with your lawyer for a moment if you like," the marshal said. "There's a process server over there with the underlying summons and complaint, if your attorney would like to see those documents, too."

Tom put a hand on Ike's shoulder. "We'll accept service," Tom said. "Can we just have a moment to review the documents?"

"Certainly," the marshal said. He retrieved a small sheaf of papers from one of the men milling about the parking lot and handed them to Tom.

"C'mon Ike," Tom said, pulling the farmer backwards. "Let's go take a look at these papers." Tom read as they walked back to the porch. Stray drops of rain fell from the sky and dampened Ike's mumbled curses.

"GenAgra is suing you for patent infringement, Ike," Tom said slowly, still reading. "They filed in federal court in Bay City. The judge has issued an order temporarily closing your stand and prohibiting you from selling, moving, or destroying any plants."

"You've got to be shitting me," Ike said loudly.

"Settle yourself, Ike," Kaye said as the men reached the porch. "Listen to Tom."

"They have the right to come on and take samples from your field for testing," Tom continued.

"Oh, for cris'sakes," Ike ranted.

Tom looked up from the papers. "We can't stop them today. If you try, that marshal over there is going to take you to jail, and I wouldn't doubt the feds would end up charging you with resisting a peace officer or something like it."

"That's just beautiful," Ike said. "What in the world is going on?"

"We can challenge it," Tom said. "But for now we're going to have to let them do what they need to do."

A tirade of curses from Ike were drowned out as the clouds let loose with a downpour.

"There is a silver lining, Ike," Tom said when the farmer had quieted himself.

"What's that?" Ike asked.

"We're going to have to file a counterclaim," Tom said, with a wry smile. "You're gonna get your day in court after all."

"That's just wonderful," Ike said, sarcastically.

Tom set the papers on the porch table, and they turned to march back toward the band of invaders in the parking lot. He was sickened as they came face-to-face with the four men that formed the GenAgra search party. The men were led by a tall, elderly man with glasses and a long white lab coat. To his right was a short man in an ill-fitting security guard uniform. The short man held a video camera that he was futilely trying to protect from the rain. The remaining two men were casually dressed. Probably lab technicians or even students.

Tom told the marshal that Ike would not impede the search in any way. Ike called back to the porch for Kaye to handle closing down the stand, as required by the court's order. And Tom and Ike accompanied the marshal as they followed the GenAgra team through the fields.

Ike restrained himself from further outbursts, but his humor did not improve in the two hours that he and Tom spent watching the men take plant samples from the farm. The men from GenAgra methodically sampled the corn field and then turned their attention to the berry brambles. They were directed at every step by the elderly man in the white lab coat. "Doctor Malec," his colleagues called him. The entire operation was filmed by the short security guard. Tom was only able to bring a smile to Ike's face once during the afternoon, commenting on the relative misery the rain caused Malec. The field was a muddy bog, sparing no one discomfort. The marshal made polite small talk at long intervals, but the search made Tom feel utterly helpless.

The group from GenAgra finally collected all their samples and retreated to their SUV. When they were gone, the marshal thanked Tom and Ike for their cooperation and wished them well, before driving off in his Olds.

Ike was openly seething once the strangers departed and wanted Tom to stay for dinner so they could discuss the case. Tom begged off. He was worn out from the excitement and chilled from the rain. He told Ike that they would need to respond to the legal papers as quickly as possible. Then he headed back to the office for a long night's work.

At the office, he ditched his wet clothes for a spare pair of khakis and a white button-down shirt he kept on hand for emergencies. Tom was angry. It had been humiliating to have to stand by and watch the search of Ike's farm. It was such a miscarriage of justice. Tom did not recognize the name of the federal judge who had signed the order, but a cursory review of the injunction made him doubt the man's fairness. Such orders, granted without notice to an opposing party, were a rare and dangerous remedy, and most judges Tom knew over the years had used them cautiously. To order Ike's entire business closed without a hearing was extreme.

Tom read the order again, trying to understand how a judge could make such a ruling. He then read the complaint over twice. He was unfamiliar with patent law and that was a handicap. Worse, his normal practice kept him almost exclusively in state courts. He hadn't appeared in a federal court for over a decade, so that was strike two against him as a defense attorney for Ike. Reading the complaint was tedious, and he quickly became frustrated at having to re-read confusing sections.

In years past, any frustrations in the office were easily remedied. He would pace for a time, and if a quiet mind did not result, he could always turn to Claire. He would walk out of his office to her desk, tell her all his silly troubles, and she would make them disappear. So he tried pacing his office. But he was utterly alone. He started for the cabinet of his credenza and then stopped halfway there. Bourbon wasn't going to make the lawsuit any clearer, he berated himself. Ike needed his help. The old man couldn't go it alone. And GenAgra, audacious enough to file this lawsuit, needed to be punished. Who in the hell did they think they were?

He looked at the wall clock. It was coming up on 6:30 p.m. He needed help, and all of it would come from people who probably went home at least an hour ago, Tom surmised. What would Claire say at a time like this, he wondered. Her voice was still clear to him. "That's a no-brainer." She would have smiled. "Let's get some dinner, get a good night's sleep, and we'll deal with this first thing in the morning." Solid advice, he thought.

"Where shall we eat?" he said, his voice breaking the unnatural quiet of the office. He listened as the silence rushed back in over the wake of his words. He waited. And a chill ran up his spine at the conscious thought that he was waiting for his dead wife to pick a place to eat. A hollow laugh escaped him, and he closed the office for the night.

Tom strolled into his office at 8:30 a.m., a half-hour earlier than the start time painted on the office doors. He wore a sleek charcoal suit with faint gray stripes, a laundered white shirt, and a blue silk tie. Dressing that morning, he had felt like a champion of the people donning armor to fight the good fight. No more laying down while the sharks swam free.

He loaded the coffee machine with life blood and jotted a "to do" list he had memorized the night before when anger would not let him sleep. Hire Wendy. Get Ryan under contract. And talk with Nell about the new posture of the case. He wanted to avoid calling Wendy too early, so he busied himself with drafting a contract and cover letter to secure Ryan's services as an expert. He pulled up forms for the paperwork on his computer and sipped steaming coffee as he worked. In a short time, he had an expert witness contract for Professor Romanelli in the outgoing mail. He crossed one item off the list and moved on to the next, dialing Nell.

"Law office," Nell answered.

"Still haven't found sufficient office help, eh, Yeats?" Tom said.

"Wow, it's nine o'clock in the morning. Who dragged your sorry ass out of bed so early?" Nell shot back.

"You're not going to believe what happened yesterday," Tom said.

"I practice law in *Alpena*, Tom," Nell said. "I would believe almost anything."

"The company we were thinking of suing, GenAgra," Tom said. "Well, they beat us to the punch. They sued my client for patent infringement in federal court."

"No shit?" Nell said.

"Yup," Tom said. "And get this. The judge issued a temporary restraining order closing my guy's business down while we straighten out their lawsuit."

"No," Nell said, aghast.

"Yup." Tom chuckled. "I was there when the suit got served. A U.S. Marshal served the order. They practically did a cavity search on my guy's farm. They brought in their little team of technicians and started carting off plants for testing."

"Unbelievable," Nell said. "Who did they have to blow to get a federal judge to do that?"

"What happened to that sweet girl I trained in my office?" Tom kidded his former paralegal.

"I'm serious," Nell said. "That sounds outrageous."

"Well, I think so," Tom said. "But, I think I'm going to need a better argument than that to try to get the judge to reverse his course. Don't you?"

"Let me guess. You don't really want to do all the research yourself, so you were hoping I might..." Nell said.

"God, I trained a bright lawyer." Tom laughed.

"All right," Nell said. "But I got a trial tomorrow. Just a one-day thing. Nasty little domestic case. It might take me a couple of days to get what you need."

"I don't have a couple of days," Tom said. "My client is seething."

"Hang on a second," Nell said, and she put the phone down. "Just grabbing my federal rules. Let me see. Rule 65—Injunctions. Temporary restraining order, yada, yada, yada. If granted, motion for preliminary injunction set for earliest possible date, yada, yada. Here we go. On two days' notice, the adverse party—you—may appear and move its dissolution, and the court shall proceed as expeditiously as justice requires. So you can't get to court without two days notice anyway."

"Come again," Tom said.

"The quickest you can get in front of the judge is two days, if you give notice today, right?"

"If you say so," Tom said.

"That's the rule," Nell said. "So fax me your stuff, I'll crank out a quick motion to dissolve this morning, and get a courier to file and serve it today. And you'll be ready to argue it Thursday."

"That's as fast as we can get there?" Tom said.

"Yes, sir. Them's the rules. And if you want me to come along to help argue it, I'm open that day."

"I think I may need back-up on this one," Tom said. "That sounds good. You know anything about patent law?"

"Not much," Nell said. "But I have one key advantage over you."

"What's that?"

"I went to law school after the advent of computer technology," Nell said. "So I'll be able to find and read the law, whereas you—"

"Wait a minute, now, young lady," Tom said. "Let us not disparage our elders. There's something to be said about learning from books."

"I'd let you argue that point, Counselor," Nell said, "if I didn't already know you have never actually looked at any book in your office."

"All right," Tom said, laughing. "If this is the best we can do, I'll fax you the stuff right now. And I'll take your help Thursday, too. So long as you take a more respectful tone in the future."

"Okay, boss," Nell said.

"You're going to get it filed, right?" Tom said. "So I can tell my client."

"Yeah, no problem," Nell said. "Just fax it. I'll fax you back a copy of the motion once I get it off to court."

"Thank you, darling," Tom said and hurried to the fax machine. He spent several minutes punching wrong buttons and subjecting himself to a symphony of painful tones, but he finally got the papers to Nell's office. At least he was fairly sure he had succeeded.

He returned to his desk and scratched off the second item on his list. It was closing in on 9:30 a.m., and while Tom thought it might still be too early to bother an unemployed graduate student, he dialed her number anyway. He was desperate. Anyone who might ensure the fax machine never again made those horrific noises was going to be an essential part of the office.

Wendy answered on the first ring and sounded alert.

"Hello, Ms. Isaacson. This is Tom Hughes, up in Milton. How are you?"

"Great, Tom," she said. "Thanks for calling back."

"No problem," he said. "It looks like I'm going to need that summer help we talked about. And after talking with you the other day, I think you would fill the position nicely."

"That's great," Wendy said. "I was really hoping you'd call. I think it'll be a great summer job for me, and I'm really happy to help out."

"I know we didn't get to talk about a salary when we spoke," Tom said, "but I was thinking about paying ten dollars an hour. Thirty-five hours a week. And I'll throw you on the health plan, if you want to take on the co-pay."

"I've got my insurance through the university," Wendy said. "But ten dollars an hour is fine."

"So we've got a deal?" Tom said.

"Sure," Wendy said. "When do I start?"

"How about tomorrow? Office opens at nine and closes at five, at least for you."

"Okay. That sounds great."

"All right," Tom said. "I'll look forward to seeing you tomorrow, then."

"Uh, one more thing," Wendy said, as Tom was about to hang up the phone. "I'm just curious. Has Doctor Romanelli agreed to work on the case?"

Strange question for a new office temp, Tom thought. But then again, he had never hired someone so near her doctorate to do routine clerical work before. He would probably have to get used to questions he didn't understand. At least for the summer.

"He said he would," Tom said.

"Sounds good," Wendy said.

Tom said good-bye and scratched the third item from his list. He sat back in his chair. There were no other files to work on, so all he could do was wait for Nell to do her thing. He decided to call Ike and give him an update.

"Stiles' residence," Kaye answered the phone.

"Good morning, Kaye," Tom said. "Is Ike around?"

"He's not coming to the phone today, Tommy. All that playing you two did in the rain yesterday," Kaye reproved, "has him in bed with his death of a cold."

"Is he okay?" Tom asked, concerned.

"Oh, he'll be fine," Kaye said. "Just needs a little honey and cinnamon. And a day off work. Which isn't a problem, thanks to our good neighbors."

"Give him my best," Tom said. "I don't want to bother him while he's resting or anything, but when he's feeling well enough, you let him know I'm having a response drafted as we speak. We should be in federal court on Thursday to get your farm reopened."

"Okay, Tommy," she said. "That'll surely cheer the old fool. I'll tell him."

Tom said good-bye. There was nothing to do but wait, he thought, but the deafening silence of the office made that impossible. Better to be active. He rose, went into his small library, and fumbled clumsily through his own dusty books in an effort to introduce himself to the wonderful world of patent law.

"I have a call from a Ms. Yale, sir," Bullard's secretary said over the intercom, distracting Bullard's attention from the spreadsheet data on his monitor. He did not instantly recognize the name and was about to scream at his secretary for failing to screen the call. "She says she's with Barnes & Honeycutt. Something about the GenAgra litigation. Shall I take a message, sir?"

"No, no," Bullard said. "Put her through."

The attorney's voice was young, clear, and powerful. He wished he had a video link.

"It's nice to speak with you, Mr. Bullard," Yale said, after initial greetings. "I was a huge fan of your show. I stopped watching CNTV for a while after they took you off the air."

"Thank you." Bullard laughed. "I guess the world just wasn't ready for that much truth."

"No," Yale said. "I agree. The way you cut through the baloney of those other talking heads on cable news and got right down to how people were really feeling. That was the best part of it."

"So you're the attorney handling our case in Michigan?"

"That's right," Yale said. "I'm with Barnes & Honeycutt. Our Detroit office. Nick Nunley at GenAgra wanted me to give you a call to keep you updated on the case."

"Yes, I spoke with Nick last week."

"I'm sorry I haven't contacted you sooner," Yale said. "We've been working non-stop on this case since we got the assignment."

"Don't mention it," Bullard said. In an ordinary subordinate, such excuses would have held little sway, but he was enchanted by Yale's voice and demeanor.

"Do you have a free minute to talk about the case now?" Yale continued. "Or would you like me to arrange a time with your secretary that's better for your schedule?"

"I suppose I could give you a few minutes now," Bullard said, feigning great opportunity-cost for his precious time. "I'm fascinated by the legal ramifications of GenAgra's product enhancement."

"Yes," Yale said. "It's an interesting area of the law. Well, let me start at the beginning and bring you up to speed.

"We got the case last week. Nick sent us the investigative reports from the research facility security team. From the information gathered it looked as if GenAgra was being investigated and that litigation was likely to follow the investigation. There was a local lawyer and a professor of plant biology that breached security at the site, and they took some illicit samples. One of our security people saw the same lawyer with a neighboring farmer, a couple of days before. The two of them were out walking the farmer's lot and spying on the research facility. And a source at a private testing facility tipped us off that the lawyer had samples tested from both the research facility and from the farmer's fields. The tests showed that the farmer was growing patented Weed-Away Corn and your project's star plant, the dietary Blackberry. Hg-Blackberry, I believe is the technical name."

"The Health-Ease Blackberry," Bullard interrupted. The time to start framing the product was nigh.

"Is that the name? Very clever. I like it," Yale said.

"My invention," Bullard bragged.

"Well, it was apparent this greedy farmer had obtained your patented blackberry," Yale said, "and had hired counsel to assist him in insulating his piracy.

"Given the importance of this product to GenAgra, we knew aggressive action was needed. We worked through the weekend and filed suit on Monday in the federal district court. We drew a very favorable judge—Michael Fuller—and we convinced him to sign a temporary restraining order shutting down the farmer's operation until we are able to prove this piracy in court."

Bullard recognized the name of the judge as one of the president's controversial appointees. He seemed to recall Fuller was given his spot by recess appointment to avoid an initial confirmation hearing before Congress.

"That is excellent work, Ms. Yale," Bullard said. "It sounds like you have the legal situation well in hand."

"Things have gone without a hitch so far," Yale said. "But the threat of this litigation is not over yet."

"How so?"

"If I might continue," Yale said. "The restraining order was served early on Monday. As I said, it closed the farm for the time being, and it also allowed GenAgra to conduct extensive testing of the fields to confirm the farmer's piracy. These samples were analyzed on Tuesday. Apparently, GenAgra's security measures have been somewhat successful, because the farmer was unable to steal enough product to plant his entire field. Our analysis indicates that only eighteen percent of his corn crop, and only forty-two percent of his blackberry crop are patented GenAgra cultivars.

"The bad news arrived yesterday. They filed a motion to terminate our restraining order. It will be heard tomorrow morning in federal district court."

"Is that in Detroit?" Bullard asked. This seemed like important litigation, and Yale seemed like someone he should work closely with on the case. His lips curled to a smile.

"No," Yale said. "It's in the Northern Division of the Eastern District. Bay City."

"What time is the hearing?"

"It's scheduled for nine."

"You'll be there to handle it?" Bullard asked.

"Yes."

"Is this hearing something we are likely to lose?" Bullard said. "I'd hate to see this farmer out there selling my Health-Ease Blackberry a year ahead of our official release date. It could be disastrous."

"Well, obtaining a temporary restraining order of this kind is an extraordinary writ, Mr. Bullard," Yale said. Bullard liked the way she lectured him. "It was not a small victory on our part. And defending it will not be easy. But I'm confident the judge will see things our way."

"I think I'd like to be there to see the matter argued," Bullard said.

"Your presence is not required," Yale said. "But it would be an honor to meet you in person, if you'd like to come."

"I'll see if I can squeeze it into my schedule," Bullard said. "Thanks for the update, Ms. Yale. Perhaps I'll see you tomorrow."

Bullard called his personal assistant in as soon Yale was off the phone. "I need to be in Bay City, Michigan for a court hearing at 9:00 a.m. tomorrow. I'd prefer a private plane, and I'd like to arrive this evening if possible. I'm traveling alone. Best rental car and best hotel accommodations available. Bill it to the GenAgra account."

Bullard dismissed his assistant and was shortly interrupted

again by his secretary.

"I've got Doctor Malec ready on video-link for your ten o'clock, sir," she said over the intercom.

"Put him through in three minutes," Bullard barked. The cur could wait, Bullard thought. "And bring me an eclair and a mochaccino." He rose from his desk and walked to the black leather couch. He let his large frame collapse.

"Here you are, sir," his secretary scurried in with his mid-morning snack.

He polished off the chocolate eclair in two bites, washing the rich pastry down with the sugary cocoa-coffee beverage. He brushed small chocolate crumbs from his black shirt, and in the next moment, Doctor Malec's perturbed face blinked larger than life onto Bullard's wall monitor.

"How are you, Doctor?" Bullard said.

"Busy," Malec sniped like a small dog.

"I won't keep you long," Bullard said, indifferent to Malec's attitude. He couldn't make the doctor like his new position as a subordinate, but as long as the man continued to do his job, his irritation was of no concern to Bullard. "I wanted an update on how things are proceeding."

"We're still preparing the final data for our APHIS report, so we can get the product approved," Malec said sharply. "It takes time."

"You can tell your people to stop twisting the data and submit the report," Bullard said.

"The report is not ready," Malec countered. "There are technical difficulties that need to be explained, and—"

"I know all about your technical difficulties," Bullard said calmly. "I had lunch with the chairman of the Senate Agriculture Committee yesterday. Senator Daniels. He is very close with the secretary of agriculture. Controls the USDA purse strings single-handedly."

"But Mr. Bullard, the berries have a potentially—" Malec said.

"I know," Bullard said, wondering when Malec was going to learn to follow simple orders. "Senator Daniels is no hack. He keeps close oversight on what's happening at the USDA. He told me all about your problem. That the protein your plant was creating was a longer molecule. That it made it farther into the digestive tract of your test mice. It's not a problem anymore. Stop writing and get the report to APHIS."

"It's not a problem?" Malec said.

"No," Bullard said. "The problem has been eliminated. There are no more delays. The Health-Ease Blackberry is going to put America on the road to a more fit future, and that is going to start sooner rather than later."

"You're going to dictate science to the USDA?" Malec asked in disbelief.

"No," Bullard assured him. "*You're* going to dictate science to the USDA. I'm just going to assure that they agree with you."

"That will make my life much easier," Malec said, hesitantly. "But you understand the cultivars are producing proteins that might pose a slight health risk to the public?"

"The USDA would never approve anything that would harm the public." Bullard laughed. "This berry is going to do more for public health than the Salk vaccine, Doctor. Your name will be in good company."

Malec appeared to brighten reluctantly.

"Now, I understand from our legal team that we did some testing to confirm that the neighboring farm is growing our berry crop?" Bullard said, turning somber.

"Yes," Malec said. "Almost half his crop is producing the Skinny Berry."

"That's Health-Ease Blackberry, Doctor."

"Yes, Health-Ease Blackberry," Malec said mechanically.

"What I want to know is this." Bullard let his voice fall low, before exploding, "Why in the *fuck* do I have to hear about what my own science unit is doing from my people on the legal team?"

Malec winced visibly, but remained silent, like a whipped dog.

"From now on, Doctor Malec," Bullard said, regaining part of his composure, "when there is *anything* going on with my project, I want to hear about it from you. And if that's a problem, I'll be happy to find someone to head up your team who knows how to communicate. Do we understand each other?"

"Yes, sir," Malec said, his head slightly bowed.

"I want you to end up like Doctor Salk." Bullard hiccupped a laugh. "But if you don't start keeping me in the loop, you might end up more like Doctor Frankenstein. Okay?"

"Yes, sir," Malec said.

"All right," Bullard said. "Now go get that report ready and get it in. And keep me posted."

Bullard clicked Malec's shaken image off the wall monitor. Keep your friends close, Machiavelli's advice popped into his mind, and your enemies closer.

Chapter Seven

Tom calculated the trip in his head as he turned eastbound on US-10. They were five minutes behind schedule, so he boosted his speed to eighty and clicked the cruise. They would easily make up the time on the freeway. He would be on time to argue his motion.

As they sped toward the federal courthouse in Bay City, Tom answered Wendy's questions about the upcoming hearing, though he didn't feel very comfortable with the subject matter himself. Several hours of study in the area of patent law had left him more confused than when he started, and less confident about Ike's chances in the case.

They made it to the city limits in just forty-five minutes. Still enough time to get to the courthouse. US-10 terminated in Bay City. The city itself was the remnant husk of a manufacturing town snuggled in the crotch of the mitten of Michigan, on the Saginaw Bay. As he approached a commercial zone, the speed limit dropped, and the highway split into two one-way roads. He continued to speed east until a large drawbridge spanning the Saginaw River came into view. His heart sank as he saw a line of cars stopped at the bridge, where two middle sections raised skyward as a large freighter drifted up the river below. He whipped out his cell phone and got through to the judge's clerk, leaving a message that he was stuck at the bridge. He hoped Judge Fuller was more reasonable in person than he was in his written court orders.

"This is not a good omen," Wendy said, lowering her window and peering out to look at the freighter.

"Omen." Tom laughed. "There are no omens in the law."

Wendy smiled. "You don't believe in omens?"

"I thought I was hiring a scientist as my new secretary." Tom continued to smile. "What's this superstitious nonsense? Bad omen."

The sun was out, and the air near the water was heavy with oxygen. Mixed with Wendy's company, the atmosphere was intoxicating. Not a bad morning so far, Tom thought, late or not.

"Hey, there's lots of stuff science can't explain," Wendy said. "The more we learn, the more questions we have. Have you read anything about quantum mechanics lately?"

The ship passed, the drawbridge slowly dropped into place, and the traffic resumed its course. Tom drove over the bridge and turned toward the courthouse. He navigated five stop lights, all red, and saw the old post office building on his right-hand side. The building was a classically designed stone structure, three stories tall, and took up an entire city block. Its limestone exterior looked yellowed in the morning sunlight. It had character, Tom thought.

He parked in an angled space in front of the building and hopped out of the car. He grabbed his jacket from the back seat, pulled it on, gathered his briefcase, and hustled to the courthouse doors. Wendy ran to keep up as he loped up a stairwell to the second floor, his lungs burning. He plopped his briefcase and keys on a conveyor at the security checkpoint and chatted politely with the guards. Wendy followed like a squire.

"About time," Nell said in a low, firm voice. She stood by the courtroom door, her posture reproachful at Tom's belated entry. "This is no way to endear yourself to the judge."

Next to Nell was Doctor Romanelli.

"Wendy. Mr. Hughes," Ryan said, with a nod of his head.

"Thanks for coming, Doc," Tom said.

"I wouldn't have missed it," Ryan said. "Not at this hourly rate anyway."

Tom took a deep breath. The four of them looked impressive, he supposed. For recreational doubles, perhaps, or a game of bridge. But no one would mistake them for a group about to engage one of the world's elite corporations in a legal battle.

"The other side is down in the conference room," Nell said. "I introduced myself to their lead counsel. She said she'd like to speak with you before we get started."

"Okay," Tom said. "Why don't you guys go get comfortable in the courtroom, and I'll be there in a minute." He walked down a dingy corridor, along the polished tile floor, anticipating his opposing counsel. He knew her only from her pleadings. A lawyer with a top law firm in the state, and a license number that said she had been around less than a decade. She was practically a kid. Too young to be a legal lion in federal court.

As he peered around the corner, Tom knew his prejudgment was wrong. She was young, but with a sophisticated beauty that conveyed instant gravitas. She was dressed in a black skirt and jacket, with a white silk blouse. Her golden hair was pulled back harshly, leaving a stray lock on either side to frame her elegant face. She stood with both hands on the back of a chair, discussing items with two seated men. The first was obviously a young lawyer, his dirty blond hair coiffed and his shoes glistening black. The second was a portly man in a casual sport coat. Tom could only make out the back of his balding head.

"You must be Ms. Yale?" Tom said, taking the initiative. He walked casually into the room and held out his hand. His eyes were drawn to hers, perfectly blue and clear.

"Yes," the woman said, her voice steely. She shook his hand. "Mr. Hughes?"

"Nice to meet you. Call me Tom."

"Hannah," she said. "This is my co-counsel, Cameron Dupree."

The young man rose and greeted Tom with a strong handshake.

"And this is Al Bullard," Yale said. "He's a representative for

GenAgra."

The fat man nodded a hello but did not rise. Tom instantly recognized him from cable news. His face had been plastered all over CNTV the previous year as a commentator during the presidential election. Tom nodded to the man, wondering how a national media figure came to represent GenAgra.

"You've met Nell?" Tom said. "She's assisting me with the case. She said you'd like to talk before the motion."

"Yes," Yale said. "Would you excuse us, gentlemen?"

Dupree led his more famous counterpart into the hallway.

"Do you mind if I check in with the judge before we get started?" Tom asked. "I got caught by the bridge, and I don't want him to think I'm holding him up."

"Not at all," Yale said.

Tom found his way past a security door and checked in with the judge's clerk. The clerk assured him the judge would not mind a delay for the lawyers to meet on the case. "Just let us know when you're ready to go," she said.

He made his way back to the conference room and again his eyes rested heavily on Hannah Yale. As he stared, her face looked familiar. Where had he seen her before, he wondered. "You've been to court up in my neck of the woods recently, haven't you?"

"Where do you practice again?" Yale said and looked down at an open file before her. "Milton. Oh sure, I was up there on a case last year. A plea hearing of some sort."

It clicked in Tom's head. She represented one of the eco-terrorists in Milton's most celebrated criminal case in decades. "A criminal matter. I remember it," Tom said. "That was a big case in our parts. You must be multi-talented. Criminal and patent law."

"Multi-talented, uh, no," Yale said in a tone of false modesty. "That case was merely fulfilling my *pro bono* requirement. It's a program we're proud of at Barnes & Honeycutt. We like to be socially responsible."

Tom suppressed laughter. Barnes & Honeycutt spent its time nuzzling in the trough of corporate and insurance company slop. They were one of the top firms representing moneyed interests in the state, and Tom was sure there was nothing about social responsibility in their secret clubhouse oath of office.

"So, I have to tell you, we were pretty surprised to get your lawsuit," Tom said. The case made him want to wretch, but he had been around the block on all kinds of heated issues, and he knew it was his job to maintain professionalism. "We had just discovered this genetic pollution on my client's property when you served us the papers."

"Genetic pollution, huh?" Yale said, amused. "We like to call it patent infringement."

"You say tomato, I say transgenic blackberry." Tom laughed, and Yale joined him.

"I'm glad to see you have a sense of humor," Yale said. "That makes things easier."

"Hey, we have to be civil to one another. We're civil lawyers," Tom said, his second effort at humor falling flat. "So, what does your client really want to do with this case?"

"Well, that's why I wanted to talk with you before we started," Yale said. "I've been authorized to make an offer."

"You know, my client is a stellar guy," Tom said, encouraging her peace offering. "He's very reasonable. I bet we could probably find a way to make this case disappear."

"Well, run this by him," Yale said. "First, our main concern is the Hg-blackberry. He'd have to agree not to sell any blackberries this season, and to either destroy the entire crop or license the Hg-Blackberry for next year.

"Second, he'd have to sign a licensing agreement for the Weed-Away Corn. And third, he'd have to pay back-royalties on the corn for three years. For his acreage, I'd say $75,000 dollars. That's ballpark."

Tom counted slowly toward ten, swallowing the vitriol that wanted to ebb from his mouth. He stopped at five. "My client is not well today." Tom kept his voice on a level plane. "He's actually bedridden, and I hate to speak for him. I'll have to convey your offer, you understand. But I don't think we are in the same ballpark. You see, my client hasn't done anything wrong. He really doesn't want your genetically modified plants in his field. I'm thinking a more reasonable settlement would be an agreement to split the cost of remediation for the pollution in his fields. You know, I'm not even sure at this point how one remediates genetic pollution. And then we would need some agreement about how GenAgra can avoid further polluting his site. That's more in the ballpark *we* are playing in."

"You're really not familiar with patent law, are you?" Yale said.

"I can't believe you'd say such a thing to an elder lawyer." Tom smiled. "I've been studying patent law for at least eight—maybe nine—hours."

She laughed again, and Tom enjoyed hearing it. He really didn't like her condescension, and the fact that she worked for Barnes & Honeycutt told him everything he needed to know about her world view. But she was superficially enchanting, he had to admit.

"I'm no patent expert either, Mr. Hughes—Tom," she said. "But Cameron Dupree out there, he lives and breathes it. He tells me that our patent case is unstoppable. So I don't really think you're bargaining from a position of power here."

"Well, there will be our counterclaim, don't forget," Tom said. "Trespass, nuisance."

"It's never been recognized in these GM plant cases," Yale said. "You're betting your novel claims against a sure winner. And you have to take that into account if we're going to settle this case."

"Look," Tom said, smiling to cover the anger that was coming over him. "Your little GM plants have run a bit wild. Between you and me, maybe there's not a lot of harm in it. I don't know. But my client is an organic farmer, and the fact that you have contaminated his crop is an immense deal to him. On top of that, you have sued him. And you are telling me you want him to pay *you* $75,000 for *his* trouble. I'm sorry, but that's not going to happen without a fight."

"If there is a fight, Tom," Yale said, "you are going to lose. And I expect it's going to cost him a lot more than $75,000. You should really encourage him to accept this offer."

"I'll convey it to him," Tom said. "And you should let GenAgra know that we've offered to let you out now if they will split the cost of the clean-up and stop their plants from spreading in the future."

"All right." She grinned. "I'll let them know. So it looks like we'll need to argue your motion, then."

"Yes, ma'am," Tom said.

They notified the judge and took their places in the courtroom.

Tom felt odd seated at the defense table, far removed from the empty jury box. He had been a plaintiff's attorney for nineteen years and preparing to defend a case was strange. Nell sat beside him, and Wendy and Doctor Romanelli sat in the gallery behind the defense table.

They rose, as demanded by the bailiff, and paid their respects to the judge as he entered. The judge had a perfect mane of sandy, graying hair, and a golden tan. He looked like he was in his early fifties and very fit. Tom thought he looked vaguely familiar, but could make no immediate connection.

"You can be seated," the judge said.

"Your Honor," Tom said. "May we approach before we go on the record?"

The judge nodded, and Tom headed to the bench, followed by Hannah Yale.

"I wanted to introduce myself, Your Honor," Tom said extending a hand over the bench. "I don't get to federal court often, and I don't believe I have had the pleasure. I'm Tom Hughes."

"Michael Fuller," the judge said, shaking his hand. "Nice to meet you."

"I wanted to apologize for being late, too," Tom said. Looking closely at the judge, he thought he recognized him from some prior case. "I forgot about your bridges here. Got caught on the wrong side of the river this morning."

"Oh, don't worry," the judge said. "I get caught a couple of times a week myself. Part of the charm of this place."

"Good morning, Your Honor," Yale said with a slight bow.

"Good morning, Counsel," the judge said. "So, this is plaintiff's—no—defendant's motion to dissolve the temporary restraining order, right?"

"Yes, Your Honor," Tom said.

"Have the two of you had enough time to talk this matter over?" the judge asked.

"Uh-huh," Tom and Yale said in unison.

"Any resolution?"

"No, Your Honor," Tom said. "Not yet."

"Okay," the judge said. "Well, we're running a bit behind, so if we're going to need to argue this motion, we might as well get started."

Tom walked back to the defense table. The judge seemed smooth and personable, contrary to the image Tom had built of him in the past two days of reading the temporary restraining order.

"We're on the record in the case of *GenAgra* versus *The Stiles' Family Berry Farm*," the judge said. "There is a notice of hearing in the court file for today's date and time, on the defendant's motion to dissolve the temporary restraining order. Counsel, can I have your appearances for the record?"

"Hannah Yale, with the law firm of Barnes & Honeycutt, Your Honor, appearing on behalf of the plaintiff."

"Tom Hughes for the defendant."

"I have reviewed your motion, Mr. Hughes," the judge said in a businesslike manner. "Would you like an opportunity for oral argument?"

"Yes, Your Honor," Tom said, rising and moving to the lectern in the middle of the courtroom.

"Please proceed, Counsel," the judge said.

"Thank you." Tom began, "Your Honor, I've brought this motion to dissolve the temporary restraining order in this case as quickly as was allowed under the court rules.

"As the court is aware, a temporary restraining order is an extraordinary form of relief, granted without notice. Had my clients had an opportunity to be present, and to fully inform the court of the factual background in this case, I'm confident the court wouldn't have issued any injunctive relief.

"In making an *ex parte* determination on this order, the court was forced to make a decision without the benefit of several key facts. I've provided affidavits from my client, Ike Stiles, and from Dr. Ryan Romanelli, to give the court a more complete picture of what happened in this case.

"Mr. Stiles has run his berry farm for over fifty years, Your

Honor. The Stiles' Farm has been certified organic for the past six years. GenAgra started doing research on the neighboring farm only three years ago at what is now called the North Central Research Center. Mr. Stiles has sworn, in his affidavit, he only planted organic seeds in his corn fields, and he has never planted or developed any genetically modified blackberry plants. Growing genetically modified foods would likely result in the loss of Mr. Stiles' organic certification, which would in turn be a major setback for his operation, considering he has held himself out as an organic farm for the past six years.

"Looking at the response to this motion from GenAgra, the court can see that GenAgra's own testing shows that eighteen percent of his corn and forty-two percent of his blackberry plants, are now genetically modified organisms, to which GenAgra claims a patent.

"One of our experts in this case is Dr. Ryan Romanelli, Your Honor. He is a plant biologist at Michigan A&T University. He indicates that, in his expert opinion, cross-pollination is the most likely explanation for how the transgenic properties of the GenAgra plants migrated into Mr. Stiles' fields. In effect, what we have here is a form of genetic pollution to an organic farm. It was unwanted. And it is harmful. We intend to file a counterclaim in this matter to seek damages for the trespass or nuisance caused by GenAgra's transgenic plants.

"In deciding whether to continue the restraining order, the first consideration the court must look at is whether GenAgra is likely to prevail on the merits of the case. Looking at their response, they contend that this case is a clear-cut infringement on their patents. Your Honor, the issues that will be presented to this court, with regard to genetic pollution, are ones of first impression. To allow GenAgra to pollute farms through cross-pollination, and then to sue the farmers they have wronged for patent infringement, is a blatant misuse of the patent. This is anything but a clear-cut patent infringement case.

"The second consideration the court must examine in determining whether to continue the restraining order is that of irreparable harm. Mr. Stiles is a small farmer, Your Honor. GenAgra is a multi-national giant. Assuming the court were to find an infringement here, there would be no harm to GenAgra that could not be remedied by monetary damages. Mr. Stiles is simply not in a position to exploit GenAgra's patent in any way that could cause irreversible harm to the plaintiff. To try to say Mr. Stiles has that much power is laughable. If anything, my client has suffered irreparable harm. The genetic pollution, and this lawsuit, are threatening his existence.

"The third consideration is whether, on balance, the hardships would favor an injunction. Again, this is a case of David versus Goliath, Your Honor. There's nothing Mr. Stiles could ever do with respect to these patents which could conceivably cause a hardship to GenAgra. It's Mr. Stiles who is suffering a hardship. The court has closed his business, Your Honor, at his peak time. In his affidavit, you'll see that Mr. Stiles' farm produces sales of approximately $15,000 per week in the summer months. As of today, he has lost revenues of over $6,000, in the three days this injunction has been in effect. This is a matter of life and death to Mr. Stiles' business, and is clearly a hardship.

"The last consideration is that of the public interest. Is the public interest served by issuance of this injunction? Clearly, no. The use of this patent in combination with injunctive relief threatens every organic farmer in this country—and every small farmer for that matter—who is not a licensee of GenAgra's GMOs.

"One last point I'd like to make, Your Honor. The breadth of this order is sweeping. The plaintiff is only claiming infringement on two plant varieties. Corn and blackberries. These crops are only a small percentage of Mr. Stiles' farming operation. This week, for example, is the heart of strawberry season. The strawberries are unrelated to this case. And yet, the court's order has simply closed down Mr. Stiles' livelihood. While I'm confident you will be dissolving this order in its entirety, if the court is even considering continuing the order, it should at least be modified so that Mr. Stiles can sell unrelated crops.

"I'd request that you dissolve this order, or in the alternative that you modify it so that it is carefully tailored to cause no more harm to Mr. Stiles than is absolutely necessary. Thank you, Your Honor." Tom sat down. The judge had looked thoughtful throughout. There was little more a lawyer could ask for.

"Ms. Yale," the judge said.

"Your Honor," she said, rising to address the court. "I would ask that my co-counsel, Mr. Dupree be allowed to address the court initially, with regard to the likelihood of success on the merits of the patent infringement case, and then I will address the other issues."

"I don't have any problem with allowing you both to argue," the judge said. "But I want to make sure that we are fair with the time allotted. Mr. Hughes used about seven minutes. So let's try to keep your combined arguments under that."

Cameron Dupree was a patent law machine, Tom thought, as the young lawyer spit out technical terms like an automatic weapon. Tom was convinced he would need a patent lawyer to stand up to Dupree's obvious skills if they were going to have any chance in the case.

In essence, Dupree explained the patent claims at issue in the case and how the Stiles' crops clearly violated the patent claims. This represented a *prima facie* case for patent infringement, absent a valid defense. Dupree enumerated the possible defenses and knocked them down one by one. He was finished in less than five minutes.

Dupree and Yale switched places at the lectern like tag-team wrestlers, and the bewitching lead attorney summarized the plaintiff's opposition to the motion.

"GenAgra has a substantial likelihood of success on the merits, Your Honor," she said. "Counsel for the defendant alludes to their coming counterclaim in an effort to confuse the court into thinking they can mount a successful defense. My research shows no case law which supports a claim for genetic pollution. This is a novel claim by the defendant and certainly not one that would cast any doubt on GenAgra's likelihood of success on the merits.

"As we made clear in our argument to obtain the temporary restraining order, there is irreparable harm to GenAgra if the defendant is allowed to continue infringing the patent. The Hg-Blackberry is a new product. It is slated for release next year. As yet, it has not been approved for consumption by the USDA. So for starters, allowing the defendant to continue infringing our patent would result in releasing an unapproved food to consumers. Now we have no doubt the Hg-Blackberry will be approved very soon, but to allow the product to be brought to market without proper approvals is a regulatory breach GenAgra would never willingly allow.

"Also, the product has unique weight loss properties. Allowing its release by a non-licensed infringer, almost a year before we will officially release the product, substantially alters the product rollout. GenAgra deserves the fruits of its patent and needs to be able to control the marketing of this product without interference from an unlawful infringer.

"We've posted a $10,000 security bond to cover any loss suffered by the defendant, in the event you later rule he has been wrongfully enjoined. The court has already scheduled a full hearing on the preliminary injunction for July 5th, less than two weeks from today. Our security bond and the early hearing date minimize any hardship involved, as the court takes the appropriate time to make a sound decision in this case.

"I also disagree with opposing counsel on the balancing of the public interests. He's asking you to remove an order that keeps an unapproved food off the market. Something that directly contravenes the public interest. The patent law, which as Mr. Dupree pointed out, almost assures GenAgra of prevailing on the merits of this case, also serves an important public interest. It protects the rights of creative invention, to give incentives to individuals and industry to keep making products that help make the world a better place. GenAgra is very proud of the products they are protecting in this case. And they believe the law should protect their scientific advances.

"Finally, Your Honor, I would respond to defense counsel's request the court should limit the effectiveness of this order by watering it down. He framed the debate as one of David versus Goliath. In this case, the stakes are very high for Goliath. GenAgra may be a world-wide corporation, but the defendant is poised to throw a stone at them which could cause serious damage. GenAgra has spent millions of dollars in producing the Hg-Blackberry, Your Honor. They are poised to capitalize on their patent, recoup their development costs, and make a profit. A profit which ultimately benefits the shareholders and our economy. If this court waters down the order and allows the defendant to re-open his operation, then GenAgra will have no way to prevent the defendant from selling the Hg-Blackberry before its time.

"The court issued this temporary restraining order based on sound reasoning. There's been nothing presented which should alter the court's analysis. The temporary restraining order should stand until this matter is fully heard on July 5th."

"Thank you, Counsel," the judge said. "Well, I've reviewed the pleadings carefully. Based on the affidavits that have been submitted to me thus far, it is clear that GenAgra does have a substantial likelihood of success on the patent infringement claim. The defendant's counterclaims, which were discussed today, do not change my opinion as to who is likely to win this lawsuit.

"I believe the best balancing in this case calls for a continuation of the temporary restraining order. GenAgra stands to be irreparably harmed if the blackberry they have been developing for years is sold out from under them due to patent infringement. And though this order is broad in shutting down the defendant's sale of farm produce, I believe it's the only practical way to ensure that the *status quo ante* is maintained until we can have a full hearing on this matter. I think the public interest is served by this order, that the order is tailored as narrowly as possible to ensure there is no irreparable harm before the court hears the matter in full, and that the inconvenience to the defendant is adequately protected by the bond that has been posted by the plaintiff.

"I am going to deny your motion, Mr. Hughes. My clerk will prepare the order. Please take a copy with you before you leave the courtroom. And we'll see both parties back on July 5th for a hearing on the preliminary injunction. Please have your witnesses and other evidence ready to go on that date.

"This court is adjourned."

The motion was Wendy's first courtroom experience. She had never fought a ticket or been in trouble with the law. She had never been sued or had the need to sue another. Before the hearing, her idea of court was drawn from television drama. But on television, the good guys were never defeated so soundly. Being a small part of the legal team, she felt guilty by association as she retreated from the courtroom loss. She followed Ryan outside as the lawyers stayed behind to take care of paperwork.

"That sucked," she said. She stood facing Ryan, together on the sidewalk, the fast-rising sun just beginning to erase the shadows cast by the old courthouse.

"Not very encouraging," Ryan agreed. She hadn't seen him for nearly two weeks, and his face had changed. He looked tired and he had a shadow of a goatee under his thin moustache. Still, even with poor hygiene, he looked good.

"I don't understand it," Wendy said. "How can they close down his farm when *they* are at fault?"

"I hate lawyers," Ryan said. "Always have. Next to car salesmen, they are the worst. They can twist anything and make it mean what they want."

She stared at him. His dark eyes rose and held her gaze for a moment. Wendy missed being around him. She missed the constant monologue he provided on all subjects and the passion he felt for everything. "How's your new lab assistant working out?"

"She's a disaster," Ryan said. "I don't remember needing to train you on anything. But with her it's like she's transferring in from the drama department or something. She has no clue about any lab protocols. No basic understanding of research, you know."

"I'm sorry," Wendy said.

"How's it going with you?" Ryan said. "Is this guy giving you enough time for your dissertation?"

"Well, this is only my second day," Wendy said. "But you couldn't ask for a better supervisor. He's very kind and considerate. Not what you'd expect from a lawyer." As she described Tom, she thought she saw a hint of jealousy in Ryan's eyes.

"Just don't forget about your thesis," he said. "Stay focused on what's important."

"I feel kind of sorry for him, you know," Wendy said, sensing an opportunity. "He lost his wife earlier this year, and he seems completely lost sometimes."

"Really?" Ryan said.

"Yeah, it's awful isn't it? Such a good-looking guy. Successful. Nice. And completely alone. A great catch for someone."

"He's a little old for you, don't you think?" Ryan said too quickly.

"Not really." Wendy smiled. It was so kind of Ryan to protect her. "Forty something, I think. But, I wasn't talking about me. I was just saying."

Tom and Nell came out of the courthouse.

"Doc, would you join us for a late breakfast?" Tom said. "Nell knows a place on the other side of the river."

"Great big slices of homemade toast," Nell said. "Yummy."

"Okay. I'll follow you," Ryan said.

Wendy rode with Ryan. She rested an arm on the center console, trying to make contact with him, but he inched away. They talked about her progress on the thesis and about the difficulties she would face defending such an anti-corporate study. Always, with Ryan, there were times when she was certain that he cared deeply for her. But the moments were rare, nestled between gulfs of indifference. It was frustrating, but her feelings for him did not seem to have faded in his absence. And she was resigned to the fact that she couldn't change how she felt.

Their group took a small booth at the restaurant. Wendy tried to jockey for a seat next to Ryan but could not manage it without being unduly obvious. She ended up seated next to Tom, with Ryan kitty-corner across the table. She ordered an omelette and ate it sparingly, looking often to the professor, whose nose was mostly buried in his own breakfast. Nell had been right about the toast, Wendy thought. It was delicious.

Tom tried hard to rationalize the morning catastrophe in the courtroom, but she felt the setback seemed like an omen of more bad things to come.

"Did you see the guy from GenAgra?" Tom said. "Recognize him?"

"Yeah," Nell said. "He looked familiar, but I couldn't place him."

"He was a political commentator," Tom said. "Had his own show on CNTV last year. He kind of did focus groups and talked politics with voters."

"Oh yeah," Nell said. "I remember, now. Bullock, er..."

"Bullard," Tom said. "Al Bullard. That's it. He was like a big pollster for the President's re-election."

Wendy did not recognize the man. As a graduate student, she had little time for either television or politics.

"What's he doing as a representative of GenAgra?" Nell said.

"I don't know," Tom said. "Strange, huh?"

Wendy let her stare bore into the side of Ryan's head. He was unusually silent. Almost sullen. She reached out carefully with her foot and softly nudged his leg. He glanced up at her, surprise registering on his face.

"So, Doc, what did you make of the arguments about the patent?" Tom said, evidently startling Ryan. "I was having some difficulty following the technical description."

"It didn't sound good," Ryan said. "It seems fairly clear that the plants growing in Mr. Stiles' fields are the same as those GenAgra has claimed under their patents. It's an abhorrent system we have when we allow companies to patent life forms, but so long as that's the case, I don't really see much of a leg to, uh, stand on in the patent part of the case."

"That's what I was trying to tell you, Tom," Nell said. "They're going to bury you. I don't think you can even get to trial. They're going to win the preliminary injunction, and then they're going to get a summary disposition. I know the law sucks, but that's the way it's going to play out."

"I can't believe that," Wendy said, letting her foot fall away from Ryan and joining the conversation. "What kind of legal system is it, if it's going to allow this happen?"

"I'm not giving up," Tom said. "This has to be a misuse of the patent. They can't go around contaminating all the fields in the world and then start suing people for royalties. Somebody's got to put a stop to it. It's absurd."

"The judge didn't think so," Nell said.

"Do you know him?" Tom said. "I thought I recognized him from somewhere, but I can't place him. He must have been an insurance defense attorney. I must have seen him on a case before."

"I don't know," Nell said. "But I can find out when I get back to the office."

"Speaking of getting back to the office," Ryan said, very obviously pouncing on the opportunity to leave. "I've got some work that needs me."

"All right, Doc," Tom said, shaking Ryan's hand. "Thanks so much for coming today. I'll call you when we're ready to go over your testimony for the preliminary injunction hearing, okay?"

Ryan gave an awkward good-bye to the table at large, and left Wendy cold. It had been good to see him again, but sharing only minutes from week to week would never do. Ryan needed to be an integral part of this case. He would need to consult Tom frequently. And as Tom's new secretary, who was in a better position to schedule regular consultations? Wendy smiled to herself and daydreamed of her beloved professor, as the lawyers chattered on.

Chapter Eight

Tom called the farm as soon as he got back to the office to break the bad news. From decades of experience, he had come to think that open communication was the biggest part of keeping clients happy. So far, Ike's case was an unmitigated disaster, and Tom could not think of a particularly good spin to put on the judge's ruling. Still, it was better to quickly pass the information on and get it over with.

Ike was still sick in bed, so Tom gave a watered-down recap of the motion hearing to Kaye and asked her to pass it along.

"All right. As soon as he's feeling a little better." Her voice sounded strained.

"Are you sure you wouldn't like him to see someone?" Tom said. "I could give Doctor Brown a call. See if he'd make a house call."

"No," Kaye said, sounding uncertain. "I think he'll be fine. But if he's not feeling better by tomorrow, maybe we will call Doctor Brown."

When Tom finished the phone call, Wendy knocked softly on his open office door.

"I called those patent lawyers," she said. "I think I've got one you'll like."

"Thanks," Tom said. It was strange readjusting to the constant presence of another human being. One who was so beautiful, he thought, staring at Wendy.

"I told him you would call later this afternoon with more details on the case."

"Very good," Tom said. "I think that's all I've got for you this afternoon. Other than catching phones. Good time to break out those books."

"Okay." Wendy laughed. "You're worse than Professor Romanelli. 'Are you sure you have enough time to study?'"

"No arguing." Tom smiled. "You're still on the clock. And this is study time."

The phone rang and Wendy darted back toward her desk. An instant later, the call rang through to Tom's office.

"It's Nell Yeats on line one," Wendy said.

"Thanks," Tom said, thinking she had gotten the hang of the phone system fast. He'd worked in the building twenty years and still hadn't figured out how to transfer a call. "Put her through."

"You calling to do a post mortem on this morning's motion, Nell?" Tom said. "Because, it's a little late for constructive criticism now that we've already gotten our ass kicked."

"Nope," Nell said. "But I think I know why this judge is screwing you over on the temporary restraining order."

"Why's that?"

"I just Googled him. The Honorable Michael Fuller. He just got appointed this year. Guess who he worked for before becoming a judge for life?"

"No idea," Tom said.

"Barnes & Honeycutt," Nell said. Tom instantly remembered why he found Fuller's face so familiar. "How do you like that? Before that, he was a prosecutor. For, like, thirty years."

"I remember him now," Tom said. "I met him when he was up in Milton last year defending that eco-terrorism case."

"Huh?" Nell said.

"He came up to Milton on that eco-terrorism case we had last year," Tom said. "You heard about that case, didn't you?"

"Yeah, okay," Nell said. "I guess I remember it in the news."

"He was the lawyer for one of the kids. Got him a very sweet deal, too," Tom said. "And GenAgra's lawyer. That Yale woman. She worked with him on that case. If that isn't a conflict of interest, I don't know what is. How could he not disclose that on the record."

"I don't know," Nell said.

"Well, let's file a motion to disqualify him," Tom said.

"Oh, no problem Mr. Hardworking Attorney," Nell said. "Just let me finish off this counterclaim I've been drafting, and then I'll have plenty of time to draft more stuff. Happy to help. It's not like I'm trying to run a practice up here."

"Thanks." Tom laughed. "Give me a call when you get that stuff done. A new judge. That's exactly what we need on this case."

He tried to return to his work but felt restless. From Claire's office, the occasional whisper of pages being turned echoed like footfalls. Tom didn't want to work. Not when there was little he could do on the office's only case. Not when a live human being was seated only twenty feet away. He doodled on a notepad for ten minutes, and when he could stand it no more, he went to use the restroom. Conveniently, he stopped to chat with Wendy on his way back.

It took him less than two minutes to convince her she needed a tour of the old Milton courthouse, one-block away. She transferred the phones to the message service, and they set out of the office together, into a perfect June breeze.

Ernie gathered his papers and stormed out of the monthly staff meeting. He had been looking forward to meeting his fellow regional epidemiologists from around the state. But Underwood was running the meeting, and it turned into a total disaster.

Underwood ridiculed Ernie in front of his peers, teasing him mercilessly with the story of how Ernie had tried to sound a statewide alarm to expose a few allergic reactions in his region. Ernie tried to laugh at himself, but it was a half-hearted attempt. He was furious with Underwood. How could anyone fail to recognize the man for a buffoon? Ernie took some comfort in the reactions of his colleagues. They laughed along with Underwood's story, but Ernie thought many of the smiling faces were wooden façades, hiding the same contempt for Underwood that Ernie felt himself.

Ernie had done little in the week leading up to the staff meeting besides working on his new syndrome. Since finding the signature of the illness in blood tests, he had labeled the disease High Eosinophil Respiratory Distress Syndrome, or HERDS, for short. Coming into the meeting, he had been prepared to discuss HERDS with his peers. But Underwood's hectoring had been too much, and Ernie only introduced himself when given the opportunity to speak.

Prior to the meeting, Underwood had made it clear the high eosinophil count alone did not sway him. He still wanted a definite source before he was going to put the entire state on alert. Still, Ernie had been prepared to take him on at the meeting, where other epidemiologists would at least have an opportunity to hear about the risk HERDS presented. And walking away from the meeting now, he felt like a coward for failing to stand up to his overbearing boss.

Ernie was lost in thought, looking at the floor as he made his way out of the health services building, and only his quick reflexes avoided a collision with a woman emerging from an office.

"Excuse me," a gracious, familiar voice said.

Ernie raised his eyes and blushed. He had almost trampled the director of the State Epidemiology Department. Underwood's boss. A woman who had hired Ernie only one month before.

"Oh," Ernie said, initially registering the surprise. "I'm sorry, Director Jones."

"Not a problem," she said. "How are you—don't tell me—I'll remember it. Mr. Vasquez. Right? How are you?"

"Excellent, ma'am," Ernie said. "Nice to see you again."

"I'm glad to see you're hustling on the job." The director laughed. Her face conveyed a genuine warmth.

"Yes, ma'am," Ernie said, still embarrassed.

"What? You're up here for the staff meeting?"

"Uh-huh. My first one," Ernie said.

"So how are things going for you?" she asked. "You liking the new job?"

Ernie hesitated, weighing out whether to tell her the truth. He hated to become an office politician in only his first month on the job, but his concern about the potential impact of HERDS was overbearing.

"Uh-oh," the director said. "I don't like that look. C'mon, talk to me." She walked him through a maze of cubicles to her corner office and had him take a seat. "You remember when I hired you," she said, closing her office door and sitting down behind her desk, "I told you, my door was always open."

"Yes, ma'am," Ernie said.

"So what's on your mind?"

"Uh, there's an outbreak," Ernie said, "I think. In my region, and I'm not sure if, um—"

"An outbreak?" the director asked, her black eyebrows arching. "What kind of outbreak?"

"Um, I'm not really sure," Ernie said. "I mean, this is my first major investigation, and I'm not really sure Mr. Underwood is taking it seriously."

"Oh, Herb, huh?"

"Yes, ma'am," Ernie said.

"Well, do you have a case definition?" she asked.

"Yes, ma'am," Ernie said. "I'm calling it HERDS, right now. High Eosinophil Respiratory Distress Syndrome. The eosinophil counts are over ten thousand."

"Is that right?" she said, looking interested.

"With rapid onset of an ascending paralysis and acute respiratory distress in most cases."

"Uh-huh," she said.

"There have been eight cases we've identified so far," Ernie said, encouraged by the director's interest. "And one death. Clinically, it's not very pretty."

"How long has this been out there? Is it communicable?"

"No, ma'am," Ernie said. "It's been developing for about a month now, and there are no reports of person-to-person infection. Only a trickle of cases really. With no identifiable source, yet."

"No source," the director said warily. "Any ideas?"

"I've done some research. There are a couple of diseases out there that are similar. They suggest it may be environmental or food-borne. Possibly a supplement of some kind. But I can't convince Mr. Underwood to raise the reporting level to yellow. So I've had my staff—my one-member staff," Ernie said, pleased to hear her laugh, "calling daily all over the region. That's how we've found the majority of the cases."

"Hmmm." The director sighed. "Well, you keep doing what you're doing, and I'll have a talk with Herb."

Ernie thanked the director and left the building, his mood much improved. The warmth of recognition from the director was like a drug. Driving from Lansing to his Mt. Pleasant office, he thought about how he would conquer HERDS. He imagined the conferences he'd attend, and the papers he would write. He imagined the made-for-television movie. He imagined saving the population from the exponential growth of a deadly syndrome, and from the panic and fear that would spread if someone was not alerted to the spread of HERDS in its early stages. The delusions of epidemiological grandeur made for a fast trip.

The smile he had worn since his meeting with the director melted as soon as he reached his secretary's desk.

"You've got three messages from Mr. Underwood," she said, frowning. "He said it's urgent. Sounds pissed."

"Thanks," Ernie said. The director had apparently wasted little time in dealing with Underwood. He closed his office door behind him and dialed Underwood's direct line.

"This is Herb Underwood." His voice was wooden.

"Hello, sir," Ernie said.

"Vasquez," Underwood said, his tone cross. "It's about time."

"My secretary said you called, sir," Ernie said, trying to let his polite voice moderate some of the heat coming from his boss.

"Damn right I called," Underwood said. "Do you know we have a chain of command in this department?"

"Uh, yes, sir," Ernie said.

"Well, tell me why you would go outside the chain of command on this so-called syndrome of yours, then?"

"I didn't mean to, sir," Ernie said. "I just ran into—"

"What do you mean, *you didn't mean to?* I just got done having a half-hour conversation with Director Jones, and she tells me that you did go outside the chain of command. Said you were in her office today, right after our meeting, telling her all about HERDS, is it? Telling her about allergic reactions."

"She asked, sir," Ernie said. "I didn't mean to say anything outside the chain of command, sir."

"How can you sit through an entire two-hour meeting and not mention something even one time, and then go to the director and try to lay some scare tactic on her? I'd like to know that."

"I don't know, sir," Ernie said. "You didn't seem to want to discuss it at the meeting. And, Director Jones wanted me to tell her. I mean, this is a serious—"

"I'll tell you what's serious," Underwood said. "You're in some serious trouble if this ever happens again. Now, I've got the director calmed down. Took a full thirty minutes, but she's under control. And she agrees with me. She's going to be sending out an e-mail about the proper chain of command to everyone, but you might as well know it is about you, Vasquez. So don't let it happen again."

"What about HERDS, sir?"

"HERDS," Underwood scoffed. "What about HERDS? I'll tell you what about HERDS. You find a simple explanation for a handful of allergic reactions, and then you report it through the proper chain of command. And we'll see where we go from there."

Ernie said nothing.

"Do we understand each other, Vasquez? If not, then we might have to have a little chat. You know, there are regions in this state more remote than Mt. Pleasant, right? Ever hear of Houghton County? Check it out on the map. You'll find it a lot closer to Canada than to Ohio. Okay? Are we clear?"

"Yes, sir," Ernie said, gripping a pen so hard the pocket-clip dug into his palm.

"Good," Underwood said. "I'll see you at next month's meeting, then."

Ernie hung up the phone and paced in front of his office window. He watched cars pass outside, straining to see the faces of the drivers and passengers. Mothers and children. Workers and students. Professionals and retirees. He was fairly certain they were all going to hear of HERDS in the near future. He hoped they would be spared a firsthand experience with the symptoms. But Underwood's stonewalling left him uneasy about their chances.

Tom overslept on Friday morning, but felt comfortable enough with Wendy running the office that he took his sweet time getting ready for work. He took a long shower, read the newspaper, and enjoyed a slice of toast covered with Kaye's honey. When he strolled into the office at ten, he was surprised by the look of concern on Wendy's face.

"You've got to get over to the hospital in Perkins," she said. "It's Mr. Stiles."

"What's wrong?" Tom asked.

"Mrs. Stiles called," Wendy said. "She didn't say what it was, just that you needed to get there fast."

Tom darted out of the office, hopped in the car, and abused the speed limit to make it to the hospital in ten minutes. At the reception desk, he was told that Ike was in ICU. He took a slow elevator to the second floor and found Kaye in one of the ICU waiting rooms. Her eyes were red, and she looked considerably older than when he had seen her on Monday. But she wasn't crying, until their eyes met.

"Oh, Tom," she said, falling against him.

"What is it?" Tom whispered. "How is he?"

"They don't know." She sniffed, leaning back and looking into his eyes. "They don't know what it is. But it's pretty bad."

"I should've never let him stand out in that rain," Tom said. "I don't know what I was thinking."

"This isn't a cold," Kaye said, her voice seemingly humbled by the magnitude of Ike's ailment. "It isn't pneumonia. He's paralyzed, Tom. And he can't breathe."

"Paralyzed?"

"Yes," Kaye said. "He started complaining about not being able to move his feet last night. And this morning they were all swollen. And it just crept up his legs. I called Doctor Brown. He told me to get him in here as quick as possible."

"Oh my God," Tom said. "They don't have any idea?"

"None," Kaye said. "But his legs have swollen up like balloons.

They're so big, the skin is splitting." She put her arms back around Tom's shoulders, held him, and cried in small sobs.

"Don't worry," Tom whispered. "He's a tough old bird."

"They think he may need a ventilator," Kaye said.

"He can't breathe?" Tom said.

"No," Kaye said. "He's laboring. And the paralysis is climbing up his body."

"I've never heard of anything like that," Tom said.

"Do you want to see him?" Kaye said, drying her eyes. "They said only family, but..."

"Do you think it's okay? I won't get him too excited?"

"No," Kaye said. "He's been asking for you."

Tom took Kaye's arm and they marched in slow steps to Ike's room. A nurse was using a washcloth to dab at gruesome fissures on Ike's bare thigh. Tom swallowed hard to keep his breakfast down.

As they approached, Ike turned his head toward them. His eyes were clear, and he focused on Tom. His breathing was slow and strained.

"They're bringing a ventilator over, Mrs. Stiles," the nurse said. "The doctor has ordered it. Just until we figure out what's going on and get him stabilized."

"Okay," Kaye croaked.

"Is this your son?" the nurse asked.

"Close friend," Kaye said. "But he's like our son."

"Okay." the nurse said. "I won't say anything if you don't. But you two will have to leave when we get the ventilator here, so we can get it hooked up and running."

"Okay," Kaye smiled. "Thank you."

Tom reached out for Ike's hand and held it; Ike squeezed back.

"I'm done with that smoking, boy." Ike wheezed and coughed lightly.

"Don't talk," Tom said. "Just take it easy." He looked at the old farmer lying in the hospital bed and had difficulty seeing the vibrant man that stalked the fields of the farm. He looked frail and nearly defeated.

A grimace came over Ike's face, and he let out a groan. "Oh, shit," he croaked.

"Cramps again?" the nurse asked.

Ike nodded.

"I'll see if I can get the doctor to up your pain medication," the nurse said.

The cramps seemed to subside after a moment, and Ike's face relaxed. But still, each breath that the old farmer drew was a battle. "Kaye said we lost," Ike whispered on the exhale. "The other day."

"Don't talk," Tom said. "We didn't lose. That was only the opening round. It's a long fight."

"Damn them—" Ike said, his words breaking into a cough.

"Someone order a ventilator in here?" an orderly said, wheeling in the high-tech gadget that would assist Ike in breathing.

"Right here," the nurse said, guiding the ventilator toward Ike's bedside.

Tom and Kaye squeezed and patted Ike, then left the room. Tom couldn't stand the thought of Ike being sick, or worse, being kept alive on a machine. In all the medical cases he'd read for his work, Tom had never come across a creeping paralysis or seen anything like the fissures on Ike's legs. He was certain that the battle over the transgenic blackberry had grown instantly irrelevant.

Bullard stretched his arms out, resting his palms on the marble tile surrounding the whirlpool. He looked down at his body. Camouflaged by the churning current, it wasn't so bad. Certainly, like most Americans, he could stand to lose a few pounds. He was a man of great appetite and little discipline. So it was natural that he would put on a little weight as he left his most active years behind him. But his shape was still salvageable.

He couldn't bring himself to use any of the exercise equipment in the Bullard Group's private gymnasium, a sprawling athletic facility that occupied a good portion of the eighth floor. But now, he would ease himself into a routine. If he could only trim a few pounds, he might be a passable companion for the lithe young lawyer working on the GenAgra case.

Bullard had judged her right on the telephone and was glad he had made the trip to see her in action. She was extraordinarily bright, ruthless in the courtroom, and had an icy beauty worthy of royalty. And given her appreciation for his wealth and power, Bullard figured that watching his weight was only marginally necessary. He had flown her back to Detroit following her court victory. She was intrigued by his political connections and seemed enchanted with the attendant luxury of the private jet. He complimented her skills and enjoyed her detailed explanation of how patent law would be used to eviscerate the farmer. Though it seemed like the most unnecessary use of his time, Bullard knew he would be paying very close attention to the litigation surrounding the Health-Ease Blackberry.

The door from the locker room opened, and Bullard's assistant came in with a rush of cooler air.

"I have the report you requested, sir."

Bullard dragged his large frame upright and climbed out of the whirlpool. He dried himself with a customized towel and took the report.

"Could you get Doctor Malec on the phone," Bullard said. "And bring me my headset. I'll be in the sauna."

Bullard ambled across the smooth marble and into the dry heat of the enclosed wooden room. The acrid air stung his nostrils as he set a towel on the wooden bench and reclined to read the document. It summarized a survey of the target market for the Health-Ease Blackberry. He scanned through the report, sucking up the highlights like a sponge. Fat people were going to love this product. Price and taste would be only marginal drawbacks, so long as the berries were minimally palatable and the pounds fell away. He was somewhat surprised by the negative numbers associated with the genetic enhancement of the product. But these negatives did not put much of a dent in the non-college educated, 18-54 market, and therefore were only a minor worry. Most Americans would herd to the trough to get at the Health-Ease Blackberry. And the product would shoot to iconic status, with Al Bullard shepherding it on its meteoric rise.

The door to the sauna opened.

"Here you are, sir," Bullard's assistant said, leaning in to hand Bullard a petite headset and microphone. "Doctor Malec is holding for you."

Bullard slid the headset on and was troubled for a moment by how he must have looked. He pictured himself as a fat and old and naked drive-thru attendant at a fast-food restaurant. But the image was fleeting and instantly caught in the undertow of his vast ego.

"Doctor Malec," Bullard said. "I got word from APHIS this morning. The Health-Ease Blackberry has cruised to approval."

"That...that's amazing," Doctor Malec said, his voice small over the phone.

Bullard thought he heard grudging respect from his chief scientist. "Nice job getting that report over there so quickly," he said.

"There was some data we needed to leave out," Doctor Malec said.

"I told you," Bullard said. "It didn't really matter."

"But it was significant, Mr. Bullard," Doctor Malec said. "One of my assistants was still putting together data from a health-effects study. We pulled it from the report, because it wasn't ready. But—"

"But, nothing," Bullard said. "Good job. That's the way we get things done in Washington, Doctor. You have to strike while the iron's hot."

"But the study," Doctor Malec said. "Fourteen of the rats died."

"Fourteen out of how many?" Bullard said, curious.

"Out of sixty," Doctor Malec said. "It's a troubling statistic. And there's really no apparent explanation."

"Those rat studies don't really mean that much," Bullard said. He remembered taking plenty of science courses designed for non-majors as an undergrad at Ohio State. And in the back of his mind, he was certain he'd learned that rat studies didn't really equate all that well to human studies. "I read the APHIS approval this morning. It said that nutritionally your berry is the same as any blackberry sold in the U.S. today. So I wouldn't worry, Doctor."

"But they didn't have this data," Doctor Malec said.

"They didn't need that data," Bullard said. "The secretary of agriculture told me that himself. They're not going to require a bunch of unnecessary testing that drives up the cost of food and keeps good healthy products off the market, when the enhanced foods have equivalent nutritional value to regular food."

"But—"

"But nothing," Bullard said. "Case closed. You turn your attention to getting this berry ready for mass production. Because next year at this time, the Health-Ease Blackberry is going to be in stores everywhere."

"Okay, sir," Doctor Malec said. "But I'm going to document this."

"You need to lighten up a little, Malec." Bullard laughed. "You'll live longer." He hung up the phone and stepped from the sauna. Though his morning routine was largely sedentary, his body was still drained from the heat. He showered, dressed, and headed upstairs to get back to work.

"You know what I want for lunch," Bullard said, as he passed his secretary. "Get me some of those sample Health-Ease Berries they sent from the research farm. I think I'm gonna give those things a try."

Tom stayed with Kaye in the ICU waiting room while Ike was hooked to the ventilator.

He kept assuring Kaye that Ike would be fine. She would nod, but her eyes were pained. Tom had always been a talker. Even as a boy. Kaye always told him he had the gift of gab. He had used that gift well in the legal world. He had made a living on little more than smooth talk. But here with Kaye, his words seemed empty, as the old farmer struggled to breathe only a few rooms away. The reality of the moment called for no words. Only silence and waiting.

Through the glass separating the waiting room from the hallway, they saw Doctor Brown walking toward them from Ike's room. They rose together to greet him.

"Hello Kaye. Tom," Doctor Brown said, his voice a strange dichotomy of professional detachment and personal kindness. "I think we have him stabilized."

"Thank the Lord," Kaye said in one expelled breath.

"He's resting now," Doctor Brown said.

"Good," Tom said. "He looked so exhausted, struggling to breathe like that."

"I'm glad you called me when you did, Kaye," Doctor Brown said. "I've seen a couple of cases like this in the past few weeks, so I had some idea of how treat it. I called ahead to the hospital to let them know."

"What is it?" Tom said.

"I'm not sure," Doctor Brown said. "It's like nothing I've seen before. Very fast acting. Very virulent. But not contagious, thank God."

"You've seen it before, though?" Kaye said.

"Just in the past couple of weeks," Doctor Brown said. "I thought it was anaphylactic shock at first. You know, like from a bee sting. But then with the paralysis. I don't know what it is. The early patients have responded a little to prednisone, though. A steroid. So I called to make sure they got Ike on that right away."

"So he's going to be all right then?" Kaye said.

"I honestly can't say, Kaye," Doctor Brown said. "I had to medevac the first patient to Ann Arbor. He's still on a ventilator. And not improving much. A young kid, too. Working on a road crew on that construction up on Main Street, and just started swelling up."

"And then there's Millie Dzurka. You know Millie, Kaye."

"Yes," Kaye said. "She comes to the farm every month. Is she okay?"

"She has responded to the prednisone very well," Doctor Brown said. "But she's still here at the hospital. Very slow improvement in her case."

"I didn't even know she was sick," Kaye said, her voice aghast.

"So we're only treating the symptoms for now," Doctor Brown said. "Until we get a handle on what it is. I've reported it to the local public health officials, and I'm still waiting on some information back."

"So we just wait?" Tom said, throwing up his hands.

"Well, I've given him something for the pain and something to help him rest," Doctor Brown said. "And I ordered the ventilator for now to ease the burden on his cardio-vascular system. We don't want him to have a heart attack or stroke as a result of the respiratory distress.

"If he responds well, and we can get him breathing normally without the ventilator, we will keep him here and treat the symptoms. Hopefully get him well enough to send home with you.

"But if I can't get him breathing on his own without the respiratory distress in the next couple of days, then we're going to have to send him to a larger hospital. They only have two ventilators here, and they're for emergencies. For long-term care he would have to go somewhere else. I'd recommend the University of Michigan. Best care in the state."

Tom trusted Doctor Brown. He had treated Tom from childhood on. From his office in Milton, Doctor Brown gave cradle-to-grave care to most people in Wabeno County, Tom guessed. He was trusted as few physicians were in the twenty-first century, on medical conditions from bunions to brain tumors. If there was no known cause Doctor Brown could share, that was because there was no known cause.

"We'd sure like it if you can keep him close to us, Doctor Brown," Tom said. "But let's get him the best care we can."

Kaye nodded and wiped her eyes. Doctor Brown gave her a hug and patted Tom on the shoulder, before setting about on his hospital rounds.

Tom took Kaye to the cafeteria. Neither of them were hungry, so they drank stale coffee. They talked about Doctor Brown's advice, and neither had any cause to disagree. They smiled bravely at each other and shared positive idioms like, "he's going to be fine" and "he's too stubborn to die." Tom knew he was lying when he said these things, and he suspected Kaye knew the same. But it was their role as caregivers, and they played it dutifully.

Ike was resting peacefully when they looked in on him later. The machine drove oxygen in and out of his body, his lungs rising at mechanical intervals. The artificiality of the scene would have disgusted Ike, Tom knew. The old man hated all things modern, even if they were sparing his life. But he did look better than when Tom had first seen him in the morning and that was something.

Tom walked Kaye to the ICU waiting room. "You should really go and get some rest," he said. "I can stay for a while, in case he needs anything."

"No." Kaye smiled wanly. "You're not the one who took a vow to that old geezer. They've got blankets right here. I might take a nap, when I'm ready."

Tom waited with her in silence for a short time until the idleness overcame him. "I think I'm going to run back to my office, then. Just to check in. I've got a new girl running the place."

"Okay, Tommy." Kaye smiled and yawned. "I'll call you if I hear anything."

Tom left the hospital and drove out of his way to pass the Stiles' farm. The afternoon sky had turned overcast. The lifelessness of the empty farm was unnatural. There were no cars in the lot. No customers at the fruit stand. No student workers. No families picking berries. Worst of all, there was no Kaye on the porch or Ike in the fields. Ike would never have allowed an illness short of death to close his farm. GenAgra and their fancy law firm and their biased federal judge would have to be stopped. Or Ike would never really be well again.

The images of Ike sick in the ICU, and the empty farm, clouded rational thought from Tom's mind as he drove back to the office. He was a combustible mixture of rage and helplessness. All the good fortune that had followed him for decades faded away like chalk drawings in a rainstorm.

As he arrived back at the office and walked to the front door, he forced the fury from his face. No sense frightening the help.

"How's it going?" he said with all the cheer he could muster.

"Great," Wendy said, raising her brown eyes from the book she was reading. "How's Mr. Stiles?"

"Not so good," Tom said. "He's on a ventilator. But they think he's stabilized."

"That doesn't sound good," she said as she stretched her arms. "What happened to him?"

"They don't know," Tom said, walking through the lobby to lean across the counter into her cubicle. "Some kind of strange disease. Pretty awful. He's kind of paralyzed. And all swollen. Can't breathe."

"You saw him?"

"Yeah," Tom said. "It's pretty bad."

"Did they give you protective clothing?" Wendy said, her thin brow line furrowed.

"No."

"A mask?" she said, leaning back slightly.

"It's not contagious," Tom said, laughing cautiously.

"How do you know," she said, "if they don't know what's causing it?"

Tom hadn't thought to ask Doctor Brown for his reasoning, and Wendy's apparent fear made him wish he had. This was not a disease he would wish on anyone. "I don't know," he said. "I guess a couple other people have had this, but it hasn't spread to anyone."

"Well, if a couple other people had it," Wendy said, as if speaking to a child, "and now Mr. Stiles has it, wouldn't that mean that is *has* spread?"

He couldn't argue with her logic. She was a bright girl. "Doctor Brown said it wasn't contagious. He's been my doctor for about forty years."

"So he's an internist or what?"

"He's a general practitioner." Tom smiled. "But I trust him."

Wendy rolled her chair back away from the counter, getting distance from Tom. "Don't mind me. I'd just like a little more info when it comes to a mystery illness that is paralyzing people," she said, returning his smile. "Maybe you should wash your hands or something, at least. Don't you think?"

"Okay. If it will make you happy," Tom said. He walked back to the washroom and quickly washed his hands.

Wendy was standing in his office doorway when he returned, holding messages in her hand. "Nell called," she said. "She faxed over your motion and your counterclaim. They're on your desk. She wants you to call her back."

"Thanks."

"And a reporter from WHIP called. Wants to talk to you about your case."

"Oh shit," Tom said.

"Sam Oster," Wendy said. "I gave him a quote. 'We expect that GenAgra will crumble any day now and file for bankruptcy protection in the face of our legal onslaught...' Hope you don't mind."

They laughed together.

"Seriously, he said he would like you to call him back ASAP," Wendy said.

"Okay."

"That's all I've got for you. Five minutes of work for you. And five hours on my thesis. Plus I had time for that Dutch apple pie at the diner. Not a bad legal assistant, huh?"

"No," he said. "Just great, I'd say."

"I've got studying to do, unless you need me," she said.

"By all means," he said, waving her away. "Go get the important work done."

Tom plopped down in his chair and shuffled through the papers from Nell. He had spent much energy in his futile efforts to comfort Kaye, and it was catching up to him. He yelled for Wendy to bring him coffee, and when she squawked about office oppression, he begged her forgiveness for being such a chauvinist. But she brought him the coffee in the middle of his apology.

Nell's work looked flawless. Their counterclaim laid out four counts, all resting on Ike's allegation of genetic pollution. It may not have been supported by current law, but it was compelling reading. Nell would forward the original, and it would be filed early next week.

The motion to disqualify was written in a dispassionate tone, but its factual allegations seemed damning enough to require the judge to step down. She had scheduled it with the court on the same day as the preliminary injunction hearing. If the judge stepped down, as he should, the case would have to be reassigned, and the preliminary hearing delayed. That would give them a chance to challenge the judge's temporary order before a less biased judge. The only work that remained was to prepare his case for the preliminary hearing on the off chance that the judge did not recuse himself.

He called Nell, caught her in the office and complimented her work. He wished she would consider coming back and practicing law in Milton, but Nell had sprouted roots in a new community. At most, she could only be a designated hitter on Tom's team. She would forward a bill and had cleared her own schedule so she could be in court with him at the hearing. All was good.

The caffeine started to work its way through Tom's capillaries, widening his eyes, at least enough so he could deal with the local media. He dialed Sam Oster.

"You've been holding out on me, Tommy," Oster said, after small talk. "You've got a case going in federal court. David versus Goliath. And I've gotta hear about it from some local who's upset he can't get his fresh strawberries."

Oster worked for Milton's only radio station, WHIP. He was a jack-of-all trades. He sold advertising, worked as on-air talent, and ran the station's independent news coverage. Oster was a bit smarmy to be a serious newsman, but his reporting really wasn't half bad. He had used Oster to plant stories in the local news as was warranted over his nineteen years in Milton, and Oster had come to expect tips from Tom as *quid pro quo*.

"I wasn't holding out on you," Tom said. "I've been buried by these bastards at GenAgra. Do you know the kind of pressure they can put on a small town lawyer, with all their high-priced legal talent? I haven't had a minute to even think about press coverage."

"Yeah, yeah," Oster said. "Cry me a river you rich SOB. You oughta try living on what they pay a radio man in this town. Don't complain about your workload to me."

"I know," Tom said. "I know. So what is it you wanted to know?"

"I'm going with a news item for the afternoon drive about the Stiles' Farm," Oster said. "I want the legal angle on it. Anything you can give me."

Tom gave him a straight case history. He didn't even have to color the facts to make Ike a compelling David. This story was biblical by nature, save for its lack of justice.

"That is ridiculous," Oster said, when Tom had finished. "You're not feeding me, like, the lawyerized version are you?"

"No," Tom said. "You could take those same facts from GenAgra's federal complaint. I mean, they use different language to couch it, but those are the facts, man."

"So when are you back in court?"

"A week from next Tuesday," Tom said. "Uh, the fifth, I think. Right after the holiday. On our motion to disqualify the judge and the hearing on the preliminary injunction."

"I may have to get over there for a remote," Oster said.

"Yeah," Tom said. "It's a good story. I'm glad you're gonna get the word out." He was thankful to have a local reporter to cover the travesty. But how much would it help if Ike couldn't make it to court, he wondered. Or if the old man wasn't around at all.

Chapter Nine

Ernie tore out of his office and made a beeline for Jill's cubicle. She was hunched over her keyboard, typing data into a spreadsheet with her index fingers.

"Come on, let's go," Ernie said, excitedly.

"Go where?" Jill said, pulling herself from the spreadsheet.

"Perkins Regional Medical Center," he said. "I just got off the phone with our good Doctor Brown up there. Case Number Nine checked in this morning."

"Perkins?" Jill said, rotating to face Ernie and visibly counting the fingers on one hand. "There's no way we can get there and get back by five."

"I'll approve the overtime," Ernie said.

"But I've got Jacqueline's dance thingy tonight," Jill said. "I can't miss it. Please, Ernie. She'd kill me."

Ernie looked at the small shrine of photos that adorned Jill's workspace, where her daughter looked expectantly at him from each photograph. He recognized that he would never rise very far in the state bureaucracy if it meant ruling with an iron fist.

"Oh, no," he said. "Of course you can't. No problem. But

do you think you could get me an interview packet together real quick, and I'll—"

"Thanks, Ernie." Jill smiled. "I'll have a packet ready to go in five minutes."

Ernie was on the road five minutes later, as promised. Once on the highway he goosed his speed up to eighty-five and set the cruise, hoping the government seal on the side panel would ward off the state troopers. Doctor Brown had given him the basic details over the phone. Elderly white male. Checked into the Perkins' hospital with the classic symptoms. Edema, pain, ascending paralysis, and respiratory distress. He was placed on a ventilator as a precautionary measure. His wife would be available for an interview at the hospital.

Speeding north, the landscape changed around him. The flat green fields of mid-Michigan, dotted by small outposts of deciduous trees, gave way to ever increasing swaths of second-growth pines. The emerald farm fields became the encroaching fauna, like oases nestled on gently sloping hills, irregularly shaped by the forests and the contours of the land. As he neared his destination, Ernie's attention was drawn to advertisements painted on roadside barns. A local berry farm begged travelers to spare a few moments from their northbound flight. The signs tugged at some wholesome instinct in Ernie, pulling him toward a pastoral space in his subconscious. There, a more fulfilling road awaited him. And if he was not in such a hurry to save the populous from a menacing disease, he was sure he would have stopped at the berry farm.

He found the small hospital with no difficulty, a mile off the highway, nestled in the rural town of Perkins. It was semi-modern, with a brown brick façade. The exterior promised far better care than it could deliver, given the facility's lack of proximity to a large population center. He parked and made his way inside, finding Patient Number Nine's next-of-kin in a second-floor waiting room.

"Mrs. Stiles?" Ernie said, introducing himself. She was a sweet-looking woman. Her gray hair was matted from hours spent sleeping on a couch, and her eyes were tired, but she still managed a genuine smile.

"Doctor Brown mentioned you'd be coming," she said. "He said you might be able to help figure out what's going on with my husband."

"I hope so, ma'am," Ernie said. "Right now, I'm gathering information. Hopefully, we can get to the bottom of this."

"I'm sure you can, dear," she said, taking his arm with her soft hand.

"I saw the Stiles' Berry Farm signs on my way in," Ernie said. "That wouldn't be your place, would it?"

"Yes, it is," she said, a smile of simple delight coming over her. "My husband and I have been running that farm for almost fifty years now."

Ernie was charmed but not distracted from his need to get quick answers. If there was anything Patient Number Nine could tell them about the cause of the disease, he needed to know fast. If he could get the answer to Underwood before five, his boss might let him issue a statewide alert before the weekend. Once he had Mrs. Stiles comfortably seated, he went through Jill's questionnaire packet. It was cold and technical, and it took Ernie some time to find a more human tone in relaying the questions. But he eventually fell into an easy rhythm.

Patient Nine, Mr. Ike A. Stiles, had no contact with any of the other patients. His illness was similar to the others, except that its onset seemed somewhat slower. He had developed a rash and swelling of his foot early in the week that had been mistaken for gout. He was bedridden the next day, his wife thinking he had a severe cold. His symptoms worsened this morning, and he was brought to the hospital immediately on Doctor Brown's advice. Mr. Stiles' diet was very healthy, with the family eating almost exclusively homegrown, organic foods from their farm. He took no health supplements except for juices and natural food products. He had lost some weight while sick, but his wife had noticed nothing before the illness. He smoked too much, drank too much, and cursed too much, but was a loving husband. Other than living in the same general area as half the other patients, there was no obvious connection.

Ernie thanked Mrs. Stiles for her information and promised her that he would not rest until they found out what was causing her husband's illness. He meant what he said, but felt a twinge of guilt, because his search so far had been futile.

He found Doctor Brown at the nurses' station on his way out, and introduced himself face-to-face for the first time.

"Nice to meet you," the elderly doctor said with a warm handshake. "So are you boys pinning this thing down, yet?"

"We've got no idea, Doctor," Ernie said plainly. "I just spoke with Mrs. Stiles, and I'm baffled. He's got no connection to the other cases we've seen."

"You know, I've been a doctor a long time," Doctor Brown said. "I was a doctor before you could get all these fancy test results back like a one-hour photo shop."

"Yes, sir." Ernie laughed politely, puzzled by Doctor Brown's comment.

"I'm kind of old-fashioned," Doctor Brown said. "I can usually tell more by looking at a man's tongue and listening to him breathe than by looking at any test."

Ernie nodded, pacifying the old doctor.

"But if I were you, I'd take a look at Ike's blood work," Doctor Brown said. "He's got an eosinophil count of over twelve thousand."

"Yes, sir," Ernie said. "All the patients have had that. We're calling it High Eosinophil Respiratory Distress Syndrome. HERDS."

"I don't care what you call it," Doctor Brown said with a smile. "But something's poisoning these people. I've never seen anything like it."

"I know, sir," Ernie said.

"So is it localized to our area?" Doctor Brown said.

"A little more than half the patients resided in Wabeno County," Ernie said. "But the other cases are spread out over a wider area. I can't narrow it down to any specific site."

"I haven't seen any notices from your department," Doctor Brown said. "If I had only treated one of these folks, it might've slipped by me."

"I know," Ernie said. "I've been trying to get my higher-ups to put out a bulletin, but they tell me the number of cases don't justify that yet. Without a cause or a source, they say this isn't distinguishable from an allergic reaction."

"What jackass said that?" Doctor Brown smirked. "Whoever it was, they've never been in an emergency room, I can tell you that. Nothing like spending a little time on the front lines to make you less cavalier."

"I can't say I disagree with you, Doctor Brown," Ernie said. "Well, I've got to get back to the office. Thanks for letting me know about this."

"No problem, son," Doctor Brown said. "You let me know when you figure something out."

"Sure thing," Ernie said. He trudged to his car with his head down, squinting his eyes against the late afternoon sun. Another fruitless trip to the field. He jumped in his car and headed for the highway. His mind sifted the data he had obtained from all the HERDS patients, turning the case histories over like coals in a fireplace, hoping for a solution to jump out of the flames. But there was no answer. He would have to wait for another patient. Another weekend. Ernie flipped on the radio and hit the scan button until he found a clear FM signal.

Finding a station that promised to play the best hits of the '70s, '80s, and '90s, Ernie was sold. He would veg-out for the trip back and maybe take the weekend off. He had heard time off sometimes assisted with insight on difficult problems. Ernie drummed out the beat to several songs and emptied his mind.

"Food fight in Perkins," the DJ said, interrupting Ernie's train of thought. "A local farmer goes to court to stop genetic pollution. I'll have your WHIP news break, at the top of the hour."

He was in the mood for music, not talk, and was about to change the channel. But the music came right back. Thomas Dolby was blinded with science for three minutes, with a backdrop of techno beats. The song was slightly before Ernie's time, but the singer's voice was funny enough to deserve percussion backup from a prematurely burned-out regional epidemiologist. As Ernie tapped out the last beat of the '80s hit, the song faded out back to the DJ's newscast.

"Food fight in Perkins. I'm Sam Oster, and this is your WHIP news break at the top of the hour," the DJ said. "The most famous tourist attraction in Perkins has been closed to the public since

Monday, after a federal judge issued a temporary restraining order requiring the Stiles' Family Berry Farm to cease operation.

"The order comes in a federal suit brought by GenAgra, a multi-national agri-chemical corporation, accusing the Stiles' Family Berry Farm of patent infringement. GenAgra claims the Stiles' Farm has grown genetically modified plants without GenAgra's permission.

"The Stiles' Farm has been growing only organic crops on its farm since 1999, according to Stiles' attorney Tom Hughes. Hughes contends that any genetically modified organisms on the Stiles' Farm are the result of genetic pollution from the nearby North Central Research Facility operated by GenAgra. He says Stiles will counter-sue the corporate giant. Hughes will be in court on July fifth, seeking to have the current restraining order lifted.

"In other news—"

Ernie turned the radio off. His mind raced to make connections, and he needed silence. He sat straight in the car seat, his head nearly touching the ceiling. The recognition that came over Ernie was nearly instantaneous. The radio announcer had mentioned the North Central Research Facility. The two Michigan A&T students with HERDS had worked at the facility. And the facility was apparently close enough to the Stiles' farm to cause genetic pollution. And now Stiles had HERDS. It was only three cases, but it was the closest thing to a geographic cluster that he had seen in the case.

Ernie called Underwood from his cell phone before realizing that it was just after five o'clock on a Friday. He let it ring, hoping that Underwood may have stayed a few minutes beyond closing time. When the voice mail picked up, Ernie hung up without leaving a message.

His normal reserve gave way to a slight smile. At least he had a lead. Perhaps the clue he needed to understand the illness was somewhere near the Stiles' Family Berry Farm.

"Al, glad I caught you at the office," Nick Nunley's cheery voice leapt across fiber optic lines from Chicago to D.C.

"Me, too," Bullard snapped. He didn't like Nunley's familiar tone. The lawyer was filled with a self-importance, like a balloon waiting to be popped.

"I was able to get through to our people at the university," Nunley said. "Your problem with Romanelli should be solved."

"Should be?" Bullard said.

"Well," Nunley said with a sniff, "GenAgra has considerable influence with Michigan A&T, but these things are not as simple as you might suppose."

"What's so difficult?" Bullard said. "Your company contributed twenty-five million dollars to their institution in the last year. It sounds to me like you need to learn how to peddle your influence a little more effectively. If you buy someone for twenty-five million in Washington, they stay bought." Bullard chuckled at his own cleverness.

"Pressure will be brought to bear on Romanelli," Nunley said. "I assure you. But they are a little more subtle in academia than they are in Washington, Al."

"You ever see *The Godfather*, Nunley?"

"Huh?"

"The movie," Bullard said. "*The Godfather*."

"Yeah."

"I don't know if I like a subtle approach on this," Bullard said. "I think GenAgra needs a war consigliere. If you see my point."

"I'm sure Romanelli will be dealt with," Nunley said.

"For your sake," Bullard said, "I hope you're right." He hung up the phone. The idea had struck him in the early afternoon. Bullard wanted to get Hannah Yale a gift she might appreciate. Something to make her clear blue eyes blaze like a sapphire sun. As ruthless as she was in court, he thought she might appreciate having the opposing expert's head served up on a platter. And in any event, even if she despised the gift, it would help out GenAgra's case. A self-serving present, Bullard thought—something he excelled at.

Nunley's subtlety had slowed the delivery of the gift. He had hoped he might give it to her this evening, as a prelude to an invitation for a weekend in the Bahamas. But now his plans were lost. Hannah Yale would have to wait.

He rose, grabbed his suit coat from a closet, and stalked out of his office.

"Good night, sir," his secretary said as he passed.

"Have my car ready," Bullard grunted.

He walked through rows of cubicles and junior offices, accepting with indifference farewells from his large staff. There was no standing order at The Bullard Group requiring any employee to stay past 5:00 p.m., yet Bullard rarely saw an employee depart before he did. And this unsolicited show of respect pleased him to no end.

He came to a corner of the office occupied by a harem of interns. Several of the group had converged around a copier as if it were a watering hole on the Serengeti plain. Three young women and an effeminate-looking young man snapped to attention from their respective resting places.

Bullard culled a prospect from their ranks. She was blonde and slightly thick. A weight problem she would surely battle soon after she matured. But she would suffice as a short-term substitute until he was able to win over Hannah Yale. He searched his mind for her name, tucked away in a file with a million others.

"Charlotte?" Bullard said, approaching her directly.

"Charlene, sir," the intern said.

"I've had a chance to look at the work you did on the tobacco marketing problem," Bullard said, pleased with his recall.

"My project is on attitudes toward child labor in the sneaker industry, sir," the intern said, blushing from his attention.

"Yes, yes, the shoe marketing problem," Bullard said. "That's right. I'd like to discuss it with you further, if you have the time. How about over dinner? Citronelle?"

The intern blushed deeper and darted her eyes to the other members of the herd for support. But they were as silent as a still night. "Sure," she gushed. "That'd be great, sir."

"I've got a car downstairs," Bullard said. He was still full from lunch, but he smiled at the intern and the thought of the appetites she might sate.

Tom suspected his method of preparing for witnesses was not the norm. He had been trained in law school that the key to eliciting valuable testimony was preparation. But through trial and error in his first years of practice, Tom learned no matter how hard he prepared for a given witness, he lacked the skills necessary to both carefully review his notes and talk intelligently at the same time. His method evolved into reading all the background materials about the case three times over, and jotting down the barest outline of prospective testimony. He then relied only on his ability to talk and his natural curiosity to discover the truth.

As he finished his first comprehensive read on Ike's file, he made a list of witnesses he expected to testify from both sides and jotted a word or two under each name. He would repeat the process two more times over the next week and a half, and he would be ready for Ike's preliminary injunction hearing. What his method may have lacked in conventionality, it made up for in ease of use. He checked his watch, surprised to see that it was half-past five.

He hadn't heard a word from Wendy and had to listen carefully to determine if she was still at her desk or had snuck out to enjoy her weekend. Waiting with his head cocked slightly, he could hear the soft shuffle of her fingers turning a page. Dedicated scholar.

Tom went to the library and slid a book off the shelf, then walked quietly into her office, copying pages at random on the Xerox just so he could watch his young employee for a moment. Her concentration on her task was admirable. Either that, or she politely ignored his gaze. Tom was not sure which.

"Would you like me to copy that for you?" she said, without lifting her eyes from her reading.

"No. It's a case I wanted to take home," Tom said. He continued his copying. "You know, quitting time is at five."

"I know," Wendy said, putting her book down and turning toward Tom. "Don't worry, I'm not looking for overtime. I was going to study here for a while. It's so quiet. Better than a library."

"No problem," Tom said. "I'm taking off pretty soon. I just thought…" Tom trailed off, afraid he was about to say something stupid.

"Thought what?" she said.

"Uh, I don't know," Tom said. "I wondered why such a pretty girl would be staying late at work on a Friday night." He was relieved when she laughed. He hadn't wanted to offend, but the question had slipped partially out before his better judgment could save him.

"I might wonder the same thing about you." She giggled. "What do you do on Friday nights?"

Tom thought of Ike, and felt guilty he wasn't already on his way to the hospital. "I've been fishing since the weather has turned nice," he said. "Up on Watson Lake. I've got a little boat."

"Cool," she said. "That sounds fun."

"But I'm going to head over and see Ike tonight," Tom said.

"Perkins, huh?" Wendy said. "I've seen that exit. All those Stiles' Berry Farm signs. But I've never stopped."

"You should sometime," Tom said. "I grew up right next door to the farm. Great place."

"I'd like to," Wendy said.

Tom felt certain she wanted an invitation out of the office, away from the drudgery of her academic life, but his feelings were a knot of confusion. He felt a tinge of guilt even having an attractive, young woman sitting in Claire's chair. The thought of asking her out, no matter how platonic his intentions, made him uneasy. And yet, Tom couldn't imagine any man who could look at Wendy and not feel desire. She was beautiful, and better, her manner was agreeable. She was like a wine complementing an excellent meal.

"You should come with me to see Ike," Tom said, letting his thoughts fade into action. "Give you a chance to see what we're fighting for. Get you away from your books for a while."

"I'd love to," she said. Her easy acceptance made Tom flush. "Mrs. Stiles sounds so sweet on the phone. It'd be nice to meet them."

"Good," Tom said, trying to sound more decisive than he felt. "Let's get out of this dump."

They straightened up the office and headed out. Tom turned off the lights and locked the door. He felt archaic when he stopped to open the passenger door for Wendy, but she didn't seem to mind. He walked to the driver's seat and wondered what he was doing. She was little more than half his age. His wife was gone only three months ago. And he had asked a mere girl, an employee no less, out for a Friday night. Tom wasn't sure what to call their excursion. Was it a date? Or was it a working field trip for her to meet clients? And he was sure he hadn't made it at all clear to Wendy what it was, either. Tom took a deep breath to calm his thoughts and climbed into the Cadillac.

"Nice car," Wendy said. "What's it get, like, three miles to the gallon?"

He laughed more hysterically than was warranted. And then he felt at ease. Wendy was comforting and alive. He would take that for what it was worth and not make more out of it than it was. "You feel like getting something to eat?" he asked, backing the car out onto Ohio Street.

"No, not right now," she said. "I'm so full. That pie at lunch was too much."

"All right," Tom said, and they were off the meet the Stiles.

Ryan Romanelli sat at a table alone, on the outside patio of the Cask & Keg, directly across the road from his office at Dryden Hall. He sipped an imported beer from the bottle and hoped he did not look as depressed as he felt.

It was officially two weeks since Wendy had left his office, and Ryan felt like a total disaster. He could not remember feeling so lovesick since his sophomore year in high school. Seeing her at the courthouse yesterday, with her lawyer friend, did nothing to ease his angst. He could not believe how much he missed her. The word "love" kept ruminating in his mind. A word for a concept he did not fully believe in, but one that was asserting itself as a real phenomenon.

He had always associated the term with petty jealousy and guilt. Emotions he thought were not prominent in his make up. But since he had forced her out, he had become aware of these lurking feelings. He was jealous of how Wendy seemed to be getting on with Tom Hughes. And he was struck with an odd attack of guilt when Hughes' rather unattractive lawyer friend had awkwardly engaged Ryan in a game of footsie under the breakfast table after court on Thursday. Ryan was horrified by the contact, feeling no attraction at all to the female attorney. And Wendy had glared at him in the same instant, seeming to see him involved in a pseudo-romantic game and causing him no small amount of guilt at being caught. If he didn't love Wendy, what was the explanation for his own illogical spate of unfamiliar emotions?

He glanced at his Seiko. Peter McPhee, the Dean of the College of Natural Science, who oversaw Ryan's department, was ten minutes late. And as miserable as Ryan felt, the waiting—alone at a table, surrounded by smiling students—was making it worse.

McPhee had called Ryan in the afternoon and asked him out for a drink after work. As socially inept as Ryan was, even he knew enough not to refuse an informal meeting with the dean. Ryan, an associate professor, had yet to make tenure. And while his stellar work put him easily on course, some basic etiquette in accommodating administrators was still required.

As Ryan ordered a second beer, he saw McPhee strolling through the cross-walk toward the patio bar. Ryan waved at the dean, and McPhee responded with a nod.

"I'm sorry," McPhee said, arriving at the table. "I got caught at the office. I honestly hate paperwork. I'd give anything to be teaching and researching again."

"No problem," Ryan said. "I hope you don't mind. I've started without you."

"No, not at all," McPhee said.

A Bohemian-looking waiter brought Ryan his second beer and collected an empty bottle.

"I'll take one of those," McPhee said to the waiter, before turning his attention toward Ryan. "So tell me, young man, how are things in the world of plant biology?"

"Can't complain," Ryan said. "I don't have any classes this summer, so I'm catching up on my writing. And trying to train a new grad assistant."

"Oh. Your young protégé has moved on? What was her name?"

"Wendy Isaacson," Ryan said. "Yeah, I pushed her out actually. Trying to get her concentrated on her thesis."

"Bright young woman," McPhee said. "Though I wonder about her research. She's the one trying to show insect resistance in the GM crops, right?"

"Yes, that's my Wendy," Ryan said, taking a gulp of his beer.

The waiter darted by, dropping off a bottle for McPhee, and then buzzing away to serve beer-guzzling students.

"She takes after her mentor," McPhee said, sipping at his beer.

Ryan nodded, his posture drooping involuntarily as the talk of Wendy made him more lonely.

"Well," McPhee said. "That's kind of what I needed to see you about, Ryan."

"What's that?" Ryan said.

"I've heard a wicked little rumor about you," McPhee said with an impish smile.

Ryan raised his eyebrows, unsure of McPhee's direction but not liking the drift of the conversation.

"I've heard you are about to embark on a career as an expert witness," McPhee continued.

"Where'd you hear that?"

"Ryan," the old professor said. "Where I heard it isn't really the issue. It's true, then?"

"Well," Ryan said, "I wouldn't say I am embarking on a new career. I've agreed to testify in one case."

"Who will you be testifying for?" McPhee asked.

"A small farmer."

"And who against?"

"GenAgra," Ryan said, his back straightening.

McPhee chuckled politely and took a long drink from his beer. "So I heard it correctly," he said, shaking his head slowly.

Ryan said nothing.

"Look, Ryan," the old professor said, "I don't need to play games with you. You know how much money GenAgra gives to this university in research grants alone. Not to mention charitable contributions and joint ventures with the faculty. They are very important to the College of Natural Science. To the university as a whole."

"Professor," Ryan said, the hair on his neck bristling at the older scholar's veiled threat, "I have never been an expert witness in a case before, and I don't plan to make a career of it. I think you know my work well enough to know I am a serious scientist. But if you're implying I should not testify as an expert in a case simply because the people I'm testifying against are big contributors to our university, I'm afraid you're overstepping your bounds, sir."

McPhee's lip stiffened. "I'm overstepping my bounds?" he said, and laughed politely. "Look, Ryan. You're a good kid. And I mean that in the kindest way. But your tenure is going to be reviewed in the very near future. Take this as friendly advice and no more. If you intend to continue as a tenured professor at this university, I think you should consider your role as an expert witness. It's unseemly, no matter who you would be testifying against. It's a distraction to our mission as a university. And it may well put an end to your career."

Ryan was deeply offended but sensed that a further direct challenge to McPhee would be a mistake. When the dean turned the discussion to lighter matters, Ryan was happy to oblige. A short time later, McPhee begged off a second beer and left Ryan alone on the patio.

The threat had been more pointed than Ryan could have ever imagined possible. The game played by academics was a political blood sport, Ryan knew from firsthand experience. But it had always been a game played with a high degree of civility. McPhee had made the threat explicit. *Go against GenAgra and you will lose your job.* The threat would have been more at home in a union fight or a mob dispute.

It was a good example of how big money was influencing all kinds of traditional institutions. Academia was no exception. But rather than intimidate the young professor, it only served to harden his resolve. If GenAgra wanted a fight, he would be happy to oblige.

Tom sat across from Wendy at the pizzeria in Perkins, laughing at her observations on small-town life. Despite her graduate studies on agricultural issues, she was a product of suburbia and had a deep, cynical sense of humor—a city-girl attitude that was playfully disparaging toward her country cousins. The post-Claire world had been a relatively humorless place for Tom, but Wendy brought him light, and the light was genuine. It was much needed light after visiting Ike at the hospital.

Ike was stable and awake at intervals, so they were able to see him. But the ventilator prevented the farmer from speaking. They sat with Kaye for the better part of the evening. Kaye gave

Tom a raised eyebrow when Wendy wasn't looking, and Tom was unsure of the look's meaning. She either approved of Tom's taste in women, or she was scolding him for robbing the cradle; she did not have an opportunity to say which. She seemed to enjoy Wendy's company, but Kaye was polite to everyone, so that was no barometer on her true feelings.

Kaye insisted on staying the night with her husband, but she gave Tom a key to the farmhouse, in case the two of them didn't feel like driving home late at night. Tom gave Wendy the nickel tour of Perkins, showing her the few sights. The high school football field where he had scored seven varsity touchdowns as a halfback. The church where Kaye and Ike had been married. And the pizzeria, where local kids had hung out since Tom was a boy. He insisted they stop for a bite. They hadn't eaten all night, and he was starving.

"So you lived here your entire life?" Wendy said, as a teenage waitress brought them a medium pizza.

"The first eighteen years anyway," Tom said. He cut out two gooey slices, serving Wendy and himself.

"That must have been," she paused, as if searching her mind for the right word, "really boring."

"Yes." Tom laughed. "It was." He tore into the pizza, sucking air to cool it down. "So what did you think of Kaye?"

"Just like I pictured her," Wendy said. "Can you imagine spending over fifty years married to someone? I think that is the sweetest thing. To find the right person like that."

Tom cringed inside. He could imagine it. "It's beautiful," he managed.

"Oh, uh, I'm such an idiot," Wendy said. "Sometimes I don't think before I say things."

"It's okay," Tom said. "You know, this is the best thing, I think. Having someone to talk to. It's okay."

A silence fell at the table. Tom finished off a second slice, while Wendy only picked at her first.

"Would you like to take a drive by the farm before we go?" Tom said. "It's my favorite place in this town."

"Sure," Wendy said enthusiastically, though Tom thought she looked tired. "How could you visit Perkins and not see the Stiles'

Family Berry Farm?"

Tom paid for the pizza with cash and escorted Wendy to the car. He was still confused about their exact status, but he was happy to share the evening with her. He drove south out of the small town, toward the farm. It was completely dark as they pulled up. Exiting the car, Tom felt small. Thousands of stars looked down on them from a pitch black sky. The milky way was a glowing band across the darkness.

"This is it," Tom said.

"Impressive," Wendy said, walking close to him in the cool night air. "I was kind of expecting more neon. And flood lights or something. But this is impressive."

They walked up the drive, back to the tractor trails Tom knew by heart, and through the unlighted fields. Tom gave her the tour by memory in the dark shadows of the night. He stopped in the open space of an apple orchard, the dew cold on his loafers, and looked up at the sky. She joined him.

"This is what I love most about getting outside the city," she said, her arm brushing against him.

Tom wanted to look at her face. To see the stars reflected off her dark eyes. He didn't know how she felt or if she felt anything at all. He could only feel his own pulse quickening. Urging him to act on a stage set by the entire world around them.

"You want to get back," he heard himself saying, his subconscious uttering words at odds with his desire.

"Sure, if you want," Wendy said, and she followed as his sure footsteps found the packed earth on the tractor trail.

"We could stay here tonight, if you want," Tom said. "You've really got a long drive once I get you back to the office…" He felt fortunate the darkness hid his embarrassment at asking her to spend the night.

"Sure, if you want," Wendy said. "I don't have anything going on tonight. And I'm kind of tired."

Chapter Ten

Wendy was smitten by Tom's old-fashioned sensibilities. Opening doors, polite conversation, and his boyish nervousness made him seem like a romantic creation of Frank Capra come to life. And if she were not so certain in her own feelings for Ryan, she might have been tempted to ease his obvious indecision.

She had been certain he was about to try to kiss her under the starlight and pleasantly surprised that he did not. And while she felt completely safe spending the night with him in the handsome old farmhouse, she did pity the man. His loneliness was palpable. She could have kicked herself for wounding him with her comment on the beauty of long marriages. And his confusion about how to act around her—whether to treat her with romantic affection or platonic friendship—was painful to watch.

"Here," Tom said, leaning into the guest bedroom and tossing her a flannel nightgown. "I'm sure Kaye won't mind if you use this."

"Thanks," she said.

"Well, I'll be down the hall," he stammered, smiling at her

with half-raised eyes.

"Tom," Wendy said. "Wait. Can we talk for a minute?"

He jerked to a halt, his expression a laughable mix of fear, guilt, and anticipation.

Wendy placed the nightgown on the dresser and sat down on the four-post bed. "Come here," she said, smiling at him, wanting to be kind in what she was about to say.

Tom sat beside her, as she pulled herself onto the bed and stretched out on her side.

"I had a wonderful time tonight," she said, feeling his stare. "That was kind of you to show me this place."

"Me, too," he said.

"If you weren't my boss—" she started but then stopped. It would have been an easy excuse, but she didn't want to lie to him. "I'm in love with someone, Tom." It was the first time she had shared this secret with anyone other than her sister. Tom said nothing in reply. "I'm in love with Professor Romanelli," she said, her smile now coming from some secret chamber in her heart. "I have been since I started working for him."

"Oh," Tom said. His face slackened, almost as if he were relieved. "I didn't know."

"Nobody does," she said. "He's really never shown any interest, and I've never told him how I feel."

"Why not?"

"I don't know," Wendy said. "I kept waiting for him. Year after year. You know. Waiting for him to ask me out. Or, I don't know—" She stopped herself for a moment, considering whether Tom was strong enough to hear what she wanted to say. And decided to trust him. "You know," she continued, "tonight under the stars. You wanted to kiss me, didn't you?"

Tom's face flushed, and he turned his eyes down. "I, uh…" He laughed. "I take the Fifth."

"It's okay." Wendy laughed with him. "I wouldn't have minded, really. But I've been feeling like that with Professor Romanelli for about three years now. The same feeling. Every day. Thinking every moment is the moment when he is going to tell me he loves me, too."

"I'm sorry," Tom said. "That must be awful."

"I thought so," Wendy said. "But now that I'm not around him every day, I miss it. I would go back to that in a minute. I love him."

"You've got to tell him," Tom said.

"I know," Wendy said. "But I don't want to. I've got some idea in my head. About how it's supposed to be."

"You?" Tom said. "Old-fashioned? Look at yourself. You're a scientist. About to be a doctor. Beautiful. You've got the whole world at your fingertips. You don't have to be old-fashioned."

"But I want to be," she said. "It's the way I am."

"Hmmm," Tom said, his brow wrinkled in thought. "Well, the guy would have to be half-dead not to like you. I mean, look at me. I *am* half-dead, and you had me won over in a little under a week."

She giggled. It was late. Tom was the older brother she never had. Someone to look out for her and protect her against all actors in bad faith.

"Well, we'll figure out a way," Tom said. "After all, the guy does work for me. I ought to be able to exert some pressure on him, don't you think?"

She leaned up and kissed him on the cheek, then watched him smile. "Thanks for listening," she said. "I really needed to tell someone."

"I'm honored you picked me," Tom said. "Though, I think it would have been a lot easier if you said this to him."

Wendy shrugged.

"We'll sleep on it," Tom said. "We can talk about it tomorrow. You ever go bass fishing?"

Ernie spent the weekend in his office. He piled his desk high with Jill's files on each of the nine HERDS patients they had identified and spent hours combing them for details that would help him sell his case to Underwood. Jill only had half the patient information entered into the database, so Ernie was left thumbing through the files by hand. The data was maddening in its ability to point in different directions, but at least shuffling through the patients' files made him feel as if he were doing something.

When he first learned that three of the cases occurred near

the Stiles' farm and the North Central Research Center, Ernie felt in his gut he had found the geographical locus of the illness. Two students worked at the center, and the farmer worked the land right next door. All three of them presented at hospitals with HERDS. That represented a third of the known cases, all with a close connection to a very specific piece of real estate.

But his weekend review gave him little additional insight. He suspected the illness was caused by some environmental factor. A chemical or fertilizer used on the crops. A toxin in the ground water. Or even one of the genetically modified plants. It wasn't beyond the realm of possibility, given his reading of the history of Eosinophilia-Myalgia. But none of these theories would explain the other six cases of HERDS. Two of the other patients had Stiles' farm products in their diet, but this still connected only slightly more than half of the cases, which would not be very convincing to Underwood. Five patients also frequented Fast Burger restaurants regularly, so he could make an equally persuasive case that HERDS was caused by a food-borne illness associated with the fast-food chain. It just wasn't very convincing.

Even after a draining weekend of searching for a phantom cause, he made it to the office early on Monday. He waited for Jill to arrive so he could bring her up to date, despite being no wiser for all his uncompensated overtime. When he saw her pull into the parking lot, he headed to meet her in the breakroom.

"How'd Jacqueline's dance recital go?" Ernie said.

"Not bad." Jill smiled. "Coffee?"

"Thanks."

Jill filled two disposable cups, then handed one to Ernie. "I wonder sometimes what I'm training her for, you know," Jill said. "I mean dance lessons, what good are they? Is she going to grow up to be a Pistons' cheerleader? Or maybe a contestant on American Idol? I'm thinking of switching her over to piano next year."

Ernie commiserated politely. He admired working parents, but felt in no way ready to shoulder the responsibility himself. "I put the field interviews from patient nine on your desk," he said, walking Jill toward her cubicle and sipping the office blend.

"How'd it go?" Jill said. "Have you solved the mystery disease?"

"I've got a hunch," Ernie said. He filled her in on the lawsuit between the two farms and their geographic connections to the patients.

"You think that's enough to get Underwood off his ass?"

"No." Ernie smiled. "But I've got to try. I'm going to go call him."

"Good luck."

"Thanks." Ernie headed for his office, then turned back. "Jill, could you try to find out what kind of genetically modified crops they're growing out at those farms? The North Central Research Center and the Stiles' farm. The contact information is in my notes in the file."

Jill nodded, and Ernie turned and headed to his office. The internalized voice of Chuck Woolery narrated his walk. "It's time to play Daily Humiliation, with your boss and mine—Herb Underwood. Our contestant today. Ernesto Vasquez." Ernie wore a self-entertained smile as he entered his office and dialed the phone. He almost hoped for voice mail, even though that would delay approval for issuing a yellow alert.

To his surprise, Underwood was in the office at a reasonable hour. But as Ernie had expected, his boss brushed off his new theory on the epicenter of the disease. "Awww, that's too bad. Well, thank you for playing—and Bob, tell him about his wonderful parting gifts," the game-show host continued narrating in Ernie's head.

Jill buzzed on the interoffice line as soon as he hung-up the phone. "So?" she said.

"Nada," Ernie said. "As expected."

"Sorry."

"Hey," Ernie said. "We'll just keep at it."

"I checked to see what I could find out about the NCRC," Jill said. "It's got a website, but there's no information on what they're growing there."

"Thanks," Ernie said. "I'm making progress on all fronts today."

"Hang in there," Jill said. "We'll figure this out. We always do."

"I'd kind of like to do that before a bunch more people get sick."

"I know," she said. "That's because you're new. And still give a shit."

"I'll take that as a compliment."

"It was," Jill said.

Ernie hung up and paced about the office, trying to relieve the anxiety he felt growing in his gut. Underwood was obviously going to wait until HERDS became a plague before he allowed any real action. The guy was a typical bureaucrat. If the problem was out of sight, it was out of mind.

He continued to pace, trying to put Underwood out of his mind. Underwood was a distraction, he told himself. He needed to focus on the investigation. Underwood would come on board as soon as Ernie broke the case.

Turning his attention to the mystery syndrome, Ernie wondered about what genetically modified plants were being fought over in court. He could call the court, but he doubted they would be overly helpful on the phone. How about the radio reporter, he wondered. What was his name? He might know the specific crops that were being grown. It was a place to start.

After a quick Internet search, Ernie found the number to the Milton radio station that had reported the case. As he dialed, a thought crept in on him. Underwood might ignore this problem when it was out of sight, but what if the story was leaked to the press? That would rachet anxiety up a notch or two—maybe enough to spur Underwood to action. It would be a clear violation of departmental policy. It might bring his budding career to an abrupt end. Underwood already had it in for him on anything to do with HERDS. An unauthorized leak might give Underwood the ammunition to get rid of Ernie altogether.

A receptionist answered and directed his call to the news director. As Ernie waited, serenaded by Bon Jovi's *Wanted Dead or Alive* in the background, his dilemma crystallized in his mind. He could be a good bureaucrat and follow departmental procedures. Or he could be a good epidemiologist and try to protect the public, even if it meant bending the rules. Ernie was pretty sure he knew the proper course.

"This is Sam Oster. Can I help you?"

What had started out as a rather disastrous date-thing on Friday night, had turned into a pretty decent weekend. Tom was much more comfortable in his role as Wendy's confidant than he was as her suitor. He quickly laughed off his own aspirations of romance as a combination of loneliness and confusion, and their weekend together turned to fishing and talk of how to land Professor Ryan Romanelli.

The finalized plan was a study in simplicity. Tom would use his position as an attorney on the case to provide Wendy ample access to Professor Romanelli. They would ply him with copious amounts of alcohol to loosen his tongue. And they would let nature take its course. Tom vowed to assist "nature" at every opportunity. Wendy, in turn, promised her quest to win the professor over would not interfere with Ike's case against GenAgra.

When they both returned to work on Monday, Tom spent the first hours in the office giving Ike's case file a second reading. The office was silent except for the intermittent sound of typing from Wendy's station. His own work went smoothly. At odd moments, his thoughts drifted toward how he could best fulfill his role as matchmaker in the Wendy-Ryan affair. And by lunch, he had a plan well worked out. He left his private office and found Wendy typing away at her thesis.

"I'm going to run over and grab take-out from the diner," Tom said. "You want anything?"

"Yeah, sure," Wendy said. "Get me a slice of that Dutch apple pie."

"That's it?"

"Yeah," Wendy said. "I'm addicted to that stuff. If I don't stop eating there, I think I'm gonna gain ten pounds."

"Well, you're doing all right so far," Tom said. She actually looked thinner than when she had started working at the office, if that was possible. "I need you to do a couple of things while I'm gone. Very important."

"Okay," Wendy said.

"First, I need you to call Professor Romanelli," Tom said. "Tell him I need to sit down with him for a couple of hours to go over his testimony. He can come here. Or I can go there. It doesn't matter. But, I'd like to do it yet this afternoon if that's possible.

Or tomorrow. Or even in the evenings. Whatever works with his schedule."

"All right," Wendy said.

"Also, I need you to contact the Doubletree Hotel in Bay City," Tom said. "I want three rooms. Checking in Saturday. Checking out Tuesday morning. Facing the river if possible."

"That's the second through the morning of the fifth," Wendy said looking at her desk calender.

"Yeah," Tom said. "Sounds right."

"Got it," Wendy said. "Anything else?"

"Nope," Tom said. "I'll be back in a flash." He walked next door to the Milton Diner, helped himself to a seat at the counter and flagged down a waitress to take his order. He browsed over a copy of the *The Milton Beacon* as he waited. The paper had picked up the story he'd given Sam Oster at WHIP. His case was front page news. He read the article. It had just enough rooting for the local hero. Just enough subtle condemnation of the unfeeling multi-national corporation. Perfect. If only a jury in Wabeno County was deciding the case, his life would be a lot easier.

The food, tucked in a brown grocery bag, was brought out just as Tom finished his perusal of the local news. He paid with a twenty and headed back to the office.

"You have a meeting with Doctor Romanelli at three o'clock today," Wendy said. "His office. He couldn't get away to come here."

"Great," Tom said.

"And you have three waterfront rooms booked at the Doubletree. Kind of pricy, though."

"Great," Tom said. "They have a pretty decent fireworks show that weekend. Place gets busy." He grabbed two paper plates from a cabinet under the coffee machine. "Come on," he said, walking to the law library. "Let's eat in here."

He unpacked the food. Apple pie for Wendy. Tuna on rye for him. Through delicious mouthfuls, Tom filled Wendy in on the master plan. "I'm going to need you to go down there with me today," Tom said. "I need someone to take notes."

"Mmm-hmm," Wendy said, through a mouthful of pie.

"When we're done, I'm taking us all out for dinner and drinks.

Unless this guy's batting for the other team, I'm pretty sure you won't be coming back with me tonight."

Wendy approved of the plan but doubted its efficacy. Still, an hour later they were on the road—headed for Michigan A&T and the professor. As their conversation dragged, Tom turned on the radio. He recognized the voice immediately.

"A Mystery Illness Lurks in Wabeno County. I'm Sam Oster, and this is your WHIP news break at the top of the hour," Oster said. "An unidentified illness has hospitalized at least eight people in northern mid-Michigan, and has killed at least one man. This according to sources in the State Department of Health.

"Officials have dubbed the illness High Eosinophil Respiratory Distress Syndrome or HERDS, and its cause has yet to be identified. Symptoms include muscle pain, skin rashes, swelling of the extremities, partial paralysis, and difficulty breathing. In early stages, HERDS patients can appear to be suffering from a serious allergic reaction.

"There is no indication that HERDS is contagious. However, persons suffering from HERDS symptoms should contact their local physician or seek emergency treatment as necessary. If you suspect you or someone you know might be suffering from HERDS, you are encouraged to contact the regional office of the State Department of Health. The number to their Mt. Pleasant office is…"

Tom looked at Wendy. Her eyes mirrored his own fear. The report was somewhat alarming—as if a tornado had been sighted. Gooseflesh raised on Tom's arms and crawled up his neck. Ike and eight other unlucky people had been stricken by a new illness, like winners in some type of reverse lottery. And though Tom trusted Doctor Brown when he assured them the disease was not communicable, something about the mystery illness made him uneasy.

"That doesn't sound good," Tom said. He reached down to change the channel to music. He wanted to put the disease out of mind.

"No," Wendy said. "Downright scary. You want me to find something else?"

Tom let Wendy take over the radio navigation. Soon she had

found a hip-hop station. Tom cruised down US-27 to an unfamiliar soundtrack. He tapped out the steady bass beats on his steering wheel, trying to rhythmically exorcize a growing panic he felt about the disease. Wendy was obviously unconcerned. She was lost in the music of her age. Tom watched her aimlessly as he drove, and after many miles, his anxiety passed to a place just outside his consciousness.

Ryan sat at the Cask & Keg patio. It was the same seat where he had been threatened by Dean McPhee seventy-two hours before. He liked his present company far better, as Wendy sat on his left with Tom Hughes across the table. He would have preferred to talk with Wendy alone, but merely seeing her made him feel more settled.

"Can you bring us another round," Tom said to the waitress, over the hum of student voices. "Two more beers and, ah…"

"I'm fine for now," Wendy said, nursing a wine cooler.

Ryan had agreed to see the lawyer on short notice partly to spite McPhee and partly out of his desire to see Wendy. He wanted to tell her in person about McPhee's threats and to warn her about the intense scrutiny she would undoubtedly face in presenting her own research. But mostly, Ryan wanted to see her. He had hoped she would be accompanying the attorney down and was heartened when he saw both their faces outside his office at 3:00 p.m. After an hour and a half of boring questions about GenAgra's patents, and the spread of GMOs to the Stiles' fields, Tom had concluded his interview. The lawyer then suggested drinks over dinner. Ryan was happy to accept, so long as it extended his time with Wendy.

The waitress brought Ryan and Tom another beer, and assured them their food would be right out.

"Thanks," Ryan said.

"*Salute*," Tom said, clinking Ryan's bottle with his own.

"So, I've been officially threatened to give up on this case," Ryan said, looking mostly for Wendy's response. "Peter McPhee, the dean of my college, told me if I go forward, I'm not going to make tenure."

A look of genuine concern came over Wendy's deeply tanned face.

"Does he have the power to make that decision?" Tom asked.

"Yes," Ryan said, turning his attention from Wendy. "In a roundabout way. He would be on the college committee that votes on my approval. He certainly has enough power to sway other votes."

"Is there a grievance process you can take?" Tom said. "I know a couple of employment lawyers. I could make calls."

"I don't want a lawyer," Ryan said. "Not yet, anyway. I'm not going to be scared off this case. I think what you are doing is right, and I'm not going to be silenced just because GenAgra is spending millions on research at the university."

"Not many people would stick their neck out like that," Tom said. "I appreciate it."

Ryan shrugged off the compliment and turned to Wendy. He prodded her about her thesis, and warned her again to couch her conclusions where academically feasible, for the benefit of the powers that be.

"Great advice, coming from Mr. Academic Conformity here," Wendy said, then she and Tom shared a laugh at Ryan's expense.

Watching them lean close to each other, Ryan saw Tom was tanned as dark as Wendy. He had been upset when he couldn't reach her by phone for the entire weekend, and seeing them together now, his jealousy peaked again.

"You guys both got a pretty good tan going," Ryan said. "Do they have tanning booths up there in Milton?"

"No, uh..." Tom started.

"Tom took me out fishing on Watson Lake," Wendy said. "That was a first."

Ryan tried to hide his emotion. He thought she might be attracted to the older lawyer, though he couldn't see any motive beyond money. The thought of them together for an entire weekend turned his heart sick.

The waitress came back with their food, saving Ryan from exposing his true feelings. Conversation quieted as they picked at the standard fare of the Cask & Keg.

"I wanted to ask you," Tom said, through a mouthful of fried fish. "Do you have any plans for the Fourth of July weekend?"

Ryan had no social life. And with Wendy gone, he had lost

even the illusion he might have a social life one day in the future. "No," he said.

"Well," Tom said. "Since we are going to be in court there on the fifth, I decided to rent some rooms at a local hotel and make it a working weekend."

Ryan was noncommittal, crunching his salad and sipping beer.

"They have a pretty good fireworks festival up that way," Tom continued, "and I've got rooms right on the water. All expenses paid. I'm hoping to get my witnesses up there for a little relaxation and some prep."

Ryan looked at Wendy, wondering if she was going. Or if she might even be sharing a room with her new romantic interest. He didn't want to ask directly in front of Tom, but it was all he could imagine. He decided he would have to find out firsthand.

"Sure," Ryan said. "Sounds fun."

There was another lull in the conversation that made Ryan feel like a third wheel. He glanced at Wendy, trying not to stare. She looked waif-like, as she picked at the Cobb salad in front of her. There was so much he needed to tell her that couldn't be said in front of a stranger. She seemed distant and uncommunicative. He wanted to kick himself for making her leave his office, but now it seemed like it might be too late to tell her how he really felt.

"You ever hear of HERDS, Doc?" Tom said.

"Herds?" Ryan said, unsure if he heard the lawyer correctly.

"High Eosinophil Respiratory Distress Syndrome," Wendy clarified. "HERDS. It's some mystery disease going around up by us."

"No," Ryan thought, searching his memory.

"Ike Stiles has it," Tom said. "He's on a ventilator. At least until tomorrow."

"High eosinophil?" Ryan said, his synapses starting to draw some connection. "Yeah, okay. Eosinophilia-Myalgia. Something similar, maybe. A disease associated with genetic engineering back in the '80s or '90s."

Tom had never seen a more inept display of courtship in his entire life. He did his best to keep the professor drinking and to encourage both of them to speak to one another, but it was like trying to force Ike to stop swearing. It was battling the natural order of the world.

As he fumbled for ways to ignite conversation between the two socially impaired scientists, the story about HERDS sprang to mind. It was out of his mouth before he could stop it. He did not really want to discuss HERDS, though he could not exactly identify his own discomfort. It was more than Ike being gravely ill, but he couldn't put his finger on it.

Tom tried to stop thinking. The professor had gone into full teaching mode, and Tom concentrated on his words. The professor's young voice spoke with a simplicity and authority that was mesmerizing. Tom imagined himself an undergrad, listening to a lecture in the hazy June heat.

"You remember about ten, maybe fifteen, years ago," Ryan said to Tom and Wendy, and anyone else in hearing distance on the patio. "There was this big scare about a supplement. L-tryptophan."

Tom shrugged. It sounded vaguely familiar, but he wasn't sure.

"L-tryptophan is the amino acid in turkey that makes you sleepy," Ryan went on. "Manufacturers made it as a supplement. People took it as a sleep aid. But then there was a big health scare. And the FDA banned it. Remember? That was the FDA version of what happened, anyway. They wanted to get their hands on regulating vitamins and amino acids. I mean, there is nothing wrong with L-tryptophan. It's natural. Might as well ban turkey.

"What you probably don't remember is why they banned it. Horrible outbreak. Thousands of people who were taking L-tryptophan. Nationwide. Eosinophilia-Myalgia. Really high eosinophil counts. And horrible pain. And people dying. I think at least thirty died. Some of the higher estimates had the death toll over a hundred, I think."

Tom sat forward, his stomach knotting, drawn in by the professor's cadence.

"So when the FDA makes its official report to Congress," Ryan said, "they blame L-tryptophan, right. Bad amino acid. Bad supplement. They were in the middle of the biotech boom, so nobody wanted to bring up any genetic engineering problems at that time. When the guy from the FDA testified before Congress about it—for their official report on this horrible disease—genetic engineering got no mention. Nada. Not at all. Just L-tryptophan is bad. Ban it.

"But the people who were actually looking into what caused the disease. The CDC. The Minnesota Health Department. They studied all the cases of eosinophilia. And lawyers handling claims for these sick people studied the disease. And it all traced back to one Japanese company.

"L-tryptophan was produced by six companies at that time. All of them Japanese. They used bacteria and mixed-in enzymes. Out of this fermenting goo they would get L-tryptophan. And other things. Toxins that had to be filtered out. But one company. Showa Denko. One of Japan's leading chemical companies. They had a good idea. They started genetically modifying the bacteria so it produced more L-tryptophan. They went through a bunch of strains. Just kept ramping it up. None of the other manufacturers did this. Only Showa Denko. A pioneer in using biotechnology for profit, you might say.

"And all the cases of Eosinophilia-Myalgia. They all traced back to Showa Denko. Surprise, surprise. They all trace back to the one company that's using genetically engineered bacteria to produce the amino acid.

"It was nothing conclusive in the end. There was no way to definitively pin it on the genetic engineering. The bacteria got destroyed before anyone ever actually tested it to see what it was making. So maybe the little GMO was producing a unique toxin. They did find a unique toxin in testing the pills. But who's to say.

"Not the FDA. They blamed it on a change in the filters used by Showa Denko, even though they knew damn well that the L-tryptophan that was being produced before the filter change was causing Eosinophilia-Myalgia, too. So in the end, the FDA blamed it on all L-tryptophan manufacturers. And they blamed it on the natural supplement. And genetic engineering wasn't even mentioned to Congress, when it all came down.

"Showa Denko paid out a couple of billion in settlements. And the biotech industry. Well, no one ever really remembered that genetic engineering was the suspected culprit. You guys don't remember any of this, do you?"

Tom shook his head. Wendy appeared just as baffled by Ryan's story. Tom knew if he had heard that GMOs produced potentially deadly toxins, he would have done everything he could to avoid them. But he hadn't even known that GMOs were in the food supply prior to his involvement in this case. So his own ignorance on the L-tryptophan did not come as a surprise.

Tom was about to order a third beer when Ike's face flashed in his memory. It was Ike lying in bed, struggling to breathe. His pained expression. A tinge of blue creeping into his face. In an instant, Tom's entire world shifted focus. He thought he heard an audible click as his anxiety fell into place with a most irrational thought. He knew why it was that listening to the HERDS report on the radio had so unsettled him. It was Ike's face, struggling to breathe. It was the same expression he had seen in Claire's dying moments.

"So you're saying that eosinophil-whatever it was in the '90s—it was caused by GMOs," Tom said, his voice overly aggressive.

"There was never conclusive proof," Ryan said. "But from the studies I've read, that would be my expert opinion."

"Could that happen with these plants Ike is growing?" Tom was leaning forward, almost out of his chair.

"In theory, yes," Ryan began. "The L-tryptophan bacteria was especially susceptible to producing—"

"So, yes these plants could cause a disease like this?" Tom interrupted.

"In theory, yes," Ryan said. "Why?"

"Because my wife—" Tom said, and his voice broke off. He felt a rush of heat and had to stifle tears that swelled in his eyes.

"What?" Wendy said, sitting forward.

"My wife," Tom said deliberately. "Claire used to love Kaye's blackberry jam. She was eating it that morning, when…" He could not say the words. He looked at his watch. Only 5:30 p.m. He jumped up from the table and stalked out toward the sidewalk.

"Wait," Wendy said, chasing after him.

"Just give me a minute," Tom said curtly. He whipped out

his cell phone, dialed information and was connected to Doctor Brown's office. He hoped the doctor was still in. Tom did not think he could take the drive back to Milton without knowing the truth.

A nurse at Doctor Brown's office told him to wait for a moment before putting him through to the doctor.

"Doctor Brown," Tom said, stopping on the sidewalk, and plugging one ear to hear better. "I'm glad you're still in. I need a favor."

"What is it, Tom?" the doctor said. "You want more of those sleeping pills, because I'm—"

"No, no, Doctor Brown," Tom said. "I need you to check something in Claire's medical records. You've still got a copy at the office, don't you?"

"Yes," Doctor Brown said. "I think I do, Tom. What is it? Are you okay?"

"Yes, I'm okay," Tom said. "Can you please get her file. I need you to check one thing for me. Please."

"Okay, okay, Tom," Doctor Brown said. "Hang on."

There was a clunk as the doctor placed the phone on a hard surface. Tom heard his old steps shuffle away. Tom looked across the road at the green treetops on campus, blowing in the wind. He remembered walking with Claire, on summer evenings, feeling the breeze together. He didn't know what answer he wanted from Doctor Brown. Tom could not imagine knowing a horrible truth. The feet shuffled back, and the phone creaked.

"Okay, Tom. I've got the file. What is it?"

"Check her blood work," Tom croaked, his voice weak. "From the last—when they took her to the hospital."

There was an eternal pause. Time stood still, forcing Tom to await a new reality.

"What's her eosinophil count, Doctor Brown?" Tom said when he couldn't wait any longer.

And the pause continued.

"Nineteen-thousand," Doctor Brown said. "Oh my God, Tommy. She had this HERDS."

"Thanks, Doc," Tom said, calmly inhaling the breeze. "Thanks for looking." He clicked the cell phone shut. He wanted to chuck it across the street and never speak to anyone. A numbness engulfed his mind and body. He felt Wendy's hand on his shoulder, but there was some buffer between her touch and his feeling. He wanted to close himself down. To cease thinking, like a computer turned off for the evening, its settings and data saved on silicon, but its existence absent until revived.

It felt like Claire had died in his arms a second time. He was waiting again for this new revelation to not be true. It was surely a cruel joke that his wife's life had apparently been snuffed out by a genetically engineered plant, so a giant company could continue to rake obscene profits.

But it was not a joke. It was real. The reality of it would not change. It felt like trailing hopelessly in a football game at the start of the fourth quarter. The clock would continue winding down to some inevitable finality. That is how the remaining years of his life seemed now. Nothing would bring her back. That thought had been trying to sink in for almost four months.

Wendy spoke to him, but her words made no sense. His head swam with alcohol and his swirling thoughts and the steady June breeze. The world spun out of control before him, as he tried to reboot. And as his consciousness came back within his control, there was a new feeling. Lying there in the dark recesses of his mind. Next to the pain of loss. It was larger. Darker. And as he explored it, he knew it. Hatred.

When asthma had been the culprit that deprived him of his mate, there had been no hate. Sorrow engulfed him. It was difficult to hate an old, familiar disease. Asthma was like a tornado or a hurricane or a bolt of lightning. It was the risk everyone took when they checked into the world. Everyone's ticket disclaimed such natural calamities. He could not hate asthma.

But now, as darkness engulfed his thoughts, he embraced the new emotion. It pushed sorrow aside. His wife had been killed by a corporation. A sheaf of papers, probably filed in Delaware, that described a fictional entity. GenAgra. This being came into the world with one purpose. Stated plainly on the front of its articles of incorporation. To engage in commerce. To earn profits. The more, the better. And, to that end—the god of profit—any means would suffice. So instead of a neutral disease that might strike anyone, Tom now had a focus for his rage. It was a fictional being, but it had real soldiers in the field. He could engage them. He could spend every ounce of his energy trying to destroy GenAgra. They took his wife. The law of the blood feud required he respond in kind.

Wendy walked him back toward the patio, still looking to him for some answer. He shuffled along beside her without thinking of his footsteps. He breathed in the air again, trying to escape the grip of his anger. Claire, the only essence of love he had known in the world, was a thing of beauty. She rarely angered. And never raged. She laughed. She thought. And she wouldn't have wanted Tom to be tormented as he was now.

She was gone. Only a sweet memory. A collage of memories. She flashed before his eyes. As she was, ten years before. Sitting beside him on their living room couch. Their bodies resting snugly against one another. Watching a movie on video, with a winter storm raging outside. He could smell her odor. Not the soap. Or the perfume or deodorant. But Claire. He could see the film. *The Shawshank Redemption.*

Tom smiled at the memory, enjoying what was left of her, and a line from the movie jumped to life as they had listened to it together. "Get busy living or get busy dying," a seemingly despairing Tim Robbins had said to Morgan Freeman.

Even from the grave, Claire could steer him. The memory wrapped around him like a shawl. It warmed him. He was alive. And he had drawn the enemy to battle. It might appear to all the world that David was going to be beaten senseless in court, but Tom had a small opportunity to affect the outcome. It was a chance to change things. A ticket to the world. And a chance to slay Goliath. Claire would at least want him to try.

Chapter Eleven

Tom drove north on the highway, Wendy sleeping in the passenger's seat. He was glad to be traveling. It helped ease the constant flood of thought. Wendy and Ryan had tried to comfort him for a time after his conversation with Doctor Brown, but there was little they could say, and Tom needed time alone.

He had tried to leave Wendy behind, both to get away and to leave her with Ryan. But she wouldn't let Tom go alone. She was worried about him. Touching concern. He had known her such a short time, yet he felt her to be a friend.

The black highway was lit at intervals by amber lamps, bleeding a sickly yellow into the night. He counted them as he passed until his mind was calm. The radio played softly in the background, competing with the sound of the tires as they bumped out a rhythm on the concrete tracks. Sam Oster came on again with a tape-delayed version of his earlier warning about HERDS. Tom's apprehension toward the report had subsided, now that he knew the connection that was lurking in his brain. And he listened analytically.

Oster's source for the report was anonymous. "Sources in

the State Department of Health," he had said. Suspected cases were referred to the regional office, housed at the County Health Department in Mt. Pleasant. They would pass Mt. Pleasant on their way home. He wondered if the Department of Health would have a night staff, given they were monitoring a strange illness. It was as good a place to start as any. He should let someone know Claire's death was a possible case. It could help save someone else's life.

Wendy stirred but did not wake as he took the sharply curving exit. He stopped at a nearby Shell station and asked the night clerk for directions to the county health department. The clerk, a marginally employable young man, shrugged and slid a phone book toward Tom. He found the address and used the map in the front of the book to figure his course. It was only a few miles off.

He drove unfamiliar roads in the dark until he found the health department building. The fluorescent lamps in the parking lot shown down on a square building, constructed with dark brick. There was no light from inside the building. Tom parked and tried the front door, but it was locked. So much for a high state of alert.

Wendy finally stirred to the point of waking as Tom got back in the car.

"Where are we?" she said, squinting under the lights and stretching.

"Mt. Pleasant," Tom said. "I was going to report my wife's case of HERDS, if they were open."

"Oh," Wendy said, still groggy.

"Nobody home, though." He drove back to the highway and was about to turn toward Milton when he saw a sign for the local casino. "Would you mind if we stopped," he said, motioning toward the billboard advertisement.

"You want to gamble?" Wendy asked, perplexed.

"I was thinking of getting a room," Tom said. "I'd like to make a report first thing in the morning. I'd kind of like to talk to someone in person. Someone in chage."

"Oh," Wendy said. "No. I don't mind. As long as you don't dock me for being late for work tomorrow."

Tom smiled in the dark and drove toward the casino. It was

a sprawling complex. Its exterior was neon, intertwined with fiberglass renditions of native American sculpture. Tom had to drive through several full rows of cars to find a space in the parking lot far from the hotel entrance.

A bellhop held the door for them as they approached, and they walked into a marble lobby, dominated by a large, central fireplace. Tom checked into a luxury suite. For mid-Michigan, the suite was opulent. He gave Wendy the master bedroom and took the hide-away bed in the den for himself.

"I'm going to go have a drink," he said.

"I'll come, too," Wendy said. She looked tired and drawn. Tom wondered whether working at the office and finishing a thesis were too much for her to handle.

They made their way from the hotel, down a giant marble hall, to the main casino. It was late Monday night, and the casino floor was packed with a cross section of the surrounding communities. The old and young and middle-aged. Men and women. Professionals. The working class. The losers. All throwing cash at various table games and rows of slot machines. The casino was like a very large mosquito, slowly suckling on the blood of invaders who had raped a once proud nation. Tom was unimpressed by the gambling patrons but happy they were donating to a worthy charity.

He found a bar at the side of the casino, paid for two beers, and watched the flat screen television as it replayed baseball highlights.

"So how are you doing?" Wendy asked, after a time.

"I don't know," Tom said. "I'm mad as hell, I guess. But it's not really doing me any good."

"You've got a right," she said.

Through the din of bells, coins, and gamblers' banter, Tom heard a familiar cell phone ringing. Wendy reached down and took the call. Tom listened to only one side of the conversation, amused.

"Hello," she said loudly, over the background noise.

"Ryan, is that you?" she said.

"What?"

"Okay," she said. "Let me ask."

She turned to Tom. "It's Ryan. He wants to know if he can

come up tomorrow and take some berry samples from the Stiles' Farm. He wants to test them for toxicity."

"Sure," Tom said. "Any time. I'm sure Ike wouldn't mind."

Wendy returned to the cell.

"Sure," she said.

"Whenever you want."

"Yeah, we're at the Soaring Eagle," she said.

"Well—"

"He wants to see someone at the department of health here tomorrow morning," she said, her voice irritated. "So we're going to stay here."

"What?"

"That's just stupid," she said, sounding angry. "You know, I really—"

"Grow up."

"I really wanted to talk with you, but not if you're going to be like that," Wendy said. "Talk to you tomorrow."

She clicked her phone shut, sipped at her beer, then turned to Tom. "What an idiot," she said.

"Doesn't like casinos, huh?" Tom smiled.

"Jesus," Wendy said. "He's being all like my big brother. Thinks you're after me."

"Well, he's looking out for you."

"If he ever showed any interest, he wouldn't have to worry," Wendy said.

"He's obviously jealous," Tom said.

"Jealous?" Wendy laughed.

Tom feigned hurt feelings.

"Oh, I didn't mean that," she said.

"At least he cares," Tom said. "You're moving him in the right direction."

They finished their beers and ordered a second round. Their clothes filled up with secondhand smoke and their minds were inundated with the sound of unfulfilled want. Tom didn't think he would be able to sleep much, so he ordered a third round. At the fourth, Wendy refused. Tom went right ahead. He drank until he forgot how to order more, then Wendy helped him stagger to the room. There he drifted into a dreamless state of unrest.

Bullard's car chauffeured him from the cable news studio to his brownstone home in Georgetown. He was tired. The intern had given him little rest over the weekend, and it had been a full Monday. He had run more focus groups on the Health-Ease Blackberry, trying to fix fears associated with the product's genetic enhancement. Then some emergency consulting on another administration nominee whose confirmation was bogged down in the senate. The latter task required him to spend the evening spinning the nominee's case on live cable television.

He opened the front door to his spacious house and walked the hardwood floors. His footfalls echoed in solitude. Bullard turned on a light in the kitchen, then walked to a stainless steel refrigerator, where he opened the door and looked in at the mostly white space. He had missed dinner, but nothing looked appealing. As he closed the door, his personal cell phone rang.

"Bullard," he answered.

"Hello," a hesitant female voice said.

Bullard waited, trying to place the voice. It was the intern.

"Just checking in," she said. "I'm up and running here."

Bullard had appreciated her weekend enthusiasm, but by Saturday evening he knew she had already proven herself far too clingy to remain in the D.C. office. He had reacted immediately, spinning out the first plausible scenario that had come to mind. He needed her in Michigan, to keep an eye on the attitudes of the locals as the patent infringement litigation developed. Her disappointment was obvious. The young girl had thought she had slept her way to the penthouse and did not want to be sent immediately to the ground floor. But Bullard explained to her the importance of the mission, and how he would need to take frequent trips to monitor her progress. She was on a plane Sunday. And now, on the phone.

"Good," Bullard said, yawning. "It's late. I was just getting to bed."

"I know," the intern said. "I saw you on the news tonight. Brilliant, as usual."

"Thanks." Bullard smiled. "If the damn president would learn how to speak the English language, he wouldn't run into these problems with his nominees. They're not that hard to sell."

"I know."

"Okay," Bullard said. "Well, I'll give you a call tomorrow to get a progress report."

"I needed to call you," the intern said. "I met with Doctor Malec, first thing, like you said. And there may be a problem. There was a story on local radio today about some disease outbreak. Malec told me about it. He's worried it might have some link to GenAgra."

"What?" Bullard said.

"Says it might be linked to the berry," the intern said.

Bullard could not imagine Malec's stupidity, for raising any potential product issues with an intern. "Were you able to analyze the news report that has Doctor Malec so concerned?"

"Yes," the intern said proudly.

"And?"

"It's pretty alarming. Mystery illness. Deadly. Local. Lists symptoms. Call if you suspect you're sick," the intern summarized.

Bullard had thought the intern's main attribute was her eager willingness to screw her way to the top. But you had to open doors in this business, and he admired her cogent summary. It was her need for emotional attachment that he couldn't stomach. "Did you get the source?"

"Regional office of the state department of health. Mt. Pleasant, Michigan."

"Got a name?" Bullard said.

"No," she said.

"Okay."

"Al," she said. "I needed to call, too, because I missed you." She giggled innocently, perhaps trying to cover nervousness.

"Okay," Bullard said. "I need sleep right now. We'll hit the ground running tomorrow. I'll be in touch."

"Okay," she said, disappointment obvious in her voice.

There was nothing like having boots on the ground in a public relations war. He called his father and in ten minutes had the name of an ally. Artie Fisher. Chief of staff to the governor of the State of Michigan. Fisher was happy to take Bullard's late-night phone call. In Fisher, Bullard found a compatriot of sorts, though on a much smaller playing field. He was a numbers man who had worked his way up to be the governor's top advisor. And he was now running the entire state government. Bullard swapped stories, dropped names, and hinted at favors. And before bedtime, Bullard had Fisher's assurance that the source of the bad story would be dealt with in one fashion or another. Not a bad day's work, Bullard thought.

Ryan slept poorly. The air conditioner in his apartment was in a terminal spiral and could not contend with the muggy June air. But it was his situation that bothered him more than the humidity. Ryan was a scientist to the core. He cared about process. He was curious about answers. And he followed the data wherever it led him. He had never let any ideology get in the way of the truth, as he was able to observe it. And Dean McPhee's threat to his career had challenged the purity of the science. If Ryan did not stand up and say the truth as he knew it on the case he was working on, then his belief in science meant nothing. And even though his personal resolve on the issue was clear, seeing power politics wielded to influence science shook his faith in the system.

Ryan was also aware his recent introduction to the corruption of academia was not the only cause of his insomnia. Gnawing at his soul, too, was the fact that Wendy had moved effortlessly away from him. If she was concealing some shared feeling, she certainly gave no sign of it. She had found a new life in the time it took a sunflower to sprout. And worse, her new life included another man.

Ryan felt sorry for Tom's situation. The attorney was obviously distraught at losing his wife. And the shock of learning that a genetically modified food may have been at the root of her death was an awful blow. But as sorry as he was, he was jealous Wendy would leave him to comfort Tom. And when he had called her later to talk about things and found her in a casino with Tom, Ryan was shattered. Something was surely going on between them. He had lost his opportunity with Wendy. The loss weighed on him heavily, deep into the night.

When he did drift to sleep, his slumber was light and restless.

He was up and showered at dawn, fixing his sights on a more concrete problem. Ryan jumped in his car and headed north toward Milton to get samples of the genetically modified blackberries at the Stiles' Farm so he could test them for toxins. Not until he was thirty minutes north on the highway, when he saw the first billboard for the Soaring Eagle Casino, did he understand the subconscious reason he had left so early in the morning.

He exited the highway toward the casino with little thought. He was going to pay Wendy a visit—to try to explain the extent of his torment. He drove a short way off the highway to the hotel and casino. Ryan was amused at the number of cars in the parking lot at 7:30 a.m. on a Tuesday morning. Though he understood the psychological component of gambling, it always amazed him at the number of people who would defy the unbending laws of mathematics in order to lose money.

Ryan parked his car and walked to the lobby of the hotel. A reluctant clerk only directed him to Tom's room after Ryan gave an academy award level enactment of a gambler down on his luck, needing the number of his friend's room so he could crash and sleep off a night of particularly heavy losses. Information obtained, Ryan hurried to the third floor suite and knocked firmly on the door, bracing himself for any eventuality. There was no response, so he pounded more forcefully. He heard rustling inside the room, then the interior lock opened and the door cracked inward. Through the crack, Ryan saw Wendy. Her hair was wet and toweled-up. She wore a white terry-cloth robe. Behind her, he could see Tom sprawled out on a fold-away bed, partially covered by a bedspread.

"What are you doing?" Wendy whispered.

"Oh, uh, nothing, I..." Ryan stammered. He thought he was ready for anything, but the sight of them together in the room stripped him of his ability to speak fluently.

"Come on in," Wendy whispered.

"No, uh, I was on my way up to Milton," Ryan said, regaining the ability to talk, if not to think. "So I thought I'd stop by, but I don't want to bother—"

"No bother," Wendy whispered. "Just keep your voice down."

"No, that's okay," Ryan said.

"Hold on a second," Wendy said. She closed the door, leaving Ryan in the hallway for what seemed like an eternity, before reappearing. She slipped out the door, the lawyer still sleeping behind her. Her clothes smelled of beer and smoke. "Want to get some coffee?"

"Well, uh, no," Ryan said. "I was headed up there to collect those samples we talked about, and, I, uh, wanted to check and see if, uh, you were okay."

"C'mon," Wendy said, heading down the hall to the elevator. Ryan followed. "I'm sorry for yelling on the phone last night."

"No," Ryan said, watching her graceful movement as she pushed the lobby button. "You were right. It's none of my business. I don't know..."

"He is a really decent guy," Wendy said. "And you saw him last night. He was shattered. I just wanted to stay with him. I was kind of worried he might hurt himself or something."

"I know," Ryan said. "I mean, I thought he was a little old for you, you know. And I didn't want him to take advantage. But, look, it's none of my business. I'm sorry for being such a jerk. I mean, I'm not your father or anything."

"Look," Wendy said, lowering her tone as they walked from the elevator, and headed down a hall toward the casino. "First, he's not too old for me—if I wanted something like that. It's condescending of you to set some age limit on men I could be attracted to. Very male of you, somehow. And second, there's nothing going on between us. He's my boss. He's having some hard times. But there's nothing there."

Ryan did not respond. He had eyes. He could see perfectly well what was going on. But he didn't want to enrage her by mentioning the evidence. She was right. She could do whatever she wanted. He had obviously missed out on any chance he ever had. They ordered coffee from the snack lounge and sat at a tall, round table. Several famished gamblers wolfed joyless meals nearby.

"What?" she whispered in animated tones. "You think because we slept in the same room I'm sleeping with him? I swear, guys are all idiots."

"Look," Ryan said, trying to stay dignified before an audience that failed to meet the minimum intelligence level required to appear on the Jerry Springer show. "We don't have to talk about this here. And you're right. It's really none of my business. I just care about you. I want the best for you."

"I care about you, too," Wendy said, softening considerably.

Ryan looked directly into her eyes as she said this. They were soft and warm, though her face was drawn. Must have been a long night, Ryan thought, wondering what exactly a long night entailed. He was unsure what she meant by her comment. She cared about him, too. Was that like care, care? But he couldn't bring himself to ask that question.

Over a half-wall that separated the snack lounge from the casino floor, a fat woman, far down the path to death by coronary heart disease, began screaming hysterically, the slot machine in front of her blasting out a mating call to all gamblers within the casino. After several seconds of staring at this typical, yet bizarre scene, Ryan drew his attention back to Wendy, her eyes now staring into her coffee.

"So are you going on this trip to Bay City?" Ryan asked.

"Yeah," Wendy said, a faint smile painting her lips. "I'm part of the team, ain't I?"

"I guess so," Ryan said.

They sipped and smiled and watched the fat woman collect her jackpot. Ryan was blind to Wendy's thoughts. Were all women such a mystery? Maybe she felt the same. Maybe not. At least the uncertainty left a sliver of hope. And this hope was far better than the thought that he had let her slip away forever. He left the casino a far happier man.

Tom was stirred by knocking at the door, followed shortly by a muted conversation. But it wasn't until several minutes later, when the sunlight slipped past the drapes and impaled his squinting eye, that he awoke to a powerful hangover. He peeked into the master bedroom. No sign of Wendy. He tried to piece together a short history of the previous night. The numbing pain of understanding Claire's senseless death. His need to report to the health department. The casino. And many, many beers. Then oblivion.

He wandered to the bathroom, sipped cool water from the sink, stripped, and let a hot shower wash away as much of the evening as was possible. Out of the shower, Tom tried to squeeze his throbbing temples into surrender, with no success. He ran hands through his hair, like small bands of soldiers trying to tame a revolution. He threw on his old clothes and heard Wendy knocking around in the master bedroom as he dressed.

"Wendy," he yelled. "Is that you?"

"Yeah," she said.

"You know what time it is?"

"Eight-thirty," she said, as Tom exited the bathroom.

"Was I okay last night?" Tom said. "I'm sorry—"

"You were fine," Wendy assured him.

"I'm sorry I dragged you away from Ryan," Tom said, rubbing his temples again.

"You didn't drag me," Wendy said. "Besides, it all worked out. He was up here this morning."

"Really." Tom grinned, despite his headache. Wendy looked tired and disheveled, but radiant.

"He *was* jealous," Wendy said. "You were right."

"Right about what?" Tom said.

"You said he might be jealous, when he called last night?"

Tom had only a hazy memory. He shrugged.

"Well, he showed up here this morning. All pissed that we were sharing a room."

"Good sign," Tom said. "Definite jealousy. And if he's jealous, he must like you, right?"

"He said he *cares* about me," Wendy said. "What the hell does that mean? My *sister* cares about me."

"Hey," Tom said, ticking at Wendy with his forefinger. "Don't be greedy. *Cares* is a good place to start."

Wendy nodded and smiled.

"Hey, I want to get over to that place and report my wife's…" Tom let himself trail off. It was a hard word to say. "You need breakfast before we go?"

"No," Wendy said. "Not if you want to get going."

Tom liked the freedom of walking out of the hotel suite with no belongings other than the clothes on his back. Traveling light was traveling right. They were at the regional health office in minutes. At 8:50 a.m. the office was already a hive of activity.

They spoke with the receptionist, tucked behind a sliding glass window, and were directed to wait in the small reception area. They watched as she ran about, taking calls, tracking staff, and dealing with the few souls that had wandered in the front door. The phone did not stop ringing the entire time they waited. After a time, a door to the main office opened and the beguiling face of a slender man leaned through.

"Mr. Hughes?" the man said, searching the reception area. His Latino features were graceful and accentuated by wide-spaced hazel eyes. His closed-mouth smile exuded warmth.

"Right here," Tom said, rising. Wendy followed.

"Good morning," the man said. "I'm Ernesto Vasquez."

Ernie held out a hand, and Tom shook it.

"Come on back," Ernie said, leading them into the busy office. They followed him past gray cubicles to a small office with a window looking out on the parking lot. Ernie closed the office door for privacy and motioned for Tom and Wendy to be seated. "I'm sorry to make you wait," Ernie began. "We've been extremely busy this morning."

"No problem at all," Tom said.

"My secretary tells me you wanted to report a suspected case of HERDS," Ernie said. The epidemiologist took a form from his desk drawer and readied himself to take down their information.

"Yes," Tom said. "From what we heard on the radio yesterday, I think my wife may have had it. She died three—almost four— months ago."

Ernie stopped scribbling notes and raised his soulful eyes to look squarely at Tom. "I'm very sorry, sir," he said. The man was either a classically trained actor, or sincere. Tom believed it was the latter.

"Thank you," Tom said, swallowing hard. "If there's something you can learn about this illness from her death, well, that would make it...better, I guess."

Ernie politely took basic background information from Tom. It was a slow, professional probe for personal details as to why Tom thought Claire died of HERDS.

"We thought it was asthma," Tom said. "She had always had it, and it looked like that. But her inhaler didn't work that day. And they couldn't get her help fast enough. When I heard the report about HERDS on the radio, I checked her old medical records. Her EE-son-uh-fill—is that how you say it—count was really high. Nineteen thousand."

"It's ee-oh-SIN-eh-fill," Ernie said. "And your wife's count was very high. Higher than what we have seen with any of the HERDS patients we've identified so far. But with the number of new calls we're getting, I wouldn't be surprised if we come away with a new understanding of this syndrome after today. "So let me get some additional information. One of the things we are trying to do is to identify the cause of this illness, so we can stop it."

"I think I know what caused it," Tom said. "I think it was blackberries she ate from a local farm. They are genetically modified, I just found out. And my wife used to eat jam made from these berries almost every day."

Ernie looked up again, his eyes widening and his eyebrows raised. "These blackberries didn't come from the Stiles' Farm, did they?"

"Yes, they did," Tom said. "I know Ike Stiles."

"Did you read about the litigation involving the Stiles' Farm in the local paper, or hear about it on the radio?" Ernie asked.

"I'm involved in the litigation," Tom said. "I'm Ike Stiles' attorney."

"Oh," Ernie said.

"I think these berries killed my wife," Tom said. "And Ike Stiles is in the hospital, too. With the same thing."

"I've met Mr. Stiles," Ernie said. "Or at least I've met his wife. I'm aware of his case."

"Ike ate that jam all the time, too. His wife makes it."

Ernie spun in his chair and pulled a file from a gray cabinet, like a second baseman pivoting on a double play. He opened it, his agile fingers shuffling through the file and his eyes fixing on handwritten notes. He then returned to the sheet he was filling out with Tom and urgently scribbled a neat note in the margin.

"These GMOs. I'm told they can produce toxins that poison people, Mr. Vasquez," Tom said.

"Yes," Ernie said. "I've been reviewing the medical literature in that area. GMOs certainly have to be considered as a suspect in this case. And I can assure you, Mr. Hughes, I will do everything in my power to get these berries off the market as quickly as I can. At least until we confirm their involvement with HERDS one way or the other."

"Thank you," Tom said. "I just don't want anyone else to have to…" His eyes moistened, and he looked out the window into the sunlit parking lot.

"If you're able, I'd like to ask you a few more questions to cover our bases," Ernie said.

Tom answered the questions. Everything he could remember about what Claire ate. Where she worked and played. What products she used. It didn't sound like Mr. Vasquez was sold on the genetically modified blackberry as the cause of HERDS, though Tom was certain in his own mind that GenAgra's blackberry was the culprit in Claire's death. And the sooner people recognized it, the sooner the disease would be stopped.

Tom trusted the young man's face, however, and wanted to give him the benefit of the doubt. Maybe he was just being diligent. Touching all the bases. And not blowing Tom off as a crackpot. Only time would tell. The only thing Tom knew for sure was he was leaving the department of health feeling better for having tried to put a stop to HERDS. He and Wendy got in the Cadillac and set off for home.

Tom pulled into the Fast Burger drive-thru before getting on the highway. "What do you want?" he said to Wendy, as he rolled up to the squawk box.

"I'm holding out for pie at lunch." She smiled.

"You've gotta eat something," Tom said.

"I wouldn't eat this crap anyway."

A static-filled transmission invited Tom to place his order. "You want to go somewhere else?" he said, but Wendy shook her head. He got an egg-bagel combo and carefully situated the meal on the center console before rolling onto the highway. Driving, he juggled his cell phone and his breakfast, wanting to call Doctor Brown's office to check what time Ike would be removed from the ventilator. He finally gave up and asked Wendy to make the call.

"Noon," Wendy said, after talking with Doctor Brown's office.

"Good," Tom said. "We'll still make it in plenty of time."

Tom drove like a zombie, his headache subsiding over the miles. He listened to the radio spinning old songs while Wendy drifted off to sleep. He looked at her as she nodded off. She had no make up, no shower, oily hair, and dark rings set below her eyes. Yet magically, she was still beautiful. Ryan was a lucky man, if he would only wake up.

Midnight Oil finished a decades-old anthem of global responsibility and burning beds, as Sam Oster cut in with the news in Milton. Tom turned up the volume to hear Oster clearly, after barely catching the words "North Central Research Center."

"Ecoterrorists Strike Again. I'm Sam Oster, and this is your WHIP news break at the top of the hour," Oster said, returning after a short commercial break. "The Earth Liberation Front has claimed responsibility for an act of vandalism at the North Central Research Center, south of Perkins. Hundreds of plants were dug from the ground at the research center last night, according to the Michigan State Police.

"An anonymous statement was sent to the WHIP newsroom claiming responsibility for the damage on behalf of the Earth Liberation Front. The statement says that the vandalism was undertaken to rid Wabeno County of unwanted genetically modified organisms, or GMOs, that are being studied at the research center.

"The attack comes almost twenty months after an infamous attack that caused severe damage to a Blue-Mart construction..."

Tom smiled despite himself as he listened to the report. He knew the likely culprit. Zeb Radamacher. Tom had worked with Zeb the previous year as he settled the young man's father's estate. Zeb had been battling for his own freedom at the time, being charged with terrorism, and later cleared, for his role in vandalizing the Blue-Mart development in Milton. Tom thought property destruction was a bit radical, but today he was happy there were people like Zeb in the world, willing to risk their lives and liberty in order to try to make things right. Tom wondered how Zeb would punish GenAgra if the corporation had killed one of his own relatives.

He drove alone with his thoughts, hypnotized by the highway, until the Stiles' Berry Farm advertisements greeted him. He had enough time to drive by the GenAgra facility to check out the damage. He drove down Perkins Road, past Ike's farm, and turned right on County-Line Road. He craned his neck to look at the gently rolling hills of the research station. Yellow police tape surrounded an area of a corn field that had been chopped from the ground prematurely. Further on, a yellow tape roped off a smaller section where blackberry brambles had been hacked to the ground. Nice work Zeb, he thought, wishing only that the boy had torched the entire place instead.

He continued down County-Line Road for a mile before turning back towards Perkins and the hospital. Once parked at the medical facility, he had to shake Wendy to wake her.

"We're here already?" she said.

They went inside and found Kaye with Doctor Brown in the ICU waiting room. Kaye hugged him. Tom, not wanting to take the focus off Ike, waited to tell Kaye about Claire's death. It was not something she needed to hear, as she awaited Ike's fate.

They walked to Ike's room as a group. Doctor Brown called for a technician and a nurse, who prepared to remove the machine that had kept Ike breathing for the past four days. Ike was awake. Obviously pained and exhausted. But in Ike's eyes, Tom thought he could see a flood of curses ready to pour out from the old farmer's mouth.

"Okay," Doctor Brown said. It was the old working on the older. The doctor removed the apparatus from Ike's airway, and the technician took the equipment and rolled it clear. The nurse monitored Ike's vitals, ready with the ventilator in case the old man could not breathe on his own. It was a medical ballet. Together they watched as Ike's lungs attempted to resume their dogged work.

Tom's own breathing ceased as he watched Ike struggle for his initial breath. The room was silent except for the sound of Ike gasping. Tom was about to demand the medical team respond, but Ike drew one shallow breath. Then another. And soon the old farmer was breathing in rhythm.

Kaye, who had been holding Ike's hand for the duration, leaned close to her mate and kissed him.

"Very good, Ike," Doctor Brown said. "You seem to be breathing a little better than when you first got here."

"Vitals are steady, Doctor," the nurse said.

Tom was drawn forward to the man who had been like his father. His eyes were wet, and he had a painful lump in his throat. He was growing sick of constant emotion. "Good job, old man," Tom said, leaning over Kaye and patting Ike's shoulder.

Ike smiled a toothless grin, his dentures removed to a cup on the bed stand.

Doctor Brown was the last of the medical team to leave, thirty minutes later. He promised Kaye the hospital staff would be monitoring Ike's breathing carefully, and they would not hesitate to place him back on the machine if he needed it. The rest of them stayed with Ike until he went to sleep. His breathing remained shallow, with a faint rattling, but he was off the machine, and sleeping comfortably.

Tom and Wendy took Kaye for a cup of coffee in the cafeteria.

"He's going to be fine," Tom said with false confidence.

"Of course," Kaye said. "Never a doubt."

"Kaye, I'm going to need you to come and testify in court next Tuesday, you know," Tom said. "There's no way Ike's going to be back on his feet before then."

"I don't know much about the farming business," Kaye said. "You know Ike wouldn't let me in the fields any more than I'd let him in the kitchen."

"Well, I'm going to need someone to lay out the case from our perspective," Tom said. "And since Ike is down, you're it."

"There's still a week, Tommy," Kaye said. "You don't worry about it. Ike will be fine. You'll see. All he needs is a little chamomile tea."

He didn't want to spoil her illusions by telling her how awful HERDS really was. He would wait to break the news about Claire. But he knew that absent a chamomile-tea miracle, Ike would be unavailable to testify.

Chapter Twelve

Ernie watched as Jill trudged into his office and collapsed in a chair. She looked as tired as he felt. It had been a crazy day, and there were still two hours to go before quitting time.

"So, where are we at?" Ernie asked, his voice quiet. The office phone rang, and Ernie answered. The receptionist tried to patch through another HERDS report. "Put them on hold, or take a message, and we'll call them back. Jill and I are on break. Just for five minutes or so. Thanks."

"Somewhere around a hundred," Jill said when Ernie got off the phone. "From one radio report, on one little station."

"How many cases meet the definition?" Ernie asked.

"I don't have it exact, yet," Jill said. "Maybe around half, I'd guess."

"You think the rest are overreacting to the news bulletin?" Ernie said.

"Could be," Jill said. "Lots of the new cases aren't anywhere near as severe as the ones we had before the news broke. Rash. Muscle aches. Coughing. Pain. Fatigue. So without blood tests, and without severe respiratory distress or paralysis, I guess I'd exclude them."

"It could be that our definition is too narrow," Ernie said. "After talking with that guy this morning. The one who's sure his wife died of HERDS caused by the blackberries. I went back and reviewed the early literature on Eosinophilia-Myalgia. Before the FDA whitewashed it, they were sure that it was caused by a toxin. Probably from genetically modified bacteria used to manufacture L-tryptophan."

"Yeah, so?" Jill said.

"Well, if we have something similar here—a previously unknown toxin made by these blackberry plants—then Eosinophilia-Myalgia is a good model," Ernie explained. "And the reaction in a population to a new toxin is not uniform. Some people will be highly sensitive. Like canaries in a coal mine. They might get sick or die-off on a single exposure. Some might tolerate the toxin better. Until it builds to a tipping point in their body. Perhaps they get minor symptoms. The rash or fatigue. And some won't get sick at all. So we'd have to broaden our definition of the illness to include the mild cases as well as the severe."

"Makes sense. But it could be that a lot of these people are bored hypochondriacs who needed to talk to us during the commercial breaks for *Oprah*," Jill said.

"That's not very scientific, Oswald," Ernie said.

"Sure, it is," Jill said. "That's why we don't report the illness without approval from Lansing. Some percentage of people will always think they're sick if you give them a bunch of symptoms and ask them to call."

"So we are going to need blood tests on all of them," Ernie said. "The news report couldn't have made their eosinophil counts go up, right?"

"I'm on that," Jill said. "I've been advising them all to see their doctor and have blood counts sent to us."

"Good," Ernie said. "I think we should get some samples of these berries, too. From the Stiles' farm and from that research center. My gut tells me that this Hughes guy is on to something."

"Okay," Jill said. "I'll take care of it."

"It's scary, isn't it?" Ernie said. "What if this is only the tip of the iceberg?"

"I know," Jill said. "Underwood's got to let us put out a release now. Even without knowing the cause. With this many reports, we've got to get some reporting system running from the ground up out in the field. Hell, the CDC should be in on this by now."

Ernie bit his lip. He had been avoiding the call to Underwood all day, even though the matter clearly had the impetus required for action. Ernie knew Underwood was going to go ballistic over the unauthorized news leak.

"Yeah," Ernie said. "I've got to call him. I want the director to shut down these blackberries. And the jam. And whatever else they make. Until we know what's causing this."

The phone rang. Ernie was disturbed that the receptionist couldn't give him five minutes to process the greatest public health crisis of his young career.

"Sir," the receptionist said when he picked up the phone, "Director Jones and Mr. Underwood are here to see you. They just barged past and they're on—"

There was a knock on Ernie's open door. He looked up and saw Herb Underwood's angry face. Underwood entered the office followed by a more subdued Director Jones.

"Could you excuse us a moment, Ms.—" Underwood said, curtly.

"Oswald, sir. Jill Oswald." Jill rose and started for the door, nodding at the director on the way out. "Director Jones."

"Hello, Ms. Oswald," Director Jones said cordially.

Ernie hung up the phone and rose from his seat as Jill left. His greeting was stopped short by Underwood.

"Where do you get off, in your third week on the job, by going to the press…" Underwood fumed.

"Now, wait a minute, Herb," Director Jones said softly. "Let's all take a deep breath. Have a seat, Ernie."

Ernie and Underwood sat down across from one another like two dogs being baited for a fight.

"Now, Ernie, first things first," Director Jones said, taking a seat. "We were informed that a report on local radio mentioned HERDS and directed people to call your office. There were no names. No named sources, so we don't know for sure, but—"

"I was the source," Ernie said, and he watched Director Jones' face morph from compassion to concern.

"I was talking with a reporter," Ernie continued, "trying to get information about genetically modified crops that might be related to the outbreak, and I guess some information slipped out. When he had follow-up questions about the illness, I was honest with him."

"That's it," Underwood broke in petulantly. "You know there's a standard operating procedure about releasing information, Vasquez. Or maybe you don't. Or don't care. But before releasing a statement to the press about a suspected illness, all regional directors must have the approval of the state office. No exceptions."

"I'm sorry, sir," Ernie said. "I did what I thought was right at the time."

"I'm sure you did, Ernie," Director Jones stepped back in, trying to reign in Underwood's anger. "And under normal circumstances—" the director paused for emphasis and shot a hot look in Underwood's direction "—this would be something we might discuss. Come up with a plan to handle it better in the future. But your office isn't the only one that has been hit with calls about this. This is a very serious matter."

"I'm sorry, ma'am," Ernie said. "But we have received over a hundred reported cases today. I think we need to take action."

"And we will," Director Jones said sternly. "But I'm afraid I have no choice but to suspend you pending an investigation of this leak to the press. With pay, of course. I'm sorry, but you're off the case."

Ernie had sensed the director was in his corner and her sudden betrayal unsettled him. "But, ma'am," he said. "I'm in the best position to go forward on this. It's a serious health threat, and I think I may finally have the source. A genetically modified blackberry—"

"Genetically modified blackberry," Underwood scoffed. "You're suspended. And if you want any hope of keeping your job, you'll keep your mouth shut about your wild theories. You've already created a panic with no evidence—"

"A hundred people are sick," Ernie fought back. "A number of them on ventilators. One, maybe two, are dead. How much evidence do you want, Herb?"

"I'm sorry," Director Jones said. "But rules are rules. Finish your day today. Turn in your badge with the office manager, and you'll be notified in writing of the proceedings to evaluate your suspension."

Ernie said nothing more. Any response seemed futile. If this was the way the system worked, he wondered if he wouldn't be better off outside it. Hostility hung in the air as Director Jones and Underwood left the office. Ernie sat for a moment, processing his short tenure as a regional epidemiologist, before Director Jones ducked back in.

"Forgot my purse," she said loudly.

Ernie looked at her with a wan smile. He liked the director and had a difficult time holding her accountable for his suspension.

"Ernie," she whispered, motioning him closer across the desk. He leaned forward. "My hands were tied on this. It comes from high up. Someone in the governor's office isn't a big fan of yours. I just wanted you to know. You might think about getting yourself a good lawyer."

"Thank you," Ernie whispered. He was shocked but appreciated the director's candor. "I'm sorry for putting you in this position."

"It's okay," Director Jones said. "I'm sure it will work out."

"It's the blackberry," Ernie whispered forcefully. "I know it. Get them off the market. And the preserves they make with them. It will save lives."

Director Jones shook his hand, nodded, then left the office, this time with her purse safely tucked under her arm.

As soon as he was sure they were gone, Ernie called Jill in and arranged his own exile.

Driving to work Wednesday morning, Tom looked at the world anew. The sun was brilliantly elevated in the early summer sky. He better understood Claire's death. Ike was breathing on his own. And Tom had a chance to go into court and battle against the people who had harmed his loved ones. He got his first restful night of sleep in weeks. And in the morning, he was eager to get to the office to finish what preparations he could.

Wendy was waiting for him as he walked in the front door.

"Mr. Radamacher has been waiting to see you," she said, nodding toward the corner of the waiting room.

Tom turned and saw Zeb.

"Hey, Mr. H.," Zeb said, jumping up and walking over to give Tom a hug.

"How are you, Zeb?" Tom asked.

"Can't complain," Zeb said. "Just have to be over at the probation department this morning, and since I haven't seen you in a while, I thought I'd stop by."

"Thanks, Zeb," Tom said. "It's good to see you."

Zeb had grown an inch or two since Tom had seen him last. But his face was still that of a boy, framed by a bushy head of blond hair.

"I heard you're working on that Stiles' Berry Farm case," Zeb said, giving Tom a mischievous grin.

"Yes," Tom said, smiling back. "I hope *you're* not working on that case, too."

"Oh no, Mr. H." Zeb grinned. "I'm still on probation for that other deal. But you heard about that direct action against GenAgra, huh? Pretty cool."

Tom laughed. "You better keep your nose clean, son."

"Don't worry, Mr. H.," Zeb said, and winked. "I will. Well, I should be getting to see my probation officer. They don't like it when you're late. Slows down the process. I'll see you around, Mr. H. Nice meeting you, ma'am." He bowed to Wendy and walked out of Tom's office.

Wendy said she liked the boy, and she wouldn't let Tom get to work until he had explained most of what he knew about the legend of Zeb Radamacher.

"So that kid basically got the entire County Commission elected?" Wendy said in disbelief, as Tom finished. "And the prosecutor, too?"

"He did," Tom said. "A regular little revolution. Right here."

"That's incredible," Wendy said. "So you think he was involved with digging up those GMOs?"

"Between you and me," Tom laughed, "I've got no doubt."

She finally let him into his own office, where he took up the Stiles' file for a last read through. Before he had gotten far, Ryan called. Tom was pleased to hear Wendy chat with the professor in civil tones for several minutes before the call was transferred his way.

Ryan wasted no time in getting down to business. "I've got results back on the toxicity testing."

"How'd you manage that?" Tom said, amazed. "It took a week to get the DNA testing done. Is this easier?"

"No," Ryan said. "Harder, actually. I had to get DNA typing done to figure out which ones were the Hg-Blackberry. I got A.J. to do it as a rush. As a favor. And I tested the berries for toxins, then matched the results up when A.J. told me which berries were which."

"So," Tom said.

"There's a distinct signature on the gas chromatograph for the Hg-Blackberry. Two peaks. I've called them Peaks B and C."

"English, Doc," Tom said. "We've got to speak English in court next Tuesday."

"Okay." Ryan exhaled. "Gas chromatography. Basically, we are running a substance—in this case the Hg-Blackberry—through a very thin tube. And separating out its molecular and chemical composition. The result is a graph that tells me a little about the composition of the tested substance."

"Okay," Tom said. "That was almost English."

"When you compare the graph of a normal blackberry to the graph of the Hg-Blackberry," Ryan said, "there's a different signature. There are extra peaks on the graph for the Hg-Blackberry. So that means there are additional substances that aren't found in the regular blackberry.

"One of the peaks—Peak B—is the molecule from the *Hoodia gordonii*. The P-57 molecule that controls the weight loss properties. I can't tell you what the other peak is yet. That's going to take a more sophisticated chemical analysis than I can make. But I would hazard a guess that the other peak—Peak C—is your culprit. An unknown toxin."

"Okay," Tom said. "This moves the ball forward. Does it help our case?"

"It might," Ryan said. "I guess. If you're going to try to show the patent is no good because it is basically killing people. Or at least capable of killing people."

"Patent misuse, it's called," Tom said. "I think. I'm getting some help on the technical aspects of patent law."

"I'm more concerned with getting this information out to the public," Ryan said. "This stuff needs to be closed down. Recalled. Stopped."

"Yeah," Tom said. "I agree. I talked with a guy at the state health department yesterday. Ernie Vasquez. I guess he is handling the HERDS investigation. He told me he was going to do everything he could to get the blackberries shut down. I haven't heard from him, though. Maybe you should be talking with him directly about this, so I don't screw up in relaying the information."

"Okay," Ryan said.

"I'll have him call you," Tom said. "You in today?"

"All day," Ryan said.

"All right," Tom said. "Hey, thanks. I'm sorry about the other night. You know. Running off. I was kind of out of it with all the—"

"That's all right," Ryan said.

"You are coming to Bay City with us, right?" Tom lowered his voice a decibel.

"Sure," Ryan said. "I'm looking forward to getting ready to testify. I don't want them to get away with this."

"Yeah," Tom said. "But I want us all to relax a little, too. Have a good time, you know."

"Well, that won't be so bad either," Ryan said.

"You know," Tom said, "I'm pretty sure Wendy is really looking forward to getting a little time alone with you."

"The thesis?" Ryan said. "Yeah, okay."

"No," Tom hissed. "Not the thesis. I think she might, you know, want to spend some time with you. There's a lot to do at this place. You guys could get out on a boat. There's a pier for walking at night. I mean, it can be pretty romantic."

"Oh," Ryan said. "Well, yeah. I appreciate you asking me. And, uh. Yeah."

"Okay," Tom said. Cupid he was not, but he was determined to get the new scientists in his life together. "I'll have that guy from the department of health call you."

Tom hung up the phone and hollered for Wendy. "Get that Ernesto Vasquez guy from the health department on the line, will you."

Wendy got up from her desk and marched into Tom's office.

"Look, I've only been here two weeks," she said, in a calm tone. "You can't be barking out orders through the office like that. That might be the way lawyers do things, but it's not civilized."

Tom frowned apologetically.

"I heard you with Ryan, too," she said. "That was laying it on kind of thick, don't you think?"

"I don't know," Tom said. "Watching the two of you together is like watching pandas at the zoo, man. I'm not sure if you're ever going to get on with it."

"Well, he *cares* now," Wendy said. "So maybe you can butt out a little."

"Okay," Tom said. "No problem."

"So he's still coming to Bay City, right?" Wendy asked.

"Yes," Tom said. "He's coming. Now go call that Vasquez guy at the department of health. Ryan's got some info on these berries to share with him."

"You got it boss," Wendy said. With a curtsey, she went back to her desk to dial the department of health.

"Chippewa County Department of Public Health," a hurried receptionist said.

"Hello," Wendy said, "can I speak with Ernesto Vasquez, please?"

The receptionist hesitated, then said, "Hold, please."

While she waited, Wendy thought of the weekend getaway. Since speaking with Ryan at the casino, she was sure she was inching toward the moment when she would be able to share her true feelings with him. And he seemed like he was inching closer toward wanting to hear it.

"Hello, this is Jill Oswald," a young woman said.

"Hi," Wendy said. "I, uh, was holding for Ernesto Vasquez."

"Yes," Jill said. "I'm sorry. He is, uh, out of the office. I'm taking his calls."

"Oh, okay," Wendy said, absently leaning to her right and

scratching at her ankle. "Is there a better time to reach him, or, uh, maybe you can help, I don't know?"

"He's on a leave of absence. I'm handling his desk for the time being," Jill said. "What can I do for you?"

"Well, uh, I'm calling from Attorney Tom Hughes's office," Wendy said. She preferred working with plants and numbers. The adjustment to talking with people in a polite manner on a daily basis was challenging. "Mr. Hughes met with Mr. Vasquez yesterday regarding the HERDS outbreak, and he wanted to speak with him again—"

"Well," Jill said. "I'd be happy to speak with him."

"Thanks," Wendy said. "Let me put you on hold a second." Wendy buzzed Tom on the interoffice line.

"I've got a woman on the line from the health department," she said. "Apparently Mr. Vasquez is on a leave of absence, and this woman is taking his calls."

"That's strange," Tom said. "He seemed fairly gung-ho about the HERDS thing yesterday. Why would he take a leave of absence?"

"Would you like to talk to his replacement?" Wendy said.

"Sure. Put her through," Tom said. "Thanks."

Wendy transferred the call.

"Hello," Tom said. His official lawyer voice was a commanding presence in the small office. Wendy did not have to strain to eavesdrop on Tom's side of the conversation.

"So you're filling in for Mr. Vasquez?"

"Lucky you. He looked kind of busy yesterday."

"I hope he's all right?"

"Well, good. I'm glad to hear there's nothing wrong. I was really hoping to talk to him, because he was heading up the investigation."

"So, if you don't mind me asking, what happened to Mr. Vasquez?"

"Leave of absence, huh?" Tom said. "Why was that?"

Wendy shifted her focus to her work. She would be glad when the thesis defense was over. She was growing tired of school and of the new routine. She was also tired of waiting for lunch. A slice of pie from the diner sounded pretty good, but it was too early.

She leaned-over to scratch at her ankle again, then returned to her reading. Fifteen more minutes of work, she bargained with herself, and then pie as a reward. But after only ten minutes, she closed the book on organic pest control and went to the diner.

Tom finished his third read through of the Stiles' case file. He was as ready as he was going to get for the preliminary injunction hearing and was almost a full week ahead of schedule. It was a luxury having only one case to worry about.

He closed the file, dropped it in his out-basket, and returned to his notes from the conversation he'd had with Jill Oswald at the health department. She hadn't been clear on why Ernie was taking a leave of absence, but she seemed pretty insistent that Tom take Ernie's home telephone number. She wanted Ernie to speak with Ryan. Tom had no idea what was going on at the department of health, but it sounded like a pretty messy operation. It was already more than twenty-four hours since he had told Ernie the blackberries were responsible for the HERDS outbreak, and Tom hadn't heard any word the berry products already in circulation were being recalled.

He dialed Ernie's home number, hoping the sincere young man he had met with yesterday could shed some light on the situation. Vasquez answered on the third ring and didn't sound too happy about being at home, excluded from the HERDS investigation.

"Leave of absence?" Ernie laughed, after Tom told him the official explanation for his disappearance from the department of health. "No, I was suspended. Not long after I spoke with you yesterday. They said I violated standard operating procedure by not getting approval before talking to the press about the outbreak."

"You've got to be kidding me," Tom said, outraged. "Isn't that what you guys are supposed to be doing? Warning people?"

"That's the way I saw it," Ernie said. "And if I had it to do again, I'd do the same thing."

"You might want a good lawyer," Tom said. "I can put you in touch with someone, if you'd like."

"Sounds good to me," Ernie said. "I've called a couple of local attorneys this morning, but no one handles employment issues around here."

"The firm I'll send you to is in Detroit," Tom said, swiveling in his chair, his fingers dancing through his Rolodex. "They're very good. And if there's anything to your case, they'll help you. You got a pen?" Tom found Franklin Putnam's number and passed it on to Ernie. "Tell him Tom Hughes referred you," he said.

"Thanks."

"So this person at your office. Jill Oswald. She said I ought to contact you with this information I have, even though you weren't officially working on the case."

"What information is that, Mr. Hughes?" Ernie asked.

"On my case against GenAgra, I've got a scientist. An expert witness," Tom said. "He's done some testing on the genetically modified blackberries. Looking for a toxin. And he says he's found something."

"Really," Ernie said. "The department was nowhere near that far along in the process."

"Yeah," Tom said. "He's a good guy. Very smart. He wanted me to talk with you directly. That's why I was trying to reach you at the office today."

"I'd love to talk to him," Ernie said. "Maybe we can still get these things pulled from the market. If somebody doesn't do something, the department is going to take its sweet time investigating this."

Tom gave Ernie Ryan's phone number. "Call him right away," Tom said. "And I'm sorry to hear about your problem at work. That's not right, what they did to you."

"I'll be fine," Ernie said. "The truth will get out. One way or the other, it always does. I'm sorry about your wife, Mr. Hughes."

"Thanks," Tom said. He hoped Putnam could help the young man. The government needed more people like Vasquez, Tom thought, as he said good-bye to the sincere epidemiologist. People who tried to do the right thing despite the political consequences.

He heard the front office door open and got up to see who it was.

"I got lunch," Wendy said as he peeked out toward the entrance.

"I didn't even hear you leave," Tom said.

"You were on the phone," Wendy said, as she marched a

brown paper bag full of food into the library. "I didn't want to bother you, but I needed some lunch. Open-faced roast beef okay with you? Because I'm not parting with my pie."

"You're a junkie." Tom laughed. "Yeah, roast beef is good, thanks. What do I owe you?"

Tom reimbursed her for both lunches, and they ate at the conference table, as was becoming their fast routine. Today's lecture was not on law or personal history or pop culture. Wendy explained her fruitworm study in all its inane detail. A story for the ages with a cast of a thousand fruit worms. And at the end, Tom knew what he had known in the beginning. Wendy was a genius.

With the work done on his file, Tom decided to take a trip to the hospital to see Ike. More importantly, he wanted to spend some time prepping Kaye. With Ike out of action, Kaye would need to lay the factual groundwork for how GenAgra's berries got into Ike's field. The expert witnesses could provide all the theory, but someone had to put on the facts. Someone had to deny the genetically modified crops were somehow stolen or accidentally used. That required Ike. Or in Ike's absence, someone with the same personal knowledge about farm operations. And Kaye was the best they could do.

Tom found Kaye in Ike's room. She was pouring a yellowish oil out of a coffee cup and onto her husband's pasty thighs.

"Damn that's hot, woman," Ike yelped, before seeing Tom.

"What are you two doing?" Tom said. "I know they call this a private room, but you could at least close the draperies if you're going to—"

"You hush yourself, Tommy Hughes," Kaye said, smiling up at him as she massaged oil across Ike's exposed leg.

"Hello, Thomas," Ike said, sounding at least like an imitation of his old self. "How are you?"

"How are *you*?" Tom said.

"Well, I'd be better if this old bat would leave me alone," Ike dead-panned. He looked better, if only because someone had replaced his dentures.

"I'll not have it, Ike," Kaye said sternly. "You know you have to get better. So you're going to do what I tell you, or so help me."

Tom enjoyed their banter. Experts Tom had heard frequently talked of the importance of respectful communication in a marriage. But if the Stiles were any role model, and Tom thought they might be the best, the experts were mistaken. Ike and Kaye had playfully fought their way through more than fifty years. And they seemed to love every minute of it.

"You certainly sound a lot better," Tom said.

"Oh yeah," Ike said. "I'm going to be out of here in no time flat."

"What's Doctor Brown say?" Tom asked.

"Oh, he don't know no better," Ike said. "He's only treating me with half the stuff Kaye's using. So he only thinks I'll get well half as fast."

"Okay," Tom said. "What's that stuff?"

"Warm olive oil," Kaye said, moving to Ike's other leg.

"My ass," Ike said. "It's hot, Tommy. Don't you let her get you with it."

"Hush up," Kaye hissed. "It's warm, for the cramps."

"It does feel good," Ike said. "Once you get used to it."

"Garlic and milk to get his breathing right. Ginseng to get his energy back up," Kaye said. "He might make it to court on Tuesday, God willing."

"Well," Tom said. "I know Doctor Brown says no way. So we're going to have to get you ready to testify, Kaye. And then if Ike can make it, that'll be fine. But we'll still be ready."

"I'm going to be there." Ike coughed hard in his rush to get the words out.

"All right," Tom said.

Kaye finished rubbing Ike's legs, and moved immediately on to the preparation of ginseng tea.

"So what's going on with our case?" Ike said.

"We're ready to go," Tom said. "I've got Doctor Romanelli ready to testify about their genetic pollution in your fields. And we'll get either you or Kaye to talk about how you planted organic crops, and didn't use or steal their genetically altered varieties. And then I've got a patent lawyer lined up to argue some of the more technical issues. All in all, I think we're ready to lay out the truth."

"Doctor Brown says he thinks it might be the blackberries that made me sick," Ike said. "I'm going to burn them fields when I get out of here. I'll not be a party to putting someone else through this."

Tom wanted to tell his old friends about Claire's death and the link to the berries. He hated hiding things from them in any way. But Ike was still in the hospital, and he didn't need any encouragement to feel bad that a product from the Stiles' Family Berry Farm may have caused her death. Not yet.

"Yes," Tom said. "I've heard about the berries. Ryan has done some tests on them. He thinks that he's found a toxin in them that could be causing this. But no one knows anything for sure yet."

"I'm almost glad the judge issued that order to shut us down," Ike said. "Because them berries were close to being ready last week. I bet they are ready now. And I don't think I could forgive myself if I hurt someone."

"It's not you," Tom said, trying to comfort the farmer. "It's GenAgra, Ike. You didn't start this. And they should have known. You can't take the blame, old timer."

"I know," Ike said. "But I'd still feel bad. Hey, you wouldn't want to run by the house and bring me my tobacco, would you, boy?"

"Ike A. Stiles," Kaye said, handing him a cup of tea. "You almost died without a breath not five days ago. This is a good time to give up that filthy habit."

Ike grimaced. But he drank the tea, then settled himself on the bed and drifted into what seemed a comfortable sleep. Tom gave Kaye a hug and rubbed her back. They watched Ike. Breathing in. Breathing out. The sight of it made Tom tired. He had not rested well these past months, and he felt the weight of his weariness.

He got Kaye to go with him to the cafeteria for a cup of coffee and they ran through the questions he would ask her in court. When he was sure she could be an adequate substitute for Ike, he ended their session. He hugged and kissed her good-bye. He wanted the Stiles to live forever. They were the last human beings connecting him to Wabeno County. When they were gone, he would be alone, like a solitary tree in a blighted orchard. Nowhere to run from his loneliness. He let her go, left the hospital, and drove home. He thought of Claire and a gnawing emptiness. And what life awaited him when this case, and when the Stiles themselves, passed him by.

Chapter Thirteen

Bullard sat across from Dean Peter McPhee. A natural light
flooded the Zimmerman Center Restaurant. The Center, a
crown jewel at Michigan A&T University, had been built primarily
with funds donated by GenAgra CEO, Wes Zimmerman. So
Bullard felt right at home. The Center Restaurant was a hub in the
new world order, connecting academia with commerce. It was a
place where businessmen mixed easily with professors, mutually
enriching one another. Commoditizing ideas.

The background noise was a soothing blend of clinking
glasses, softly clanking silverware on ceramic plates, and hushed
conversations. Bay windows in the dining area invited patrons to
admire the green expanse of Michigan A&T's campus. As Bullard
looked from McPhee to his intern, he could see she was intoxicated
with the atmosphere.

"I'm afraid I don't understand," Bullard said, finishing a
bite of his salad. "This Romanelli character has ignored your
instructions. And there's no accountability?"

McPhee wiped his mouth with a linen napkin. "Professor
Romanelli is a rising star at this university," he said. "I've done

what I could to encourage him to act responsibly. Unfortunately, he's called my bluff. He doesn't intend to back down from this case. And there's little I can do to stop him."

Bullard leaned back in his chair and sighed. "Look around," he said, sweeping a hand as if introducing the Zimmerman Center. "Our partnership has brought an era of prosperity, Dean McPhee. Your university has thrived in a time when government funding has been cut back. GenAgra has profited from excellent research being done right here. At *our* facilities, Peter."

"Mr. Bullard," McPhee said. "We appreciate what GenAgra has done. I appreciate what Wes Zimmerman has done for this university. But there's nothing I can do. Ryan Romanelli hasn't violated any school policy. He's been an exemplary scholar and teacher and researcher. Perhaps GenAgra could benefit from the knowledge he is uncovering. Not only can I not punish him for his participation in the case against GenAgra, I can't credibly oppose his gaining tenure. Not in good conscience."

"Look," Bullard said, leaning forward and resting his flabby chin on his folded hands. "I'm not *asking* you to act on this. GenAgra is not *asking* you to act on this. Wes Zimmerman is not *asking* you to act on this. Our corporation and your university are going to be doing business for decades to come, Mr. McPhee. The real question is whether *you* are going to continue to be a part of that partnership as we move forward."

"Are you threatening me?" McPhee hissed, taking his eyes from Bullard and shooting an annoyed glance at the intern, whose lips were drawn to a fine line on her pale face.

"No." Bullard laughed politely, sitting back in his chair. "I'm encouraging you to continue your fine work on behalf of this partnership."

McPhee said nothing, but disgust oozed from him.

"I'm here to help today, Peter," Bullard said, taking a thin envelope from inside his jacket and placing it midway on the table. "It seems that one of Professor Romanelli's assistants is having some difficulties with the professor. This is her statement on the matter. Rather unfortunate for the poor young woman."

"How did you come across this?" McPhee said, not moving to take the envelope.

"I don't know the details." Bullard smiled. "But she applied for one of the highly regarded positions at the North Central Research Center. Do you know what students who do their training there make in their first year after graduate school, Peter? It's astounding. Someone she communicated with there felt strongly enough about what Professor Romanelli is doing to this poor girl to report this. I understand she is making a formal complaint to the university as we speak."

McPhee picked up the envelope and placed it in his own pocket. His face was shriveled like fruit withered on the vine.

"Thank you for lunch," Bullard said, standing. The intern rose a half-beat behind him. "I trust you will take care of our mutual problem."

McPhee said nothing, and Bullard sauntered out of the restaurant to a waiting limousine.

"That's hardball," the intern whispered, getting into the backseat ahead of Bullard.

"It's a dog-eat-dog world," Bullard said, squeezing in behind her and placing a hand on her thigh. "You have to decide whether you are going to eat or be eaten."

"Grand Rapids, sir?" the limo driver said, through the rolled-down glass partition. "WTLK?"

"Yes," Bullard said.

"That'll be about one hour, sir," the limo driver said before rolling up the glass.

"I can't believe you're going to be on *The Studs Nolan Show*," the intern said, her eyes sparkling. "I listened to that all the time back home before I came to D.C. My friends thought I was crazy, but he is so right about everything, you know."

"First rule in PR," Bullard said, lecturing his fawning scribe. "Never ignore the story. Good or bad, you've got to get out there and put it before the American public. And there's no better place to start than on his show."

Nolan's program was the fastest-growing conservative talk-radio show in the Midwest and was ranked number three nationally. He was becoming a star, mostly because he stayed on message and let the right people get their spin out unfiltered. If Nolan hadn't found his own niche in the market, someone like Bullard would have had to invent him as the perfect tool.

The intern continued blathering about her own proximity to a world she had always wanted to penetrate, as Bullard's greedy hands groped her in the privacy of the limousine. She was still an adequate substitute for his sexual desire toward Hannah Yale, and when she finally shut her mouth, Bullard was better able to concentrate on his fantasies of the most attractive lawyer he had ever seen.

Bullard was pleasantly surprised when Yale called on the cell and interrupted his afternoon tryst. "Hannah," he said, answering the phone while trying to disentangle himself from the semi-nude intern.

The intern took a nip out of his neck when he said the name, much to Bullard's annoyance.

"I got your message," Yale said.

"Yes, thanks for calling," Bullard said. "Listen. I'm on my way to do an interview for *The Studs Nolan Show*, so I can't really talk."

"Nolan, huh?" Yale said. "Impressive."

"Yeah. Getting some good press for our case, actually. But, I wanted to call," Bullard said, finally clear of the intern, who sulked in the corner of the limo. "I wanted to check your schedule. I'm flying into Detroit on Friday the first, and I wanted to make sure you're going to be available that weekend. There are some public relations items I want to go over with you, to put them in a legal context, so we're working in unison on this thing."

"Oh, yeah. I'll definitely be working that weekend," Yale said.

"Well, try to clear your calender," Bullard said. "Double your rate, or whatever, because there is a lot I want to cover to be ready for the Tuesday hearing."

"Will do, Mr. Bullard," Yale said.

"Call me Al." He laughed.

"Okay," Yale said. "Al. Right."

"Well, I have to run," Bullard said. "I'll talk to you Friday."

The intern sulked for the rest of the trip to Grand Rapids, and Bullard didn't bother trying to console her. She would need to develop a thick skin if she was going to be able to whore her way to the top in this racket. Bullard smiled to himself, looking out the smoked glass at the small city that sprung from the heartland. It looked clean. Steel and glass glinting skyward. He felt at home as the limo whisked him to Nolan's studio.

Nolan's assistant greeted them in the lobby, which was plush by radio standards. They were escorted to the studio where Bullard's intern was directed to a waiting room, and Bullard was led into the bowels of the operation: Nolan's broadcast booth. The live show was underway. Nolan's assistant showed Bullard to his seat.

"Up next, we've got a gentleman in the studio with us who really needs no introduction," Studs Nolan told radio listeners across the land. "He's a man who has been instrumental in building the policies that have helped shape this nation. His influence is felt in the White House, on Capitol Hill, and throughout the media. He's flown in from his offices in Washington, D.C., today, to speak with us here on *The Studs Nolan Show*. I told you we would have a special guest today, Nolanites. I'm excited to have a man of his stature joining us on the Superior Radio Network. We will meet him and take your calls, after we pay the bills with these commercial messages."

Nolan pushed his microphone aside and shook Bullard's hand. "We're clear for two minutes," he said. "Thanks for coming."

"Pleasure," Bullard said, noting that Nolan's face made it certain he would never cross-over into television.

"So, you're doing private consulting now?" Nolan said.

"That's right." Bullard nodded.

"And we're going to talk about a case you are handling with GenAgra against some of these goofy organic farmers?"

"That's about it," Bullard said. "These nuts would end the American dream if they could."

"All right," Nolan said. "It's an honor to meet you. I love your book. Though I'm not sure if you weren't borrowing on my ideas when you wrote it." Nolan laughed and chatted nervously, until the theme music led him back to the only place he was not generally annoying, Bullard thought. Talk radio.

"And we're back," Nolan said, welcoming the audience in a well-practiced tone—deep, rich, and devoid of intelligence. Bullard had a hard time pairing the voice with the slight man before him. "This should be a treat for you Nolanites out there. As you know, we frequently talk about enviro-fascists on this show. How they sip their lattes, and drive their Priuses, and condemn honest, hard-working Americans who don't have the luxury of worrying about whether some lab rat is getting, quote unquote, humane treatment during a scientific study.

"Well, today I have with me in the studio a very intelligent man. A close advisor to the president and vice president of the United States. I would go so far as to say if it were not due to this man's understanding of the core values we all share as Americans, and his tireless efforts at fighting these lunatics on the left, I don't think the president would have been elected last year. He's here with me today to talk a little bit about his involvement in a case with these enviro-fascists. One you might not have heard about yet. One that is still flying under the radar of the liberal media. But we'll talk about it here first. I am pleased to welcome Al Bullard, president and CEO of The Bullard Group, Washington, D.C.'s premiere public relations firm. Welcome, Mr. Bullard, to *The Studs Nolan Show*."

"Glad to be here," Bullard said. "Thanks for having me on the show. I don't get a chance to listen to as much talk-radio as I'd like, but my staff keeps me up to date, and they tell me I'm a Nolanite at heart, even if I don't know it yet."

"As any thinking person is." Nolan clucked with faux laughter. "Thank you, sir. Now I want to talk about this case you're involved in. It is a case in federal court, as I understand it. Not being covered by the liberal media, just yet. But I think we can help get it the attention it deserves. It's the case of GenAgra versus..."

"GenAgra versus the Stiles' Berry Farm," Bullard said.

"That's right, I lost that name somewhere in my notes here," Nolan said. "So this farm is being sued by GenAgra, and the suit tells us they have stolen a plant developed by GenAgra—GenAgra has spent millions of dollars and several years of research, if I understand it correctly—and this organic farmer has essentially stolen their work. And is now going to profit from his theft—if a federal suit had not been filed to stop him. Tell us about your involvement."

"Well that's right, Studs," Bullard said, taking Nolan's

national stage. An opportunity to pre-program an entire audience of Americans so they would understand how to believe the story as it unfolded before them. "You've stated it pretty well. You've got GenAgra. A great company. Involved in feeding the world, really. They spend millions. Hundreds of millions, really, on research. To make American farming the best in the world. The most productive. The safest. And this farmer comes along and basically steals their product. And the products we are talking about are plants. Corn and blackberries in this case. Products that are self-replicating, really. So this farmer is pirating these plants, which he can then turn around and mass produce and sell. Both as food and as plant stock. And if it is not stopped, well, then companies like GenAgra will not be able to continue to produce these miracle plants—because that's what they are—and we are all going to pay for it."

"So now, how did you come to be involved in this case?" Nolan asked.

"Well, my firm does both government and private sector consulting. As you so kindly said, we spent a good deal of our time last year helping the president get elected," Bullard said. "Because it was an important election. Your audience knows that better than anyone. It was an election about the safety of our nation. But once we accomplished that mission, I wanted to set my sights on getting back to the private sector. To help America move forward and compete in the global marketplace. And this opportunity presented itself to work with GenAgra. So I felt really lucky. Because I've been fairly successful. I don't just take clients for money anymore. I get to work on things I truly believe in. And that is just great."

"So, like a true patriot," Nolan said. "A citizen-leader, if you will. Like George Washington. Or Thomas Jefferson. Those folks didn't spend all their time in Washington running the government. They were citizens. Patriots. Farmers, really. And they worked. Private sector, folks. So that is kind of what you've done here. You've spent a good deal of time serving your country—nobly, I might add. But now you are moving back to where the world really works. And helping private sector companies."

"Exactly, Studs," Bullard said. The guy was really good.

"I'm helping GenAgra get their story out there. About the good things that they are doing. And, that is what GenAgra is all about. Putting people to work. Feeding America and the world. Being a world leader in global trade. And they are making these products. Enhanced foods. They are making corn so farmers can spray less pesticides and herbicides. They are making crops that are drought-resistant and have higher yields. And they are making products that will make America healthier. The new Health-Ease Blackberry, for example, which has been approved for sale to Americans by the USDA just last week. That product will help revolutionize health in this country. It will help Americans who want to lose weight. And as we all know, obesity is becoming a problem in this country."

"You know," Nolan said, "you've touched on a point that bothers me here. These enviro-fascists are out there. Organic farmers. Anti-free trade. I got word of a story yesterday, not picked up by the national media because they're cowards. But just the other day a bunch of these ecoterrorists were out again, vandalizing property at a GenAgra facility. Digging up plants on private property. And what are they saying? They're saying these foods are genetically modified and that they're bad. Well, I have had about all the nonsense I can take from these people. These foods are perfectly safe. They've been approved by every government agency there is—talk about over-regulation. And not only are they safe, but they're actually helping the environment. They're cutting down on the use of pesticides. They're cutting down on the use of herbicides. And, they're—you know—this is what gets me, too. Without these foods brilliant people invent, at companies like GenAgra, and others. Without these foods, the average American would be spending three times as much on his grocery bill every week. How would all you Nolanites like that? 'What did you spend on food this week, honey?' 'Oh, Studs, it cost me four hundred and fifty dollars. But I won't have to go out again until next week.' And I read the other day, that, in fact, more people get sick eating organic food, than have ever been sickened eating these wonderful products.

"Now, you've got me off on a rant here. Because these enviro-fascists are driving me insane. With their lies. With their hyperbole.

With their rhetoric. But you and GenAgra are fighting back. And I want to talk to you more about your case.

"We're going to pick this up in a moment," Nolan said. "We'll hear more from Al Bullard about his case. And we'll take your calls. After we pay the bills with these commercial messages."

Bullard smiled. He couldn't have written a better script than Nolan's impromptu rant. If the herd in the heartland didn't understand the rightness of GenAgra's case after a few weeks of a media pounding like this, then there was no controlling them.

Tom considered staying home on Thursday. He wasn't sure if he could take two more office days waiting for the hearing. At least there would be distractions over the weekend. But waiting around in the office was going to drive him mad. After a long breakfast and an hour reading the paper, he realized the boredom of home might be even worse. So he went to the office late. Wendy looked happy to see him.

"Phone has been ringing off the hook," she said. The bags under her eyes had deepened since Tom first noticed them two days before.

"You feeling okay?" he said. "You look exhausted. Maybe you should take the rest of the day off. Heck, even tomorrow."

"No, I'm fine. I've been up late working on this thing," Wendy said, holding up a tattered stack of loose papers—her thesis in progress.

"All right," Tom said. "It's been so slow around here, I thought you might like the time off."

"Slow," Wendy said, handing him telephone messages. "You've got bunch of people to call back, mister."

"There's three." Tom laughed, looking at the phone messages. "Man, I'd hate to see you in a real office. We used to get three messages every five minutes around here."

"I'm not talking ancient history," Wendy said. "Three is a lot for us. Here and now. And I've been telling them all you'd be in shortly, and that you'd call them right back. And you're not going to make a liar out of me."

"I don't know if I mentioned this," Tom said, "but it is a job requirement for a legal secretary that you be able to lie to people calling on the phone."

"You're not paying me enough to compromise my principles," Wendy shot back. "Now get."

Tom went to his office, chuckling at the strange ideals of his new secretary. He thumbed through his messages. The first was from a salesman pushing research materials. Tom crumpled it and shot it into a nearby wastebasket. The second was from Felix Hrdina, the patent lawyer he had hired to handle the technical aspects of the case. And the last was from A.J. McCoy at Michigan Genetics. He needed to speak with both men.

He called Hrdina back first, wanting to get the worst of the conversations over with quickly. Tom had learned next to nothing about patent law in his first two decades of practice. And with his recent exposure on this case, he was glad he hadn't learned it before. Hrdina droned on about technical details Tom did not understand and legal principles that sounded foreign. When he couldn't take another second, Tom politely cut him off.

"A couple of things," Tom said. "First, give it to me in English, because I'm not following the technicalities. That's why I'm paying you. What are our chances of convincing the judge they have no likely success on the merits under their patent claim?"

"From my review of the file," Hrdina said after a brief pause, "not much. It looks like a clear case of patent infringement to me. The argument you want me to make, about this blackberry being toxic and polluting, and how that is a misuse of the patent, is not really supported in the law. Not that I've seen. It's really a novel claim. Not a bad one, considering you've got no other leg to stand on. Just unusual."

"Okay," Tom said, "so what am I paying you for, exactly?"

"I can't change the facts or the law," Hrdina said defensively. "I'll argue the novel issue the best I can, but you should recognize your case on the patent infringement claim is exceedingly weak."

"Okay," Tom said. "Just try not to be defeatist in court, all right?"

"Never," Hrdina said.

Tom had never heard a more monotonous attorney in his life. Putting Hrdina in front of a jury would be like subjecting them to sensory deprivation. "Second thing," he said. "Do you ever take time off? Because you sound kind of wound up in the details of this thing."

"It is a fascinating area of practice," Hrdina said.

"I know," Tom said, trying hard to avoid the sarcasm that was slipping out. "That's what I'm thinking, handling this case. But I'm wondering if you get much time off?"

"When I need to, sure," Hrdina said.

"Well," Tom said, "I wanted to invite you to a kind of rolling party this weekend. If you'd like to come. I'm having everyone involved in the case up to Bay City for the holiday weekend. Luxury hotel. Big fireworks festival. All expenses paid. Close to the courthouse where we're appearing on Tuesday. Food. Drink. The works. So we can relax and enjoy. And maybe work a little if we want to. I'd love it if you could come."

"Well," Hrdina said hesitantly. "I was going to spend a good part of the weekend in the office. But since it's a holiday, I guess I could get away. There'll be space to work there, right?"

"Oh, I'm sure," Tom said. "Bring your laptop. Have a ball. It's a great weekend show, too."

"What day?"

"Check in's on Saturday afternoon. I can have my secretary fax you directions, if you want to come."

"That's very nice," Hrdina said, perhaps tearing up, Tom thought. He imagined for a moment the poor, technical lawyer had never been invited anywhere in his life. "I'll check my schedule. Maybe we'll see you there."

"Great," Tom said.

He hung up the phone. "Wendy," he hollered through the office. "Fax the directions for this weekend to Felix Hrdina. His number's in the file."

"What have I told you about yelling?" she yelled.

"Just this once," he yelled back. "I've got *so* many people to call back. I need your help." He crumpled the Hrdina message and tossed it toward the wastebasket, watching with great disappointment as his shot rimmed out. Wouldn't have been like that in his days as a shooting guard at Perkins High, he thought, shaking his head. Tom dialed A.J. McCoy.

"Just returning his call," Tom said to a receptionist.

A moment later A.J. was on the phone. He sounded sharp and direct, and Tom had no worry he would be a good witness to cover the DNA testing of the crops.

"I wanted to touch base with you about this subpoena I received," A.J. said.

"Standard procedure that we send them out," Tom said. "Nothing to worry about. It covers us with the court."

"So we are still on for Tuesday at nine, right?" A.J. said.

"That's right," Tom said. "The federal courthouse in Bay City. Do you need directions?"

Wendy walked into the office head down, reading a sheaf of legal papers. She laid the papers in his in-box with a perplexed look.

"No," A.J. said. "I can find it. I'll meet you there."

"Okay," Tom said.

"I wanted to call to make sure you didn't have any questions about my testimony," A.J. said. "I testify in so many cases now, it's kind of like old hat to me. But sometimes the lawyers want to go over some things in advance."

"I've gone over the report you sent for our file," Tom said. "It's very comprehensive. I haven't taken much DNA testimony in the past, but I feel pretty comfortable with it, given your summary."

"Yeah," A.J. said. "Lots of lawyers tell me that my summary works well for them."

"So, I don't really have any other questions," Tom said. "It's a preliminary injunction hearing, so no jury. I'm not too worried about it. I'm sure we'll get by just fine."

"Okay," A.J. said.

"I don't know if Ryan has mentioned this to you," Tom said, "but I've invited everyone working on this case up to Bay City for the holiday weekend. Kind of a working party. We've got some nice hotel rooms. And there's a Fourth of July festival up there that's nice, if you'd like to come along."

"Already have plans," A.J. said. "But thanks."

"All right," Tom said. "I guess we'll see you up there, Tuesday."

"Sounds good," A.J. said.

Tom hung up and immediately reached for the papers Wendy

had placed in his box. The papers were from the GenAgra case. He read the title on the cover page:

Plaintiff's Motion for Summary Disposition

He paged through the meticulously drafted motion. Several clerks, associates, and partners at the law firm of Barnes & Honeycutt had apparently spent hours upon hours crafting this inspired work of legal art, Tom thought derisively.

The motion was GenAgra's attempt to score the equivalent of a first-round knockout. The motion laid out the precise facts and legal groundwork that required the judge to not only throw out Tom's counterclaim, but to declare GenAgra's own patent infringement case was unassailable. The motion was to be heard on the first Monday in August. And irrespective of what happened at the preliminary injunction hearing next week, if GenAgra's motion was successful, the case would be over. The Stiles would officially be declared the loser without the benefit of a trial. Nothing left but a possible appeal.

Historically, motions for summary disposition were rarely granted. But over the course of Tom's career, as the courts had become more conservative and more dominated by business interests, these motions were now routinely filed by insurance companies and big corporations. And routinely granted. In Tom's view, these motions represented the slow erosion of the time-honored American tradition of a jury trial for righting civil wrongs. And given that Judge Fuller had already granted a dubious temporary restraining order, Tom was not eager to face the judge on a summary disposition motion. But they would cross that bridge when they came to it. Or better yet, Tom would have someone else think about crossing that bridge.

"Wendy," Tom yelled. "I need you to fax something to Nell."

Ernie sat in a booth at Fast Burger, a folded USA Today held close to his face. Bright sunshine flooded through a window to his left, reflecting off his newspaper. Through his dark sunglasses, the sunlight registered as a dull brown. He was dressed in his best American casual. A black t-shirt tucked into faded jeans. Ernie felt like a spy waiting for his contact. He liked the feeling.

He sipped coffee and glanced furtively from the newspaper to the entrance, waiting for Jill. As a lunchtime rush started to press down upon the Fast Burger staff, he saw her maroon mini-van pull into the parking lot. She entered the restaurant and Ernie caught her eye.

"You getting some lunch?" Jill said, approaching his table. Her lack of candor shattered Ernie's delusions of espionage.

"If someone sees you having lunch with me, you're liable to be suspended, too, you know," Ernie said, inviting Jill to speak more softly.

"It's a free country," Jill said. "And I don't give a damn anyway. Screw them. You getting some lunch?"

"No," Ernie said. "I'm sticking to coffee."

"I gotta get something," Jill said, and she joined the throng of working-class sheep waiting for their noon meals.

Ernie read an article about Mad Cow Disease, and when Jill returned with a Fast Burger and fries, he wondered about the safety of the meat patty she was about to devour. "You're not going to eat that," he said.

"I sure am," Jill said. "Go get a salad if you want one. You can tell me what I'm going to eat after you're a single mom for a week, knucklehead. I haven't got time to pack a lunch every day."

Ernie laughed. He missed seeing Jill at work. "So how's it going there?"

"Fucking zoo," Jill said, mashing a chunk of burger into her mouth. "Underwood's come up to oversee things. But at least the CDC's been brought in."

"They should've been brought in right away." Ernie shook his head.

"Yeah, well," Jill said. "They got an alert out nationwide as soon as they were notified. Cases have popped up everywhere. Like two hundred and thirty-something—under an expanded definition of the disease. Lots of them aren't as serious as what we've seen."

"Really?" He was surprised the cases were that widespread. He had started to view the outbreak as tied to the GenAgra research facility. It was funny what could be turned up if things were investigated properly. He shook is head at the thought of Underwood's obstinance. "How spread out?"

"Most of them still in our region," Jill said, using the multiple fry method to polish off her side dish. "I think we're over two hundred clustered in mid-Michigan. Then there's a cluster in upstate New York. And one in Oregon. And a trickle in a few other states. Ohio, Indiana, California."

"Wow," Ernie said, trying to wrap his mind around the consequences of a nationwide threat.

"The CDC kept your name," Jill said. "HERDS is the official name of this bad boy."

"Great," Ernie said sarcastically. "I'm honored. I wish Underwood would have listened to us two weeks ago. Maybe we could have saved some people."

"Yeah," Jill said. "That guy is a tool."

"So are they following up on the Hg-Blackberry?" Ernie asked.

"Well," Jill said, "if you want to call it that. The legal department is looking at how to procure samples, then the forensics department will take a week to test it. But because it looks national, I don't think they are concentrating solely on the blackberry right now. Too many other possible causes. I don't know. That is CDC info. Need-to-know basis kind of shit."

Ernie gave the idea of other possible causes much thought. But it was the blackberry that stuck in his craw. There was something about the certainty in Tom Hughes's voice, as he relayed the story of his wife's death. It was a hunch. And Ernie knew hunches were not good science, but Tom had convinced him.

"I have to get on the road in a few," Ernie said. "I'm meeting this plant biologist down at A&T. He says he has already found the toxin in the blackberry."

"How long's he been working on it?" Jill said.

"I don't know. A few days," Ernie said. "But he's moving a little faster than you guys."

"Hey, don't lump me with them," Jill said, finishing her lunch in minutes flat. "I've got to get back, too. Underwood's cut lunches to thirty minutes. Asshole."

"Well," Ernie said. "Keep me in the loop."

"You keep me in the loop." Jill smiled.

Ernie gave his friend a hug and headed for his meeting with Ryan. A&T was only a short drive south on US-27. Since he no longer had the luxury of a government car to avoid speeding tickets, Ernie set his cruise at five over and got to Ryan's office in forty minutes. Parking on the campus was brutal, even though it was summer. Ernie couldn't imagine finding a spot when all the students were in town. At least not without a road-rage incident.

Once parked, he walked to the third floor of Dryden Hall and found a young man in a lab coat looking over reports in the back office of a laboratory.

"I'm looking for a Professor Romanelli," Ernie said.

"Hi," the young man said. "That's me. Call me Ryan, please."

Ernie was surprised by the professor's youthful appearance.

"You must be Mr. Vasquez," Ryan said, walking to Ernie and shaking his hand.

"Yes," Ernie said.

"Thanks for coming down," Ryan said. "Let me get the chromatographs." He spun around in his chair and searched a mountain of loose paper on a desk at the back of the office. Finding the large graphs he was looking for, he returned to his main desk and laid them before Ernie. "This is the chromatograph of a regular berry," Ryan said, pointing to one chart. "And this is the chromatograph of the Hg-Blackberry. Look at these spikes. B and C."

"That's a pretty clear signature," Ernie said.

"Yeah," Ryan said. "I can't believe the guys at GenAgra would miss something like this if they were testing their own berries. The B spike is definitely the molecule they sought to introduce into the blackberry from the *Hoodia gordonii*. P-57 it's called. But this other spike, Peak C, is some unknown molecule. I'd say a toxin."

Ernie thought for a moment. It was impossible for him to conceive that any scientist would allow a genetically engineered product anywhere near human consumption if faced with data indicating an unknown toxin might be present. No one would overlook test results like these.

"Maybe it's something that happened after their own testing,"

Ernie said, working out a theory. "Like a post-production mutation or something."

"That's not impossible," Ryan said. "But highly unlikely. Unknown toxins don't just spring up in subsequent generations like this. I don't buy it."

"Well," Ernie said, "I'm no plant biologist, I was only thinking out loud."

"So what do we do with these results?" Ryan said. "You're the public health expert."

"Well, I was." Ernie laughed. "Tom didn't tell you? I was suspended on Tuesday." He laid out the story to Ryan's disbelief.

"That's typical of our government," Ryan said. "Anything to protect these damn corporations. To hell with the people getting sick."

"Well," Ernie said, "I don't know if I would go that far. I know a lot of people in government, myself included, who would never intentionally let something like this happen."

"It doesn't look like that from where I stand," Ryan said. "So do you have anybody at the department of health who you can get these results to, ASAP, so we can stop this thing?"

"I'm told that they don't want to narrow it down to the blackberry," Ernie said. "There are a number of cases appearing nationwide now, completely unconnected, since the CDC has put out a bulletin on the disease."

"Well, this ought to stop them from that speculation," Ryan said, holding up the chromatograph of the Hg-Blackberry.

"Yeah," Ernie said. "Maybe. And maybe not. I think there may be too much resistance in my old office. But maybe there's another way to get the word out."

Ernie laid out his plan for Ryan, and the young professor seemed to agree. Sometimes bureaucrats needed some prodding.

Ryan liked the plan. He didn't really trust the press, but they served a purpose. And he trusted the government even less—all the way down to the bureaucratic level of the health department. Ernie seemed like a smart man, and Ryan had no reason not to trust his instincts. So if Ernie didn't think the health department would act quickly to keep the blackberry away from people, Ryan had no basis to second guess him. Getting the information to Ernie's reporter seemed like the right call. It would almost certainly free the government to do its job.

"You take these then," Ryan said to Ernie, folding up the chromatographs. "Get them to your contact quick. The sooner we get this information out, the sooner they'll have to pull the plug on these berries."

"Excellent work, Professor," Ernie said. "I'll get on it."

"Good," Ryan said, rising from his chair to walk Ernie out of the lab.

"I'm still troubled by the fact that we're getting other cases unrelated to the blackberry though," Ernie said, pausing in the lab. "How do we explain that?"

"I can't explain it," Ryan said. "Could be these people were exposed to the Hg-Blackberry in some way you can't identify yet. Or it could be there are other causes. Or it could be this toxin I've identified isn't the culprit you're after. But you know what?"

Ernie shrugged.

"It isn't a bad thing you'll be getting these berries off the market. This is a real toxin," Ryan said, pointing to the chromatograph. "And it could cause damage, even if it turns out not to be the cause of your little epidemic."

"Thanks, Professor," Ernie said, slapping the graphs on his hand.

"Keep me posted," Ryan said, walking Ernie to the door.

"Will do." With a wave and a smile, the epidemiologist was gone.

Ryan returned to his office. His supposedly soft summer schedule had not turned into the easy workload he was expecting. There was the case against GenAgra. And the funk he felt in Wendy's absence. But these distractions weren't the primary cause of his overwork. He was always a man who knew how to set distractions aside. He had an uncanny ability to focus on the task at hand.

Ryan's summer had been busy for one simple reason. Nancy Freeman. Wendy had practically run the lab since she had come on board as Ryan's grad assistant. But Freeman was far less competent. She didn't understand the basics, so it was frequently easier for Ryan to do her tasks than to take the time to explain them to her. And if her lack of competence wasn't bad enough, her attendance record was the kicker. Today she had apparently decided to blow-off work altogether. No call. No notice. And no answer when Ryan had tried to reach her. She just didn't show—something that no grad assistant had ever done in his seven years as a professor. So Ryan fumed as he was left to read through all the background research she was supposed to be doing for an upcoming paper. He missed Wendy in more ways than one. And he couldn't wait for the weekend when they would finally get a chance to talk to one another.

Ryan was pulled from his thoughts by the sight of an unfamiliar man in a gray security uniform walking toward him. As he looked up, he saw Dean McPhee was accompanying the security guard.

"Ryan," McPhee said, the lines on his small leathery face drooping toward the ground. McPhee turned to the security guard, "Could you wait in the hallway, please. I need a moment with the professor."

The security guard gave a militaristic nod and headed for the hallway.

"Ryan," McPhee said again, walking toward the back office.

"What's with the rent-a-cop?" He had seen enough of McPhee for the year. If the dean kept on bothering him, Ryan would have to skip the department Christmas party.

"I'm afraid I'm here on rather unpleasant business, my friend," McPhee said.

"What kind of business requires a security guard, Peter?" Ryan said. "My God, what are we coming to at this university."

"I know, I know," McPhee said. "It's overkill. I wouldn't have brought him if it wasn't required by university rules."

"What?" Ryan said.

"I'm here to ask you to leave, Ryan," McPhee said. "You are going to be placed on administrative leave by the university, pending an investigation."

"What?" Ryan said, stunned. He collapsed into his chair, his hand making a controlled bounce off the front panel of his dictaphone. "An investigation of what?"

"It's all here in this letter," McPhee said, taking an envelope from his coat pocket and patting it in his own hand.

"What?" Ryan said. "Let me see that."

"Not yet," McPhee said. "I'm going to try to be a friend here, Ryan. I've already tried once, and it's gone beyond me now. But I'm going to stick my neck out and try to clear this up. If you'll listen for a minute."

"Clear what up?" Ryan said. "I don't even know what the— what are you talking about, Peter?"

"There's been a formal complaint filed against you for sexual harassment. Now, I'm—"

"For what?" Ryan raised his voice, indignant. It was the most laughable thing he had ever heard.

"Sexual harassment," McPhee said. Ryan tried to let the words sink into his brain. "Now, I'm reasonably sure this can still be resolved. A formal complaint has been filed, and I mean, there will be some process followed because of it. But if you'll follow my advice, I think I can probably get this dropped. Perhaps resolved with you attending sensitivity training or something."

"I've never—" Ryan started, his voice angry. "Who is it I supposedly harassed?"

"That's not really important right now," McPhee said, his voice strained. "You'll know soon enough. I have to give you this letter, and then I have to close your lab. Your papers. Everything. Sealed. That's what the security is for. But my point is, will you let me help you?"

"I think you've helped me enough," Ryan spat the words out. "This is all about GenAgra, isn't it?" McPhee's silence answered the question sufficiently for Ryan. But he asked again for the record. "It's all about them, isn't it?" Ryan demanded.

"What do you think, Ryan?"

"Who did I supposedly harass?" Ryan said.

"Ryan, if you would stop being so obstinate, there's a chance to save your career, here," McPhee said. Ryan found the pleading tone in McPhee's voice odd. Almost sincere. "Just stop what you are doing. Don't go to court next week. You don't need to be an expert witness. You are a very gifted man, Ryan. Talented. And you will go far here. I know it. But you're destroying yourself. Just walk away from that case. Take a couple of days off. I'm sure

I can talk to the administration—maybe even the girl. This doesn't have to be the end."

"You know this is bull—" Ryan stopped himself. "Baloney."

"I know there's been a formal complaint filed," McPhee said. "And I also know *they* are calling the shots on almost everything around this place. You know how much money they're pumping in, Ryan. It's part of the new atmosphere in academia. A partnership with business. That's just the way it is. And you're going to have to learn to work within it—if you want to continue to be a professor and a researcher. If you want to make tenure."

Ryan put his head down. "Can you give me a minute," Ryan said. He didn't need a minute. He didn't need a second. It was all he could do to keep from lunging across the table and choking McPhee. The old man was the poster child of corruption. Perhaps not active corruption, Ryan thought, but the insidious corruption of inaction. A corruption that happens over years of failing to uphold a sharp line between those things that are right and those things that are wrong.

"Certainly," McPhee said, handing Ryan the sealed letter. "I'll go get security. But please. Do something for yourself, Ryan. You'll only get to make this decision once." McPhee turned and walked slowly out of the office, toward the hallway.

As soon as McPhee was gone, Ryan popped the small cassette tape out of his dictaphone. He rose and stuffed the tape in his front pocket. Then, unsure about whether the guard would search him for property, Ryan clandestinely fished the tape from his pocket and stuffed it into his underwear. He straightened his waistline, looking to see if the dean had returned. He hoped the little tape, now resting uncomfortably against him, had recorded the conversation well enough.

Ryan looked around the office. There was only one other thing he wanted. He opened his desk drawer and pulled out a yellowed news photo, cut from an old campus paper. He and Wendy smiled in the photograph, celebrating a grant they had received to study fruit worms. Ryan remembered his smile in the photo and no one could ever smile with such feeling over funding for the study of insect larvae. He stuffed the photo in his pant pocket as McPhee re-entered the office with the security guard in tow.

"So?" McPhee said.

Ryan collected himself. "You, GenAgra, and this goddamned university can stuff it right up your ass." He marched past McPhee. Ryan knew he wanted one other thing as he passed the dean. He wanted a photograph of the old bastard's face. The look of shock was priceless. But Ryan knew he'd at least have the memory.

"Sir," the security guard said. "It's my job to secure the premises, your papers and effects. May I see what you were putting in your pocket?"

Ryan pulled out the old photograph of himself and Wendy and showed it to the security guard, registering as much disgust as he could with body language alone.

"Oh, sorry, sir," the guard said, in humbled retreat.

The dean's faith that Ryan would compromise himself must have been great, Ryan thought, because the elder man's face was still slack-jawed as Ryan turned to walk out of the lab.

Walking to his car, the sun beating down on him, Ryan stepped gingerly, dealing with the uncomfortable positioning of the cassette tape. As he walked, he opened the letter from the university. His accuser was a young woman he had never touched, barely knew, and who had not bothered to show up to work today. He never thought ill of grad students in general, but Nancy Freeman had earned his contempt.

Chapter Fourteen

om liked Nell's opinion about the motion for summary judgment even less than he liked his own.

"It's what I've been telling you from the beginning," Nell said over the phone. "You never stood a chance in this case. I don't even think the preliminary injunction hearing matters, Tom. Come August first, this judge—or whatever judge replaces him—is going to grant their motion and dump your case."

"I'm paying you to represent *our* side in this, Nell," Tom said. But he knew Nell was only giving him a straight answer.

"Oh, I'll come up with a response for all of it," Nell said. "Don't you worry. I just don't think anyone's going to buy it. Your claim is presenting a question of first impression that no trial court is going to be eager to put before a jury. And their case is cut-and-dried. No matter how screwed up it is that they've patented the damn plant and that it's capable of boundless self-propagation. The law allows it."

"Well, try to get some response put together in the next couple of days, if you can," Tom said. "I'll read it and sign it over the weekend. You're still coming, right?"

"Oh, I'll be there," Nell said. "Do you know how I celebrate the Fourth in Alpena?"

"Nope," Tom said.

"There is a family of four on my block," Nell said. "The young girl lights off a package of sparklers, and her older brother tries to hold firecrackers for as long as he can before tossing them. All while the parents watch in delight. Great show. Best bet this year is that the kid is going to be brave enough to lose a couple of fingers. I'll hate to miss it."

"Well, I don't know if we can top that," he said, "but we'll try."

"See you there, Tom,"

"All right," Tom said. "And thanks for the help."

"No problem."

The motions for summary judgment troubled him even more, given the second opinion. If Tom didn't secure a less biased judge, he figured his case would be history in little more than a month. But for the present, he would have to put those thoughts aside and concentrate on the preliminary injunction hearing.

As he sat thinking about his case, Tom could hear Wendy taking a call. At first her voice was too low for him to make out much of the conversation. He could not figure who was calling. But after a very short time, her voice became a thunderstorm.

"Sexual harassment!" Wendy yelled. "With her!"

There was a pause before she continued screaming at the caller. Tom was confused. His mind raced over possibilities, in some strange calculus. It must have been a call from a new client. Someone had found his number in the book. They were looking to file a sexual harassment claim. But why on earth would Wendy be screaming at a potential client? Even if Tom really wasn't interested in taking new cases, she was far too composed—far too smart to behave like that.

He got up from his desk and moved quickly to the reception area, trying to ease her anger with hand signals. Her voice lowered, but she continued spitting hatred into the phone. Tom mouthed the words, "Who is it?" in her face.

"Ryan," she said loudly. "He needs to talk to you."

Tom was thoroughly confused. Wendy handed him the

receiver, got up, and walked out of the office. Into the street.

"Ryan," Tom said. "What's going on? What's got Wendy all in a tiff?"

Tom listened as Ryan recounted his suspension.

"So is there any truth to it?" Tom said, when Ryan had gotten the story out.

"None at all," Ryan said. "This is all GenAgra. And I think I have the dean admitting that on tape."

"On tape?" Tom said.

"Yeah," Ryan said. "As soon as he told me what was going on, I started my dictaphone so I would have a record of it. And—I haven't had a chance to listen to it yet—but I know the jackass admitted it was GenAgra who was behind it."

"You're saying that GenAgra has set you up with a sexual harassment claim?" Tom said.

"You don't think they're capable, Mr. Hughes?" Ryan said. "They aren't playing games. There are billions of dollars at stake. And they're going to take out whoever's in their way."

"God, Doc," Tom said. "I don't want any of this. You should've just quit the case. I'd find someone else. Is it too late to talk to him?"

"I'm not quitting the case," Ryan said angrily. "This is how they bully everyone, everywhere. And their bullying is not going to change the truth. Not this time. At least not as far as I'm concerned."

Tom listened the professor's bravado. It made him feel guilty. Tom would have taken almost any opportunity to avoid the case in the beginning, because it was the practical thing to do. And here was a mere witness who was ready to give up his career to defend the rights of an old farmer he had just met. The abuses by GenAgra made Tom's blood boil, and he was a little more confident with Ryan on his side.

"You're a good scientist, Doc," Tom said. "A good man. And if you got that dumb son-of-a-gun on tape saying that he fired you because of GenAgra, then you've got a better case than Ike Stiles ever thought of having."

"You think?" Ryan said.

"I'll get you in touch with a friend who handles employment

issues," Tom said. "He'll know for sure. We'll fight the bastards."

"Oh, I'm doing that," Ryan said.

"So they locked down your office, huh?" Tom said.

"Yeah," Ryan said. "Everything except this cassette."

"All your materials for trial?" Tom said.

"All sitting right on my desk," Ryan said. "I couldn't leave with anything. But I did get those toxin reports to that guy from the health department. Vasquez."

"Well," Tom said. "That's something."

"I don't need anything for the hearing," Ryan said. "I could testify blindfolded."

"So what's with Wendy?" Tom asked.

"I'm not sure," Ryan said. "I think she's a little jealous of this new grad assistant—the one they are using to make this claim against me. So she must think the worst of me, I guess."

"Don't you believe that for a minute," Tom said. "Between you and me, I think Wendy likes you a lot more than you would ever believe."

"You do?" Ryan said.

"Yes, I do," Tom said. "You might be right about the jealousy, though. But I'll explain this to her."

"You will?" Ryan said.

"Sure," Tom said. "And thanks, Doc. I'm sorry they did this to you. But I'm glad you are on our team."

"Nothing I wouldn't do for anyone," Ryan said. "Those people. They have no respect for anything. Not for life. Not for people. They have to be stopped."

"You still on for the weekend?" Tom said.

"Wouldn't miss it," Ryan said.

"Good," Tom said. "See you Saturday, then."

"Okay, bye," Ryan said.

Tom hung up the phone and went to look for Wendy. He had a pretty good idea where she went. He walked next door to the Milton Diner. At the counter, she sat devouring a slice of apple pie.

"Mind if I join you?" Tom said, sitting down on the stool next to her.

Wendy mumbled something incoherent through a mouthful of apples, crust and glaze.

"What are you having?" the waitress said.

"I'm all set, Marnie," Tom said.

"Did I overreact a little?" Wendy said, swallowing.

"Just a little."

"Am I fired?"

"Fired?" Tom said. "Who would help me get through this working weekend if you were fired? We're going to court on Tuesday. We're a team."

Wendy smiled at him.

"He didn't do anything," Tom said. "You know that, don't you?"

"He didn't?" Wendy said. "They can't just suspend a guy for nothing."

"Sure they can," Tom said. "GenAgra's suing Ike for nothing, right? Just because someone makes a claim doesn't make it true."

"I've had a feeling about that girl all along," Wendy said. "I knew there was something. She's the one he hired to replace me, you know?"

"He's got the dean on tape," Tom said. "This is a total set-up. GenAgra was trying to run him off the case. Now our expert is a suspended professor who stands accused of sexual harassment. It's all a big game to them."

"Really?" Wendy said.

"Really," Tom said. "You've got a big weekend ahead of you."

"You think?"

"Yeah," Tom reassured her. "Everything is going to be all right."

When she finished her pie, they went back to the office.

"You're going home early," Tom said. "Pack up and get out of here."

"I'm okay," Wendy said. "I promise. No more outbursts."

"Look," Tom said. "You're taking the afternoon off."

"You are a tough boss." Wendy smiled. "I am kind of tired."

"Good," Tom said. "Get some rest. Don't work on your thesis. Don't think about this place. And we're closed tomorrow, too.

You're not coming in."

"Are you sure?" Wendy said, picking up her purse.

"Yes," Tom said. "It will be a good rest for us both. Just be ready to go Saturday. We're meeting here at one."

"All right. I'll see you then," Wendy said, heading for the door. She stopped in the waiting room. "I'm sorry for the blow-up, Tom. That wasn't like me. It's Ryan. And I've been tired."

"It's all right," Tom said, with a warm smile.

Wendy left, and Tom headed for his office. He kicked his shoes off and propped his feet on the desk. He was more amused by Wendy's outburst than anything. Working with women. He had forgotten the pleasure. He breathed deep and thought about taking Friday off. A day on Watson Lake. He enjoyed the motion of the boat in the water. He enjoyed the silence, save for the natural humming of the planet around him. After Claire was gone, he had been lonely. But now, after only a month back on the job, a day alone on the lake sounded good.

Tom plopped his feet on the floor, pulled closer to the desk, and grabbed the Stiles file. If he was going to spend Friday on the lake, he needed to make sure things were ready to go for the weekend. He opened the file and paged through it, performing a mental checklist.

The state of the case was poor. His star witness, Professor Romanelli, would have a new introduction to the court. Instead of distinguished and esteemed professor, he would be branded disgraced and suspended professor. Not a bonus in terms of credibility. His most crucial fact witness, Ike, lay in a hospital bed. His best treatment seemed to be herbal tea and hot-oil massages. It was unlikely the court would even get to hear his firsthand account of how GenAgra's crops had blighted his fields through no fault of his own. Instead Tom would be forced to rely on the testimony of Kaye, and she would be vulnerable when it came time for cross-examination. She was as involved in operations as any farm wife, but she was not with Ike in the fields day by day. And this lack of personal knowledge could be exploited by a deft attorney.

The witnesses' shortcomings were not the worst of it. The technical side of the patent case was in shambles. His own legal experts had predicted failure. And his office was hemorrhaging money.

If the state of the case wasn't bad enough, almost every person involved was being punished. Ryan's career was in jeopardy. Ernie had been removed from office. GenAgra had its corporate boot on Ike's throat, exactly like they did over the rest of the population of planet Earth. Tom was just more aware of it in this case. And he wished he could return to a state of blissful ignorance.

Despite it all, Tom still felt hope. He still had a voice. If people like Ryan and Ernie could stand and fight for what was right, so could he. They might lose the battle. But Tom believed that humanity would prevail over corporate interests in the long war.

He closed his case file. He felt ready to fish and think and float on a small lake. The little part of the planet that brought him peace.

As soon as he left Professor Romanelli's office, Ernie called Sam Oster at WHIP. The receptionist said he was busy, and Ernie left a voice mail asking Oster to return his call. Ernie needed to get the story onto the WHIP news no later than four o'clock if his plan was going to work. Unable to reach Oster on the phone, he made a beeline to the WHIP newsroom. On the way, he called Jill.

"Can you talk?" Ernie said.

"Yeah, why?" Jill said.

"I need your help."

"All right."

"Director Jones is up there every afternoon, right?" Ernie said.

"Yeah," Jill said. "She's already here. It's good to see her riding Underwood a little."

"Make sure you get her by a radio at four o'clock."

"What?" Jill said. "You've looked at the toxicology reports? It's the berry?"

"There is definitely a toxin in those Hg-Blackberries," Ernie said. "With the information I've got, I would have to say it is the probable cause."

"What about all the cases outside of this area—where no blackberries are involved," Jill said.

"I don't have all the answers yet, Jill," he said, "but these reports are enough to stop the public from eating these berries."

"So, four o'clock?" Jill said. "You got your radio guy to broadcast another story?"

"I'm hoping," Ernie said. "Just get Director Jones by a radio, whatever it takes. 106.5 FM. I want this to happen today. It's been too long already."

"All right, Vasquez," she said. "But you're going to owe me, when you get re-hired and promoted. I want donuts. Every Friday. And I want a big fat raise. Do you know how much piano lessons cost?"

"You got it," Ernie said.

He pressed the accelerator a little harder, hoping the traffic gods would spare him a patrol officer. He tried Oster again, but only got voice mail. He hoped his newsman was in the office. His mind wandered as the miles slipped by. He had been suspended, but he was still an epidemiologist. His pay was even continued. It made Ernie wonder what was important about a job. Was it something people did for money? Because even if he weren't getting paid, he knew he would still be on his way to Milton to try to stop a possible epidemic. Did he work for the state, or did he work for his fellow man? It was clear to him he was driven by the need to help people. To try to protect them. The world was a scary place. There were no ultimate protections from anything. But Ernie knew his mission in life was to try to help. And in this knowledge, he took pride. He would be an epidemiologist somewhere, whatever the outcome of his suspension process, until his reputation was so tarnished by trying to do the right thing that no one would have him.

As he neared Wabeno County, he saw the signs advertising the wholesome Stiles' Berry Farm. In a little more than an hour, people seeing those signs would not think of wholesome fruit. Instead, they would recoil slightly and wonder when they had last eaten a blackberry. At least if Ernie's plan succeeded. It was too bad for the organic farmer. But the berry was in the stream of commerce now, and it had to be stopped.

Ernie exited onto Milton Road and found the station a half-mile to the east. It was a small brick building abutting a large FM antennae that stretched skyward. Ernie pulled into a tiny parking lot, found a space, and jogged toward the front doors, chromatographs in hand.

Greeted by the front receptionist, Ernie insisted on seeing Oster. The receptionist calmly pointed Ernie to the waiting room. Surrounded by fake plants and magazines, Ernie tapped his toes on the laminate floor. Minutes passed like a slow summer breeze, until Oster finally greeted Ernie in the lobby.

"Mr. Vasquez," Oster said, shaking Ernie's hand.

"I've got something you need to see," Ernie said. "Information that might save lives if you can get it to the public fast."

Oster's face went from a plastic smile to vague frown, his moustache visibly weighed down by the gravity of Ernie's tone. He led Ernie into his news office and offered him a seat. Ernie took it.

"The story you ran on Monday," Ernie said, wasting no time. "I was suspended because of it."

Oster said nothing, but his moustache drooped even farther, threatening to slide from his face.

"It's nothing you did," Ernie said. "Just a turf battle."

"I'm sorry," Oster said. "That was an important story, I thought."

"Well, the one I'm about to give you is even more important," Ernie said. "These are chromatographs that have been done by a professor at Michigan A&T."

Oster grabbed a pad of paper from his desktop and started taking notes.

"This one is for a regular blackberry from the Stiles' farm," Ernie said, pointing to one of the graphs. "And this one is for the genetically modified blackberries that have migrated over from the NCRC."

Oster looked up, confusion apparent on his face.

"The NCRC. GenAgra's North Central Research Center," Ernie said, and Oster's confusion dissolved. The reporter became a note taking frenzy. "You see these spikes here. These are proteins that are present in the Hg—in the genetically modified blackberries. And this spike in particular—this is the toxin that is likely causing HERDS."

Oster processed for a moment, his eyes lighting up, then

narrowing. "So why are you bringing this to me?" he asked. "Shouldn't your office be putting out an official statement?"

"Here's the problem," Ernie said. "I was suspended for coming to you because of some internal power struggle. My boss, for whatever reason—let me be charitable, and call it an abundance of caution—has not wanted to believe HERDS even exists. So he's hardly ready to tell the world that not only does it exist, but we have identified a probable cause. I would take these tests to him and give him that opportunity, but I'm worried he'll bury it."

"Okay," Oster said, understanding showing on his face. The radio journalist may not have been overly quick, Ernie thought, but his heart was definitely in the right place.

Once convinced of the graph's authenticity, Oster wanted to run with the story. Ernie sat with him for twenty minutes more, helping him craft an accurate news release, before heading back to Mt. Pleasant. On the ride back, at 4:00 p.m. sharp, Sam Oster broke the news to the mid-Michigan listening audience.

"Mystery Illness Solved? I'm Sam Oster, and this is your WHIP newsbreak at the top of the hour," the radio reporter said. "The deadly mystery illness, HERDS, that has sickened dozens across mid-Michigan, may be caused by consumption of a genetically modified blackberry. This according to an employee at the Michigan Department of Health. Tests performed by Michigan A&T plant biologist, Dr. Ryan Romanelli, show the genetically modified blackberry, known as the Hg-Blackberry, produces a previously unknown toxin. Toxins such as those produced by the Hg-Blackberry have in the past caused illnesses similar to HERDS, according to WHIP's source with the Michigan Department of Health.

"This is a breaking news story. The Michigan Department of Health has not yet issued an official statement. Please stay tuned to WHIP news for further updates. We'll pass along all information on this breaking story, as it becomes available."

"In other news…"

Ernie smiled. The ball was squarely in the department's court now. He hoped Jill had gotten the director in front of the radio. Even more, he hoped Underwood was near enough to hear. He imagined the pinched look on Underwood's face, when his cell phone rang.

"Hello," he answered.

"Ernie," Jill said.

"Hey, did you get her to listen?"

"Um, Director Jones would like to speak with you," Jill said, followed by the muffled sounds of a phone being jostled.

"Mr. Vasquez?" Director Jones said.

"Yes, ma'am," Ernie said, unsure of what to expect next.

"This is Director Jones," she said. "Ernie, *you're* the employee at the Michigan Department of Health who told that radio announcer we've found the cause of HERDS, aren't you?"

"I'm not sure if I should answer that," Ernie said.

"Are you the source of that story or not, Vasquez?" Director Jones said, uncharacteristically cross. "Jill tells me you might know something about it."

"I heard the story," Ernie said, deciding to hedge his bets. "I know Professor Romanelli."

"So you are the source," Jones said.

"I didn't say that," Ernie said.

"But you have access to the test results showing a toxin?" Jones said.

"Right here next to me," Ernie said.

"I need to see them, Vasquez," Jones said. "If you heard the news report I heard—oh, who am I kidding? You made the report. And you know darn well we're going to have to take action. So I want you to get your butt in here ASAP and help me deal with the shit-storm you unleashed."

"It's going to take me a while," Ernie said. "I'm driving back from Milton."

"Uh-huh," Jones said. "Just happens that's where the news story broke, huh?"

"Strange coincidence," Ernie said.

"Uh-huh," Jones said. "Well, it's probably better you get here later anyway. It'll give me time to calm Underwood down after I give him the news. I'll try to shuffle his butt out of the office. The two of you are like cats and dogs, I swear."

"Does this mean I am un-suspended, Director Jones?" Ernie asked.

"No," Jones said flatly. "You are still in a world of hurt. You've pissed off someone at the top. I'm still trying to piece it together myself. But someone in the governor's office wants your ass for breaking this story. And this little stunt isn't going to help matters."

"It's got to be GenAgra, ma'am," Ernie said. "They're the ones who are going to get pummeled by this story."

"Yes, I suppose that could be," Jones said. "The CDC is sure trying not to step on their toes. GenAgra won't even cooperate with us to get some of their blackberries down to our lab. Something about proprietary secrets and whatnot. We might actually have to go to court to get samples."

Ernie was fairly certain that Director Jones was in his corner, and he disliked deceiving her. "I did leak the story," he said. "Because I wasn't sure what would happen if I brought the chromatographs to the department. I thought if I made it public first, it would put more pressure on Underwood to act."

"That was good thinking," Director Jones said. "There's no doubt we are going to have to act fast now. I'm shutting these blackberries down first thing in the morning. You get here now, and we'll go over those chromatographs—figure out our strategy."

"Thank you," Ernie said.

"Thank you, Mr. Vasquez," Jones said. "Not many people in this department would have given this kind of effort. And I'm pretty sure none of them would do a damn thing if they were on paid leave."

Ernie stepped on the gas. Surely the traffic gods would not impede someone on whom fate smiled so kindly. Ten minutes later, he was parked on the side of the road. His charming smile did nothing to convince the state trooper a warning would be sufficient. Ernie took his ticket and drove cautiously to meet Director Jones, now uncertain where fate smiled.

The GenAgra jet had Bullard to the Detroit Metropolitan Airport ahead of schedule on Friday morning. The intern waited for him with a limo on the tarmac. The only thing wrong with the picture was the pruned look on the intern's face. It was not the ass-kissing look that had drawn him to her a week before. It had morphed into a serious, bitter face. Bullard worried she had taken their sleeping together to mean she had risen above her bottom-feeder rank in the corporate order.

"I've got some bad news, Mr. Bullard," she said, and now he recognized her look as one of nausea. It was the look of a messenger bearing bad tidings.

"Tell me in the limo," Bullard said. "I'd like to make it to Barnes & Honeycutt by noon."

The driver held the door, and they were whisked away from the airport.

"The Michigan Department of Health held a press conference today. They are pinning this HERDS outbreak on the Hg-Blackberry," the intern said, her eyes averted from direct contact.

"Health-Ease Blackberry," Bullard corrected her. "What did they say?"

"The Health-Ease Blackberry is producing an unknown toxin that may be associated with the disease," the intern said. "They said their testing was not conclusive, but they ordered that all Hg—I mean, Health-Ease Blackberries or products made from the blackberries be prohibited from sale or distribution."

"Has the story hit the wire?"

"Yes, sir," the intern said, her head bent low in shame. "It's global."

"Shit!" Bullard said. "When did this happen?"

"Press conference was at nine," the intern said. "Wire service just picked it up. I—"

"Why didn't you call me?" Bullard said.

"I tried, sir," the intern said. "Your cell was out of service."

Fucking planes, Bullard thought. Time was of the essence in dealing with any public relations crisis. Though he had never thrown a punch in combat, he thought public relations was very much like what he had heard about a fist fighting: hit first and hit hard. There was little to be gained from further interrogation of the intern. Perhaps he had over-evaluated her PR instincts. A better person on the ground might have avoided this fiasco.

"Their testing was inconclusive?" Bullard said, his mind setting up a perimeter around the potential public relations disaster as he went.

"Yes, sir," she said. "They were acting out of an abundance of caution, pending further testing. That was their take."

"There's nothing wrong with the Health-Ease Blackberry," Bullard said strongly. "I've been eating it myself for a couple of weeks. I've never felt better."

"Yes, sir," the intern agreed. In her current state of terror, she was nearly useless.

"The USDA gave it their stamp of approval," Bullard said. "The best safety standards in the world."

"Yes, sir," the intern said.

Bullard had his first line of defense. The Michigan Department of Health was full of shit. The Health-Ease Blackberry had met the highest standards of safety and testing. Next, he needed to shore up his flank. He flipped open his cell phone and got his secretary on the line.

"Get me Wes Zimmerman," Bullard said. "I'll hold for as long as it takes. I need to speak with him immediately. It's urgent. And while I'm talking to Zimmerman, you track down my father. Tell him he needs to hold. I've got to speak with him."

"Yes, Mr. Bullard," she said, and promptly put him on hold. He listened to classical Muzak for a full minute before his secretary returned. "I'll put you through to Mr. Zimmerman, sir." And with a click, the distance between Detroit and Chicago was eliminated.

"How are you, Wes?" Bullard said gregariously.

"I'm in the middle of a shit-storm," Zimmerman said, as if he were talking to a copy boy. "How's your morning going, sport?"

"I called to tell you about a distraction that has popped up, here," Bullard said, still hoping he had gotten to Zimmerman first.

"A distraction?" Zimmerman said. "That's what you call it in Washington when a fucking state agency announces one of your products is potentially deadly and your stock price falls ten percent!"

"No, Mr. Zimmerman," Bullard said, sidestepping. "I just touched down in Detroit and got the news. You were my first call. I wanted to assure you this is a bump in the road. I've already got a strategy ready to roll out. This should be old news by tomorrow, and I'm sure—"

"I should fucking hope so," Zimmerman raved. "I've seen the expense account you've been submitting to me. I expected I was paying for a first-class ride on this little cruise. I didn't expect to get shafted by a podunk little bureaucrat in a third-rate state."

"Consider the bump ironed out, sir," Bullard said. "Give me twenty-four hours."

"I sure as hell hope so," Zimmerman said, then let loose with a grunting sigh. "Do you know where I'm going to be next month, Mr. Bullard?"

Bullard fell silent in the face of Zimmerman's tirade. The old man needed a kick in the balls to get a grip on himself.

"I'm going to be in Brussels," Zimmerman said, raging on. "Biggest talks GenAgra has ever had. We are within an inch of cracking the European resistance to our current product line. Do you know how much money that means? If Europe caves and starts accepting GMOs, like America does, we are talking billions. Corn. Soy. Canola. You name it. And that's not going to get fucked up because some piss-ant holds a press conference. Do we understand each other?"

"Yes, sir," Bullard said, breathing deeply to suppress his own anger. He would eviscerate Zimmerman in due time, after this battle was over. All things in due time.

"Good," Zimmerman said. "I need to talk with my board on Wednesday. I want to hear from you no later than Tuesday night. Sooner, if you can't clear this shit up pronto."

Bullard hung up and dialed his secretary.

"I still haven't gotten your father, sir. Do you want to hold?" she said.

"Yes," Bullard said, and was again forced to listen to Vivaldi on his cell phone. The limo pulled up to the Renaissance Center as he waited on the phone. He looked up at two columns of steel and glass that rose high into the Detroit sky. The offices of Barnes & Honeycutt were tucked somewhere inside the giant structure. Traveling without an assistant, and too busy to do it himself, he ordered the intern to retrieve Hannah Yale and her baggage. The intern hustled out of the limo, apparently intent on redeeming herself for breaking the bad news. Bullard watched as she disappeared into the monolithic building.

Shortly after Vivaldi had been ruined, the Muzak set about destroying Mozart. Until his secretary mercifully patched him through to his father.

"Sir," Bullard said, sweating through his suit in the air-conditioned backseat of the limo. "You're getting harder to reach."

"It's summer, son," Bullard's father said. The old man was the most well-connected rancher in America. He had known the Vice President since before compassionate conservatism was cool. And while Bullard believed his own achievements were gained through his own talents, his father's connections were part of the equation. "Me and Elsie are going to skip out of town early and head for the ranch." Elsie was wife number four. The wives changed in approximately decade-long intervals, to the best Bullard could calculate. The old man had lived the American dream.

"Dad, I'm in a spot," Bullard said. "I'm going to need some help." He explained the mess that had been created by the Michigan Department of Health. And the havoc it was playing with GenAgra's stock.

"Holy Christ," Bullard's father said. "Food scares will shock the market. I imagine old Wes is fit to be tied."

"An understatement," Bullard reported.

"I should probably give him a call."

"It couldn't hurt," Bullard said. "But so long as I fix the problem, I think he'll get his nose bent back into shape."

"All right," his father said. "Let me spend some time on the phone this afternoon. It's going to be tough—Friday you know—but we'll get something rolling. The power of the federal government. We ought to be able to make those locals dance."

"Thanks, Dad," Bullard said.

"No problem. Chin up," his father said, then hung up the phone.

Bullard hated to rely on the old geezer. It was like showing weakness. But tough times called for tough measures. And his father never failed him.

Ten minutes after she left, the intern returned with Hanna Yale in tow. Bullard practically salivated over the lawyer as she walked to the limo. The intern struggled with Yale's bags in the lawyer's wake. The driver was out of the car in good time to attend to Yale and her luggage.

"Hannah." Bullard smiled warmly, moving over to make just enough room for the lawyer.

"Hi," she said. "So where are we off to on this mystery trip? I've been dying to find out."

The intern walked around to the other side of the limo, and the driver eventually got there to open the door for her.

"Uh-uh," Bullard said, turning to the intern. "I want you to take a cab back to the airport. Rent a car and get back up to Milton. I need you to be my eyes and ears on the ground while we fight this thing out." Bullard expected hurt to flash in the intern's young eyes, but the emotion was clearly anger. Things did not look like they would end well for her.

"Yes, sir," she murmured, as she backed out of the limo.

"Detriot Yacht Club," Bullard said to the driver.

"Yes, sir," the limo driver said.

"Yacht club?" Hannah said. "Now we're talking."

Bullard watched the intern's dark stare out of the corner of his eye as they pulled away. They rolled on, and she was out of sight. And she had never truly occupied any significant part of his mind. He happily turned his attention to Yale. Blackberry crisis or no, this was going to be a pleasure cruise.

Chapter Fifteen

Tom took his boat out on Watson Lake at sunrise and fished all day. He caught his dinner early. A twelve-inch largemouth that would have fed both him and Claire. He released two others, and when the fish calmed down under the noon sun, so did Tom. He laid down his rod, ate sandwiches from the cooler, and drank beer. He read from a tattered copy of John Steinbeck's *Travels with Charley*, admiring the great author's indomitable spirit. As the sun started its descent, Tom moved the boat near the shoreline, searching for the crafty bass hiding among the reeds. He lost a few lures, caught no clever fish, and gave up at dusk. He drove home happy. Tom fried his fresh catch, steamed asparagus, and ate in pure silence. He drank more beer, until his sun-drenched body demanded sleep.

He woke late Saturday recharged. He showered, packed his things, and met Wendy at the office at 1:00 p.m. for their weekend trip. She was there ahead of him, leaning against her car, her bag beside her. He saw an eagerness in her eyes. She was clearly ready for an eventful weekend.

"You're looking chipper," he said, getting out of his car and popping the trunk.

"Amazing what a couple of days off will do," Wendy said. "You got some sun."

"Took the boat out," Tom said, walking around to grab Wendy's suitcase. He heaved it into the trunk, next to his own bag and a large cooler. "I gotta grab some stuff out of the office."

He unlocked the office, found an old box-like briefcase in a back closet and loaded it with everything he might need in court on Tuesday. The file, pens, paper and rules of court. Wendy paced the sidewalk in front, waiting.

"Okay, let's hit it." He tossed the briefcase in the trunk and started for the highway, stopping only at the Super Foods store on the way out of town to fill his cooler with party essentials.

The trip was shorter to Tom, since he had driven it only a few weeks before. His mind grasped the passing exit signs like landmarks, breaking the journey into small chunks of highway that were devoured in bites. Wendy fretted about Ryan and the weekend to come. Tom laughed and smiled and said little. He had done enough. This weekend was, in a way, his present to Wendy. She had her opportunity to finally connect with Ryan. Tom didn't know the outcome, but he was pleased to play his small part.

As they neared their destination, a crush of tourists made for heavy traffic. Minivans, cars, and trucks battled to enter the small town to celebrate the nation's independence. It was a warlike festival, recreating the rockets and bombs of America's infancy. A country born in war, aged in war, and dying in war. He drove carefully through the traffic toward the downtown and the Double Tree Hotel.

Crossing the bridge over the Saginaw River, the swollen population of the town was on display. Thousands milled under a hot sun. Kiddie carnivals. Live music. Softball games. Boat tours. Helicopter rides. People marching up and down the boardwalk along the river. Families staking out seating on green lawns, hours before the first fireworks would explode. Northern rednecks tailgating in the back of open truck beds, parked among an ocean of vehicles. Retirees sipping beverages under the canopies of their RVs. Children running and shooting each other with massive water guns, manufactured in lands not celebrating liberty. Police officers on bikes and in cars and on foot. Blocking and directing traffic. Shepherding the flock toward a safe and painless celebration.

Traffic stalled on the bridge, and Tom was able to look upon the scene below for a time. He was at once nostalgic for the summer celebrations of his youth and appalled by the wretched excess of his countrymen. All things a carnival.

Across the bridge, he followed a sign for hotel parking. He found a space in the crowded lot. Nearby a maze of orange security fences turned the waterfront into a series of gates and walkways for the milling herds. Together he and Wendy lugged their bags and supplies to a waiting bell hop at the front door, and Tom checked in.

They had three adjacent rooms on the third floor, all overlooking the water and the evening's festivities. Tom was expecting to arrive early enough to set out some food and drink for a reception, but Ryan had beaten them there. Apparently Wendy wasn't the only one eager about the weekend.

"This place is great," Ryan said, emerging from the middle room. "I hope it's all right, I took this room. I can move if you want."

"You're fine," Tom said. "I'm going to take this one here. Wendy, we'll put you and Nell down at that end, okay?"

"Sounds good," Wendy said.

The bellman delivered their luggage as they talked in the hallway and Tom tipped him generously. Wendy took her bag to get settled in, and Ryan followed Tom.

"That was great yesterday about the blackberries, huh?" Ryan said, helping Tom lay out a smorgasbord of deli food from the cooler.

"What about them?" Tom said. "I was out on the boat all day."

"You didn't hear?" Ryan said. "The press conference?"

"No, what?" Tom said.

"Ernie got my reports to that radio guy up by you," Ryan said. "They did a story on the toxins I found in the Hg-Blackberry. And Ernie got the Department of Health to issue a recall yesterday. I can't believe you missed it."

"I don't get much news on the lake," Tom said. "That's kind

of the beauty of it. But that's great. You guys really lit a fire under them, huh?"

"Yeah," Ryan said. "I hope you don't mind, but I invited Ernie to tag along this weekend. He wasn't doing anything, and I figured he could have my bed if he needs it. He's got some great insider knowledge, and I thought he could help us prepare."

"No," Tom said, wishing he'd have thought of it himself. "A.J.'s not coming until Tuesday, so Ernie can use that bed. No problem."

Tom cracked open two icy beers, handed one to Ryan, and walked over to survey the mass of humanity from the hotel window. Wendy came in a few minutes later with Nell.

"So this is party headquarters?" Nell said, walking over and giving Tom a hug.

"I guess so," Tom said. "Welcome. Glad you could make it."

Ernie Vasquez and Felix Hrdina found their way to the room in rapid succession, and with the gathering complete, Tom made the formal introductions. Tongues were loosened by drinks, and spirits lifted by stories from Ryan and Ernie about how they had combined to expose GenAgra's dangerous product.

Tom treated the small company to dinner at the hotel restaurant. More drinks heightened their euphoria. They were a small team, united against a giant, but in a moment of group intoxication, Tom was sure that they each individually believed they could win. After dinner, the group was sobered by a walk in the late afternoon heat. Amongst a growing crowd, they found a spot near a brick wall, close to an open-air stage. They listened to blaring rock-and-roll acts, one after another. Nell and Wendy danced to the cover tunes, with Ernie joining in on songs that appealed to him. Tom kept company with the less rhythmic men, holding up the brick wall with their backs, talking law and politics and business and war. Tom knew he would have joined the dancing, had his lovely wife been with him. He could imagine her graceful movements, luring him clumsily off the wall. But he couldn't dance with a memory.

As darkness approached, the group headed back for the air conditioned room and their bird's-eye view of the fireworks. Beer ran smoothly down Tom's throat. The day ran together in his buzzing mind. It was a mixture of pleasant victory and hope and good feeling. He was warmed by the intoxicants, but more by the group of strangers drawn around him. They were all good, different people. Pulled together in common cause. And for a time they had helped him forget Claire's absence.

Tom looked around the room as his new friends jockeyed for position at the bay window, the darkness almost complete. The first stars punctured a clear and blackened sky. He was pleased with the atmosphere he had created. He wiggled himself next to Wendy and pulled his chair close to the window, sitting to watch the show.

The conversations that had run throughout the afternoon died away slowly, in anticipation of the fireworks to come. Soundless, Tom saw a ripple ascending in the night sky. He followed its ethereal path high into the air. It exploded in a gold umbrella, silent through the hotel window, spreading out to subdued cheering from the landscape below them. One after another the fireworks mushroomed before them. Red, white, and blue. Green and gold. Their own "oohs" and "ahhs" and appreciative commentary provided the only soundtrack, punctuated by the rare thud and cheer strong enough to penetrate the glass barrier that kept the hotel room safe from reality. The explosions built in climactic peaks, and fell away, until a final gluttonous orgy of pyrotechnics lit the night sky, now stained with drifting smoke.

Tom felt the sting of a tear in his eye and was thankful the lights were out. It was not a tear for his horribly misguided country, blinded by a warlike patriotism. It was not a tear for a system run amok, where good people were ground up on unbalanced playing fields by giant corporate enemies. It was a tear of understanding.

Tom had not known the truth about why he scheduled this weekend retreat. But, sitting in a roomful of new friends, watching the show, it came to him like a splash of cold water. He and Claire had sat in a nearby room at the same hotel only a year before. And though he had been aware of this fact, he had failed to grasp the trip he had planned under the guise of a working weekend was his own futile attempt to recreate a moment that was gone, never to return. He was stung by this truth and felt lonely, though surrounded by friends.

"Good show, Tom," Wendy said, beside him. "You were right.

They do put on a good show here."

A chorus of thanks praised him, and before he had a chance to sulk in his own pain, someone turned on the lights. Tom wiped his eyes quickly and saw to another round of drinks. Below them, Tom watched the crowd disperse *en masse*, as if guided by an unseen shepherd. Wendy walked toward him and put a hand on his shoulder.

She leaned closed to Tom's ear. "We're going to take a walk," she whispered. Tom said nothing but smiled as she and Ryan slipped out of the room together.

Ernie, the diligent civil servant in exile, had drunk himself into an early stupor. His ability to track conversation was noticeably off. His eyes were glazed. And Tom laughed as he guided the young epidemiologist to a comfortable bed.

With Ernie sleeping, the party was down to three. Nell was fawning over Felix Hrdina. A nickel-and-dime practitioner from Alpena and a brilliant-but-boring patent lawyer from metro-Detroit. Tom said nothing but watched them with the same interest he would have given a Discovery Channel documentary on the mating rituals of a strange species in the Amazon rainforest. Tom had to cover his amusement as he imagined the potential offspring from the bizarre pairing. He thought of trying to stop them for the good of humanity but quickly chastised himself as a jerk. He had no right. "Let no man put asunder," a preacher boomed in his own drunken head, and Tom laughed out loud. Fortunately, Nell and Hrdina were too engrossed to notice him. Nell excused herself on the pretense of fatigue, and predictably, Hrdina grew tired only minutes later, leaving Tom with only Ernie's snoring for company.

Ryan and Wendy slipped out of the hotel lobby and into the dispersing crowd. For the entire day, and perhaps for as long as he had known her, Ryan had been trying to find time alone with Wendy. Time not dictated by their academic relationship. Time not infringed upon by others. They cut across the crowd toward the river, fighting a steady stream of people leaving the fireworks display. They crossed a wide grassy embankment sloping down toward the water. The grass was trampled and litter covered the ground.

The silence between them raged. Ryan felt that if he did not speak soon, he would pass a point from where he and Wendy might never speak again. "That was really great," he blurted out the first random thought that came into his mind.

"Yeah," Wendy said. "I'm so glad Tom invited us."

Tom again. Since she had left, every time he had seen her, it was always about Tom. Even here, alone on a beautiful night, it was Tom.

"Is there anything..." Ryan said, and stopped.

"What?" Wendy asked. They climbed up a steep slope near a bridge abutment, and joined a trail of people crossing the river.

"Do you like Tom?" Ryan said. "I mean, is there something between the two of you?"

"What?" Wendy said. "No. I mean, I like him. He's great. But no. There's nothing."

They walked along, up the arch of the drawbridge. Over the water, a cool wind kicked up.

"Why do you ask?" Wendy said.

"I don't know." Wendy was struggling to keep up with his pace, and Ryan had to slow his stride considerably.

"I'm sorry for yelling at you the other day," Wendy said. "I should have known better than to think, you know, about them firing you."

"Suspended," Ryan said. "Yeah. You know me. I'd never. The only time I ever thought about touching Nancy Freeman was to choke her for not getting anything done in the lab. She was absolutely worthless."

"Yeah," Wendy said, "Tom told me you guys talked after I blew up. I'm really sorry. I just..."

"What?" They reached the down slope of the span and Ryan had to lean back to slow his pace going downhill.

"I don't know," Wendy said. "I mean, I completely believe you."

"Thanks," Ryan said.

"I know you would never," Wendy said. "That's all. I was being stupid."

They walked under the west abutment of the bridge, on

a boardwalk that ran along the edge of the river. "See that pier up there?" Ryan pointed upstream, a half-mile down, where the boardwalk jutted at a right angle toward the center of the black water.

"Yeah," Wendy said.

"Want to walk up that way?" Ryan asked.

"Sure."

They walked along, Ryan looking over the wooden rail at the river. It softly reflected yellow street lamps and white moonlight at him, like a Monet. The crowd had thinned, but cars and people still struggled to get away in knots of congestion. Wendy paused at intervals, scraping her left shoe against her right ankle.

"Stone in your shoe?" Ryan said.

"No," Wendy said. "Bug bite, I think. Right on the ankle."

"Oh," Ryan said. "Worst place."

"Yeah."

After a long, mostly silent stroll, they turned onto the pier. It jutted two hundred feet into the river and was crowded with pedestrians. Two dozen people. And Ryan wanted to be near none of them. He wanted her to himself so he might finally tell her how he felt.

Halfway out, Wendy slowed considerably. "Do you mind if we stop," she said, pointing toward an empty bench near the wooden railing.

A gaggle of teenagers clowned nearby, braying loudly about a world they surely didn't understand. Ignorance was truly bliss. "No," Ryan said, lying. He wanted to be anywhere on the planet but around the teenagers. "That sounds good."

They sat down and together stared up the river. Wendy leaned down to scratch her bug bite, and when she sat back up, Ryan turned to look at her. Under the soft amber lamplight, she was a dream. He had missed seeing her face every day. Its angular perfection. But she looked tired now, and Ryan was again guilty for letting her go. She could have stayed in his lab. She could have worked on her thesis from there. There would be no false sexual harassment claim to deal with. Life would be as it was. And that would be good.

But there would have been nothing driving him to this moment, where he was certain he needed to tell her the secret he held in his heart. Whether she shared his passion or not was no longer the question. Ryan needed to say it.

One of the teenagers had broken from his pack and approached. He looked like a seagull about to accost a fast food patron for a french fry. "You guys are over twenty-one, right?" he said.

"Yeah," Wendy answered, before Ryan could say anything.

"There's a party store up the road there," the shadowed adolescent said. "We really need someone to get us some beer for a little party we got going on, and was wondering…"

Ryan started to get up, taking Wendy's arm.

"We could give you twenty bucks, man," the boy said.

"Can't do it," Ryan said. "Might get busted."

"Shee-it, man," the boy shot back. "We ain't no five-oh." A chorus of teenagers cackled.

Ryan and Wendy walked farther down the pier.

"Muh-fuckuhs, man," the boy murmured in their wake.

Ryan stopped three-quarters of the way down the pier and leaned nonchalantly against the wooden railing. He looked at Wendy, and she returned his smile.

"You muh-fuckuh." She giggled.

Ryan laughed so hard a dam in his heart seemed to break. "You know," he said, his laughter checked by the look in her eyes, "I've missed you so much since you left."

Wendy smiled wider, her laughter dying away. She tilted her chin upward, drawing perceptibly closer to him. "Really?" she said, her voice solemn.

"Yeah, I can't stand that you're away from me," Ryan said. He leaned close to her, drawn by a force not described in the biological literature. He felt a soft wisp of her breath against his face. He closed his eyes. Waiting to feel her. His pain receding.

Wendy ignored the sore on her ankle and the tightness in her chest. The sore was her own fault, she thought, from constant scratching. The tightness—she attributed to something she ate at the party. And she had no intention of letting indigestion get in the way of this moment. Standing on a pier above a gently flowing river, Ryan was going to kiss her. It was a moment she had dreamed of for years. Too perfect for distraction.

He leaned toward her, and she rolled up on the balls of her feet, wanting to meet him more than she had ever wanted any man. The true pain started as tightness in one fiber of muscle in her foot. It could be ignored, for a moment. In their life after the kiss, she would have time to tell him everything. Shopping lists. Bad hair days. Minor aches. All could be shared. But nothing could interfere with this kiss.

In the milliseconds that separated her from Ryan, the one complaining fiber grasped hands with a neighbor on either side, together forming the taut nucleus of a knot. The tiny nucleus latched on to more fibers in all directions, like a growing crystal, and the knot swelled to life. Wendy could almost feel Ryan's lips on her own, separated by microns. But the knot gripped into a tightly wound ball that seemed intent on wrenching itself away from her bones. Her foot contorted with the unusual flexion, and the cramp spread, like a run in her hose, to her calf. She was unaware of her own screams.

Wendy realized, as her body could no longer support her weight, and as the distance from Ryan increased, the pain in her foot had only been a prelude—an overture—of the symphony of hurt to come. Her calf seized instantly. Its graceful length replaced by a muscle resembling a child's fist, selfishly squeezed around forbidden candy. The contortions of her lower leg unbalanced her and she tumbled, bouncing her head off the wooden railing, the new aching bruises a welcome sideshow to the monster that devoured her leg.

She collapsed at Ryan's feet, the lower part of her right leg rigid and wooden and sending a constant scream of pain through her mind. Wendy panted, drawing shallow breaths between waves of pain, trying to collect her mind and will her leg to relax. To let go of the insanely tight revolution that had started as a twinge.

"Wendy!" Ryan said, somewhere close beside her as she drifted, eyes closed. "What is it? What's wrong?"

She opened her mouth but her leg seized again, and a scream rolled out in place of the words her mind tried to form. Feet thudded on the pier, bouncing her face against the boards that had become her pillow.

"What's going on, man?" The teenager's voice. More human now. "What'd ya do to her, dude?"

"Wendy," Ryan said, his hands rolling her over, his face a sheet of horror. "What? What? What happened?"

The tide of pain rolled out, leaving a residual ache like ocean waste on the beachfront. A warning of more to come. "I don't know." Wendy panted. "Cramp in my leg. Help me."

"What'dya do to her, man?" the teenager was more emboldened.

"Shut up!" Ryan screamed.

Wendy felt his hands run down her legs to the dead feeling in the cramped stump that rested below her right knee.

"God!" Ryan said. She felt his hands like an echo, and the tide of pain rolled back in, and she screamed again. "God! Wendy, I'm going to call for help. Okay?"

She tried to nod her head. Tried to adjust to the pain. But was left with no release but to scream again.

"See that cop!" Ryan yelled. "Get him now!"

More thudding footsteps, bouncing the boards under her face.

"Wendy," Ryan said. "Wendy, your leg is swelling."

"No." Wendy moaned. "It's a cramp."

"Are you allergic to anything?" Ryan said. "That bug bite?"

"No," Wendy said, and a tinge sparked in her left foot. The fear of the pain that was to follow was more than she wanted. She screamed readily with the wave that rolled up her left leg.

"Wendy," Ryan said, hovering somewhere over her. "Have you eaten those damned berries?"

Gripped in pain, she tried to shake her head.

"What's wrong?" A different voice. Calm and authoritative.

"I don't know," Ryan said. "She says a cramp, but—"

"Jesus!" the authoritative man said, hovering over her, the calm having departed from his voice.

Another wave of pain. Both legs. She bit down on her lips against the screaming, feeling sweat trickling down her cheek.

A radio crackled. "I need an ambulance down here on the River Walk Pier," the authoritative man said. "Adult female. Anaphylactic shock, I think. Med-one."

"Med-one," a crackled voice said. "Copy, that. En route."

Wendy's mind recessed to a calmer place. Turmoil still raged in her body and around her was chaos. But she found the rhythm of the black water below her, through the cracks in the boardwalk. And rode it to oblivion.

Tom was startled from sleep by the blaring pulse of an unfamiliar telephone. The shades were drawn, the room hidden in pitch blackness, as he struggled to orient himself. The phone shot off another two bursts of sound, and he reached for it on the bedside table.

"Hello," he said, sleep still clouding his voice.

"Tom, I need your help." It sounded like Ryan, only more rapid. "I'm at the hospital…" there was a muffled sound from the phone and talking in the background "…Bay Medical Center. I need you to get down here. Fast."

"Ryan?" Tom said, swinging his legs onto the floor.

"Yeah," Ryan said. "It's Wendy. I think she might have HERDS, Tom, and nobody will listen to me because I'm not a relative."

"HERDS. What?"

"She's got severe cramping and swelling in her legs," Ryan said. "And a rash. It looks like HERDS to me, but nobody around this place has even heard of it."

Tom's waking mind struggled to make sense of the call. Wendy was in trouble. "I'll be right there," he said. "Where are you again?"

"Bay Medical Center," Ryan said.

Tom pulled on his dirty clothes, put his tennis shoes on bare feet and headed for his car. He stopped in the lobby to ask directions and got to the hospital in five minutes. He found Ryan and Wendy in the rear treatment area of the emergency room.

It hurt him to look at Wendy. The lower half of her beautiful form was misshapen with swelling, and her lovely face, asleep, had been gashed below the right eye. Ryan got up from the chair by her bedside.

"C'mon," Ryan said, grabbing Tom by the arm and dragging him through the treatment room. "These doctors won't listen to me because I'm not family. So you're going to have to do your lawyer mumbo jumbo to get it through their heads this isn't an allergy."

Tom's head was still swirling. He had only slept an hour, thanks to Ernie's drunken snoring, and he hadn't fully awakened. Worse, Ryan seemed to be operating under at least two misconceptions: first, that Tom knew what was going on; and second, that anyone at the hospital was going to take orders from a lawyer.

"What happened?" Tom said, as Ryan led him around, searching for the right physician.

"She's got HERDS, Tom," Ryan said. "She has a rash on her leg and severe pain and swelling. This isn't an allergy. She says she hasn't been eating those blackberries, but there's another cause out there. Lots of cases out there Ernie can't link to blackberries."

"So what do you want me to do?" Tom said, as Ryan swung him in front of a young doctor in a white lab coat.

"Doctor," Ryan said. "This is Tom Hughes, Ms. Isaacson's attorney."

"Look," the doctor smiled with something less than enthusiasm and did not offer his hand, "it's been a busy night around here. With the holiday, it's probably going to get worse. Now, Mr.—"

"Romanelli. Doctor Romanelli," Ryan said.

"Doctor Romanelli," the doctor said. "I have treated thousands of cases of anaphylactic shock. I know it can be scary to look at when it is someone you love, but please trust—"

"This is not anaphylactic shock, Doctor," Ryan said.

"I can assure—" the doctor started.

"Have you checked her blood count?" Ryan asked.

"I don't need her blood count to tell you quite well what this is," the doctor said.

"Listen to me—Doctor Knowles, is it?" Tom broke in, reading the young doctor's name tag. "You need to check that woman's blood count. You are going to find her eosinophil levels are way too high. Over ten thousand."

"That's highly unlikely," the young doctor said. "And who are you?"

"I'm the lawyer that is going to be suing you for malpractice," Tom snapped, "if this woman dies because you don't know how to read the latest bulletins from the CDC, my young friend."

The doctor was muted for a moment. "What bulletin?"

"Go look it up," Tom said. "High Eosinophil Respiratory Distress Syndrome. HERDS. It's probably in your latest bulletins. And it's deadly. You can't treat this case like a normal allergy. That girl will be going into severe respiratory distress at any moment."

The doctor's look went from irritated to skeptical. He walked to a nurses' station separated from the emergency treatment area by thick glass. Inside he spoke with a nurse and plucked a large three-ring binder off a shelf. The young doctor opened the binder, paged through, and stopped to read for a time. When he looked up, he barked an order at the emergency nurse, before returning to join Tom and Ryan.

"I'll have the blood work back shortly," the young doctor said. "There's probably nothing to worry about, but we'll take a look at her eosinophil levels."

"Thank you, Doctor," Tom said. "I don't know if it's mentioned in the bulletin, but some HERDS patients have responded well to prednisone."

"Let's get the tests back first," the young doctor said, trying to save face.

Tom and Ryan waited by her bedside. The minutes passed like days. Wendy's sleep was restless. Her face winced in pain. And her legs continued to swell. The young doctor returned with a white paper.

"You're right," he said to Tom. "Eleven thousand. I'm going to start her on a prednisone drip. We'll admit her right away and monitor her closely. If her breathing gets bad, I'll make sure we have a ventilator on stand-by."

"Thank you, Doctor. We've seen a number of cases like this over in our neck of the woods, or we wouldn't have known either," Tom said, trying to soften the blow to the young doctor's ego. He didn't want the physician to spend time worrying about being wrong. He just wanted him to save Wendy.

"Where are you from?" the doctor said, stepping aside for a nurse to administer an IV.

"Milton," Tom said.

"I wonder if there's someone there I might talk to," the doctor said.

"Dr. Donald Brown," Tom said. "He's in Milton. His patients are over at the Perkins Regional Medical Center."

The doctor jotted a note to himself. "Thanks," he said. "Now, if you'll excuse me a moment, I've got to report this to the CDC. Someone should be here to take her up to a room in a minute."

"Thanks, Doctor," Ryan said, shaking the doctor's hand.

Tom and Ryan waited together in the bedside chairs.

"I swear," Tom said. "I think GenAgra is trying to pick us off one by one."

Ryan shook his head and rubbed a hand through his wiry, black hair.

"First Ike," Tom said. "Now Wendy. And you and Ernie both suspended. Who's left?"

An orderly came and took Wendy to her room. Tom and Ryan followed. Tom could feel Ryan's heavy heart, as the young professor sat by her side. It was a feeling so familiar, Tom could not stand it.

"I'm going to get back to the hotel and get some sleep," Tom said, after an unbearable time.

"I'm going to stay," Ryan said, though Tom didn't need to hear it. It was apparent Ryan loved the broken young woman lying in the hospital bed.

"She's going to be okay, Doc." Tom clapped Ryan on the back and turned to leave. He passed through the sterile hallways, his vision still bleary from lack of sleep. A chill ran through him, causing him to shudder. It was difficult to see someone as young and vibrant as Wendy struck down.

Tom drove back to the hotel on deserted streets, signals flashing yellow and red at empty intersections, waving wayward travelers home again. He parked in the hotel lot, then turned off the ignition and sat in the car, looking out at the river before him. The sky overhead was black and clear. Bright stars poked through the ambient streetlight, making the heavens look like a jewel.

The embankment, where a mass of humanity had teemed hours before, was lifeless. The heavy silence and emptiness near the center of the small town enveloped him. Wendy's illness felt like an additional weight piled atop Tom's formidable load. Another ball to juggle for Tuesday's circus. Only this ball was an intelligent young woman with a limitless future. And Tom was no juggler.

He had reacted like a lawyer when presented with the stubborn young doctor. It was a way of being, ingrained by years of study and practice. See the problem. Analyze the problem. React to the problem. And start over. Quick decisions executed without hesitation.

But lawyers were not supposed to feel for their clients. In order to see and analyze and react, Tom needed professional detachment. Clients were abstractions in an equation to be manipulated for the desired end. They were guarded abstractions, to be sure, because they paid the bills. But their problems had to be dehumanized for any lawyer to function effectively.

Ike's case had become far too personal. The anger of injustice at the beginning. The compounded rage when Ike fell ill. The ire at Ernie and Ryan being misused. The fury now that Wendy was struck down with the same disease. And all of it encircled with the mind-numbing knowledge that Claire would be alive if GenAgra had not produced this abominable plant.

Tom could never empathize with the lunatic shooters that popped up on the news every few months. Seemingly random shots fired at the nation's courthouses or factories or schools. But the strain of this case, and his inability to separate it from his personal feelings, was making him crazy. For the first time in his life, he thought he might be within viewing distance of the mindsets of those deranged gunmen. Perhaps they all went through a similar phase. An insane desire to stop the world and step down from the ride.

Looking at the black water of the river before him, Tom felt a surge of emotion. His breathing tightened. His chest ached. He felt warm tears running down his cheeks before he knew he was crying. He burned with shame, thinking what Ike would say if he saw him there. Bawling alone. In a car by the river. But tasting the salt of his tears, the shame evaporated. Tom let go and sobbed. He held his face and had the fleeting thought that he was not fit to go on as Ike's attorney.

His breathing relaxed after a few sobs, and to his surprise, Tom's mind felt more clear. Not transparent, but clear enough to think. To try and remember how to juggle, so he might keep all the balls in the air. It is what Claire would have wanted. It was what Ike needed. It was what Ryan and Ernie were doing. He wiped his tears with his hand.

Nell and Hrdina slept on the third floor of the building to his left. Perhaps they slept together, Tom thought randomly. Together, the three of them were a legal team. Perhaps they were not formidable. They might not strike fear into the likes of the legal all-stars at Barnes & Honeycutt. But they were a team. And they had a game to play. And greater odds had been overcome. They had to take their shot. And hope that giants would fall.

Chapter Sixteen

Bullard stood on the deck of the sailboat and scanned the river. A cool breeze blasted at the back of his balding head. In forty-eight hours he had guided the old wooden craft up the coast, around the thumb, and into the Saginaw Bay. With only a high-maintenance attorney for a crew. Hannah Yale would not have made it as a sailor. But she had earned her passage as his carnal consort.

Sailing up the Saginaw River, he felt very much like a Colonial explorer entering the virgin swampland of Michigan. Of course, the vast marshes and thick woods that had once dominated the land were gone, Bullard could see, replaced by garbage dumps and power plants and condominiums. But he tingled with the thought he was like the early white men who had come to this land. Triumphant. Like conquering heroes destined to turn the wild into a habitable paradise.

"You've got the life," Yale said, crawling up from the cabin and laying a hand on his shoulder. "I would do this every weekend if I could get away from that damned office."

Bullard knew that Yale's chief attractions to him were his

wealth, his power, and his proximity to Washington's elite. She
was candid about her growing distaste for Barnes & Honeycutt,
though she was well on her way to making partner. Yale wanted
to be introduced to an entire new level of affluence. She aspired to
the world of limos, private jets, and yachts. And she wasn't likely
to attain that level as a partner at the firm. She would top out at the
level of Hummers, first class coach, and annual Caribbean cruises.
And it wasn't enough.

The yacht was borrowed from a friend of the family. A
GM exec who had escaped the company in a golden parachute
before the collapse of the SUV market. It was far too much boat
for Bullard, who was in fact a poor sailor, with a poorer crew.
Fortunately the weather had been fair, and he managed to tack the
yacht up the river on the last leg of the journey. They docked at
the local marina.

Bullard hadn't spent the entire weekend chasing Yale and
fumbling to control the yacht. He worked his cell phone like a
sailor in a storm and managed to pull together a cogent response
to Friday's public relations disaster. His intern had regained her
composure and did yeoman's work analyzing the scope of the
problem. His father had come through again, ensuring Bullard a
Tuesday morning press conference by the USDA was going to
solve the health scare that plagued GenAgra's stock. Zimmerman
had been pacified with the good news. And Bullard had even
hatched his own emergency plan to neutralize the Michigan
Department of Community Health and their attack on his Health-
Ease Blackberry.

After securing the yacht, Bullard looked up the dock and saw
Malec waiting to usher them to the hotel. Bullard struggled to get
the bags to the waiting SUV.

"How are you doing, Doctor Malec?" Bullard said, puffing
the last yards of the way.

"Peachy," the doctor said, making no effort to cover his
distaste for Bullard, nor to help him with the bags.

"I'm sorry to drag you out," Bullard said, cheery from his trip,
despite Malec's continued insubordination.

"Hello, Doctor Malec," Yale said, shaking the doctor's hand.

Malec drove them off the river, through the grimy remains

of a once thriving manufacturing town. Bullard was disappointed when Malec drove up to the puny eight-story hotel near the river.

"Is this the best they have to offer?" Bullard said.

"I don't know," Malec said. "This is where your secretary booked your room."

"Well," Bullard said, rolling his eyes toward Yale and throwing his hands up at the injustice. "I guess we'll have to make do."

Bullard checked in, escorted Hannah to the room, grabbed his portfolio from his own bag, and excused himself for the remainder of the afternoon. According to his own plan, Bullard set out with Malec for a quick trip to Mt. Pleasant to meet with the fine government officials who had torpedoed GenAgra's stock with their impromptu press conference on Friday.

"Did you bring the toxicology reports?" Bullard said.

"They're gas chromatographs, actually," Malec said, a smug smile sneaking across his face.

"Did you bring them?" Bullard demanded.

"Yes," Malec said, thumbing toward the back seat. "They're in my case."

"Let me see them," Bullard said.

"Grab them yourself," Malec said. "I'm busy driving."

Bullard reached behind the passenger seat with great effort, and flailed for Malec's briefcase. When he finally snagged it, he tugged it angrily to the front seat. He opened the briefcase and found a large, folded chart amongst the doctor's papers.

He took the chart and opened it carefully on his lap, his eyes unable to distinguish anything significant about it. It could have been an EKG or a line scribbled on graph paper by a kindergartner for all Bullard's untrained eye could see, but he studied it carefully, wanting to impress Malec with his grasp of detail. Peaks and troughs skipped across the graph paper from one side of the chart to the other—meaningless data to Bullard.

"So this version more accurately reflects the lack of toxicity in the berry?" Bullard said.

"I made the changes you asked for," Malec said. "I'm not happy about it. But I made them."

"Doctor Malec," Bullard said. Malec's eyes remained squarely on the road as Bullard turned in the passenger seat to stare at him.

"This health scare represents a significant threat to GenAgra. I don't think I need to remind you of that, do I? How much money did you lose on your stock options during Friday trading?"

"This isn't about stock options," Malec said. "I've done things I'm not proud of while working for this company, but you made us rush through the approval process, Mr. Bullard. This berry should not be on the market. Not yet. I told you that with the last reports we submitted to the USDA."

"And I told you, Doctor Malec," Bullard roared, "if you want to continue your cushy job at this company, you are going to do what I say. We had a green light for approval, and we took it. Our product is officially safe. It has the gold standard. USDA approved. And I don't need any of your ethical fretting. You put that berry in the field. You've put it into the stream of commerce. And it is good. Don't start backpedaling on me now. You know the Health-Ease Blackberry is going to save lives. You know how many obese children we have in this goddamn country? Not to mention the lard-ass adults."

"You read the memo from our last round of testing," Malec said, disdain dripping in his voice. "You know this guy from A&T is only confirming a toxin we knew about. You prevented me from sending that report to the USDA. If you'd have given me two years, I could have made another berry that would have let people lose weight without fucking killing themselves."

"I didn't have two years," Bullard said. "And there's no proof the Health-Ease Blackberry is causing anything, for fuck's sake. I've had someone working on it all weekend. The CDC has cases of this being reported around the country, Doctor. California, Washington, Oregon, Ohio, Indiana, and New York."

"I'm aware," Malec said. "That's three clusters. Centered in Michigan, Oregon, and New York, you ignorant son of a bitch. Did you ever bother reading the background paper my staff compiled at your request? Our research center isn't the only test site. Wanna guess where the others are? Do you think their locations might have anything to do with this epidemic?"

Bullard wanted to fire Malec on the spot. The scientist had rubbed him the wrong way from day one and had never assumed his proper role under Bullard's rule. But the open hostility drove

Bullard mad. If he were more prone to violence, he might strike the doctor for using such condescending language. But Malec was essential to today's plan and Tuesday's hearing. After that, Bullard would be pulling the trigger on some changes, before proceeding to market the Health-Ease Blackberry.

"No, I don't know where your other facilities are," Bullard said. "Why don't you tell me."

"Michigan is our main facility," Malec said. "But how did you suppose we were going to make it up to marketing speed when we gained approval? Every experimental plant we're growing here is being grown on a larger scale at our sites in Oregon and New York. Commercial fields."

Bullard hadn't given any serious thought to the idea the Health-Ease Blackberry really might be deadly.

"This new thing. HERDS," Bullard said dismissively. "It can't be caused by the Health-Ease Blackberry. I've been eating those samples you sent me every day. For two weeks now. And I'm fine."

"Did you ever take a biology course?" Malec said, raising his eyes from the highway for the first time to stare icily at Bullard. "Do you know how toxins act in the human body?"

Bullard said nothing. He wouldn't give Malec the satisfaction of displaying his own ignorance on the subject.

"I didn't think so," Malec continued, taking Bullard's silence for what it was. "Toxins are poisons, Mr. Bullard. And they affect different people in different ways. All kinds of factors play into how a particular person will respond to the poisoning. The dose of the toxin, length of exposure, weight, liver function. Hell, genetics even. Some might not be affected at all. And not everyone exposed is going to collapse and die. There will be mild cases of poisoning and other cases that result in death. That have *already* resulted in death. And everything in between. And I don't want to be a part of that. I wouldn't let my own children eat these berries."

Bullard's throat constricted at the thought he might have been ingesting a poison for the past two weeks, but he tried to relax, figuring Doctor Malec's rant was done for exactly that effect.

"I've given you the chromatograph you asked for," Malec said. "It shows something much closer to a regular blackberry.

The peak that shows the toxin has been toned down. But I'm not
going to be a party to any more of it. You use it how you will. I'm
through."

"The hell you're through," Bullard said, gathering himself.
He folded the forged chromatograph and placed it in his portfolio.
"If there are problems, we're going to fix them, Doctor Malec.
And we're going to take this product to market. And we're going
to make money. Lots of it. But you aren't going anywhere. You're
in this, Doctor. Your name is on those reports submitted to the
USDA. Do you know what they do with people who lie in official
documents and end up killing people? I don't think there's a death
penalty in this state, but I'm sure there are some pretty hellacious
prisons."

Malec said nothing for the rest of the trip. Bullard didn't
like his instability. He wished Zimmerman could have seen the
disloyalty in his own ranks. It was sobering. And Bullard was sure
the old tycoon would agree with his decision to fire Malec when
the time came.

Without conversation, the trip dragged. The freeway turned
into a four-lane highway, and Malec slowed the SUV to the lower
speed limit. Bullard looked out at the paltry rural homes that
dotted the landscape, separated by farm fields and islands of basic
commerce. Gas, food, videos, and lottery tickets. He wondered
how one lived in this part of the country. Boredom must have been
endemic.

Bullard was thankful when they arrived at the Chippewa
County Department of Public Health. He and Malec waited
briefly in the empty lobby before they were met by Artie Fisher.
Fisher was a short, balding man, who sported a prolific paunch
that ballooned forward over his belt, making him look like the
world's only fifty-year-old pregnant man. He looked so ridiculous
that Bullard would have considered telling him so, were it not that
Fisher was the governor's chief of staff. Bullard decided to tread
respectfully.

"Thank you for meeting with us on a Sunday, sir," Bullard
said, kissing Fisher's ass."Not a problem, Mr. Bullard," Fisher
said. "Your father was a good friend to Governor Howell when he
was in Washington. The governor wants to assist in this crisis in

any way possible."

"Thanks," Bullard said. "We truly appreciate the governor's help. Mr. Fisher, this is Dr. Otis Malec."

Malec nodded and shook Fisher's hand.

"Nice to meet you, Doctor," Fisher said. "If you'll both follow me, we're assembled in the conference room."

The conference room was substandard. Low grade industrial wallpaper and a dropped ceiling housed a long table of the finest particle board covered with a thin veneer. The chairs reminded Bullard of the lawn chairs he had used during his fraternity days at Ohio State. If someone could whip up a keg of beer, it would be a party.

"Mr. Bullard, let me introduce Kathy Jones," Fisher said. "She's the director of our Department of Community Health. And this is Dr. Herb Underwood, manager of the Bureau of Epidemiology."

Bullard nodded to the underlings, a portly black woman and a horse-faced white man.

"This is Al Bullard and Dr. Otis Malec," Fisher said, completing the introductions.

"Thanks so much for seeing us on a Sunday," Bullard said to the state workers. "I would have never requested such an inconvenient meeting if the matter weren't urgent."

The black woman smiled in a way that discomforted Bullard. He sensed she could see directly through the bullshit he was spewing. The epidemiologist, on the other hand, nodded as if he were the only sinner at a revival sermon, soaking in all that Bullard said. Bullard placed his portfolio on the table.

"Like I said, the governor has instructed us all to give you our full cooperation," Fisher smiled. "And we've been working around the clock on this health crisis, anyway."

"Well thanks, Artie," Bullard said. "I appreciate it. Since I heard about this on Friday, I've wanted to sit down with the people who are out there on the front lines, in terms of public health. You know, safety is the key component in all products developed by GenAgra. We're a company built on ensuring safe, reliable products for consumers. And anything as serious as this, well, we naturally want to sit down and cooperate with the appropriate authorities. So we can clear up any problem and avoid something—something like what happened to our stock price on Friday, for instance."

Bullard, Fisher, and the epidemiologist laughed.

"If GenAgra wanted to cooperate," Director Jones said, "why have you been stonewalling our request for berry samples? We'd like to test them for toxicity and get this all cleared up."

"GenAgra would never stonewall your office, Ms. Jones," Bullard said. "Of that I can assure you. We have complied with all government regulations in the development and testing of the Health-Ease Blackberry, and as soon as our lawyers are satisfied that providing you with samples will not disclose any proprietary information, I'm sure you will get your samples. You have to understand, we are in the middle of litigation with a farm that is pirating our product. And everyone at GenAgra has a lot riding on this berry."

"What did you call it?" Director Jones said. "The Health-what?"

"The Health-Ease Blackberry," Bullard said, his face a model of sincerity. "It's an unbelievable new weight-loss product. One serving and your appetite disappears for an entire day. Just won USDA approval. Perhaps you would like to try some samples." Bullard smiled broadly at her, but Jones's own expression was still icy toward him.

"As I was saying, we would be happy to cooperate with your state's investigation, *but*," Bullard paused for effect, "I understand the ban you've imposed on the Health-Ease Blackberry is actually without a shred of scientific basis."

"Without a shred?" Director Jones openly scoffed.

"Kathy," Fisher said diplomatically. "Now, we might have to agree to disagree on some interpretations of the evidence here. But the governor has asked we be gracious enough to hear GenAgra's side of this, and we're going to do that."

Kathy nodded at Fisher and pursed her lips.

"Thank you," Bullard continued. "It has been brought to my attention that many, many cases that have been reported nationwide are not related in any way to the Health-Ease Blackberry. Now that fact alone should have been enough to give a prudent investigator pause before sending our stock into a panic." Bullard watched as the epidemiologist nodded along with him. He had one sure ally inside the enemy camp, anyway.

"Well, we have a chromatograph showing an unknown toxin in your *healthy* berry," Director Jones interrupted again. "We haven't traced it to all cases yet, but how could we not act on that evidence? We've got to protect the citizens of our state, Mr. Bullard. Surely you understand our mission."

"I haven't had a chance to see that report," Bullard said.

"Well, I've got it right here, if you'd like to," Director Jones said.

"I would, as a matter of fact," Bullard said. Jones handed him two folded graphs. Bullard unfolded them on the table. One graph showed the test results for a normal blackberry, and one showed the test results for the Health-Ease Blackberry. Even to Bullard's untrained eye, there was an obvious difference between the graphs. The Health-Ease Blackberry's graph showed two extra peaks—two unknown substances. "Are these the originals?"

"Yes," Director Jones said. "I can run you a copy if you'd like."

"No, that won't be necessary," Bullard said, looking over the charts. He showed the graphs to a disinterested Doctor Malec and refolded them as he spoke. "Thank you. I can see how one might be tempted to jump to interpretive conclusions while searching for an answer to this dreadful disease, but I'm afraid we do have a different idea about what these graphs show. And I'm not alone in my conclusions on this. I understand the USDA and the CDC will be making a joint statement Tuesday morning rejecting the idea that HERDS is caused by the Health-Ease Blackberry."

"What?" Director Jones said. "How is it you know that? I've been working closely with the CDC this week, and they are hotter on the trail than we are."

"GenAgra is a multinational corporation, Director," Bullard said, as he deftly placed the director's original graph into his portfolio and replaced it with Malec's forgery. "They have contacts all over the world. Believe it or not, they even make substantial contributions to your governor, if I'm not mistaken. The man who appointed you.

"We have access to a much wider web of information than you might appreciate. But from our vantage point, it's clear you have jumped the gun on this. And it was a painful mistake to us. However, you might still have time to make amends."

Jones bristled at Bullard's words, but Fisher and the epidemiologist seemed ready to draft a letter of apology.

"The information from the CDC is very helpful," Fisher said. "I'm sure that might make a difference in the course we take from here. But you understand we have some diverging views within the department, and we are going to need some time to come to a decision."

"Of course, Artie," Bullard said. Fisher was obviously a man who would play ball. "Of course. I'm only pleased to have had this opportunity to sit down and get our views on the table. In the future, I hope we can work better together beforehand so we can all avoid these pitfalls."

Bullard could feel the heat coming from Director Jones. He wondered what she would be doing when her career in public service came to a close. That time was certainly not far off. He considered posing the question directly but decided against it. Though he loved to gloat, she looked as if she might be dangerous in the wrong setting.

"Thank you again for having us, Mr. Fisher," Bullard said rising. He slid the folded forgery back to the director. His plan was complete. "I don't want to keep you any longer than necessary. Please let us know after you've had a chance to talk this matter over."

"We sure will," Fisher said.

"And give my best to the governor," Bullard said. "I understand his name has been floated as a possible candidate."

"Well, you'll get a no comment on that." Fisher laughed, practically blushing.

Michigan was definitely in the bush leagues. The only thing moderately attractive about the state was Hanna Yale, and he planned to take her away as soon as he could get clear of the godforsaken place.

The weekend had fallen apart after Wendy fell sick. Ryan had not left the hospital, and the rest of the ragtag legal team had visited Wendy in shifts on Sunday. The doctors called her stable, but she still battled bouts of severe muscle pain. The pain medicine didn't seem to be helping much, and it was difficult to watch her endure the agony.

Tom called for an official strategy meeting for noon on the Fourth of July. He meant no symbolism in picking this date. The preliminary injunction hearing was one day away and Tom wanted at least one opportunity to talk with everyone about the case. He pulled the dining table next to the couch, doing his best to make an impromptu conference room.

Ernie took a seat on the couch. Nell and Hrdina dragged chairs up to the table. This was it. This was his all-star legal team. Ryan had promised to make the lunchtime meeting, but Tom wasn't surprised by the professor's absence.

Tom grabbed his file from his boxy briefcase and sat across from Ernie. The group was casual. Collegial. Comfortable. No need for anyone to pound a gavel.

Nell got things rolling. "Felix and I have been talking." The pair had been inseparable since Saturday night. Their chairs were nearly touching. "The only real shot we have is to show misuse of the patent. Even that's a long shot, but that's where we have to concentrate our efforts."

"Not only misuse," Hrdina said sounding more confident to Tom. "But misuse because they had knowledge the product was a threat to public health."

"Okay," Tom said. "That is something to start with. What are we going to need to put in as evidence?"

"First, prove the blackberry is a threat to public health," Nell said.

"Yeah," Tom said. "That's not so hard. We've got Ryan's testimony that he tested it and found the toxin. But how are we going to show they had knowledge of that?"

"They're GenAgra," Nell said. "They're evil. Of course they had knowledge of it."

Tom and Ernie laughed.

"Too bad the judge isn't going to take judicial notice of that fact," Hrdina said stiffly. His absurd lack of humor brought more laughter.

"Okay," Tom said. "You're right about that, Felix. So we're going to have a hard time showing they had knowledge. I'll get what I can on cross, and we'll go from there."

There was a knock on the hotel room door, and Tom rose to answer it. It was Ryan, and he looked like a vagrant panhandling in the hall.

"Hey, how you doing?" Tom said, guiding the professor in. "How is she?"

"The same," Ryan said, defeated. "Paralysis in the legs, and pain. I don't think they're doing enough to manage the pain."

"Still stable, though?" Tom said. "She's breathing okay?"

"Uh-huh," Ryan said. He walked into the room and sat on the couch next to Ernie. "Sorry I'm late." There was a chorus of absolution from the small group.

"We're just getting started," Tom said, taking his seat at the table. "Okay. So we're going to have a hard time showing they had knowledge of the toxin."

"You know," Nell said. "You can always fall back and argue it was what they knew or should have known. I mean, if this toxin was so obvious that Ryan could find it in a couple of days, then they should have known. Constructive knowledge. Even if we get no evidence they actually knew."

"That's good thinking," Tom said, jotting a note in his file. "Where did you intern again?"

"The best little personal injury office in the country," she said, smiling at her old boss.

"All right," Tom said. "So if we put in solid evidence of the toxin from Ryan, then I cross their people on their knowledge of the toxin, even if I can't get anything out of them, I still have a good fallback argument based on constructive knowledge. Right?"

"Good," Nell said.

"Might work," Hrdina said. "It's the best argument you have."

Ryan's tired face turned to a look of worry. "Ernie, you have my chromatography reports, right?"

"Nope," Ernie said hesitantly. "I gave them to the department of health."

"Oh shit," Ryan said, rubbing his hands through his wiry hair. "Those were my originals and I don't have access to my office to reprint the results."

"Oh no," Tom said. "We need to get those reports in evidence to establish the berry is toxic. I mean, I can probably get your testimony in, but without the reports…"

"Let me make a call," Ernie said. "Maybe I can get them here before tomorrow." He rose and paced by the door as he called Jill on his cell.

"Honestly," Nell said, "I don't even see how this is going to go forward tomorrow, Tom. There's no way that judge can say there is no appearance of impropriety. He's sitting on a case tried by the firm he just left. I don't see it. He's going to DQ himself, and we'll get another judge. Tomorrow's going to be adjourned."

"Yes," Hrdina agreed. "It would be most unusual for him to hear the case."

"I don't disagree," Tom said. "But you know, I wouldn't put anything past these people. We'll just be ready, and we'll go from there."

"Ready or not, Tom," Nell said, "if he stays on the case, how are you going to win? Fuck, why even have a court? Let's just let Barnes & Honeycutt do whatever they decide to do."

"I can get the report," Ernie said, returning to the couch. "Is a copy good enough?"

"Yup," Tom said. "That'll work fine."

"All right," Ernie said. "I've got to go pick it up later this afternoon at my office. My old office."

"We'll get you back there, Ernie," Tom said. "Don't you worry. The state is going to be begging you to come back when we get through with them."

"All right." Ernie smiled.

"Okay," Tom said. "What else have we got?"

The group hashed over the case, point by point. Tom ordered room service for lunch, and the meeting dragged on. No one point covered by the group made him any more hopeful about his case, but Tom knew he had pulled together a good team. He wished Wendy could see them in action.

"Tom, if you don't mind, I want to get back to Wendy," Ryan

said when he had finished his lunch. "I want someone to be there to stay on top of the staff. The holiday weekend, you know. I want to make sure they're changing her meds and monitoring her breathing and—"

"No problem," Tom said. "Go. Just make sure you're in court tomorrow. Nine o'clock. You know where it is, right?"

"Yeah," Ryan said. "I'll be there." He stood, shook hands with his colleagues, then headed for the door.

"Ryan," Tom said, remembering just in time to stop his friend. "Before you go, I need that tape you made of the dean. I need to listen to it so I can fit it in."

Ryan patted his pockets and shrugged. "It's in my coat," he said. "I must have left it at the hospital."

Tom looked a Ryan's face. The professor obviously needed to get back to Wendy. "Just go ahead," Tom said. "Forget it. Remind me to listen to it tomorrow before the hearing."

Ryan gave Tom a thumbs-up and headed out the door.

The lawyers and Ernie talked on, gnawing on second-rate hotel food. No case Tom could remember had ever been decided before the lawyers got to courthouse and had their say. He was as ready as he wanted to be. Tomorrow his little legal team would take its best shot.

"Hi, Ernie!" the little girl said, running to him in the health department parking lot. Jill's daughter shrieked with delight as Ernie picked her up and spun her around.

"Hello, princess," Ernie said, setting Jacqueline safely back on the ground. Looking at the joy in the little girl's face, Ernie was overcome with a quasi-parental love.

"We have to hurry up," Jill said, jiggling her key in the lock to open the front door. "I've got to get her over to her dad's."

"We're going to see fireworks!" Jacqueline said.

"Oh, you are so lucky," Ernie said. "I am going to miss it. You're going to have to remember everything and tell me about it later."

"You can come, Ernie," Jacqueline said. "I'll ask my daddy."

"No, I have to work," Ernie said. "But you remember all about it, and you tell me. The colors and the sounds and all the people.

Everything. Okay?"

"Okay!" Jacqueline said, excited with her new mission.

Jill slipped inside the front door of the office and punched a code into the keypad to disable the alarm. Ernie followed her back to his old office, still piled high with the junk he had left behind. And emerging stacks of new junk.

"Underwood's been using it," Jill hissed.

"Mommy, can I play on your 'puter?" Jacqueline asked.

"Go ahead, sweetheart," Jill said, touching her daughter's chin. "But we're only staying a minute." Jacqueline sprinted off, her tennis shoes clapping on the thin carpet as she ran.

"She already knows how to use the computer?" Ernie asked, surprised.

"Oh yeah," Jill said. "They have one at her preschool. Gotta get them started young."

"So a copy is okay, right?" Jill said, opening a filing cabinet and pulling the folded chromatography reports out.

"Yeah, great," Ernie said.

Jill took the reports and walked out. He heard her turning on the copy machine near the reception area. Ernie walked slowly around his old desk, feeling like an intruder in a most familiar space. He sat in his old chair and let his eyes search over the papers scattered on the desk. Ernie didn't like the marks Underwood had left in his territory. He was beginning to doubt whether things would ever be set right, and was trying to console himself with the fact that at the end of the day, when all was said and done, Underwood would still be a jerk, no matter who won or lost. This small truth comforted him little.

Ernie's eyes settled on one of the new stacks of paper. Atop the stack was a faxed report of a new HERDS case, and Ernie's attention was drawn to the name of the victim. Wendy Isaacson. He picked up the report and paged through it. It had been completed by the treating physician at the Bay Regional Medical Center. White female. Twenty-six. Suspected HERDS. Mild presentation. Edema. Myalgia. Cramping. Ascending paralysis. Controlled with prednisone. Eosinophil count of 11,000. He turned the page and found a listing of foods she had consumed in the week before her illness. Wendy had been on a strange diet. She had eaten only

Dutch apple pie for the entire week, receiving her daily fix from the Milton Diner in doses of one slice per day.

Ernie leaned back in his chair. It wasn't blackberry pie, so there was no direct connection to the Hg-Blackberry. But if certain assumptions were made, Wendy's case was like a Rosetta Stone for solving the HERDS puzzle. Assuming Wendy's HERDS was caused by a food-borne pathogen and the incubation time of the disease was less than a week, there was only one possible cause. It had to be the pie. These were broad assumptions. But if he were working the case, it was a theory that would have been checked out two days ago.

"Here you go," Jill said, returning and handing Ernie a large manilla envelope. "I put your copies in here."

"Thanks," Ernie said.

As Jill filed the originals away, Ernie mulled over his Dutch apple pie theory. His mind pulled a detail from weeks before. The very first case of HERDS had been a construction worker from Milton. Hadn't he eaten at the Milton Diner? Ernie searched his desk, and found the construction worker's file at the bottom of a stack, exactly where he had left it. He opened the file and paged through it. The man had eaten Dutch apple pie from the Milton diner three times in the week before his illness. Hair raised on Ernie's arms. He thought he may have cracked the last mystery of the HERDS outbreak, and he wasn't even officially working the case.

"The Milton Diner," Ernie said. "Does that sound familiar to you?"

"Yeah," Jill said. "They were one of places selling that blackberry jam. In gift baskets. I had to contact them on Saturday to get them to pull it. Why?"

"I don't know," Ernie said. "How many cases ate there? Do you know?"

"Quite a few," Jill said. "I mean, looking at the Michigan cases, Wabeno County is the epicenter. And that diner is one of the only restaurants up there, besides Fast Burger and a few other chains. A lot of the HERDS cases from that area have eaten at the diner. I don't have a breakdown, but I could get one."

"Jill, I think there may be something in their pie," Ernie said.

"The Dutch apple pie. Or maybe something with the packaging. Or the pans. I don't know. Can we get them on the phone?"

"I've got to get Jacqueline to her dad's," Jill said, her brow knitted. "You don't know how he gets if I'm late. Big fight. I don't need it."

"Daddy gets mad," Jacqueline said, from Jill's cubicle outside the office.

"Just a quick call," Ernie said, tilting his head and giving her puppy-dog eyes. He saw the look of resignation before she spoke.

"Okay, but you're going to have to hurry," Jill said.

He followed Jill to her desk. She searched through a stack of messages and gave Ernie the number. He dialed quickly but was disappointed by a recorded voice. The Milton Diner was closed for the holiday.

"Shoot," Ernie said, hanging up the phone. "Can you contact them tomorrow? Something about that pie is making these other people sick. I don't know what it is, but I think we have this thing narrowed down to one restaurant. One food. Can you get there first thing tomorrow and get all the information you can about their Dutch apple pie. Ingredients. Recipe. Everything."

Jill looked at him impatiently. "Will you let me go drop my daughter off if I say yes?" she said.

"Yes," Ernie said. "I'm sorry. But we've got this thing. I know it."

"Okay. I'll do it for you," Jill said. "C'mon Jackie, let's get going."

"Thank you," Ernie said, wanting to hug Jill, but laying a hand on her shoulder instead.

"You know," Jill said. "You don't work here anymore."

"I know." Ernie laughed.

"You're still taking me to Lansing when you get Underwood's job." Jill smiled.

"Absolutely," he said. "Chief Investigator for the State of Michigan."

"It's not the title I'm after," Jill said. "I just miss having you around."

Chapter Seventeen

Tom paced back and forth in the courthouse hallway. With each
round, he stopped to peek inside the courtroom. The judge
had yet to take the bench, but the other pieces were mostly on the
board. Yale sat at the plaintiff's table with her co-counsel and the
GenAgra representative, Bullard. Tom still didn't understand how
it was that a cable news pollster wound up heading this biotech
project. It was a strange world.

Nell and Felix sat at the defense table, along with two empty
chairs. Kaye had promised she'd be ten minutes early, but she
hadn't arrived. She had no cell phone for Tom to call. Unlike a
criminal trial, the defendant in a civil case had no obligation to
attend hearings. But not having a human face representing the
Stiles' farm would be a disaster both of form and substance. Tom
wouldn't look good crying all day about his poor clients, if they
weren't even concerned enough to be present at the hearing. Worse,
when it came his time to produce evidence, he needed Kaye to
take Ike's place as a witness, or they would have no chance of
convincing the judge to lift his injunction.

Tom paced the hallway twice more and peeked into the

courtroom again. Still no judge at three minutes after nine, he thought, looking at his watch. Tom inventoried the witnesses. Behind the plaintiff's table was the doctor who had come out to take the samples from Ike's farm, his white lab coat replaced with a jacket for his court appearance. Next to him was a younger twin—probably another academic in GenAgra's employ. Nearer the center of the gallery sat A.J. McCoy, who had showed up on time, as commanded by Tom's subpoena, although he would likely not testify until much later in the day. Further to A.J.'s left, squarely behind the defense table was Ernie.

Notably absent was Ryan. Tom had left him at the hospital the night before, still watching over Wendy, her condition unchanged. Ryan had promised to be at the hearing on time, but was nowhere to be seen. He wouldn't testify until after the lunch hour, Tom was sure, so he tried to cut the heartbroken young professor some slack.

"They didn't start without me, did they?"

Tom heard a gravely voice behind him. It was instantly recognizable. He turned to confirm that his ears had not deceived him. "Ike," he said, hugging the old farmer. "Holy Christ!"

"Tom," Kaye reproved, as she entered with Doctor Brown. "Not in court. That language should be left at the pool hall."

Tom didn't have the heart to tell Kaye that pool halls had gone the way of disco. "How are you feeling?"

"Never better," Ike said, though his appearance suggested otherwise. He was still bent with some kind of pain. "Doc Brown here didn't want me to come, but I told him I was. So he offered to come along."

Tom exchanged greetings with Milton's long-time family practitioner. "Why didn't you tell me, Kaye?" Tom said.

"I didn't know until this morning." Kaye shrugged. "Stubborn old fool."

Tom surveyed Ike with a careful eye. "Is he going to be okay to testify, Doctor Brown?"

"Well, I've taken away his pain medicine, so he'll be lucid. And I don't think being here worsens his condition, if that's what you mean. So long as I'm around to keep an eye on him. But I would have serious doubts about my lawyer, if he ever called such a pig-headed man to the stand," Doctor Brown said.

"To hell," Ike said. "This is my farm, and I'm not going to miss my day in court to save her."

Tom patted the now frail farmer on the back gently and led him to the courtroom. It was time to get this case under way. On entering the door, Tom could see Judge Fuller had taken the bench. Nell was halfway toward the door, in an effort to fetch Tom from the hallway.

"Sorry, Judge," Tom said, slowly escorting Ike to the defense table. Kaye and Doctor Brown split away and took a seat behind Ernie.

"Can we get under way now?" Judge Fuller said.

"Ready, Your Honor," Yale said, her slender frame rising from the chair as she spoke.

"Yes," Tom said. "We're ready, Judge."

"Would counsel approach, then," Fuller said, beckoning the lawyers forward to the bench. The bench was old hardwood, probably walnut, Tom thought, running a hand on its warn edge. It had seen a legal battle or two, and Tom was eager for it to see one more.

"Off the record," Fuller said to the clerk on his right.

"Morning, Your Honor," Yale said with a sultry smile.

"Judge," Tom said, nodding. Fuller was no older than Tom and deserved no great respect in Tom's opinion. He had been elevated to the lifelong position only because of political connections, Tom surmised. Further, if the temporary restraining order Fuller had issued against Ike was any guide, the judge was hardly a fair jurist.

"Morning, counsel," Fuller said. "Has there been any effort to resolve this thing?"

"Our position is strong," Yale said. "I honestly can't imagine the court not ruling in our favor, so there's little we'd be willing to offer."

"My client cannot resolve this, Judge," Tom said, "unless they'd be willing to agree to a dismissal of their claim, a concession on liability, and a hearing on damages."

Yale scoffed good-naturedly.

"Well, I can see that was fruitful," Fuller said derisively.

"Okay, how many witnesses can I expect today?"

"Two, maybe three from our side," Yale said. "Should easily be able to get them in this morning."

"Three at this point," Tom said. "Not very long ones, though."

"So you're telling me this is going to be an all-day hearing," Fuller said. "I've got a golf league at five."

"Well, there is our motion to disqualify, Judge," Tom said with a smile. "If you grant that, or we can stipulate to it, then you won't have any problem making it for golf."

The joke did not rest easy on Fuller, and Tom regretted it at once. The man was already hostile enough, and the extra prodding was like enraging a staked bear.

"We don't agree with the motion, Your Honor," Yale stepped in to spread salve on the judge's ego. "There's no legitimate basis for disqualification, and I'm prepared to argue it."

"Okay," Fuller said. "We'll take up the motion first and then proceed from there. Let's move things along, okay?"

The lawyers moved back to their respective tables. "On the record in *GenAgra* versus *The Stiles' Family Berry Farm*," Fuller said, his voice commanding the courtroom. "We are here today for a hearing on the plaintiff's petition for a preliminary injunction and on the defendant's motion for disqualification. Will counsel please place their appearances on the record."

"Hanna Yale representing GenAgra, Your Honor. With me today are co-counsel, Cameron Dupree, and Al Bullard for GenAgra."

"Thomas Hughes on behalf of the Stiles' Family Berry Farm, with Ike Stiles, and attorneys Nell Yeats and Felix Hrdina."

"Thank you, counsel," Fuller said. "Let's take up your motion for disqualification first, Mr. Hughes."

Tom moved to the lectern in the center of the room with no paper or file. He looked for Judge Fuller's eyes, but was left staring at the top of his head. The judge's head was cocked down toward the court file, possibly reading the motion.

"Your Honor, our motion is straightforward," Tom said. "It is laid out in the attached affidavit. In their response to the motion, I believe GenAgra has conceded all the relevant facts to deciding this motion.

"As the court is well aware, Your Honor was only recently appointed to the federal bench. Up until that time, Your Honor had been a partner with Barnes & Honeycutt, counsel of record for GenAgra in this case. While I cannot point to any actual bias, the appearance of impropriety is certainly evident if Your Honor were to continue to sit on this case. There are other judges to whom this case can be transferred. There is no danger of prejudice that would inure to plaintiff GenAgra should this court recuse itself. Simply put, justice requires this court step aside and allow this case to proceed without the unnecessary appearance of impropriety."

"Thank you," Fuller said. "Ms. Yale?"

Yale replaced Tom at the lectern, looking past Tom as their paths crossed. "Your Honor, this motion is governed by 25 USC 455," Yale said crisply. "Section (B)(2) is the only specific provision that would require recusal in this case. Recusal would be required only if you served in private practice as a lawyer on the case in controversy, or if you served in association with myself or Mr. Dupree while we were handling this case.

"For the record, Your Honor, GenAgra retained our firm for this litigation after you had left Barnes & Honeycutt for the federal bench, and you have never served with either myself or Mr. Dupree in any capacity regarding this litigation. What the defendant is trying to do is essentially disqualify you from any case where Barnes & Honeycutt would be lawyers appearing before you. This would be an unnecessary burden on the court and on our firm. We handle a great deal of litigation in the Northern Division, Your Honor, and barring you from handling any of our cases is not required or prudent under the applicable statute.

"Without a specific exclusion, defendant is relying on Section (A) of the statute, which requires disqualification if a judge's impartiality might reasonably be questioned. The United States Supreme Court has expanded on that part of the statute, Your Honor, and the standard under Section (A) is clear. It requires removal only if there is a personal bias, prejudice, or wrongful partiality. Nothing in the defendant's affidavit even alleges an actual bias on the part of this court. Their motion must be denied."

As Yale sat down, Tom admired her, as one might admire a

shark. She cut gracefully through the water and killed without remorse.

"I am going to deny the motion," Fuller said magnanimously. "Our docket in the Northern Division is extremely crowded, and we are short-staffed. Ms. Yale is right when she says there has been no allegation of actual bias. And I can assure you and your client, Mr. Hughes, I have no bias, prejudice or interest in the outcome of this case, other than to provide a fair hearing and to make decisions according to the law. Your motion is denied."

Tom was not surprised. Fuller had been about as plain as possible at the bench. He had planned to spend the day taking testimony, and no threat of a lengthy hearing interfering with his tee time was going to make him remove himself from the case.

"Now, Ms. Yale, that brings us to your petition for a preliminary injunction," Fuller continued on without pause. "I understand from speaking with counsel at a bench conference that we will be taking testimony today on this matter. I have set aside the better part of the day to hear the relevant testimony before making a ruling on your request for an injunction. Do you have opening remarks, or should we proceed right to testimony?"

"The court has read the pleadings?" Yale asked.

"I have," Fuller said.

"Well then, I'd waive any opening remarks, if counsel is agreeable?" Yale said, gesturing to Tom.

"That's fine, Your Honor," Tom said.

"All right," Fuller said. "Ms. Yale, you can call your first witness."

"The plaintiff would call, Dr. Tate Cannaert," Yale said, leading the younger of GenAgra's academics from the gallery to the witness stand.

Yale used Cannaert, the assistant director at the North Central Research Center, to lay out GenAgra's hard luck story. Poor downtrodden corporation. Years spent toiling in research to patent corn and blackberries that might help mankind. The painful regulatory process to get the products approved for market. And the betrayal at learning their hard work had been foiled by Ike Stiles, when the old farmer had appropriated their genetically modified plants just as they were being readied for market.

When Yale finished revealing Cannaert's powerful narrative, she turned to her co-counsel to flesh out the technical patent aspects of the case. Tom had no objection to allowing Dupree a turn with the witness, as he himself would need to rely on Felix Hrdina later in the case.

Dupree led Cannaert crisply through the patent for the Hg-Blackberry, or Health-Ease Blackberry as the product would be known if ever brought to market, and the patent for Weed-Away Corn. Cannaert laid out a strong and simple message. The Hg-Blackberry and Weed-Away Corn were the patented property of GenAgra. Almost one-fifth of Ike Stiles' corn, and nearly one-half of his blackberries, were in violation of the GenAgra patents. To legally grow these patented varieties, a farmer needed a license from GenAgra, a luxury that Ike Stiles had not procured. Growing the patented crops without a license from GenAgra, whatever the old farmer's methods or motives for the piracy, was an infringement of GenAgra's patents, Cannaert assured the court.

After forty-five minutes of convincing direct examination, Dupree finally surrendered the witness to Tom, who shifted eagerly in his seat awaiting the opportunity. But as anxious as he was to get into action, Tom wanted Felix Hrdina's technical questioning to go first.

Watching Hrdina cross-examine the witness was even more painful than watching the direct examination. Tom, who had studied the case in some detail for the past weeks, had difficulty understanding Hrdina's questions. And he was sure from the look on Fuller's face the judge was understanding almost nothing. Felix Hrdina was clearly a very smart lawyer, but smart and skilled were two entirely different things in the courtroom, and Hrdina had no future in litigation. He ended fifteen minutes of pointless, tedious questioning with a whimper and turned Cannaert over to Tom. Tom sprang from his chair and hoped to put a stop to the bleeding.

"Doctor Cannaert," Tom said amicably, "you testified you have worked for GenAgra—and formerly Midwest Chemical—for the past fifteen years."

"Yes, sir."

"During that time, you have seen both the Hg-Blackberry project and the Weed-Away Corn project from start to finish."

"Correct," Cannaert said. "Well, the Health-Ease Blackberry will not officially be on the market until next year, but yes, I've been with both projects since the beginning."

"Well, since you bring up the marketing of the Hg-Blackberry," Tom said, resting both hands on the lectern. "You are aware the Michigan Department of Community Health ordered the berry and its derivative products be pulled from the market, correct?"

"Yes, sir."

"You're aware, Doctor, the reason for this action is the Hg-Blackberry is producing an unknown toxin?"

"I can't speak for the department of health or their reasoning," Cannaert said. "But I would disagree the Hg-Blackberry is producing a toxin."

"Doctor, how long has the Hg-Blackberry been in development?" Tom asked, releasing the lectern and beginning to pace slowly behind it.

"Well, field testing at the North Central Research Station started in 2003," Cannaert said. "But the initial phases of the project started in 2000. So that's almost five years now."

"During that time, Doctor, the Hg-Blackberry was subjected to rigorous testing, correct?"

"Yes, sir," Cannaert said. "From the beginning this was a product meant for human consumption, and that meant it had to meet the standards of the USDA, the FDA, and the EPA with regard to final approval. These agencies don't let unsafe products onto the market."

"I'd move to strike that comment," Tom said, turning to Fuller. "It was non-responsive, and this witness isn't in position to make such a blanket statement about the safety record of these agencies."

Fuller drew a deep breath and looked at his watch. The judge had yet to awaken from the boredom induced by Hrdina's questioning.

"Denied," Fuller said. "Mr. Hughes, this is going to be an abbreviated hearing. I've got to make up my mind on this preliminary injunction, and I've only got today to take evidence. So I may restrict the scope of things. There will be time for discovery and a full trial as this case progresses. *If* this case progresses. But if you have something to tell me about the likelihood of success on the merits, or lack thereof, or something about the existence of irreparable harm to one of these parties, I would be happy to hear about it. I haven't heard it yet."

Tom returned to the lectern to regroup. It sounded as if Fuller's mind was already made up, and that was not good. Tom needed to make his point quickly, or the case might be lost before Ike or Ryan ever took the stand.

"You tested the Hg-Blackberry for toxins?" Tom said, returning his focus to the witness.

"Yes, sir," Cannaert said. "We submitted those results to the USDA, and the product was approved last week."

"So your testing at GenAgra showed no presence of toxins in the Hg-Blackberry?" Tom asked.

"No, sir," Cannaert said.

So much for pinning GenAgra with actual knowledge the product was harmful. He was again pacing behind the lectern. His eyes met with the older scientist in the gallery, behind Hannah Yale. The doctor's stare was so intense it caused Tom's concentration to falter. "No presence of toxins in GenAgra's testing?" he repeated.

"Objection," Yale sniped.

"Sustained," Fuller said. "If you have no new ground to cover, Counsel, perhaps we could move on to another witness."

"Just a few more questions, Your Honor," Tom said, forgetting the doctor's stare from the gallery. "Doctor Cannaert, would it be fair for me to say your testing of the Hg-Blackberry was comprehensive?"

"Yes, sir. Very comprehensive."

"And if it turned out the Hg-Blackberry was producing a toxin, would that—"

"Objection," Yale said. "Facts not in evidence, and calls for speculation."

"I intend to present evidence the berry is producing a toxin," Tom argued. "And I intend to ask Doctor Cannaert his expert opinion, Judge."

"I don't see the relevance of this," Fuller said. "This hearing isn't to judge a products liability case, Counselor. If the berry is toxic or is not toxic, is not the question. The question is simply whether there has been an infringement of the patent."

"Judge, this is relevant to the likelihood of success on the merits in the patent case," Tom said, hoping to salvage a single point. "I intend to show the Hg-Blackberry is toxic, and GenAgra should have known about this toxicity, and their contribution in spreading this toxic product is a misuse of the patent, not entitled to protection under the patent laws."

"That sounds far afield, Mr. Hughes," Fuller said, with another sigh, "but, if it will get you to the end of your cross any quicker, I'm going to allow it."

"Doctor, if it turned out the Hg-Blackberry was producing a toxin," Tom said, "would that be something you would have expected GenAgra's comprehensive testing program to uncover?"

"Yes, sir," Connaert said. "But the comprehensive testing showed exactly the opposite. The Hg-Blackberry is substantially the same as any non-genetically modified blackberry. That's why the USDA approved it for human consumption."

"And if your testing program somehow missed a toxin being produced by the Hg-Blackberry, you would be surprised, correct?"

"Yes, sir."

"Your testing program should have caught any toxins?" Tom said.

"Correct," Connaert said.

"And if it failed to do so, that would be a failure of your testing program, wouldn't it?" Tom said.

"I don't believe our testing program failed," Connaert said.

It was the best Tom would get from GenAgra's own witness. Enough to argue GenAgra should have known about the toxin, but probably not enough to convince a judge like Fuller, who was so obviously inclined to rule in GenAgra's favor.

"No further questions," Tom said.

"Thank you," Fuller said, rubbing his temples. "Ms. Yale, any redirect?"

"No, Your Honor," Yale said.

"Good," Fuller said. "We will be in recess for ten minutes.

Let's have your next witness ready at ten-thirty, Ms. Yale."

The weight of probable failure was beginning to mount on Tom. It was compounded as he turned to leave the courtroom and looked square into Al Bullard's ape-like grin. The failed television pundit winked at him, and Tom was thankful he was not within striking distance. The only way for today's hearing to be worse would be for Tom to spend a night in jail for contempt of court after decking GenAgra's representative. He swallowed his pride and walked from the courtroom, surrounded by his legal team.

Ryan had nodded off in a chair by Wendy's bedside sometime before dawn. The tension of waiting with her had taken its toll. He slept, dead to the world, until he was awakened by one of Wendy's screams. He grunted, slipped from the chair, and landed his butt on the hard tile floor. He jumped up, almost in one motion, and was at her side. "What?" he said. "Are you okay?"

Wendy groaned. He saw her eyes roll up before she squeezed her lids tight. Ryan looked at the IV bag of pain medication. It was empty. He tried to comfort her with one hand rubbing on her forearm, as his free hand stretched to hit the call button.

"She needs another bag of the pain medication," Ryan scolded the nurse, as she entered. Ryan was sure his appearance had suffered during his vigil at Wendy's bedside, and could only imagine what the hospital staff thought of him. He'd had no shower. Not enough rest. And his every moment was filled with the sheer terror he might lose the most important person in the world.

"It just ran out," the nurse tried to explain. "I'll get another one hooked up right away."

"Are you okay?" Ryan said, leaning his head down close to Wendy's ear.

"Hurts," she moaned, through clenched teeth. "Legs."

"I know," Ryan said, stroking the hair from her face. "They're going to get you something for it. Just hang on a second."

The nurse scurried back with another bag and reloaded Wendy's pain medication. In a few moments, Wendy stopped simpering, and drifted off into a light sleep. Ryan rubbed his hands through his hair, looking toward the window. The light streaming through the blinds was brilliant, and Ryan felt a moment of panic.

He looked at his watch. After ten. Tom was going to kill him. He bent to kiss Wendy's forehead, grabbed his coat from the back of the chair, and ran out of the hospital.

The mid-summer sun had risen high enough to burn away any hint of morning cool. Sweat beaded on Ryan's skin as he jogged to the visitors' lot and his car. He drove like a madman through the small town, then parked in front of the courthouse. He looked in the mirror and was put off by a three-day growth and ratty hair. Ryan spent two seconds using his hands as a comb, succeeding at nothing, and raced from the car to the court. He pulled his summer jacket over a collared shirt as he ran.

Ryan sprinted up the stairs to the second floor, sweat beginning to seep through his shirt. The security guards eyed him suspiciously, but after a brief search he was waved through the checkpoint. And as he sprinted for the courtroom, the door opened, and he collided squarely with the exiting Tom Hughes.

"I'm sorry," Ryan said, holding onto Tom for balance.

Tom said nothing, his face at first startled, then angry.

"I fell asleep," Ryan said. "And there was a problem with her pain medication this morning."

Beyond Tom, Ryan saw the exodus of people leaving the courtroom. Ernie and Nell and Hrdina. Then Kaye Stiles. Then Ike walking toward him, slightly bent and assisted by Dr. Brown.

"Oh my God," Ryan said. "Ike. How are you?"

"Pissed," Ike spat. "Goddamn judge."

"Take Ike outside," Tom said to Kaye. "This judge is hostile enough. I don't need any more help today."

"C'mon, you old fool," Kaye scolded Ike. Together with Doctor Brown, the old couple walked slowly to the elevator.

Tom's face seemed to regain some of its composure, and he pulled Ryan further aside for private words. "Look," he said in a soft voice, "I understand what you're going through. Really. I lost someone. Okay. I know. But, I need you now. Today. Ike needs you. Let's let the doctors take care of Wendy, just for today. All right? And we're going to concentrate on this case."

"All right," Ryan said.

"Come on. Let me get you a cup of coffee," Tom said.

They walked to a lounge off the courtroom hallway, where

Ernie, Nell, and Hrdina were crowded around a television set mounted high in the corner of the room. Tom fixed Ryan a cup of coffee, and Ryan migrated to the television, his mind willing to accept any distractions that would allow escape from the present.

Ryan looked up at the screen. It was tuned to CNTV. A large red graphic at the bottom of proclaimed: "CDC: No Health Threat Linked to Blackberry." Above the graphic, the Director of the CDC and the Secretary of Agriculture stood side-by-side in front of a blue backdrop. The director read a carefully worded statement ensuring the American public the recent health scare related to enhanced blackberries was overblown. The berry had been tested and approved by the USDA. There was a small health crisis called HERDS, but the blackberries did not appear to be causing the disease. More than half the reported cases had no link to the blackberry. The CDC was investigating around the clock, and the public should be comforted that an answer would soon be found.

Ryan tried to listen to the questions being hurled by reporters following the director's statement, but was thwarted by Ernie, who was muttering loudly.

"This is insane," Ernie ranted. "How can they come out and make that statement? Have they seen the chromatograph of the berry? Of all the irresponsible things in the world, I absolutely can't believe this."

"That's the USDA," Ryan said. "They've been approving genetically modified foods for ten years. What do you expect them to do? Hold a news conference and announce their department is responsible for approving foods that kill people? Of course they're going to toe the company line."

"You look like crap," Ernie said, noticing Ryan's appearance. "You really need to work on the personal hygiene a little. I used to be a health officer. I know these things."

Ryan laughed weakly. "When you get your job back, you can come and arrest me," he said. "Until then, worry about your own hygiene."

Ernie's cell phone rang, and it was impossible for Ryan not to eavesdrop in the small lounge. Ernie pulled a small notepad and a pen from his jacket pocket and started scribbling notes as he talked.

"Man, I think I might have found something to tie up all these random cases," Ernie said, after hanging up the cell. "Last night, I got a chance to look at some of the incoming HERDS files at my old office. I saw Wendy's on the desk. She was living on Dutch apple pie for a week straight before she got sick."

"Yeah, from the Milton Diner," Tom said, handing Ryan a cup of coffee. "It's right next to my office."

"Yeah. That's right. From the Milton Diner," Ernie said. "So it reminded me of the very first case. I took the report. That guy was eating Dutch apple pie from the Milton Diner, like three times in the week leading up to the onset of HERDS. I wasn't able to get the numbers, but I think a significant portion of the people who don't have direct contact with blackberry products were in the Milton Diner. I think it may be the apple pie."

"Not apples," Ryan said. "No connection with the blackberry there. I was thinking there might be some problem with the raspberries, though. They can cross-pollinate with the blackberries."

"Well, it's only a hunch, but I had Jill from my office go talk to the people at the diner this morning," Ernie said, flipping open his notepad. "To get a list of ingredients for the pie. Check out the way it's made. I was thinking maybe they were using a blackberry product in the pie. But I guess maybe my hunch was wrong."

Ryan looked at the ingredients on the list Ernie had copied. Northern Spy apples, flour, salt, eggs, sugar, milk, honey, and cinnamon. No blackberries.

"Everything is homemade there," Tom said. "From scratch. They try to use local ingredients. And God, it is so much better than any of these goddamned chains that are everywhere now."

A switch went off like a circuit breaker in Ryan's tired mind. "Do they use Stiles' Farm products at the Milton Diner?" he asked.

"Yeah," Tom said. "They sell Kaye's gift baskets. Jams, fresh fruit, honey."

"Yeah," Ernie said. "When the department of health shut down the blackberry sales on Friday, that was one of the biggest retailers of the blackberry products."

"Let me see that list of ingredients again," Ryan said, grabbing

Ernie's notebook. "Kaye is a beekeeper isn't she? She collects honey right there on the farm?"

"Yeah," Tom said. "She's been doing it forever. They need the bees to keep the berry crops producing—"

"Does the Milton Diner uses her honey in the apple pie?" Ryan said, running a finger down the list of ingredients in Ernie's notebook.

"Why?" Tom asked.

"It's the fucking honey," Ryan said. "Bees pollinate plants for miles around."

"What?" Ernie said.

"They bring the pollen back from the plants and use it to make honey," Ryan said. "So if they take up pollen from a genetically modified plant, they bring it back to the hive. The toxin isn't *just* in the berries, it's in the *pollen*. And that means it's in the honey. And that means it's in the pie."

"Are you serious?" Ernie said. "That sounds a little far-fetched."

"Serious as a heart attack," Ryan said. "I can't believe I didn't think of it before. Christ, Europe has practically eliminated honey imports from Canada because the honey is being produced with pollen from genetically modified Canola."

Ernie was dialing Jill back on the cell phone as Ryan spoke, to check what brand of honey the Milton Diner used. But Ryan already knew the answer.

"They use Kay Stiles' honey," Ernie said, snapping his cell phone shut.

"We've got to shut down the honey sales," Ryan said.

Tom looked at his watch. They needed to be back in court in one minute. He did not want to make Judge Fuller wait for a second time that morning, so he needed to make a quick decision. Having Ernie available to testify in the afternoon was a luxury to Tom. The case was already going poorly, and Tom needed every possible advantage. But Ernie looked at him for permission to leave and fight the spread of the disease. And Tom knew the answer was really very simple. Ernie had discovered an additional cause of HERDS—knowledge that might save lives if it were placed in the proper hands. Having Ernie as an ace in the hole for this hearing paled in comparison to the chance to save a life.

"Yeah," Tom said. "Ryan is right. We've got to shut down that honey. Can you get someone at the state to stop the honey distribution, Ernie?"

"I don't know," Ernie said, gesturing up to the federal officials who were touting the safety of the Hg-Blackberry on TV. "But I can try."

"Well get going then," Tom said. "And don't come back until you get the job done."

"I'm out of here, then," Ernie said, already starting for the door.

"All right," Tom said. "Good luck."

Ernie marched out of the room, down the corridor, and out of the courthouse.

"C'mon," Tom said, clapping a hand on Ryan's back. "Have a seat in the back of the courtroom and soak in what you can from their witnesses, so you can be ready to testify later."

Ryan plodded beside Tom, slurping coffee, and they slipped into the already packed courtroom. Ryan took his seat, and Tom made his way to counsel's table. Judge Fuller and his clerk came in just as Tom was taking his place next to Ike.

"All rise," the clerk said, echoed quickly by a "be seated" from the judge, still walking to the bench.

"We're back on the record in the case of *GenAgra* versus *The Stiles' Family Berry Farm*," Judge Fuller said, plopping down in his seat behind the bench. "Ms. Yale, another witness?"

"Thank you, Your Honor," Yale said. "Plaintiff calls A.J. McCoy to the stand."

Tom's eyebrows drew together in puzzlement. He had subpoenaed A.J. as *his* witness. His testimony was not terribly important, but technically it was necessary to enter the DNA testing results Ryan would use as the foundation of his own analysis and testimony. It was not a violation of any rule to call an opposing party's witness in a civil case, and was in fact common practice in certain settings, but it certainly caught Tom by surprise. He could not imagine how Yale expected his witness to benefit her case. As Tom puzzled over Yale's motive, A.J. was already shooting comfortable answers to questions, like the professional witness he was.

"I'm the president and CEO of Michigan Genetics Labs," A.J. said, in response to Yale's question.

"What services do you perform at the Michigan Genetics Labs, Doctor McCoy?" Yale asked.

"Testing and analysis of commercial food crops accounts for about ninety percent of our revenue," A.J. said. "Academic and other plant testing accounts for the other ten percent."

"Were you engaged to do testing related to this case?"

"Yes, I was," A.J. said. "I was contacted by Professor Ryan Romanelli, from Michigan A&T University. He put me in touch with Attorney Tom Hughes."

"That is Attorney Tom Hughes, here in the courtroom," Yale said. "The attorney for the defendants in this case, correct?"

"Yes, ma'am," A.J. said. "Mr. Hughes hired my lab to test plant samples he and Professor Romanelli had obtained."

"What types of samples were these?" Yale asked.

"Blackberries," A.J. said.

Tom followed along, happy to let Yale take the testimony he himself would have been forced to offer to an obviously bored Judge Fuller.

"What type of testing did you perform on these samples?" Yale said.

"I performed a DNA PCR test on each of the samples," A.J. said.

"And Doctor McCoy, what are your qualifications to perform this testing?" Yale said.

"Hold on a minute," Fuller said, sitting up in his chair. "It sounds like we're getting into foundational questions for an expert, Ms. Yale?"

"Yes, Your Honor," Yale said.

"Okay," Fuller said. "Just to speed things along. Is there anything controversial about this witness's expertise?"

"Not that I'm aware of," Yale said.

"I'd stipulate he is an expert in genetics and DNA testing," Tom said.

"So we can skip the curriculum vitae, anyway," Fuller said.

"Now what about the testing he has done? Is there anything unusual or contested about the testing, or his reports on the testing, if he has made a report?"

"He has made a written report on his test findings, Your Honor," Yale said. "We don't doubt its accuracy and would seek to admit the reports."

"We'll stipulate," Tom said, happy to get A.J.'s testimony out of the way.

"Okay, let's have those marked as what?" Fuller said. "Plaintiff's Exhibit B, right?"

Tom looked through his own file and was removing A.J.'s reports, and was surprised to see Yale approaching the clerk with a neat stack of stapled paper, plucked from the corner of her desk. "Yes, Your Honor," Yale said.

There had been no discovery made by either side at this early stage of the case. The only documents Tom had acquired had been those he was able to get his hands on, not ones compelled from the opposing side. It struck Tom that he had not disclosed A.J.'s reports to Barnes & Honeycutt, either.

"Your Honor," Tom said, rising to address the court. "Could I see the reports we are marking as Exhibit B?"

Yale paused, turned, and offered Tom the documents. He looked at them closely. They looked like exact copies of A.J.'s original report in his own file. Yale had gotten her hands on his witness's reports in some way, even without the formal discovery that would take place later in the case. Tom was puzzled by this development, but since the reports were accurate, he handed them back to Yale and allowed her to enter them into evidence with no fight.

"I'm handing you Plaintiff's Exhibit B," Yale said, walking the papers from the clerk to the witness stand. "Do you recognize these reports?"

"Yes," A.J. said, flipping his thumb through the stapled papers. "These are the DNA results for the tests I performed for Professor Romanelli."

"Could you briefly describe these results for the court," Yale said.

"Ms. Yale," Fuller interrupted. "If the reports are in evidence, do I need a description from the witness?"

"Just very briefly, Your Honor," Yale said. "If I may?"

Fuller rolled his eyes and nodded.

"*Very* briefly, if you could summarize your results," Yale said.

"All samples submitted were an exact genetic match," A.J. said hurriedly. "The Hg-Blackberry. The samples submitted were an exact match."

"And what did you do with these test results?" Yale said.

Tom felt Ike shifting in the chair next to him.

"I sent the original report to Tom Hughes and copies to Professor Romanelli," A.J. said, "and GenAgra."

Tom was uncertain if he heard A.J. correctly. The witness was less than twenty feet from his table, but Tom's mind had difficulty grasping what his *own* witness had just said. He sent a copy of the DNA test results to GenAgra? Tom's legs elevated him from his seat of their own accord, without any conscious order to do so. His mind searched for the proper objection.

"Why—" Yale began.

"Objection, Your Honor," Tom said, pausing. He had still not grasped the proper objection. He was coming up on two decades of practice, and never before had he been in any hearing or deposition where his own witness exposed himself as some sort of double agent.

"What's your objection?" Fuller growled, turning a suspect eye to Tom.

Tom thought for a beat. And then two. But there was no proper legal objection. Under the weight of Judge Fuller's stare, he was forced into an awkward retreat. "Withdrawn," he said.

Fuller shook his head twice and let out a small groan.

Yale had turned to look at Tom during the objection, and he could clearly see the corners of her mouth upturned. She was circling. She had planned this very moment, he was certain, for his embarrassment.

Yale turned back to the witness. "Why did you send a copy of the report to GenAgra?" Yale said.

The lawyer in Tom's mind was now screaming, "Objection, relevance," but Tom was so interested in the answer, he didn't bother to stand and utter the phrase.

"Michigan Genetics has a contract with GenAgra that requires my company to report any positive tests for plants patented by GenAgra," A.J. said. "It allows GenAgra to confirm whether the person submitting the sample is licensed to grow the plant. Part of their patent infringement security system."

Tom did not move or let his face show surprise. It was a reflex from many appearances in front of a jury. A poker face could fool an untrained juror, though it probably wasn't going to get by Judge Fuller. And behind a quiet mask, Tom was roiling. His own expert witness was under contract to GenAgra.

His legs told him to stand and object, but there was no legal ground. A.J. was certainly being unethical, but without knowing more, he had no way of arguing that what had happened broke the law or any rule of evidence. He would have to wait for an opportunity to question Benedict Arnold.

"Now you had no role in collecting the samples that were taken, Doctor McCoy?" Yale continued on.

"No, ma'am," A.J. said.

"Were you told the methods used to collect the samples?" Yale said.

"Yes," A.J. said. "Professor Romanelli told me that he and—"

"Objection, hearsay," Tom said, his reflexes functioning again.

Fuller looked up toward Yale.

"I'm offering it conditionally, Your Honor," Yale said. "I believe it will be inconsistent with testimony given by Professor Romanelli when he is called. I'd ask the Court to take the testimony, and exclude it later if it turns out not to be inconsistent."

"Anything to move this case along," Fuller said. "I'll accept the answer, and exclude the testimony from any decision if it turns out to be inadmissible hearsay."

"What did Professor Romanelli tell you about collecting these samples?" Yale pushed forward.

"He told me that he and Tom Hughes had snuck onto the NCRC and stolen known samples of Weed-Away Corn and Hg-Blackberry from GenAgra's stock," A.J. said.

Tom felt an immediate heat rush to his face. He had always tried to practice law in a fair manner. Honest to courts and juries, and straightforward in his dealings with witnesses and evidence. He had never been ashamed while standing in the cold light of the courtroom, when his name was dragged into proceedings by a witness, for he had nothing to hide. But the words A.J. had spoken were true, and Tom had been involved in a theft. He hadn't even thought about it at the time. He was getting samples in the only way he knew how, so he could better advise Ike. It was like eating one grape at the market, before purchasing the entire bunch. Technically stealing, yes. But done without any ethical qualm in the mind of the shopper. But now, hearing about his own misdeed in open court, Tom felt like crawling under the table.

Fuller sat up, abandoning his indifferent posture. "Did you just testify that Mr. Hughes stole these samples?" Fuller said to the witness.

"Uh-huh," A.J. said, turning to face the judge.

"Will the lawyers approach," Fuller said. The judge asked his clerk to make a side record as Tom and Yale reached the front of the bench. Fuller hissed at Tom, "Is this allegation true?"

Tom thought about taking the Fifth. It had been a long time since he had studied criminal law, but he probably had a right to invoke his privilege against self-incrimination. "I was with Professor Romanelli when he collected the samples," Tom said, opting for a careful crafting of the factual truth.

"At a minimum, that makes you a witness in this case, Counselor. At worst, you are accused of a crime," Fuller said, disgusted. Tom could read the subtext clearly. *You had the nerve to try and disqualify me from this case*, was the sentiment bubbling beneath the judge's words. The judge turned to Yale. "I will tell you I'd be inclined to grant a motion to remove Mr. Hughes as the attorney in this matter. But I don't want to waste this entire day of testimony."

"Nor do I," Yale said. "We have our witnesses here. And I would never dream of dragging Mr. Hughes into these proceedings as a witness today. Trial might be another story."

"All right," Fuller said. "We'll plow through. But I'll be reporting this to the state bar, Mr. Hughes. Ms. Yale, I'll leave it to you to advise your clients, should they want to report this suspected theft to the proper authorities. Let's go back on the record."

Tom's face burned. He tried to keep his head high as he returned to the defense table, but it felt like a lead weight.

"Ms. Yale," Fuller said, when the lawyers had resumed their positions, "you may proceed."

"I have no further questions," Yale said, turning prettily and sitting alongside Bullard, who smirked at Tom.

Tom rose weakly from his chair and made his way to the center of the courtroom. He leaned forward, supporting his weight on the lectern. Yale had accomplished all of Tom's ministerial points with the witness. Tom was left with a cross-examination driven solely by curiosity. He was too stunned to recognize the obvious danger of a lawyer asking questions just because he wanted to know the answers.

"You've testified here you were under contract to both GenAgra and to myself, correct?" Tom said.

"Yes, sir." A.J. said. His face was passive, completely composed. In contrast, Tom's own expression was contorted with emotion.

"And you knew I was the attorney for the Stiles' Berry Farm," Tom said.

"Yes, sir."

"You and I have discussed this case, correct?" Tom said.

"Yes, we have. On several occasions," A.J. said.

"And you never informed me you were working for GenAgra, did you?" Tom said.

"You never asked," A.J. smiled slightly, and it made Tom's anger boil.

"I'm paying you two hundred dollars an hour to be here in court today on behalf of Ike Stiles, correct?" Tom said, his voice rising up.

"Yes, sir."

"One question, then," Tom said. "Are you double billing us?"

"Objection, argumentative," Yale said smoothly.

"Sustained," Fuller said. "We're going to keep it civil in my court room, Mr. Hughes."

Tom paused. "Are you billing both GenAgra and my office for this time?"

"Not technically, no," A.J. said.

"What do you mean, not technically?" Tom said.

"Well, I am under contract to GenAgra to report any suspected patent infringement," A.J. said. "As a part of that contract, I have agreed to provide reasonable testimony for the information I disclose to them."

"So how much do they pay you for this service?" Tom said.

"GenAgra pays four thousand dollars a month for monitoring patent infringement at Michigan Genetics facilities throughout the Midwest, and that fee includes my testimony as it is required," A.J. said.

"I guess they pay you a little better then, huh?" Tom said.

"They are paying for the truth," A.J. said. Yale had risen to object to the question, but sat down and let A.J.'s professional answer suffice. "Just like you are. I'm not some hired gun. I provide accurate testing."

"And you believe this is ethical behavior, for an expert witness to take money from both sides in a dispute," Tom said.

"These matters are disclosed in the contract you signed with me," A.J. said.

"My question was whether you believe this practice is ethical, Mr. McCoy," Tom said.

"Objection, relevance," Yale said.

"I'll take the answer for what it's worth," Fuller said. "If we can move this along."

"Mr. McCoy?" Tom said.

"Yes, it's ethical," A.J. said. "Michigan Genetics is a for profit company. We do accurate testing. And I'm going to give the truth in court, one way or another, no matter who's paying the bill. Nothing about the fact that I am employed by both sides has impacted my testimony in any way."

"Nothing further," Tom said, returning to his seat like a fighter who has taken a savage beating.

"No redirect, Your Honor," Yale said.

"Thank you, Mr. McCoy," Fuller said. "You are excused. Do

you have another short witness we can get in before the lunch hour, Ms. Yale?"

"Yes, Your Honor," Yale said. McCoy avoided Tom's eyes as he left the courtroom. "We'd call Phillip Stevens to the stand."

Tom listened to the testimony from a fog. He had never been through three worse hours in court. His attention flagged. It was all he could do to focus long enough to understand where the testimony of the next witness was heading. He was the director of marketing at GenAgra. And he talked like a used car salesman. Only instead of selling Tom another Cadillac, he was selling the judge on the idea that Ike Stiles' pirating of the Hg-Blackberry was akin to stealing the crown jewels. GenAgra would lose millions if the theft was allowed to occur, and there was no way to stop it without an immediate injunctive order.

"I want you to take this one," Tom whispered to Nell. "I need a break."

Nell nodded her head. Relieved of the burden of following every detail from the witness stand, Tom tried to relax. He hadn't expected to make any real headway with GenAgra's witnesses, he told himself. Nothing that had happened in the morning session had damaged his case irreversibly. He needed to collect his thoughts, and tear into the judge with Ike's side of the story after the lunch hour. Fuller had shown no signs he could be fair, but Tom still had a chance. How could anyone listen to Ike's story and not be moved? But looking up at the judge, and over at the eternally smirking Al Bullard, Tom was sure some people did not have the capacity to care.

Chapter Eighteen

Wendy looked down at her own body. The hospital bedding had been stripped away, leaving only her small frame, partially covered by a flannel hospital gown. She was relieved to see the swelling in her legs was almost gone. The creases where her skin had ruptured were healed. She looked normal.

But a feeling of dread came over her despite the fact that all looked well. She could not move her toes. There was no pain. Almost no feeling. And it was not only her toes. She struggled to move a knee, but it felt as if it were weighed down by an anchor. She couldn't move her upper leg. With each failed attempt at movement, her sense of despair grew by orders of magnitude. Her stomach would not move voluntarily, but only in rhythm with her breathing. She could not sit up in bed. And she realized that her arms were stuck in invisible cement, all the way to her fingertips. She tried to call out for help, but even her lips were frozen. Only her eyes moved.

Looking back down to her toes, Wendy was mortified to see a tiny green worm struggling between them. It was a tomato fruitworm, the star of her thesis. But it wasn't a single specimen.

Several worms squirmed up through the cracks of her toes, with more still burrowing out of her pale shins. All with no pain. No sensation at all. The mass invasion of the fruitworms worked its way up her legs to her thighs, and as it approached the hem of her hospital nightgown, Wendy finally loosed a scream for the on-duty nurse.

Wendy's eyes opened with the scream. Her breathing was panicked. She looked down to see her lower body hidden under a wrinkled hospital bedspread. Her mouth was closed. There had been no scream. The worms were a dream. But the nightmare of her hospitalization was very real. With consciousness came her new constant companion. Pain. She had lived the past days, how many she had lost count, in a constant fog of pain, medication, and restless sleep. Her head ached. She looked around the room, but it was empty.

Wendy could not remember how many times she had awakened. From dreams. From nightmares. From black unconsciousness. And each time she had opened her eyes, Ryan had been there by her side. His dark eyes, gentle and swollen. His smooth forehead crinkled with compassion. Though he hadn't said the words, Wendy was sure Ryan loved her. But he was absent now, and she felt lost.

Sun streamed through the opened blinds. A lunch tray sat waiting for Wendy near the side of the bed. But the room was silent, save for the hum of the central air vent. In the silence, Wendy laid back on her pillow and felt her body. The pain was moderate, compared to what she had come to expect. But an uneasy numbness had seemed to rise all the way to her pelvis. She could almost feel it rising, as she lay still, attuned to her body. Wendy focused on her breathing. Her lungs were expending noticeable amounts of energy drawing breath. Was she having difficulty breathing? Panic swallowed her mind.

She looked down at her body, fearful she might see worms. Her legs were swollen. She rolled her head looking for the call button. She found it behind the headboard and pressed it. And as she arched to reach the button, she felt her bladder let loose. There was no control. Just a rush of urine. The smell of ammonia acrid in the air. Wendy started to cry.

"Help," she said, at first softly and then louder. "Help!"

The feeling of pressure inched up her body, pressing her like a vice. Up over her stomach. Into her solar plexus. It was far less pain than the cramps that had tormented her legs, but Wendy knew she was struggling for breath now. She willed air into her lungs, and gasped another softer call for help on her exhale.

She reached back with her hand again, searching for the call button. She could hear her own shallow panting. And then footsteps. But it was not a nurse.

"Oh my God," Ryan said, his face registering shock at Wendy's condition.

"Help," Wendy gasped, hurt by the revulsion in his eyes. How could he ever love her, deformed as she was. Wendy cried both for fear and for loss.

Ryan turned and ran out of the room as Wendy tried to say no. There was no air left to say any word to him. Her vision seemed to redden in increasing shades. Her thoughts swirled—feeling oxygen slipping away. She laid back in bed, her body now asphyxiating. She heard Ryan yelling in the hallway, and she thought how she would like him to touch her, just one more time. His earth-worn hands would be warm and gravelly on her face.

Wendy saw a rush of activity around her. Hands. White coats. Perhaps the tufts of Ryan's wild hair. She could hear him somewhere. Crying. She loved a man, once, she thought. And the red faded to purple. The purple to black. And silence fell on her thoughts.

Lunch at the grill across from the courthouse had only confirmed Tom's fears. Nell and Hrdina knew the case was a disaster, as surely as Tom did. They tried to comfort him, commiserating about the injustice of A.J.'s backstabbing testimony. And they didn't think the theft allegation against Tom would ever amount to more than grandstanding by Yale. But they could not remove the facts that had come into evidence. Everything said in the morning court session told Judge Fuller that GenAgra was right, and the Stiles' Berry Farm should be shut down until the case could wend its way through a full trial.

The only thing good to come of the break was a chance for

Tom to clear his mind. And when he returned to court and sat by Ike's side, ready to start the defense case, he was serene. There were two sides to every story, and Fuller had only heard one of them. There was still time to convince him to do the right thing. Tom looked back at the gallery as they waited for Fuller to take the bench. GenAgra's rooting section had grown by two business executives Tom did not recognize. One, a barrel-chested elderly man in an impeccable suit, the other, a young assistant. Tom's cheering section had shrunk. Ernie was on the road to try to stop HERDS from spreading further. Ryan had visited Wendy over lunch and had not returned. But Ryan would not stand him up twice in one day, Tom thought. The professor would be in court ready to testify when the time came.

Tom's attention was called by the court clerk, as Fuller took the bench. The judge called for the defense, and Tom called Ike to the stand. The old farmer slowly made his way across the courtroom to a raised witness platform. The court clerk gently adjusted the microphone, and Tom had a lengthy conversation with his good friend.

It was as easy as talking on the porch, over beers and a warm summer breeze. Ike, sans profanity, was softer. Even more charming. Almost cuddly. And the substance of his testimony was powerfully highlighted by his folksy wisdom. Ike explained the farm's history, his decision to go organic in '99, and the care he and Kaye had given to the project. He explained the husbandry of the berry patches, and orchards, and leaf crops, with the patience of a grandfather passing wisdom to his kin. Even Fuller's seeming boredom was overcome by the magic of Ike's storytelling, Tom noticed. The judge had perched on the edge of his chair and leaned in to listen to Ike. He was rapt by the old farmer's testimony.

After laying out the background, Tom shifted Ike to the problem. The strange behavior of the deer and the birds in their avoidance of genetically modified foods—testimony that was accepted by the entranced judge over Yale's objection. Ike's certain knowledge that genetically modified crops had polluted his fields, confirmed by Ryan's testing. The devastating impact the genetic pollution would have on his organic operation—that it had already had on his organic operation. The hardship of losing the only work he had known for sixty years.

Tom rounded third and headed for home. He eased Ike into his own battle with HERDS. He let the old man described the painful disease in the plain language of a man who spent all day, every day, with plants and trees and brambles. He described the hopeless sensation that came with struggling to breathe against an unseen toxin. Again, the testimony was accepted over Yale's objection— the judge with a look of true concern for the storyteller. When Tom finished his questioning of the old man, the courtroom was silent. Only applause from an adoring audience was missing. It was a direct examination from heaven.

"No other questions, Your Honor," Tom said, and surrendered the witness to Yale. He turned slowly and smiled at Bullard and Yale, whose faces were more sober. As were the faces in the gallery. Reality was sometimes sobering. His triumph was tempered as he realized Ryan had still not arrived back at the court. Taking his seat, Nell gave Tom a smile that said more than any praise. Ike may have pulled them back to within striking distance, if he could withstand Yale's cross-examination.

Yale rose and stalked to the podium with the grace of a predator. Her face was calm, and her piercing blue eyes were fixed on the old farmer with no malice or mercy. "Let me start by making sure I understand the limits of your testimony," she said evenly.

Tom considered objecting to Yale's editorializing, but decided to see how well Ike could fend off the shark himself.

"First, you aren't here testifying about the patents GenAgra holds on Weed-Away Corn and the Health-Ease Blackberry, are you?" Yale said.

"I'm here saying they are wrong," Ike said. "How can you patent a, uh, plant? It's ridiculous."

"So you do have some knowledge you would like to share with the court about these patents?" Yale said.

"Yes," Ike said. "They're wrong. It's wrong to let them make a crop, and have it spread all across the green earth."

"Have you read the patents, Mr. Stiles?" Yale said.

"No, I haven't," Ike said. "I don't need to. That's why I hired a lawyer."

"You would agree with me that the plants growing in your

field are Weed-Away Corn and the Health-Ease Blackberry," Yale said.

"Yes, isn't that why we're here?" Ike's face started turning red like a strawberry, and his breathing was audible from the defense table.

"And you testified you had no permission from GenAgra to grow either Weed-Away Corn or the Health-Ease Blackberry, isn't that correct?" Yale said, quickening her pace.

"No," Ike said, his face angry and pained. "I testified I wouldn't have their goddamned plants on my farm."

"Mr. Stiles," Fuller said, the judge's stern yet amused voice barely audible over Kaye's gasp. "This is a court of law. I will admonish you to keep your language civil."

"There's nothing this court can do to me that my wife wouldn't top," Ike wheezed, with a wink and a smile at the judge.

Fuller seemed convinced of the truth of his statement. "Please watch your language, Mr. Stiles. Do you have more questions, Ms. Yale?"

Fuller actually seemed to be encouraging Yale to stop torturing the old farmer. Tom thought he saw Ike grimace when the old man turned to look back at Yale. He considered asking the judge for a recess, before Yale cut off his thoughts.

"Just a few more questions, Your Honor," Yale said, and launched an immediate attack. "You would agree with me that Weed-Away Corn has advantages over organic corn, wouldn't you?"

"No, ma'am," Ike said. Tom could now see sweat on the old farmer's brow. "I think you need to spend a few more years working in the fields before you're qualified to make that judgment."

"Organic farms cannot use chemical pesticides, isn't that true?" Yale pressed on.

"Yes," Ike said.

"And you're aware that Weed-Away Corn produces its own organic pesticide. Bt, right?"

"Yes, ma'am," Ike said, his breathing strained. Tom looked back at Doctor Brown, who gave a concerned shrug. "It produced a bunch more than *I* would ever put on any crop."

"So by having Weed-Away Corn on your farm, you gain the

benefit of having a crop with built-in pest resistance, isn't that correct?"

"Nothing about what GenAgra is doing is any benefit to me, ma'am," Ike said.

"It is true, is it not, Mr. Stiles, that the State of Michigan has issued an order closing your farm's operations until it has finished investigating the alleged toxicity of the Health-Ease Blackberry?"

"Yes," Ike said. "Another great benefit of having GenAgra's crops on my land."

"You are complying with that order from the State, aren't you?" Yale asked.

"Yes," Ike said.

"You haven't made any challenge to that order?"

"No," Ike said. "I think it may save people's lives, ma'am."

"So there is really no financial harm to you in continuing this preliminary injunction until that State order is removed, is there, Mr. Stiles?" Yale said.

"Perhaps you'd like it if the court closed your firm, too," Ike said, grimacing again.

"Your Honor," Tom said. He felt like a cut-man in the corner of a title bout. He would throw in the towel if it meant keeping Ike safe. "May we approach."

"Yes," Fuller said. "The witness may stand down for a moment, but please remain in the courtroom, Mr. Stiles."

Ike rose and walked gingerly toward the defense table, Doctor Brown coming out of the gallery to meet him.

"Your Honor, Mr. Stiles has been out of the hospital for about six hours," Tom whispered to the judge. "He's the only HERDS patient I know who has made it out of the hospital. And I don't want him being cross-examined to death."

"Maybe Mr. Hughes should have thought of that before he put Mr. Stiles on the witness stand," Yale snapped cruelly. Even Fuller seemed taken aback by the beautiful lawyer's venom. "I have the right to fully cross-examine any witness they present, and I'm not waiving that right."

Fuller sighed and folded his hands, his eyebrows drawn together in contemplation. "This whole hearing is moot, isn't it?" he asked, finally. "At least until the State was to lift its order banning the farm's operations."

"That goes to a balancing of the harms," Yale said. "There's no harm to them in continuing the order, but I'm not asking the court to stop this hearing. We've already wasted thousands of dollars getting to this point. I don't want to come back and do it again later, when the state finally figures out this blackberry is completely safe."

"I just want to protect my witness," Tom said, shrugging.

"Well, why don't we take a recess. And you can see if you can get him—"

The relative quiet of the bench conference was broken by a crisp thud from behind Tom, and the sound of instant commotion. People rushing about. He turned to see Ike collapsed by the defense table, Doctor Brown beside him.

"Could someone call an ambulance," Doctor Brown said, his voice cool and firm, above the general din. Tom rushed to Ike's side. The old farmer was conscious but gasping for breath. Doctor Brown leaned over Ike and to check his airway, and Kaye leaned over the bar, reaching for her husband. Even the old scientist from GenAgra looked concerned, crowding in close to Kaye. Tom met his eyes again. Malec was his name, Tom remembered. And in his eyes, there was a story.

Bullard stood at the plaintiff's table watching them attend to the ancient man. The thought of crediting the blackberry with his collapse crossed Bullard's mind but was quickly shunted away. Still, he might stop eating those berries until the entire matter was cleared up. Yale seemed to accept him as he was—rich and powerful. Bullard smiled, glancing at his pet attorney. Not many people at Washington dinner parties could brag about their dates literally cross-examining a witness to some state near death. Now that was an ice breaker. His smile grew.

Zimmerman's assistant tapped Bullard lightly on the shoulder.

"Mr. Zimmerman would like to see you and Ms. Yale," the assistant said.

The court recessed to clean up the mess Yale had left behind, so Bullard and Yale weaved their way through the chaos and followed the assistant into the hallway. Zimmerman waited for them in a conference room, standing at the head of the table. Doctor Malec was seated to his right. The assistant closed the door as he left.

"That was quite a cross-examination," Zimmerman said to Yale. "I don't think I've ever seen that in a courtroom before. And I've been getting sued regularly for the past fifty years."

Yale smiled but said nothing. Most people would not take pleasure from the old farmer's collapse, but it was clear to see Yale had enjoyed herself. Bullard's pride swelled, but it was washed away when Zimmerman's demeanor changed.

"But the old fucker was killing us in there before he collapsed," Zimmerman scowled. "Was that some kind of Hallmark moment we were having?"

Bullard steamed in silence. He thought the old mogul would have been pacified completely by the news from the CDC and the USDA, not to mention the shutout they were pitching in court.

"I'm very confident we have this thing in the bag," Yale said, flashing Zimmerman a cold smile. "I wouldn't worry about those theatrics. I know Judge Fuller well, and I don't think there is any way we lose this hearing at this point."

"Well, I'm glad to have someone of your skill handling things," Zimmerman's mood swung again, but he was far from totally mollified. "So what do you think is left?"

"They have to call an expert," Yale said, "if they want to even have something to argue to Fuller. I expected them to call Professor Romanelli, though I haven't seen him in court this afternoon. I'm ready to blow his testimony away, though. Or whoever they put up. This is as close to a slam dunk as a case can get."

"Well, thank you for the legal briefing," Zimmerman said. "Now if you'd excuse us, I need to speak with Doctor Malec and Mr. Bullard for a moment."

"Yes, sir," Yale said, shaking Zimmerman's powerful hand. "Pleasure to meet you."

"The pleasure was mine," Zimmerman said.

Yale left swiftly, leaving Zimmerman and Bullard standing on opposite sides of the table, with Doctor Malec seated between them.

"I trust you saw the CDC news conference earlier, sir?" Bullard said calmly, testing Zimmerman's odd mood swings.

"I trust you've seen the Wall Street fucking opening," Zimmerman shot back. "GenAgra's down another ten percent this morning right out of the fucking gate."

"I'm sure it will bounce back," Bullard said, yielding no ground. He knew the big dogs didn't like to see weakness.

"Goddamn right it will bounce back," Zimmerman said. "It's you I'm worried about. GenAgra will survive. But if you don't win this fucking case and stop the bad press we've been taking, I don't know if you will. That old farmer's testimony was like watching Ol' Yeller. And I've taken about enough of it. For what I'm paying you, I could've bought the old bastard off at the start."

"Sir," Bullard said curtly. He did not want to buckle to Zimmerman's pressure, but he knew he was walking a fine line. "With all due respect, it would be very expensive to buy your way out of the problems in this case. If not for my intervention, I don't see how you would have staved off a full crisis surrounding this berry."

Zimmerman was silent for a moment, letting Bullard's comment sink in. "I've gotten a pretty clear picture of how you're running this operation," Zimmerman said icily, nodding toward Doctor Malec. "And I can't say I approve of your methods. Unlike the public relations industry, we still have to make products that don't actually kill people. If we kill off all of our customers, they tend not to buy our products anymore. No matter how we spin things, okay?"

"Mr. Zim—" Bullard started but was silenced by the power of Zimmerman's rising voice.

"Now you listen," Zimmerman continued. "I am going to be very frank with you, young man. Which is probably more than you deserve, given the things I've heard about what's been going on here. I gave you the advertising account and the lead on this Skinny Berry project because I am an old friend of your father's. He said you needed more private sector clients, and I was happy to help him out."

Zimmerman's words bit into Bullard's ego, making Bullard

feel like a helpless child. If he'd have thought he could have pulled it off, he might have tried to end Zimmerman's speech with a good right cross.

"Now, I adore your father," Zimmerman said. "He is an old-time businessman. And I mean that in the best way. He knew how to take care of customers and make a fuck of lot of money at the same time. But I don't like him so much that I'm going to put up with the crazy bullshit you've been doing while managing this project. So here's the deal. You win this case. And set things in order. And make amends to those you have been fucking over in my company. And we can continue to do business together. But if you lose this case, or fail to make things right, or fuck up my trip to Brussels and the EU negotiations, then I don't think there's going to be much work for you anywhere on this whole goddamned planet." Zimmerman paused. "Do we have a deal?" the old man asked.

Bullard was actually afraid of the stout little CEO. There was a power within him that was great. But Bullard's pride required him to try and fight back.

"The Bullard Group is hardly as desperate as my father might have let on, Mr. Zimmerman," Bullard said calmly. "He is getting on in years, so I forgive him some misunderstandings. But I am personal friends with the Vice President of the United States. And you understand the kind of power he has. My contacts in the White House and on the Hill make me either a very great friend or a formidable enemy."

He stared right into the old CEO's eyes. They did not flinch. "I have enjoyed working with GenAgra, Mr. Zimmerman," Bullard continued. "But with all due respect, I think you may need me more than you realize. And I don't appreciate being threatened."

Zimmerman laughed off his words. "Son, you aren't even old enough to understand that the government is only the shadow of big business's ass. I own more senators than you know. And I've got friends in every industry. Hell, we are the government. So if I were you, I would close my goddamned mouth and take care of business. Do we understand one another?"

Bullard paused. "Yes, sir," he said.

Tom watched as Ike was raised on a gurney and taken from the courtroom. Doctor Brown and Kaye had to hurry to keep pace as the old farmer was whisked away, still breathing on his own. Tom hadn't had a chance to say so much as good-bye to his client in the commotion. And he stood in the courtroom with only Nell and Hrdina by his side. The judge and GenAgra's entourage had recessed as Ike was treated.

"Are we going to throw in the towel, boss?" Nell said, her voice quiet, as she put a hand on Tom's shoulder. "I can make the closing argument if you want to get to the hospital."

Tom was out of witnesses. Ryan had not come back from his lunch visit to the hospital. Ernie was fighting to save the world. And Ike had just given up his health, if not his life. Tom didn't even have enough facts in evidence to argue his case without Ryan's testimony. And even with Ryan's testimony, it was a long shot. Would Ike, preoccupied with illness, care if Tom let the case come to its pathetic and inevitable conclusion without a fight? The answer in Tom's head was immediate and clear.

"I've got to get Ryan," Tom said to Nell. "I need him to testify."

"I've already tried his cell," Nell said. "It's out of service."

"He's probably still at the hospital," Tom said. "Maybe he lost track of time. He was kinda out of it this morning."

"Yeah," Nell said. "I don't know if putting him on is going to help much, to be honest."

"I've got to put him on," Tom said. The clock was ticking, and Tom hatched a plan like those drawn in the dirt from childhood football games. "Nell, I need you to do whatever it takes to keep the hearing going. I'm running over to the hospital to try to get Ryan. I'll be back as soon as I can. Twenty minutes maybe. I don't know how long before the judge will take the bench again. Just stall him."

"Okay," Nell said, looking like a soldier ready to flee the battle.

"You can do it," Tom said. And he sprinted from the courthouse. Tom sped through the small town, cursing red lights, and praying it was not quota day for the traffic patrol. The hospital was only a short drive, but Tom could imagine Nell struggling to keep Judge

Fuller from calling a close to the hearing so he could get in extra practice swings before his golf league.

Tom parked in the visitors' lot and ran to the hospital doors. The mid-afternoon heat was searing, and Tom could feel sweat soaking his dress shirt. He jogged to the elevator, pushed the button repeatedly, and rode the slow machine to the third floor. He found Ryan in Wendy's room, his eyes red with exhaustion or tears. As Tom entered, he heard the mechanical whir and hiss that had become familiar in the past days. He brushed aside a curtain and saw Wendy unconscious. Prone in bed. Her lungs being force fed sustaining oxygen by a machine.

Ryan snapped from a trance as Tom approached. "Oh, Tom," he said, dreamlike.

"What happened?" Tom said. Wendy had been stable when Tom had seen her the previous night. But now she was the picture of lingering death.

"They let the prednisone run out," Ryan sniffed. "While I was at court this morning. She went into acute respiratory distress. If I wouldn't have made it here at lunch…" Ryan swallowed off his last words.

"What is wrong with these people?" Tom said, approaching Wendy and laying a hand on hers. "Is she going to be all right? What have they said?"

"I don't know," Ryan said. "They're keeping her sedated and on the machine while they get her meds going again. But I can't leave her again, Tom."

Tom walked over to Ryan and laid his hand on the top of the young professor's wiry hair. "This isn't your fault," Tom said softly. "You *know* who did this to her."

"It doesn't matter who did it," Ryan said. "I almost let her die. And I can't live with that."

Tom thought of turning around and heading back to court. Ryan was right to want to stay. But Tom could not give up on his case. And time was running out. "I'll be right back."

He ran from the room to the nurses' station. A matronly woman helped him locate Ike, and Tom ran down the corridor like a schoolboy. Down a flight of stairs. To the cardiac care unit. He found Ike admitted to a private room, with Kaye and Doctor

Brown by his side. Ike was attached to an IV and an oxygen tank, but looked slightly improved.

"Is everything okay?" Tom said, surprising the group.

Ike nodded and croaked. Kaye walked over and hugged Tom. "What are you doing here?" she said. "Shouldn't you be in court?"

"Is he okay?" Tom asked.

"Mild heart attack," Doctor Brown said. "They are going to do some testing, but he should be fine—" and the doctor turned to Ike "—if he stops smoking, like I've been telling him for twenty years."

"Oh, God," Tom said. He was about to describe the news of a mild heart attack as "great," but checked himself. "Doctor Brown, could I borrow you for a second?" he asked. "I need to get back to court, but I need your help."

Tom and Doctor Brown hurried to the third floor ICU and into Wendy's room.

"Ryan, get your jacket," Tom said. "Doctor Brown is going to wait with her. Watch her. We're going to court."

"I, uh—" Ryan started.

"I can handle it, son." Doctor Brown smiled, reassuring Ryan.

Tom grabbed the professor by the hand and pulled him from his seat. "C'mon, we're not going to let them get away with it."

Ryan allowed himself to be dragged from the room, looking back on Wendy until they were in the hallway.

"We've got to hurry," Tom said, urging Ryan to a trot. "We're already late."

They jogged back to the car, and Tom retraced his path, catching the same traffic lights, uttering the same curses, until he was parked before the courthouse. They jumped out of Tom's car, ran to the second floor, and into the courtroom, with only a brief pause at the security checkpoint.

Tom's eyes searched the courtroom for clues. Fuller was on the bench and that was a good sign. But his face was hostile. The judge's eyes were boring into Nell, who was at the center lectern. Nell was in mid-sentence as Tom and Ryan entered.

"...don't have authority at my fingertips, Your Honor," Nell said, "but I can assure you that in rare cases, lawyers have been allowed to testify."

"Well, I've never seen it," Fuller spat. "And I've been practicing for over thirty years now. I'm not going to let you call Mr. Hrdina as a witness, and that's the end of it. So if you don't have any other witnesses, we're going to move on to closing statements."

Tom took his cue. He marched past the bar to the defense table. "We have one final witness, Your Honor," he said. Nell whipped around, saw him, and shrugged. "The defense would call Dr. Ryan Romanelli to the stand." Then he whispered to Nell as she walked past him to her seat, "Nice job."

Fuller asked about Ike with genuine concern, and Tom assured the judge the old farmer's condition was life-threatening. It was good to leave the judge emotionally torn about Ike, Tom thought. Fuller's concern lasted all of sixty seconds, though, before he pressed on with the hearing, still determined to make his tee time.

Doctor Romanelli was not the picture of a credible expert. He was disheveled and unshaven. He wore a rumpled coat, literally slept in. Early in his testimony, his words were no more organized than his appearance. But Tom masterfully guided him to a point of comfort, as he had done with witnesses for twenty years. Just having a chat and a cup of coffee, without the coffee.

After ten minutes where Tom worried that Judge Fuller's boredom and exasperation were going to explode, Ryan settled into a rhythm. The young professor talked to Tom as he had through the weeks they had known each other. Confident, but not cocky. Sure in his vast knowledge of the plant world. Ryan filled in the theory around the facts that had been laid out by Ike. It was true the farmer's corn and blackberry crops were infested with the patented GenAgra plants, but it was perfectly implausible that Ike had intentionally stolen the plants. Ryan drove this point home with a statistical analysis of the fields. If Ike had wanted to pirate the plants, as GenAgra had claimed, why would the old farmer plant only a small percentage of his fields with the genetically modified crops? And more importantly, why would the genetically modified crops be intermingled with the organic plants in a semi-random pattern? The answers were simple and apparent to any rational scientist, Ryan concluded. He ended the first portion of his testimony with a simple explanation of how the genetically modified crops cross-pollinated in Ike's field. It was the only rational explanation for the unusual percentage and unique distribution of the genetically modified plants on the old farmer's land.

Tom was pleased. Though it was late in the day and the testimony was somewhat technical, Fuller seemed to have followed it clearly. Tom confidently moved to the second major point he wanted to make with Ryan's testimony.

"Now Doctor, you have had the occasion to test the Hg-Blackberry for toxicity?" Tom said.

"Yes," Ryan said. And the professor launched into a lucid explanation of his methods and procedures.

"Thank you," Tom said, after Ryan had explained the background of the testing so any third grader could have followed. "Now with that testing, you compared known samples of the Hg-Blackberry and the organic blackberries that were growing on Ike Stiles' farm?"

"Yes," Ryan said.

"And in your expert opinion, are there differences between the two berries?"

"Yes," Ryan said.

"And what are those differences, Doctor?"

"Well, the most obvious difference is the Hg-Blackberry has been modified to make a molecule that is normally manufactured by the *Hoodia gordonii* cactus. This molecule—called P-57—is associated with Hoodia's ability to suppress appetite. And the molecule is readily observable in the tests I performed. So that is the first major difference between the berries."

"And are there other differences?" Tom said.

"Yes," Ryan said. "My tests showed that in addition to the appetite-suppressing molecule, the Hg-Blackberry was also producing a previously unidentified toxin."

"And can you describe the significance of this finding, Doctor?"

"Well, as you are aware, the Michigan Department of Community Health has been investigating an illness in our state called HERDS," Ryan said. "While clinically I am not qualified to say this new toxin in the Hg-Blackberry is certainly the cause of HERDS, it is the leading candidate. More testing will need to be done to establish the exact pathology of this illness and to confirm the link between the toxin I discovered and HERDS. But it is safe to say people should not be consuming this toxin. And GenAgra should have known about its existence."

"Objection," Yale said. "Speculation."

"I'll allow it," Fuller said, concerned by the testimony.

Tom pulled the two chromatographs out of a manilla envelope from his file. He showed them to Yale and had them marked as exhibits by the court clerk. He then handed them to Ryan.

"I'm handing you two charts marked as Defense Exhibits One and Two," Tom said. "Do you recognize these charts?"

Ryan glanced at the chromatographs. "Yes," he said. "These appear to be copies of the chromatographs showing the berry's toxicity."

"Any objection to entering these?" Fuller asked, looking at his watch. "I got the gist of it from his testimony."

"None," said Yale.

"Mr. Hughes, you were going to offer them in evidence?" Fuller said impatiently.

"Yes, sir," Tom said. "I was going to have Doctor Romanelli explain briefly—"

"I get the gist of his testimony," Judge Fuller said. "If I have additional questions about the reports, I can always put him back under oath. But it's three-ten, and we still have cross. And some closing argument. It's not getting any earlier."

"All right, Judge," Tom said. "I'd move that Defense Exhibits One and Two be entered."

"Without objection, Defense Exhibits One and Two are entered into evidence," Fuller said. "Any more questions, Mr. Hughes?"

"No, Judge," Tom said. "That's all I have."

"Cross-examination, Ms. Yale?" Fuller said.

"Thank you, Your Honor," Yale said. She bolted forward to attack Ryan. "You would admit GenAgra's Weed-Away Corn was growing in Ike Stiles' field this summer, correct?"

"Yes," Ryan said.

"And you would admit GenAgra's Health-Ease Blackberry was growing in Ike Stiles' field this summer, correct?"

"The Hg-Blackberry, correct." Ryan said.

"And both these plants are patented by GenAgra to the best of your knowledge, correct?" Yale said.

"Yes."

"And to the best of your knowledge, Ike Stiles never had a license to use these patents, correct?" Yale said.

"No," Ryan said.

"Now, it was your opinion on direct examination these GMOs got into Ike Stiles' field through cross-pollination, correct?"

"Yes," Ryan said.

"But that is only an opinion," Yale said. "A guess, correct?"

"It is an educated guess. The only hypothesis that makes any sense," Ryan said.

"Looking at the same data, it is also possible Ike Stiles obtained patented seed stock and cuttings and planted them selectively throughout his fields, is it not?" Yale said.

"I've talked with Mr. Stiles," Ryan said. "He would have no reason to do that. It would have cost him his organic certification."

"My question was whether it was *possible*, looking at the data, Ike Stiles could have selectively planted GMOs he obtained in some fashion," Yale said.

"Well," Ryan said. "I guess anything is possible, Ms. Yale. But it's not a plausible explanation."

"It is *possible* he selectively planted the GMOs to increase the yields in his crops, isn't it?" Yale said.

"That wouldn't make sense," Ryan said. "He'd lose his certification."

"It's possible the reason he planted the GMOs in such a fashion was to avoid detection when his fields were certified organic, isn't it?" Yale said. "He could try to ensure his crops were still certified organic by directing the testing to the organic parts of his field and still get the benefits of increased production in the genetically enhanced portion of his field."

"Anything is possible," Ryan said. "But I've spoken with Mr. Stiles, and I wouldn't believe that."

"Thank you," Yale said. "Now I'd like to turn your attention to your position at Michigan A&T, Doctor Romanelli. You testified earlier you were a professor of plant biology there?"

"Yes," Ryan said.

"And you are currently employed as a professor of plant biology there?" Yale said.

"Technically," Ryan said. "Yes."

"And why would you qualify your answer, Doctor?" Yale said.

"I am currently inactive," Ryan said.

"Inactive?" Yale said. "Are you on a sabbatical? Writing, perhaps?"

"I've been suspended with pay," Ryan said.

Ryan was struggling, and it was Tom's own fault. With better preparation, he would have had Ryan ready to answer these painful questions more smoothly, but the run up to the hearing had been anything but smooth. Ryan was going to have to get through things as best he could.

"Suspended?" Yale said. "Why is that?"

"I've been accused of sexual harassment," Ryan said angrily. "But it's a lie. They are trying to retaliate against me because of pressure from your client, Ms. Yale. GenAgra had me suspended."

"Oh," Yale said. "I see. GenAgra has had you suspended. Because of your participation in this case?"

"Yes," Ryan said. "And I can prove it."

Tom remembered the audio tape. He had completely forgotten about it.

"That's very nice," Yale said, moving on from the unknown danger. "I'm sure you can. But I would appreciate it if you would simply answer my questions. I want to move on to your assertion that the Health-Ease Blackberry is in some way toxic. You said you came to this conclusion based on testing you conducted?"

"Correct," Ryan said.

"And specifically, those tests results are compiled in what has been admitted as Defense Exhibits One and Two?" Yale said.

"Yes," Ryan said, fumbling with the chromatographs. "Yes, One shows the normal blackberry. And Two shows the Hg-

Blackberry."

"Might I approach the witness, Your Honor?" Yale said. Fuller waved her forward. Yale swam directly to her prey, Tom thought. She took Exhibit Two from Ryan, examined it, and handed it to him. "This is the graph that shows, in your opinion, the Health-Ease Blackberry is toxic?"

Ryan glanced at it again. "Yes," he said, "it says Hg-Blackberry at the top. This is a copy of my chromatograph."

"And you shared this with the Michigan Department of Community Health," Yale said.

"Yes," Ryan said, "It was an urgent matter of public health."

"That was your opinion," Yale said.

"Yes," Ryan said. "It is scarcely an opinion, though. The test results are clear."

"Well, Doctor," Yale said, "I don't mean to be obtuse, but I guess I'd like you to show me, looking at this Exhibit, how exactly you concluded the Health-Ease Blackberry was toxic."

Ryan looked down at his chromatograph, his face annoyed to be challenged by a mere attorney on a matter of science. But Tom watched in horror as Ryan's expression devolved into a look of confusion. Ryan shuffled back and forth between the two chromatographs.

"This is not my work," Ryan said, agitated. "It looks like a copy, but it has been altered."

"I'm sorry, Doctor?" Yale said. "These are the reports that have been admitted by you, correct?"

"Yes," Ryan said. "But this report on the Hg-Blackberry has been altered. In my original report there is a spike. A toxin was clearly present. But this copy—"

"Yes, Doctor," Yale said. "Defense Exhibit Two, your chromatograph on the Health-Ease Blackberry. There is no evidence it is toxic in that graph, is there?"

"Uh, not in this copy, but it has been changed..." Ryan stammered. He looked to Tom and then to the judge and then to Yale.

"I suppose GenAgra has somehow altered the chromatograph you submitted into evidence?" Yale said sardonically.

Ryan looked like a deranged conspiracy theorist. Before this revelation in Ryan's testimony, Tom had thought Fuller might open his mind and actually consider ruling in Ike's favor. But now, Fuller looked like a man whose entire day had been wasted by the incompetence of others.

"No more questions," Yale said.

Tom rushed in to try to repair the damage. "May I approach the witness, Your Honor."

Fuller disgustedly waved Tom forward.

"So, in reviewing Defense Exhibit Two," Tom said, "it is your conclusion that someone has altered this copy of your chromatograph."

"Unmistakable," Ryan said. "The spike from the chromatograph that showed the unknown toxin has been removed."

"So your original report showed a spike, which was consistent with an unknown toxin?" Tom struggled.

"Yes," Ryan said. "It was clear."

"And this graph. Altered, as you say," Tom was drowning, "it in no way changes your opinion, Doctor? The Hg-Blackberry is toxic?"

"No," Ryan said stolidly.

Tom remembered the tape. It was a last hope to show there really was a grand conspiracy afoot. "You said earlier you could prove GenAgra was responsible for your suspension at Michigan A&T," he said. "How is that?"

"The dean of my college, Peter McPhee," Ryan said. "He told me so."

"Objection, hearsay," Yale sniped from the plaintiff's table.

"Sustained."

"I'm not offering it for its truth, Your Honor," Tom said. "He taped the conversation with McPhee. I'm offering it to show its effect on the listener. This is not some delusional conspiracy theory that is being woven by Professor Romanelli."

Fuller sat back in his chair momentarily, almost bouncing with impatience. He checked his watch. "If you've got a tape, I'd consider it for that purpose," Fuller said, annoyed. "But I'm not going to take his hearsay testimony."

Tom looked at Ryan, who pulled the tape from his coat pocket. It was a micro-cassette, commonly used for dictation. Tom had no device to play the tape and looked helplessly to the judge. Fuller shrugged. Tom turned to the defense table first. Yale's eyes showed a small amount of fear. Bullard looked terrified.

"Here," Nell said, pulling a small dictaphone out of her purse. She tossed it to Tom.

Tom put the tape in and hit the play button. The tape hissed with white noise. Tom found the volume control and turned it up. There were sounds of a conversation, but the only audible words came from an agitated Ryan Romanelli and they were hardly proof of anything.

"Do you have any other questions?" Fuller asked, again bouncing in his seat.

"No," Tom said, defeated. "I've got nothing further."

"Any redirect, Ms. Yale," Fuller said.

"No, Your Honor," Yale said.

"Good," Fuller said. "I'm going to take a five-minute break to use the little judge's room, and then we're going to get this hearing over with." Fuller stalked out of the courtroom.

Tom turned and headed for the hallway. Nell and Hrdina patted him on the back, but it did nothing to soothe him. Though he knew Ryan was a decent and brilliant professor, his testimony had been that of a wild-eyed lunatic. The outcome of the hearing was no longer a mystery. And beyond this hearing on the preliminary injunction, the fate of the case against Ike looked sealed as well.

Chapter Nineteen

E rnie's first call after leaving the courthouse was to Jill. He caught her on the cell phone as she was getting back to the office. She gave him a run down on the director's agenda for the day. She and Herb Underwood had been called to Lansing to meet with the governor himself, to bring him up to speed on the HERDS investigation, and the CDC's sudden abandonment of the Michigan public health effort. Ernie explained Ryan's theory about the honey and the need to get it off the market.

Jill said she would do all she could to get Ernie in to see the director at the governor's office, and Ernie sped through summer construction on his way to Lansing. He made the trip in an hour and a half, battled for another fifteen minutes to find a parking space next to the governor's office building, and sprinted into the offices in search of Director Jones. Jill's behind-the-scenes work had paid off. Director Jones had left a message at the reception desk. Ernie was escorted into the heart of the state's executive offices.

"Ernie," Director Jones said, rising from an upholstered colonial chair in the governor's reception area. "Glad you were able to make it." A dour-faced Herb Underwood was seated next to Director Jones.

"Director," Ernie said. "I've got some new information—"

"Why don't we step out into the hallway. I'll be just outside if the governor needs me," Jones said to the secretary. She gently pushed Ernie into the hall outside of Underwood's earshot. "Jill said you had news."

"Yes, ma'am," Ernie said.

"If you don't stop calling me 'ma'am' you're going to have to find another department to work in." Jones smiled at him. "It's Kathy."

"Kathy," Ernie said hesitantly. "Yes. I think I've found the secondary cause to HERDS. My investigator is running the numbers this afternoon, but I'm pretty certain that it's honey polluted with the toxin from the Hg-Blackberry. I think it will account for almost all the cases in Michigan."

"Listen to you," the director said. "Suspended for a week and still giving orders to your staff."

"Yes, uh, Kathy," Ernie laughed self-consciously, "it was too important to sit on. I really think once she compiles the data, we should put out an immediate order stopping honey distribution from any sites near the GenAgra research facility."

"Okay," Jones said. "But have you seen the CDC's statement this morning? Five hours ago I would have shut down honey distribution on your word. But now, I don't know."

"Yes, ma'am," Ernie said, to the director's gently reproving look.

"And now I've got the governor calling me on the carpet," Jones said. "He wants some definitive answers, like, yesterday."

"I understand," Ernie said. "What can I do?"

"Well, Herb has been trying to shut this investigation down since the beginning, you know," Jones said. "So I'm pretty sure what spin he's going to give the governor. I want to let the governor hear both sides of this, so I'm letting Herb have his say. But I want to put forward the best case to shut down the berry, and the honey, too. That's why I'm going to let you speak on behalf of the department."

Ernie let the words sink in, and then flushed with satisfaction.

A month ago he was a new epidemiologist, and now he was the director's designated hitter on an important outbreak investigation—going to brief the governor, no less. Energy ran through him. Both pride and fear.

The governor's secretary poked her head into the hallway. "The governor is ready to see you, Director Jones," she whispered.

Ernie marched into the governor's office side-by-side with Director Jones, feeling like an interloper who would be forcibly detained at any moment. The office was decorated in shades of brown; heavy wood tones and soft light. Ernie immediately liked the surroundings. It was a place where silent reflection could have resided, had it been a desired tenant.

"Kathy," Governor Roger Howell said in a rich voice. He shook the director's hand. He was an elegant-looking man in person, but his presence seemed hollow. "Thank you for coming today. Come in. Come in. Sit down. You know Artie."

"Mr. Fisher." The director nodded to a man Ernie had never seen before. A short man, obviously hidden from the public light, but clearly accustomed to crawling comfortably in the halls of power.

"Kathy," the little man said, shaking the director's hand.

"I've brought some help along," Kathy smiled. "So you can make the most informed decision. This is Dr. Herb Underwood, manager of our Bureau of Epidemiology. And Ernesto Vasquez, the regional epidemiologist who headed up the early part of the investigation."

Handshakes were exchanged by all, and everyone was seated around the governor's solid mahogany desk. Ernie basked in the comfort of the upholstered chair that supported him, excited, feeling like the ultimate insider.

"Kathy," Howell started. "I've brought you in today to get a handle on this thing. Artie says the numbers make this a very sensitive issue. This could be a political nightmare. And that is not something I want to deal with, obviously. Plus, with this federal stuff coming out this morning—I want to know what the hell is going on, so I can get through this crisis all right."

"Yes, Governor," Kathy said. "That was a very strange news conference by the CDC this morning. I'm at a loss. But I want you to make the best decision possible. That's why I've brought along Doctor Underwood *and* Mr. Vasquez. Because they represent a diversity of opinion that exists on my staff. So I thought you'd benefit by input from both sides."

"Excellent," Howell said. "All right. Bring me up to speed and tell me where we are going on this, so Artie here can craft me a message that gets us through it. Who wants to start?"

Underwood raised his head high and his eyebrows higher. He was recognized by default.

"Governor, as you know, we're facing a serious health crisis," Underwood said, doing his best impression of a statesman, but sounding constipated. "We are up to two hundred and sixty-two cases of HERDS in Michigan. Three-oh-eight nationwide. The numbers have gone up fairly steadily since the blackberries were removed from local sources on Friday. So we are unsure there is any causal connection between the Hg-Blackberry and HERDS—"

"Just a minute," Director Jones interrupted Underwood firmly. From her file, she pulled out the folded chromatographs which had been provided by Ryan. "Now these are technically beyond my paygrade, but you reviewed them, Herb. And you told me yourself, before Friday's press conference, they show a toxin."

The interruption punctured his attempts at formality. "If I might continue," Underwood said. "I have had a chance to look at them more closely, Director Jones, and I am far less certain today there is even a toxin in the Hg-Blackberry, let alone with the conclusion the blackberry is causing HERDS."

"That's not what you said just—" the director shot back, her voice rising.

"Hold on. Hold on," Howell said magnanimously. "More light, less heat, Kathy. Let's let Doctor Underwood have his say."

"Thank you, Governor," Underwood said, his head bobbing up and down in a near curtsey to the chief executive. "As I was saying. You can look at the chromatograph yourself, Governor. I believe my initial conclusion may have been flawed. I don't even believe the Hg-Blackberry is toxic at this point.

"And my point here is strengthened by the fact that nearly fifty percent of the cases statewide have no connection to the Hg-

Blackberry. So if we are starting from the hypothesis that we, one, have a toxic blackberry, and two, it is causing HERDS, that would mean we would also have to believe there is another cause out there, independent of the blackberry. And that would be highly unusual in the history of epidemiology. To have two independent causes of the same illness, arising at nearly the same time. So I am doubtful we've identified the right cause."

"Hmm." Governor Howell sighed. "That's not good. So in your opinion we've misidentified the cause, created a food panic, and torpedoed GenAgra all based on an error."

"I'm afraid that's my conclusion, sir," Underwood said.

Howell and Artie Fisher turned to one another and shared a disturbed look.

"So where would you advise we go from here?" the governor asked.

"We go back to square one. Investigate this matter as it should have been handled from the beginning," Underwood cocked his head slightly to Ernie, insinuating his underling's incompetence. "Track down the real source of the disease *before* we issue another statement to the press. And from listening to the CDC's press conference this morning, that is the direction they are going in."

"How long's that going to take?" Howell asked.

"I don't know, sir," Underwood said. "But we have to follow scientific processes if we want to come to more prudent answers to this crisis."

"All right," Howell said, smiling briefly. "Well Artie, I think our friends at GenAgra might be happy to hear that opinion. You said there was another side to this story, Kathy? Let's hear it."

Jones nodded to Ernie, urging him to speak. Ernie sat frozen for a micro second, unsure if any sound would utter when he moved his mouth. But he thought the people of the state needed some kind of voice at this meeting, and so he found his own.

"Thanks," Ernie said to the governor. "Sir, I couldn't disagree with Mr. Underwood more. I think it is clear Michigan has been out in front on this. Ahead of the CDC or the USDA. We have found the cause of HERDS, sir. It *is* the Hg-Blackberry. It *is* toxic, and it has the potential to kill people if we allow it back on the market."

"What about all these other cases that aren't caused by the blackberry?" Artie Fisher asked, swiping a broadside at Ernie's opening comment. Ernie was startled to handle questions from multiple directions, but he relaxed and adapted. He knew the truth, and he knew Underwood was full of shit. And that was enough to make anyone confident.

"I'm glad you asked," Ernie said. "I've spoken with Professor Romanelli this morning. He's the plant biologist who discovered the toxin. It's his belief the toxin is being spread not only by direct consumption of the Hg-Blackberry, but also through honey that is being made from the pollen of the Hg-Blackberry. I've got someone from my office working on that theory now, and they should have a definitive answer this afternoon. But my initial look tells me the blackberry and the honey are going to account for over ninety percent of the cases. It will take some legwork, but my gut tells me the other ten percent of the cases will eventually be linked to the toxin in the Hg-Blackberry. Consumed either through the berries or the derivative honey."

"You have someone working on it from *your* office," Underwood said, irritated. "*You're* suspended. *You* don't have an office."

"This is the kid who went to the press?" Artie Fisher barked, rolling his eyes.

"Kathy?" Governor Howell said.

"Yes," Jones said. "He is. And you know what? I believe him. His going to the press saved lives. So he speaks for me on this issue."

Howell and Fisher exchanged another cautious glance that Ernie could not read.

"All right," Fisher said finally. "So you say you may have solved the causation problem. What do you say about Doctor Underwood's point that the Hg-Blackberry isn't even toxic?"

"Frankly," Ernie said, considering the consequences of his next utterance only briefly, "it's bullshit. I've examined the chromatographs. No scientist could look at them and fail to see the toxin. So I don't know where he's getting that interpretation."

"Right here," Underwood said, frothing. The head epidemiologist grabbed the folded graph from Director Jones and fumbled awkwardly to get them open. When he finally managed to open the graph on the Hg-Blackberry, Ernie saw the change immediately. The peak of the toxin Ryan had shown him five days before was erased from the chart, as if it never existed.

Ernie was stunned momentarily. "That's not the same chromatograph I gave you last week," he said to Director Jones finally.

The director shrugged.

"Sir," Ernie said, turning to the governor. "That document is not the same chromatograph I received from Professor Romanelli. The toxic signature of this Hg-Blackberry was unmistakable on the graph I saw. I saw it. Professor Romanelli saw it. Even the press reporter I shared it with saw it.

"He saw it, too," Ernie continued, gesturing to Underwood. "And if he's here trying to heist this forgery on you, you have a problem, Governor. If you don't keep this blackberry off the market, if you don't get this honey off the market, people are going to continue to die. And Governor, you don't want to see this disease. It is ugly. I've seen it up close, and I wouldn't wish it on anyone. I can't imagine the voters would be too happy if they ever find out you had the right information about what was killing them and didn't act on it."

Howell leaned back in his chair and rested his hands on top of his head. His face was a contorted mix of puzzlement and anxiety. "So what are you proposing, Mr. Vasquez?" Howell asked. "What would you say is the correct course of action?"

"Have another toxicology report done on the berries, ASAP," Ernie said. "And on the honey. If you put your weight behind it, sir, I bet you could still get results today. You'll see that I'm not lying to you about this Hg-Blackberry. It is the problem."

"And what if we go with Mr. Underwood's plan?" Artie Fisher said.

"Well, that's your prerogative," Ernie said. "But I'm going to get these products tested again, one way or another. And if you leave it up to me, I've got nowhere to go but the press."

Fisher and Howell shared a third look, this one more agitated than the first two. The team from the Department of Health was shown the door, and the big men were left alone to plot a course of action.

Tom walked into the courthouse restroom, bent over the sink, and brushed cold water onto his face. He stood up and regarded himself in the mirror. His eyes were bloodshot and highlighted by small black pouches. Tom could see every line that fifty-four years had left, most of them coming since he had been licensed to practice law, and many from as recent as Claire's passing. He wondered if he had taken a different path, whether his face might not be so written with age. Tom thought of how awful Ryan's testimony had really been, and he laughed out loud at the absurdity of it. He had to cut himself short when the door to the restroom opened. The older academic with GenAgra, Malec, walked in. He approached and stood at an adjacent sink.

As he paused next to Tom, their eyes met in the mirror, and Malec took an object from his pocket. He set it on the countertop. The object made a hollow plastic clack as it was placed on the faux marble. A micro-cassette. Tom assumed the doctor had retrieved it from Nell's dictaphone and was returning it, in some perverse victory dance. A dangerous rage built up in Tom, but it was silenced when the doctor spoke.

"You need to listen to that tape," Malec said simply. "I'm taking a copy of it with me to the U.S. Attorney's office tomorrow. But you need it today. Now."

Tom looked at the tape more closely. It was not the same one he had played so humiliatingly in court only moments before. "What is it?" Tom said.

"Listen to it," Malec said. "And don't let the bastards get away with it."

Malec turned and left the restroom. Tom hesitated before moving. Was this another great moment in legal history? He could scarcely imagine how the hearing could be made any worse. He took the tape and started after Malec, but the scientist was already leaving the courthouse through the security checkpoint.

Tom walked quickly to the lounge and found Nell talking with Hrdina. Their conversation died away as Tom approached. He could only imagine their shame at being associated with what was quickly becoming the worst one-day hearing in the history of the legal profession.

"You okay?" Nell said, trying to smile.

"Yes," Tom said. "Let me borrow your dictaphone again."

"Ryan left for the hospital," Nell said, ignoring his request. "He wanted me to tell you."

"Let me see your dictaphone," Tom said again.

Nell fished the dictaphone out of her purse. "What have you got?" she asked, as Tom took the new tape from its case and slipped it into the small recorder.

He pressed play, adjusted the volume, and listened. "I don't know," he said, trying to understand the conversation that was clearly recorded on the tape. He strained to orient himself to the speakers. Two men talking about chromatographs. Both voices vaguely familiar to Tom. One speaker identified in the conversation as Doctor Malec. And the second identified moments later as Al Bullard. The voices seemed genuine—it was clearly Malec and Bullard. The tape was no fake. And the content of what the men were saying made the hair on the back of Tom's neck rise. He looked from Nell to Hrdina, their faces mirroring the "holy shit" look that Tom knew he was himself wearing. They knew about the toxin all along. They faked Professor Romanelli's chromatograph. Sometimes there really was a conspiracy.

Tom sent Nell to the ladies' room, to transcribe the short conversation as best she could in private. He paced the hallway, peeking in the courtroom, waiting for Fuller to return to the bench. He had a bombshell, and he could not wait to lob it at GenAgra. Bullard and Yale brushed past him on their way back into the courtroom, their smugness oozing from them like cheap cologne. Tom smiled cheerily at them. Bullard in particular.

The chambers' doors in the back of the courtroom opened, and Fuller and the clerk entered. Tom sprinted for the restroom and knocked impatiently for Nell.

"I got most of it," Nell said, emerging. She handed him the dictaphone and a legal pad containing the basics of the conversation, as the two of them dashed up the hallway and into the courtroom. Fuller was carping at the helpless Hrdina, demanding an explanation for Tom's whereabouts when Tom and Nell entered.

"Sorry, Your Honor," Tom said loudly, as he and Nell hurried to the defense table.

"Mr. Hughes, could we kindly get started," Fuller said, his impatience bordering on pathology. "I assume you have no other witnesses and we can have some brief argument."

"Ah, I'm sorry, Judge," Tom said. "I do have just one other witness. Very short, I think."

Fuller leaned forward and fixed Tom in a maniacal stare. "Mr. Hughes, the court has been very patient with your case so far," Fuller said. "But I'm not sure where you have left to go here. What topic are you going to cover with your next witness?"

"Your Honor, the defense would call Al Bullard to the stand," Tom said. The few remaining participants in the courtroom led out a collective breath. Bullard straightened noticeably in his chair.

"And what is the purpose of this testimony?" Fuller said. "If you are fishing for discovery here, it is something you should really do by way of deposition."

"No, Judge," Tom shook his head, needing to laugh, but only able to smile. "This is directly relevant to today's most unusual hearing."

"Well, I'll agree with your characterization of the hearing." Judge Fuller chuckled, and the GenAgra team collectively joined in. "But I'm not sure I understand where you are going with this witness."

"Judge," Tom said. "I'll be brief. Five minutes at most."

Fuller looked at his watch. "Okay. Proceed."

Bullard walked to the witness stand, a picture of hubris. Tom was delighted. The smug, fat man was sworn to tell the truth, the whole truth, and nothing but the truth. A proposition that again made Tom stifle laughter.

"Mr. Bullard, you are the agent representing GenAgra at today's hearing?" Tom said.

"Yes, I am," Bullard said. "I am actually an independent contractor with GenAgra, but I have been assigned to oversee the Health-Ease Blackberry product."

"Are you or are you not the agent for GenAgra here today?" Tom asked curtly.

"Yes," Bullard snipped.

"How long have you been heading up the Health-Ease Blackberry project?" Tom said.

"A little over a month now," Bullard said.

"And Health-Ease Blackberry, so I am clear, is the name GenAgra has given to its Hg-Blackberry, correct?" Tom said.

"It's the name I gave the Hg-Blackberry, Mr. Hughes," Bullard said proudly.

"They're one in the same. The Hg-Blackberry in the patent is what you now call the Health-Ease Blackberry, correct?" Tom said patiently.

"Yes," Bullard said.

"Now I want to ask you some very direct questions, okay?" Tom said.

"Certainly," Bullard said. "It's the best way to communicate."

"Good," Tom said, smiling at the doomed man. "You are aware GenAgra's stock price fell dramatically last Friday, correct?"

"Yes," Bullard said. "Thanks to the claims of your Professor Romanelli. Rather unfounded claims, as it turns out, I must say."

Team GenAgra murmured approval in the background.

"Can we get to a point here, Mr. Hughes," Fuller directed.

"Yes, Your Honor," Tom said. "Would it be fair for me to say you thought Professor Romanelli sounded like a bit of a conspiracy theorist in his testimony today, Mr. Bullard?"

"I wouldn't say a *bit* of one," Bullard smiled. "I think the facts clearly showed his theories for what they were."

"Conspiracies, right?" Tom said.

"Your words," Bullard smiled larger. "But I wouldn't disagree."

"You are familiar with a Doctor Malec at GenAgra, aren't you?" Tom asked.

"Mr. Hughes," Fuller snapped. "Is there a point here, or should we get to your closing arguments and be done with this?"

"There is a point, Your Honor," Tom said forcefully. "And if you will give me a few more questions, I think it will be clear."

Fuller sighed and leaned back in his chair.

"You know Doctor Malec?" Tom said

"Yes," Bullard said. "He is the director of the enhanced

products division at GenAgra."

"Does he have involvement with the Hg-Blackberry, Mr. Bullard?" Tom said.

"Yes. He invented it," Bullard said dismissively. "He was in charge of the project before they brought me on. The project is shifting from development to marketing."

"He told you GenAgra knew the Hg-Blackberry was toxic, didn't he?" Tom said.

"What?" Bullard said, his smugness melting away. The fat man shifted in his chair.

"It was a simple question," Tom said again. "Doctor Malec told you GenAgra knew the Hg-Blackberry was toxic, didn't he?"

Bullard's eyes shifted from left to right. He looked at Yale. The burden of his own silence seemed to weigh on him, until he finally said, "No. That's preposterous."

"It is conspiratorial?" Tom said.

"Yes," Bullard said.

"Doctor Malec never told you GenAgra knew the Hg-Blackberry was toxic?" Tom said.

"No," Bullard said.

"And Doctor Malec never told you he would have needed another two years to make the Hg-Blackberry fit for human consumption?"

Bullard's face turned a brilliant crimson. "Never," he said, very conscious of his denial.

"Let me ask you this, since it goes to the heart of Doctor Romanelli's testimony," Tom said. "You never asked Doctor Malec to alter a chromatograph in connection with this case, did you?"

Bullard's pauses grew exponentially longer. "That's ludicrous," he said.

"It would be a conspiracy, wouldn't it, Mr. Bullard," Tom said. "Pure fantasy?"

"Yes," Bullard said.

"And you would never be involved with something of that sort, even if it did exist?"

"Objection, Your Honor," Yale said.

"Sustained," Fuller said. "I'm reaching my limits here, Counsel. If you have anything else relevant to my decision, you'd better get to it quick."

"I will, Judge," Tom said, removing the dictaphone from his pocket, to a chorus of light snickering from Team GenAgra. "I'm going to play you a tape, Mr. Bullard, and I'd like you to identify the voices you hear."

Bullard's eyes grew wide and the courtroom grew silent as Tom played the full tape Malec had handed to him during the break. Bullard wouldn't acknowledge the sound of his own voice, but the damage was well done. And nothing Yale could do during her frantic questioning could save the buffoon on the witness stand.

Ryan was still staggering from his performance in the courthouse, as he parked in the visitors' lot and headed inside the hospital. He felt like a zombie. The only parallel he could draw was to his days as a graduate student, when he had stayed awake for the better part of four days studying for his comprehensive exams. He was still unsure about what had happened to him on the stand. Somehow Tom had handed him a fake of his own chormatograph, and Ryan hadn't had the spare mental capacity to answer any of the questions effectively. He was quite sure he had cost Ike his case. And this saddened him. But even after his thorough embarrassment on the witness stand, he could only think of Wendy. He drove immediately to the hospital.

Doctor Brown was waiting patiently by her side as Ryan made his way into the ICU.

"How'd it go?" Doctor Brown asked, rising from his chair.

"Is she okay?" Ryan said.

"She's been in and out of consciousness," Doctor Brown said. "With the medication and the respiratory distress, that's normal. But once they got her back on the prednisone, I think she stabilized very well."

"Is she going to be okay?" Ryan asked, the hissing of the ventilator like a constant reminder of death.

"It's hard to say, son," Doctor Brown said. "This illness is still very new. Recoveries I've seen have been slow. But we've got

Ike to look at. If a seventy-seven-year-old man as stubborn and unhealthy as him can get well, I don't see why this young woman can't."

"Thanks for watching her," Ryan said.

"Oh, it was my pleasure," Doctor Brown said. "And I've had a talk with the doctor on duty. I don't think you're going to have to worry about Wendy's medicines being changed."

"Thanks, Doctor Brown," Ryan said.

"Well, I think I'd better head down and check on that old billy goat I brought in here." Doctor Brown laughed and shuffled to the doorway before turning. "How did it go in court? Ike might want to know."

"I'm not a lawyer," Ryan said. "But I think Ike is screwed."

"Well, at least you're honest," Doctor Brown said. "That's better than a lot of witnesses I have known in my day."

With that, Doctor Brown was gone, and Ryan turned his attention to Wendy. He walked to her bedside and kneeled, bringing his face level to hers. The ventilator moved her lungs in rhythm. Slowly in. Slowly out. He reached out with his hand and let the back of his fingers brush the soft skin of her cheek, before sliding a strand of wayward hair back off her face. Ryan lost track of time watching her, wishing she were with him consciously. He needed to tell her again. Wanted to know that she knew. Wanted to hear his love echoed back in her voice or see it in her eyes.

Ryan's knee went numb on the hard tile, and a sharp pain was threatening to make him stand and leave his post, when Wendy's eyelids flickered. He moved his head left, into her field of vision, not wanting her to have to spend an ounce of energy to find him. Her soft brown eyes fixed on his. She was awake. She was still Wendy. He was sure.

"I love you," he whispered, and then said it again to be sure the words were not drowned out by the ventilator. He saw her throat strain against the ventilator, struggling to speak, and he stroked her hair softly. "Shhh," he said. "Don't talk."

She continued to look straight at him, and Ryan felt a warmth spreading inside his chest.

"I love you," he said again. "Nothing else matters."

Wendy's eyes watered, and a single tear spilled down her

cheek.

Tom sat down. At its heart, his argument was as simple as it was short. He told the judge that what GenAgra had done to Ike was wrong. They should never prevail in front of a jury on such horrendous facts. They should never have been entitled to a temporary restraining order. And the court should certainly deny their application to convert their temporary order into a preliminary injunction that would remain in effect until trial. When he sat down, he felt as if a great burden had been lifted from him. He smiled and wondered how David had felt when he had felled Goliath. Perhaps it was more a sense of relief than a sense of joy.

Consumed in his own thoughts, he did not hear Yale's rebuttal argument. Despite the cataclysmic meltdown at the end of her case, she had still asked the judge to grant her petition in her first crack at argument, stating that regardless of the facts that were elicited during the hearing, the law allowed GenAgra to proceed as it had, and prevented the Stiles' Berry Farm from growing the patented plant, regardless of anyone's intention. But in her rebuttal, her tone was shrill, and Tom tuned it out. It had been a long day, a very long week and an unbearable four months. Tom would be glad to leave this behind.

Judge Fuller wasted little time in ruling once Yale sat down. He flipped through a few pages on a legal pad he kept behind the bench, and read from a judicial manual he kept near him, before speaking.

"I'm going to rule from the bench in this case," Fuller said, sitting up in his chair and looking from one table to another as he talked his way through the decision. "The only issue before me here today is whether to grant GenAgra's petition for a preliminary injunction. GenAgra has asked me to convert the temporary restraining order that currently prohibits the Stiles' Family Berry Farm from conducting all farm operations into a preliminary order that would be binding until this case was finally resolved.

"There are four elements this Court must consider in deciding whether to grant a preliminary injunction, and a failure to find that any one of these elements is met dictates a decision in favor of the Stiles' Berry Farm. GenAgra bears the burden of proving each of these elements at this stage in the hearing.

"For the sake of argument, I will assume GenAgra has met its burden on the first two elements. I am making no decision in this regard, but simply assuming GenAgra is indeed likely to succeed on the merits of their patent infringement case. It is an unusual case, to be sure. One where it appears to me Ike Stiles is an innocent actor whose organic farm was invaded by genetically modified plants from GenAgra's facility. But it is not clear to me that the patent law requires any bad intent on the part of Ike Stiles to have, in fact, infringed on GenAgra's patent. His intention may make a difference with regard to the ultimate damages GenAgra might collect for this infrigement, but the fact is admitted by all sides that patented plants were being grown by Ike Stiles without a license. It is a very interesting legal question. One we may have to answer later in this case. But for the time being, I assume GenAgra would likely succeed in their claim.

"I also assume GenAgra would be irreparably harmed by someone selling this Hg-Blackberry before they are able to bring it to market themselves. I'm ignoring the controversy about whether or not the Hg-Blackberry causes HERDS, because if in fact that turns out to be the case, then I don't see how GenAgra could ever market this product. There is certainly evidence the berry has an unknown toxin. Evidence that GenAgra's agents tried to hide. But I can't say on this record whether that toxin is the cause of HERDS. So I'm assuming there would be irreparable harm to GenAgra if Ike Stiles was not enjoined from the sale of these patented products.

"I make these assumptions because it is clear to me the last two prongs of the test for granting a preliminary injunction are clearly not met. First, this court would have to find a balancing of the relative hardships between the parties would favor the issuance of injunctive relief. The evidence suggests just the opposite to my mind. GenAgra is a multi-national corporation with billions in revenue. Revenue from the Hg-Blackberry, if any, would not represent a sizable share of their overall profits. I see little hardship that would fall upon GenAgra if I fail to grant this relief.

"On the other hand, Ike Stiles runs a relatively small organic farm. The injunctive relief is crippling to his business. There may be continuing orders by the Department of Community Health which prohibit him from operation, but this court is not going to grant GenAgra a preliminary injunction.

"Finally, so there is a clear record for any appeal, this Court looked at the impact on the public interest, and whether it favors the granting of an injunction in GenAgra's favor. I would say this. This was one of the most unusual hearings I have ever witnessed. And I have never seen so much evidence of potential malfeasance on the part of a corporation or its agents as I have seen in this case. The record suggests—there is strong evidence to this effect— that Al Bullard, the agent of GenAgra at this hearing, may have lied under oath, and may have conspired to forge documentary evidence in this case. I will be having a copy of this transcript made, and I will personally ensure it is turned over to the Office of the United States Attorney for review.

"In addition, though the evidence actually before the court is not clear, someone at the Michigan Department of Community Health has seen enough evidence to pull the Hg-Blackberry from the market under suspicion it is producing a toxin that causes HERDS. And evidence on this record suggests GenAgra quite possibly had prior knowledge of this toxin. Given the irregularities on this record, and the danger I believe GenAgra may have subjected the public to, this Court cannot find the public interest is served by granting an injunction.

"For these reasons, GenAgra's petition is denied. I understand from my clerk we have motions scheduled in this case for August 1st," Fuller said, rising as he spoke. "I will see you back in court on that date. This case is adjourned."

The clerk stopped the recorder and Fuller continued. "Are we off the record?" he said to his clerk. "Good. Will counsel approach."

Tom rose and walked to the bench as if riding on a cloud. It was no knockout, but a better result could never have been expected. GenAgra was in a crippled position, thanks to the deceit of Al Bullard, and Tom could press that advantage at his leisure.

"I'm still going to make my golf league." Fuller smiled, unzipping his robe while still behind the bench, revealing a yellow golf shirt and pressed khakis.

"Glad to hear it, Judge," Tom said. It was always easier to be magnanimous in victory.

"I just wanted to give a word to the wise," Fuller said to Yale. "That is outrageous, what that clown did in this case. If I were you, I would be telling my client to settle this thing, because I don't think a jury is going to like what it hears at trial."

"I'll mention it to them," Yale said, her face wrecked.

"Chin up," Fuller said. "That wasn't your fault. Clients sometimes get what they deserve." Fuller waved as he walked out of the courtroom, headed for the first tee.

Tom was normally gracious to opposing counsel, but his dislike for Yale was too much. He turned without offering a handshake or a smile or a word of encouragement. He thought Fuller was probably being too generous in Yale's case, because Tom suspected she might have known the truth GenAgra had tried to suppress all along.

Nell and Felix Hrdina were smiling and waiting to escort Tom from the courtroom like a triumphant general.

"Oh, you guys are all smiles now," Tom said with a laugh. "Nervous Nell and Mr. I-Don't-Like-Your-Chances Hrdina. A couple of fair weather fans if I've ever seen them."

Neither of the young attorneys said anything. His comment probably struck too close to home. They walked down the corridor toward the security checkpoint, and were about to leave when someone called out behind them.

"Mr. Hughes," said a booming voice from the end of the hallway. "Mr. Hughes."

It was the impeccably dressed fire-plug of a man who had sat in GenAgra's corner from midday on. "You guys go on to the hospital and check on Ike," Tom told Nell and Hrdina. "Give him the good news."

"I'm Wes Zimmerman," the old man said, as Tom walked back to meet him. "I'm the CEO of GenAgra. I wanted to speak with you for a moment."

"What brings the CEO of a giant like GenAgra out to the courthouse on a case like this?" Tom said, curious.

"This is no small case, my friend," Zimmerman said. "I've got a board of directors to keep happy, and this issue is bread and butter to them. I am wondering if we could take a few moments to talk settlement."

"Well," Tom said. "I'd love to, but I would normally do that with your attorney, since GenAgra is represented."

"By all means," Zimmerman said. "I've got her seated in a conference room up the hall. She wasn't really up to talking with you, I'm afraid."

"Okay," Tom said, following Zimmerman back to the conference room. Tom had a strange sense about this dynamic old man. He seemed much like Ike in some way. Determined. Stubborn. Tom was sure he wouldn't trust Zimmerman as far as he could throw him across the hall, but he did sense the CEO was a practical man with whom one could talk business.

"Ms. Yale, Mr. Bullard," Zimmerman said. "You know Mr. Hughes." Yale and Bullard sat at the conference table as dejected as scolded puppies. Tom nodded and said nothing.

"Ms. Yale," Zimmerman said, "Mr. Hughes is one of the ethical members of your profession who insists you be present while we discuss a settlement."

Yale nodded and said nothing. Tom was surprised at how heavy the loss weighed on her. He had thought her a striking woman when the case started, but now she looked defeated. Ugly.

"Mr. Hughes," Zimmerman said, not taking a seat. "I won't beat around the bush. I'm ashamed of some of what I heard in the courtroom today—" the old man shot an evil look at Bullard "—and I'm going to be ordering a thorough internal review of this matter. There is going to be transparency about what has happened. And I can assure you right now I'm going to share the results of that investigation with you. I can't afford to be running a business that way. Not the way I heard about it in there."

Tom said nothing. He discounted the old salesman's words instinctively and waited for him to get to the point.

"As I am sure you will understand, one thing GenAgra is very sensitive about is bad publicity," Zimmerman said. "I simply cannot afford to have a product line that scares the public. And I can't afford a lawsuit that ends up with the headlines I'm sure are capable of being created after today's little fiasco. We have too many irons in the fire at GenAgra to get sidetracked on an issue like this.

"So let me make it simple," he continued. "What is it going to take to settle this matter?"

"Well, at the beginning of today's hearing," Tom said, smiling and glancing at Yale, "your attorney indicated GenAgra was unwilling to offer much of anything to settle."

"Well, things have changed," Zimmerman said. "I'm asking you. I'm not saying the sky's the limit. That would be foolish. But I want to talk turkey. What's it going to take?"

Tom had honestly given the matter no thought. He paused before speaking, wanting to sound rational before he finally opened his mouth. "This isn't merely about money to my client," he said. "And I can't make any binding offer without speaking to him first."

"Of course," Zimmerman said. "Of course. But let's put our cards on the table and see where we can get."

"GenAgra stops producing the Hg-Blackberry," Tom said. "Project over. And you pay for whatever it costs to clean up Ike's farm."

"Hell, I'd buy his farm," Zimmerman said, not batting an eye. "And if what I heard in there today is right, I'm not so sure we won't be pulling the old plug on the Skinny Berry anyway."

The old man was buying Ike off like GenAgra bought everyone off. The thought of them buying Ike's farm offended Tom, but he kept a poker face. "You set up a fund to fully compensate the victims of HERDS," Tom said, reaching higher.

"Whoa now." Zimmerman smiled. "We don't even know what's causing HERDS, and we sure as hell don't know how many people might get sick. I can't buy a pig in a poke here. I told you, I do have a board to answer to."

"A victims' fund depending on proof of a link between the Hg-Blackberry and HERDS, then," Tom said.

"And we'll talk about valuation of the fund later?" Zimmerman said. "When we get some final numbers on who's sick and how bad."

"Okay," Tom said. He could imagine Zimmerman hawking snake oil at a carnival. He was a salesman and irrepressibly likeable. "And..." Tom thought of the most outrageous sum he could ask for on Ike's behalf, and then multiplied by five, just because Zimmerman had talked about buying the farm, "…fifty million dollars."

Zimmerman exhaled deep from his barreled chest, as if absorbing a body blow. "Ouch," he said. "That is pretty steep. You want fifty million for your client alone."

"I think that might put my client somewhere in the ballpark of not wanting to drag your corporation kicking and screaming to trial," Tom said.

"So you think that deal would do it, then?" Zimmerman said.

"It would put us in the ballpark," Tom said. "I'd have to run the exact specifics by my client, assuming he is still alive."

Zimmerman swallowed at the talk of Ike being dead. "I'd have to run it by my board, too," the old CEO said. "But I'd say we might be in the same ballpark. Why don't you draft a formal proposal and submit it to Ms. Yale here, and we'll iron out the details."

"I will," Tom said.

"Very impressive in there today, Mr. Hughes," Zimmerman said, offering his hand. "You were a real bulldog."

Tom shook his hand despite himself. He felt he was selling out, and Claire wouldn't have liked it. Except for the size of Tom's contingency fee, which probably would have made her laugh. Tom left the courthouse and went to see Ike.

Chapter Twenty

The door closed. Tom Hughes was gone. Bullard was shaken by being called to the stand and forced to lie under oath. He was not sure how, but he knew he would pay Hughes back with interest. But first he had Zimmerman to deal with, and the old CEO was breathing fire.

"You see that man?" Zimmerman said, walking up behind Bullard's chair. "He knows more about business than you will ever know. I imagine this could have been handled with a few million dollars before you took over."

"Sir, GenAgra is a brand name," Bullard said. "You are making life better. You can't roll over for these shrill people who are standing in the way of that mission."

"Making life better," Zimmerman scoffed, placing his hands on Bullard's shoulders. "That's a slogan, son. You see, you still don't get it. There's a difference between a slogan and real life. A good marketing campaign only takes you so far. At some point you have to have a product. And at this point, you've destroyed the product."

"Mr. Zimmerman—" Bullard started.

"Let me say this as nicely as I can," Zimmerman said. "Out of respect to your father. Son, you need to find yourself the best criminal defense lawyer you can. And judging from what I heard on that tape in there this afternoon, I'd start having the old man make some calls to find you the right federal prison. Because I've seen it before, and I've got no doubt that's where you're headed."

Bullard said nothing. His head was weighed down by the truth of Zimmerman's prediction. He had never felt so exposed as he was on the stand. Even as the spin was coming from his mouth on the stand, Bullard had sensed the danger. But he couldn't stop. And now he was going to need his father's help again. That was certain.

"Your association with GenAgra is over," Zimmerman said. "You can work out the details with our in-house legal team. But The Bullard Group no longer represents my company."

Zimmerman slapped Bullard on the back and started for the hallway. At the door, he turned. "Ms. Yale," the old CEO said, "I'd like to spend some time with you hashing out the details of this settlement. He said fifty million, but I know he'll take half that."

"Okay, sir," Yale said, composed.

"I've got my jet at the airport." Zimmerman smiled that salesman's grin. "I'll fly you back to Detroit, and we can talk about it on the plane."

"It would probably get me home quicker," Yale said. She stood, grabbed her briefcase, and left with Zimmerman. She did not look back at Bullard.

The intern waited for Bullard in a rental car outside the courthouse. His flight was first-class out of the Tri-City airport. No private jet was available, his secretary had explained.

"So your flight isn't until later, right?" the intern said, driving him across two-lane asphalt roads that creased fields of green corn.

"Ten o'clock," Bullard said, looking out at the corn. Eighty percent of it was enhanced, he thought.

"So I think we've done a pretty nice job with the spin on this," the intern said cheerily. "Did you see that press conference this morning?"

"Yeah," Bullard said. "You've done an excellent job here, but we're packing up the operation."

"What?" the intern said.

"Tough day in court," Bullard said. "This berry of theirs. It's no good. At least that's what the judge said."

"The focus group numbers you showed me were excellent," she said, not understanding.

"I know," Bullard said, turning to look at the intern, seeing a hint of Hannah Yale in her chubby profile. "It's a shame. But it's good, too. I'll be glad to have you back in D.C."

The intern smiled at him, and it made him forget about federal prison momentarily. He wanted to forget more.

"What about Hannah Yale?" The intern pouted, but it was a hopeful pout.

"That was just business," Bullard lied.

The intern smiled and drove. The corn gave way to an open field, surrounded by a military fence. Runways. Planes. A squarish cement terminal. Aluminum hangars. And an airport motel across the roadway.

"I am exhausted from court," Bullard said, stifling a yawn. "Why don't you pull into that motel there, and we'll catch a catnap."

The intern looked at him with an impish smile. She did not speak, but she eased the car off the road and into the motel lot. Bullard got out and saw a small jet taking off, flying overhead. It looked like GenAgra's Lear. Hannah Yale chasing another large fish. More power to her. People used people. It was a fact of life.

Bullard used the intern. He forgot about his humiliation at the hands of Tom Hughes, and about the sting of being slapped down by the old CEO, and mostly about the impending certainty that, absent high-level intervention, he might be spending his nights in the unpleasant company of felons. But he did not forget about Hannah Yale. She had been a specimen of pure beauty, like none he had ever known. He saw hints of her everywhere in the intimate closeups of the intern. The color of her hair. The connection of her neckline to her shoulder. Bullard closed his eyes to the intern and imagined Hannah. He was oblivious to his surroundings. A cheap motel in the middle of a lonely cornfield. Overhead, jets raced to ferry the people of sleepy towns to the world's most majestic cities.

"Get the fuck off me!" the intern screamed, kicking at Bullard, and wholly interrupting his fantasy. "Get the fuck off, you pig." The intern forced him aside and slid out of bed.

"What?" Bullard managed.

"What?" The intern said, attacking the night stand. Her hands moved with cartoonish speed, and she chucked everything in reach at Bullard. A lamp. His wallet. The wall phone, dangling its cord as it flew through the air. A small pad of paper, slicing a small incision on Bullard's chin. His cell phone, narrowly missing him, destroyed as it smashed somewhere beyond him.

"What the fuck are you doing?" Bullard screamed.

"You called me fucking *Hannah*!" the intern said. "You fucking pig! I am not a piece of meat!"

She was crying. Screaming. Raging. Bullard got out of bed, seeing his own naked body in the mirror. He was not a pig, he thought, and smiled at his reflection. Those berries had taken off a few pounds.

"Hon—" Bullard started.

"My name is *Charlene*!" the intern screamed. "Asshole!"

"I didn't say…" Bullard sputtered. "I didn't call you…you must…"

"You fucking did!" she seethed, finding his shoe as she crouched, then chucking it at Bullard, hitting his raised arm. Her pose on the floor was very unflattering. The poor girl would lose all shape in her thirties and would rue the day she let this opportunity pass her by.

"Stop that," Bullard said. "That hur—"

Bullard's words were interrupted again. Not by the intern, but by pain. Not by the dull ache where the shoe had struck his arm or the small cut on his chin. This was a pain that was previously unknown to Bullard in his forty-four years. His words were interrupted by his own scream. From some primal place in the brain. The place in the brain that directed human beings to run from predators.

His lower legs went wooden with the fiercest cramps he could imagine, tightening themselves to a death grip, as if they had become boa constrictors. Bullard fell like a tree. Face first. His arms only partially muting his fall.

"Help," he sobbed through the pain. "Help me."

"Fuck you!" the intern screamed. "You fuck off! Why don't you ask Hannah Yale for help, you fucking dick!"

Bullard looked up at the intern, trying to place a pathetic mask over his own deathly fear so the young girl would stop. Talk to him. He saw her gathering her clothes, heading for the door. Bullard tried to tell her to stop but was gripped by another contraction. This time the snake had wound its way to his thigh and buttocks. His words were a desperate scream. The door opened and slammed shut.

"Don't go." Bullard panted. "Help me."

He tried to yell, but even in the recess of the sharp pains, the residual agony sapped his breath. He felt the next wave move up his body. Bullard pissed on the carpet uncontrollably, and screamed as his body convulsed and left him prone again on the urine-soaked floor. His lungs began to burn with effort. The rasping sound of his own breath was like the scream of a scorned lover. Bullard looked for his cell phone. The room had gone from stark white to shades of pink. He could see pinprick shadows falling like rain before his eyes. His last moments of sight were a kaleidoscope. The Skinny Berry was like crack cocaine, he thought, as the room faded to a very early sunset. It practically sold itself. But it was very hard on the consumer.

Ernie felt the sweat on his forehead. In his dreams of glory, he had never imagined the actual heat of the spotlight. Television lighting. Photo flashes. It was intense. He was glad his position on the podium made him only a prop, and that the governor wouldn't ask him to speak.

"Thank you all for coming this morning," the governor began. He was dressed in a sleek black suit, and spoke with the authority of Ceasar, though having seen him behind the scenes, Ernie knew Howell was not all that impressive. "As you know, my administration has been working around the clock this week to deal with a public health threat that has cropped up in Michigan, and indeed in several states throughout the U.S.

"High Eosinophil Respiratory Distress Syndrome, or HERDS,

as many of you know, is a serious illness. As of this morning, there have been three hundred and twenty-nine suspected cases reported nationwide, and four deaths. This is a terrible tragedy, and my personal condolences go out to the families of those who have been struck by this syndrome.

"This morning, I have several positive developments to report in our battle with this cruel illness. Thanks to the hard work of scientists within Michigan's Department of Community Health, most notably Director Kathy Jones and regional epidemiologist Ernesto Vasquez, who first identified HERDS, we have confirmed that a toxin found in a very limited quantity of blackberries and blackberry plants is associated with almost every identified case of HERDS in Michigan. It is too early for our scientists to say the toxin is the cause of HERDS, but the early evidence suggests that it is. And testing is ongoing to confirm this causal relationship.

"Now I want to stress that this toxin is found in only a tiny proportion of blackberries in this state. We have isolated the farms where these blackberries were grown, and we are actively recalling any products connected with these blackberries. The commercial products of concern are any fresh or frozen blackberries from the North Central Research Center or the Stiles' Family Berry Farm. In addition to fresh or frozen blackberries from these particular farms, anyone who has purchased Kaye's Famous Blackberry Jam or Kaye's Famous Honey should discard those products, as they may contain traces of the toxin. But I stress, all other blackberries from any other source are completely safe to eat. We have already ensured that, as of today, any of the tainted products will be recalled and not offered for sale.

"Finally, I'd like to reassure the public that HERDS appears to be treatable. Doctors throughout our state have been able to stabilize HERDS patients. Those who are sick continue to recover. The symptoms of the illness are described on the Department of Community Health website, and I would encourage anyone who has any questions about whether they may have contracted HERDS, or questions about whether they may have come in contact with the described blackberry products or honey made from the pollen of these specific blackberries, to call our state hotline or see their local physician.

"I'll take a few questions now," Howell said. "Don, why don't we start with you?"

Ernie's attention drifted with the questions. He swayed gently next to Director Jones, remembering to keep his back straight, his chin high, and a pleasant expression on his face. He felt like an actor on the stage, and it struck him that he would never advance far along in his career with the state. Everyone he had met who had achieved the upper echelon of government work had become an actor to some extent, and Ernie was content to be behind the stage.

Questions kept coming, and the governor kept swatting the easy pitches and ducking the rest. Ernie was growing weary, when the governor finally uttered, "That's all I have time for today, and thank you for coming."

The governor walked off the stage, followed by Director Jones and Ernie.

"Mr. Vasquez," the governor said, as they reached the staging area behind the pressroom, "you were very courageous in your advice yesterday. That can be a very valuable commodity to someone in my profession."

It could also get you fired, Ernie thought, but decided on a more political response. "Thank you, sir," he said.

"I'm going to keep an eye on you," the governor said, shaking his hand. "Now if you'll excuse me, I need to go take care of some angry campaign contributors." The governor chuckled quietly to himself as he walked back toward his office.

Director Jones led Ernie through the labyrinth of the George W. Romney building and out to the street.

"So are you happy to be back in your job?" Director Jones said, smiling as she raised a hand to ward off the sun.

"Yes," Ernie said, stopping to talk with the director on the stark, sun-lit sidewalk. "Thank you, ma'am."

"What do I have to do to get you to call me Kathy?" the director said, and laughed with Ernie. "Give you a job in Lansing?"

"No, ma'am," Ernie said consciously.

"You know, Underwood is out after that stunt he pulled in front of the governor?" Jones said.

"No," Ernie said, surprised.

"There was no way he couldn't have recognized that chromatograph as a forgery," Jones said. "Howell wants him gone."

"Honestly, I can't say I'm sorry to hear it," Ernie said, contemplating the opening Underwood's departure would create.

"Me either," Jones said. "There's some talk he might get a spot with GenAgra as a consultant. I'm sure they'll need an epidemiologist to sort through the storm that's headed their way."

"Makes sense, I guess," Ernie said.

"You know, I can't give you his job," Jones said. "You don't have the experience to become the state's chief epidemiologist."

"I understand," Ernie said. "It's an important position."

"Oh, I have no doubt you'd do a fine job in that role," Jones said. "But this is Lansing, and positions like that require some politicking. And I'm afraid you just aren't there yet."

"No, ma'am," Ernie said. "I don't know if I'll ever be there."

"You know," Jones said, "the person hired for that position usually gets to select their own staff. Secretary. Investigators. A chief assistant epidemiologist."

"Really," Ernie said.

"I'm quite sure I might be able to persuade the next chief to name an assistant I've handpicked." The director's eyebrows rose and she smiled. This was the game of bureaucratic politics. The words were not direct. But maybe he could get used to it. And there was good to be done. Had he been working in Underwood's office, fewer people would have gotten sick, Ernie was sure.

"I wonder," Ernie said, trying out his political skills, "does a chief assistant in Lansing get to appoint his own investigator, too?" It felt uncomfortable, but he could learn.

"I think that would require the support of the Director," Jones said.

"That sounds like a great position," Ernie said. "I am sure a person in the Lansing office could do a lot more than us poor folks in the out-counties."

"There is no doubt," Jones said. "I'll definitely call you as the process unfolds."

Ernie held out a hand to the director.

She grabbed it, and pulled him toward her for a hug. "Nice

job, Ernie," she said. "Thanks."

"Thanks, ma'am," Ernie said. He left the director and strolled along Ottawa and then Capitol Avenue, looking at the majestic state house, and its monuments to war strewn across a wide green lawn. He pulled out his cell phone and called Jill at the office.

"Jill Oswald, can I help you?" she said.

"Did you see the press conference?" he asked.

"Yeah," Jill gushed. "Everyone was gathered around the TV in the break room. You're our hero, Ernie."

"Hey," Ernie said. "How would you like a position as the investigator to the chief assistant state epidemiologist?"

"Are you serious?" she said.

"Maybe," Ernie said. He didn't know. And if he was going to become a politician, he guessed he would have to learn to live with the uncertainty. "But I think it's possible. And I think it would mean a raise for you."

Wendy was wheeled off the elevator by Doctor Brown. The old doctor took her slowly across the white tile, around a corner, and through the lobby. Her body ached to get out of the chair. She could not stand the idleness. After three weeks of relative immobilization, she needed to move.

Doctor Brown had visited weekly, keeping the local doctors on their toes. And Wendy was happy to see him. He embodied the cordiality she had known in her adoptive town of Milton, and if she could have found a way to clone the old doctor, she would have given him as a holiday gift to her favored friends.

Tom and Kaye had been frequent guests as well. Kaye came daily that first week, while Ike recovered from his heart attack. Wendy credited Kaye's warm olive oil massages, and alternating brews of gruesome garlic and milk, followed by pungent ginseng tea, with her relatively speedy recovery. The doctors had said that some of the HERDS patients were not nearly as fortunate as she had been. Medical science set it down to Wendy's sound and youthful health before she was exposed to the toxin. But Wendy had her own ideas.

Kaye's medicine was second to only one thing. Ryan had been her constant companion for twenty-five consecutive days, since she was brought in from the pier. And many nights too, she thought, a smile warming her face. Wendy had never felt as loved as she did with Ryan at her side. He had whiled away the time reading and playing cards. But mostly they talked about all the things they hadn't said to one another over the years. They laughed at one another's misimpressions. And they loved. And Wendy was certain that his love was the true medicine that healed her.

Doctor Brown rolled the chair out through the automatic doors. Ryan had pulled the car around. He parked and ran to open the passenger door for her. She loved the intensity of his movement. His wild brown hair. The aura of integrity that surrounded him. Wendy got up from the wheelchair and walked to his long embrace. Where she felt at home.

Yale looked like she had bounced back well, Tom thought, as he sat across from her in the small conference room.

"You've been getting some sun," Tom said, meaning to ease his way into their negotiations.

"I've been out boating on Lake Michigan about every weekend," she said, flashing a pure white smile.

"Oh yeah," Tom said, uncomfortable playing nice-nice—as he doubted he could ever forgive this shrew of an attorney for what she had done to Ike. "Where at?"

"Chicago," she said.

She was a regular jet-setter.

"So what did your clients think of our latest proposal?" Yale said, knocking pleasantries aside.

"They thought they could probably do better at trial," Tom said. The offer GenAgra had laid on the table was generous. Almost total capitulation. Far better than Tom believed he could do with a jury. They were paying just to avoid trial. And the bad publicity that would follow.

Yale laughed openly at him. "You know that's not true," she said, when she regained herself. "What is it? You want more than twenty-eight for your clients alone? You know that is an obscene figure for this case."

"I know GenAgra's fear of going to trial is worth more," Tom said, stone-faced.

"This is it," Yale said. "This is my last offer today. Your clients don't want it, I'm arguing my motions for summary disposition and going home.

"Agreement not to market the berry. Compensation fund of two hundred and fourteen million for the victims, their reimbursement from the fund subject to a waiver of all liability. GenAgra's research center is leased to your stupid nonprofit for a ninety-nine year term, at the agreed price of one hundred thousand dollars for the term of the lease. And your clients get a cash settlement of thirty million. That's it. Take it and run."

"I'll talk to them," Tom said. "It's all I can do. Some things are a matter of principle." Tom got up and left Yale alone in the conference room. He walked to the courtroom and found Ike and Kaye seated in the gallery. "You miss this place, Ike?"

"Hell no," the old farmer barked.

"Come on," Tom said. "Let's take a little walk, if you're up to it."

The three of them walked through security and down the stairs. A haze grew up from the heated concrete in the small town, and threatened to turn into a summer storm. They walked in front of the old postal building, and Tom explained GenAgra's final offer.

"I don't like it, Tommy," Ike said. "It's like letting them put one over on the public. Without their misdeeds ever seeing the light of day."

"Well," Tom said. "There's the criminal investigation. Though I think now that Bullard's dead, that might not be going far. And there's the press. They've taken a shellacking in the press, Ike."

"What about Claire?" Ike said. "Do you think she would think this was justice?"

"Ike, I told you," Tom said, "this isn't about her. It is nice you're forcing them to set up a compensation fund for victims in this case, but that's just window dressing. This case is about making you whole.

"And do you know what I've been thinking, Ike? Now that you bring her up. I think Claire liked a good settlement more than anything else in the world. Settlements paid our bills for a lot of years. Nobody ever gets anywhere trying cases."

"That's a lot of money," Kaye said. "Doc Brown's been after

you to stop this farming. With that money, we could get a little cottage."

"I don't want to leave the farm," Ike grumbled.

"Ike, you could afford a little cottage and the farm, too," Tom said. "If that's what you want."

"They're going to be setting up that organic research project at the old facility under this deal," Kaye said, winking at Tom behind Ike's back. "Right Tom? The one Ryan and Wendy are going to run."

"Yes, they are," Tom said. "The Stiles' Family Organic Research Center. S-FORCE. I've already got them a nonprofit set up, just waiting for this settlement. That's another nice thing you'll be doing, Ike. It is really quite remarkable."

"Well, it'll be nice to get rid of that accursed place," Ike said and spat. "Frankenfoods." He pulled his pouch of tobacco from his pocket, forgetting himself.

"Where did you get that, you stubborn old fool," Kaye said, snatching the tobacco from him. "Doctor Brown would fall down dead if he saw that. What is the matter with you? One heart attack is not enough? Lord have mercy."

They walked on, Ike chastised to silence almost the entire way around the old postal building.

"Tell me this, Tommy," Ike said. "What happens if we reject this offer?"

Tom reflected for a moment on the problem he had been thinking about for almost a month. What would happen if they went to trial? Almost certainly a worse financial deal for all involved. The only thing satisfied would be their need to demand justice, and that might not pan out in a courtroom.

"It's hard to say, Ike," Tom said. "We'd have to argue the motions for summary disposition today. And frankly, the way the law is, our case might get dismissed. I haven't wanted to believe it from the beginning, but the law just might allow them to plant their damned patented genetically modified crops—even ones that might hurt people—and let them spread wherever, and then sue any farmer they want for patent infringement. Nell and Hrdina still tell me that is a possible result, even with the judge believing you didn't intentionally steal anything, and even though their plant turned out to kill people."

"It is a world gone mad," Ike said.

"Yes, it is," Tom said. "But the leverage we have is them not wanting any more bad press. And I've worked it as far as I can. They could just dismiss their case, Ike, and admit our allegations, and ask for a trial on damages. And I don't see how a court would ever award you thirty million dollars. Your whole farm is worth what? Two million? Two and a half? And there wouldn't be any compensation fund or organic research facility. This is a phenomenal deal. I just don't see doing any better."

Ike walked on, obviously thinking about everything. Nearing the doors to the courthouse, he turned to his wife. "What do you think woman?" he asked. "You want to be married to a rich old bugger like me?"

Kaye smiled.

"All right, Tommy," Ike said. "What do we have to do to get this thing over with."

Tom walked them into the courthouse. The settlement was on the record in a matter of minutes, to be confirmed by a written agreement. And the case of *GenAgra* versus *The Stiles' Family Berry Farm* was over.

Epilogue

T om loaded his tackle box into the boat and went back for
the puppy. Scout was Tom's new companion. He was a gift
from Ryan and Wendy, and at fourteen weeks old, the little yellow
Labrador Retriever was irrepressibly adorable. Tom stopped on
the dock and watched as Scout tramped off the shore and into the
shallow water. The puppy took tentative steps, wading in like a
dancing stallion. Scout looked into the water, perhaps seeing a
fish or simply a late afternoon shadow, Tom thought. The little
puppy cocked its head from side to side, trying to get a fix on
some mystery in the shallows. Just as Tom was about to go and
pick the dog up, Scout shot his head into the water. Tom waited for
the puppy to come up with whatever curious object floated below,
but the pup stood face down in the water for one second. Then
two seconds. Then ten seconds. Scout's head drew back after an
eternity, and the little dog coughed and sputtered and shook. Tom
laughed loud and long, while Scout tried to get his bearings.

When the laughter had left him, Tom scooped up the puppy and
placed him in the boat next to the tackle box. Tom got in carefully,
unmoored, and rowed out to his favorite spot for evening bass

fishing. The trickle of water against the aluminum hull, and an occasional whimper from Scout were the only sounds to compete with the wind through the trees, and the early-evening frogs. The air was growing chilly. A preview of fall and winter to come.

No fish bit on his repeated casting, and Tom rowed farther along the lakeshore. He looked back at his dock and the cottage he had purchased with his part of the settlement money. The bulk of the money sat in the bank, despite warnings from Tom's accountant about the shortcomings of Tom's investment strategy. But now that the practice was officially closed, Tom did not care. All the money in the world could not buy another Watson Lake.

He cast into the reeds and slowly reeled in the line, yanking the rod high when a fish hit. The fish had been small or timid. It missed the bait. Looking back toward the shore, at the cabin next to his own, Tom saw Ike march out and light a grill. The old couple had bought the cabin next door, as much for Tom's sake as for their own, he thought. Kaye came out of the cabin and joined Ike. And they embraced. The sun set on the lake. It was not a brilliant light, but it struck Tom's eyes and wetted them. Through watery eyes, he watched as a single duck swooped down from the northern sky, flying like the wind across the sunset.

Claire's memory was fading like the season. He had to think for longer periods of time to remember the light in her eyes and the sweet smell of her hair. Her voice, angelic in simplicity, came to him with less frequency. Tom remembered her thoughts, but they were disembodied now. He hated her slipping away, but knew it was natural. As natural as the little puppy's yawn as he raised himself in the bottom of the boat, circled three times, and nuzzled up against Tom's fishing boot. Scout was companion enough. For this season of life. And the season would turn in its own good time.

Other Books By Terry Olson

Direct Actions

Printed in the United States
108548LV00001B/153/P